A SLENDER MAN WALKED ONSTAGE

He wore black jeans, but the shirt was disappointingly beige. His hair was black, too. He wore it loose and very Viggo Mortensen, which was fine for *The Lord of the Rings* but seemed affected for a resident of Vermont rather than Middle Earth. But at least it was clean. Was I the only woman in the world who had watched that movie and wondered why the dwarf always had clean hair while the king looked like he shampooed with lard?

Rowan's vampiric pallor fit nicely with my preconceived image. His stature did not; he was only an inch or so taller than fairy godmother Helen. But he radiated a quiet self-assurance that gave you the sense that he was in control of himself, the theatre, and everyone in it.

"If there are no questions, I will turn you over to your director, Rowan Mackenzie." With a flourish of his clipboard, Reinhard stepped back, allowing Rowan to assume center stage.

"Thank you, Reinhard. On behalf of the entire staff, I'd like to welcome you to the Crossroads Theatre."

That voice. Yesterday's nerves had kept me from fully appreciating it. Soft and intimate, as if he were speaking only to you, yet each word carried clearly. He augmented its power by allowing his gaze to roam slowly across the front rows, ensuring that each person felt embraced by his welcome.

"I had a chance to meet you briefly yesterday. In the weeks to come, I hope to get to know you better."

Forget about directing. He should have been a therapist. Or a hypnotist. Or a snake charmer.

You are getting sleepy . . . sleepy . . . you want to join our company . . . you want to turn your life savings over to me . . .

"Svengali," I whispered.

SPELLCAST

BARBARA ASHFORD

DAW BOOKS, INC.
DONALD A. WOLLHEIM, FOUNDER
375 Hudson Street, New York, NY 10014

ELIZABETH R. WOLLHEIM
SHEILA E. GILBERT
PUBLISHERS
http://www.dawbooks.com

First Printing, May 2011
1 2 3 4 5 6 7 8 9

DAW TRADEMARK REGISTERED
U.S. PAT. AND TM. OFF. AND FOREIGN COUNTRIES
—MARCA REGISTRADA
HECHO EN U.S.A.

PRINTED IN THE U.S.A.

ACKNOWLEDGMENTS

Bear with me. A lot of people helped me create this book and I'm going to thank all of them!

My writing friends who provided feedback and critiques: Dr. Karl Korri, Michele Korri, Kate Marshall, Michael Samerdyke, Shara Saunsaucie White, Susan Sielinski, Dave Stier.

My friends and colleagues in the theatre who filled in the blanks, refreshed my memory, and corrected my technical errors: Sargent Aborn (Tams-Witmark), Jay Dias, Richard Ginsburg, Andrew Gmoser, Michael Kamtman, Richard Norton, Buck Ross, Steven Silverstein.

The helpful residents of the Green Mountain State who assisted with research, in particular: Patricia Buck (Dover Historical Society), Julie Moore (Wilmington Historical Society), Ned Phoenix (Estey Organ Museum), Stephanie Ryan (*The Bennington Banner*).

My sister and niece—Cathy Klenk and Carter Klenk-Morse—for details of Wilmington and Brooklyn. And menu suggestions! And my brother-in-law Ellis Underkoffler whose photo inspired the appearance of the Crossroads Theatre.

My editor, Sheila Gilbert, who said, "You know, you should write a fantasy that draws on your theatre background." God forbid I think of it!

And the actors, staff, and crew members I've been privileged to work with, especially my husband, David Lofink. Our long run began after we starred opposite each other in *Bedroom Farce* at another barn theatre—the Southbury Playhouse. He is the inspiration for everything I write, and this book is dedicated to him.

To learn more about the world of the Crossroads Theatre
and get a sneak peek at the sequel to *Spellcast*,
visit www.barbara-ashford.com.

CONTENTS

OVERTURE

IT HAS BEGUN. The annual migration to this small corner of the world.

Tomorrow, they will arrive, just as they have for so many years. Bewitched, bothered, and bewildered, to quote the old song title.

Most will find a logical way to explain why they have come here: an impromptu desire to travel, a chance turning at a crossroads, a series of unremarkable coincidences that brought them to this place on this day. Only a few will simply accept what is happening and embrace it. The world looks upon them as dreamers or mystics or fools. But they are the ones who come closest to grasping the truth.

ACT ONE

WELCOME TO THE THEATRE

ON A SCALE OF ONE TO TEN, the day had registered 9.5 on the Suck Scale even before I climbed into the bathtub with my bottle of Talisker. First, the "I'm sorry, but the recent merger means that we'll have to let some people go" speech at work. Then, the horrifically exuberant letter from some college classmate that exclaimed, "Hurry, Maggie! Only a few days left to register for our tenth reunion!"

Now, it appeared to be snowing. Inside my bathroom.

I gazed heavenward and frowned. A few moments ago, the crack in the ceiling had merely struck me as a depressing metaphor for my life. Now, it had blossomed into a giant spiderweb.

Mesmerized by whisky and the sheer improbability of yet another disaster, I watched the web expand. Like a character in a movie who stands on the frozen lake while you're shouting at the screen, "The ice is breaking up, you moron!"

When the first chunk of plaster struck my knee, I grabbed the Talisker and scrambled to safety. Seconds later, a chunk the size of my microwave plummeted into the tub, sending a small tidal wave lapping across my feet.

I stared at the icebergs of plaster floating in the tub, at the gaping hole in my ceiling, at the water racing down the hallway. Then I did what any strong, self-reliant New Yorker would do after surviving the loss of her job and the reminder of ten years of lackluster achievement on both personal and professional fronts. I cried.

After which I blew my nose, drained the tub, mopped up the mess, dried myself off, and called Jorge, the super. By the time he rang the doorbell, I was already packing.

━●━

I reviewed my options to the accompaniment of Jorge's sorrowful ruminations in Spanish.

No way was I staying in my apartment. It was just too damn depressing.

I could scurry down to Delaware, but I knew I'd run afoul of my mother's bullshit detector. Realizing that some major life crisis had prompted my spur-of-the-moment visit, she'd interrogate me ruthlessly until I came clean. And then I'd have her desperation to deal with on top of mine.

A colleague's apartment? Half my coworkers had lost their jobs in today's bloodbath. The rest felt guilty about hanging on to them. Either way, they didn't need me showing up on their doorsteps, and I didn't need to relive the whole saga with them.

Friends from college? The few I kept in touch with were scattered around the country.

Friends in the city? None.

Still clutching the pair of socks I'd been rolling up, I sank onto my futon. Two years in the city, zero friends. There were the other residents of my brownstone, most of whom I knew by sight rather than name, my colleagues at HelpLink, a few blind dates that my colleagues had arranged, but no real friends. The nice West Indian greengrocer who occasionally tossed an extra mango in my bag didn't really count.

I hauled out the stash of travel books I'd been collecting since I got the job at HelpLink. I'd never gone anywhere, but I had two weeks severance and two years of meager savings, and if ever I needed to escape Brooklyn, it was now.

I weighed the relative merits of Southern hospitality, Rocky Mountain vistas, and Pacific coastlines before deciding I couldn't afford to splurge on airfare. Then I picked up a guide to New England's bed and breakfasts.

And bing! I had the answer.

What could be more New Englandy than Vermont? The perfect place to retreat, relax, regroup. Patchwork quilts on the bed. Rocking chairs on the porch. Groves of maples. Babbling brooks. Cows.

Normally, I would have spent hours researching amenities and prices. But if I was going to spend the next God knows how many months winging it, I figured I might as well start now.

The next morning, I threw an overnight bag into my ancient Honda Civic and headed north. My spirit of adventure faded somewhere on I-91. Everyone in Connecticut and Massachusetts seemed to be fleeing their respective states. It was like gold had been discovered in the Green Mountains or I'd inadvertently entered an alternate universe where lemmings could drive. After six endless hours, I bailed onto a two-lane road and set off in search of a quaint country hideaway.

The road wound through dense stands of trees that still wore that new-leaf green that had adorned New York a month earlier. Eventually, the forest gave way to rolling countryside that looked like it had posed for a *Vermont Life* calendar. Stone walls surrounded fields where black-and-white Holsteins grazed. Purple wildflowers ran riot in a meadow, while daffodils hugged the foundations of a dilapidated shed.

I passed farmhouses and barns, a Buddhist meditation center and a blacksmith's forge, but the closest thing to a town was a collection of rundown mobile homes that had definitely not posed for a *Vermont Life* calendar. I was beginning to regret the whole winging-it thing when the road came to an abrupt end.

A sign informed me that I had reached the township of Hillandale, evidently Vermont's version of the Twin Cities since Hill lay a mile to the north and Dale three miles to the south. Logic and my sore butt called for a right turn toward Hill, but the same instinct that had made me bail told me to turn left.

As I rumbled over a wooden trestle bridge, I glimpsed a man crouched on a slab of rock on the stream bank below. A little girl clung to his hand, staring intently at the opposite bank.

"Who knows what might be under those tree roots, Maggie! Pirate treasure. Or a family of gnomes. Or a gateway to another world."

I pulled over, astonished and angry to find tears burning my eyes. A couple of deep breaths banished the unwanted memory, but my first glimpse of Dale was a little blurry.

Once it came into focus, it proved to be the quintessential New England town, minus the fall foliage. White church steeples. Open fields. Virgin forest. A stream gleaming like polished brass in the last rays of sunlight still peeking over the mountains.

A green-and-white sign welcomed me to Dale, founded in seventeen-something-or-other. I felt like I'd reached the promised land.

I passed a deserted lunch stand and a well-manicured cemetery. Then I spied a large white barn in a meadow. My foot came off the gas pedal as if it had a mind of its own.

It wasn't your typical Vermont barn. Narrow windows along one side formed five Gothic arches. A tall cupola with the same slatted windows sprouted from the roof. Atop it, a spire pointed heavenward, furthering the barn's odd resemblance to a cathedral. Or a Wiccan house of worship. For under the steep central gable, there was an enormous five-pointed star.

I hit the brake. Architectural anomalies aside, I had the weird feeling that I'd seen the barn before. But that was impossible. I'd never been in Dale in my life.

"Need help, miss?"

The words jolted me out of my reverie. A pickup truck had pulled up next to me. An old guy in a John Deere cap regarded me from the passenger side, patiently awaiting my response. It was such a far cry from the typical New York reaction that I just stared at him. Then I stammered, "No. Thanks. I was just . . ."

Gawking at a barn like a stupid tourist.

"If you're looking for the crossroads—"

"Coffee. I could really use some coffee."

"Chatterbox Café. Next to the hotel."

A hotel sounded promising. Maybe I'd skip the bed and breakfast and crash there.

As I continued down the road, the rearview mirror reflected the shrinking image of the barn. It seemed forlorn somehow. But that was as much a product of my overactive imagination as that earlier moment of déjà vu.

The town looked anything but forlorn. White clapboard houses lined the street, most with porches and many with rocking chairs. No B&B signs on the front lawns, just an elderly couple sitting in a pair of Adirondack chairs and a little boy throwing a Frisbee to an enthusiastic golden retriever.

There were a surprising number of cars on the road, most heading in the opposite direction. Traffic slowed to a crawl at the village green. I circled the roundabout, fighting the absurd desire to take another look at the barn. After my second circuit, I became absorbed in the town.

The tree-lined street, neat shops, and small white Congregational church created a setting so perfectly Norman Rockwell that I began to suspect it was secretly Ira Levin. But the women looked normal enough in jeans and sweaters. Nary a Stepford Wife in sight.

As I escaped the traffic circle, the Norman Rockwell aura imploded. A screaming pink neon sign advertised Hallee's. Judging from the lingerie in the window, Hallee's was a shopping mecca for New England hookers. Two doors down, a gingerbready building with dragons flanking the front door turned out to be the Mandarin Chalet. Bea's Hive of Beauty and a pub named Duck Inn revealed a strange local penchant for puns.

The Golden Bough Hotel turned out to be a colonnaded edifice that looked like it had been transplanted from a Tennessee Williams play. Next to it, as promised by my Good Samaritan, was the Chatterbox Café.

Placards in the front window announced "Free WiFi" and "Bikers Welcome," neither of which I'd expected in a country town like Dale. I slowed as two ladies exited the café and got into their car. Their flowered dresses and elaborate hats suggested they were off to a revival meeting. I waited for them to back out, then whipped into the vacated parking space.

My arrival seemed to be the cue for a general exodus from the Chatterbox. In addition to bikers, Dale's tourist trade included Goths, Renaissance fair refugees, and a small Asian street gang.

Time warped as I stepped inside. Patrons and décor seemed to have escaped from the set of *Happy Days* or *Bye Bye Birdie*. In one of the booths lining the left wall, an AARP couple hunkered down over their early bird specials. A noisy group of tweens crowded around the table in the front window, gobbling ice cream sundaes. The linoleum counter with its soda fountain stools reminded me of the Eckerd's drugstore Nana used to take me to when I was little. Same red vinyl seats on the stools. Same glass domes covering the cakes and pies. Same pleasantly stout waitresses in powder blue uniforms.

One of them ambled over as I slumped onto a stool.

"Long day, huh?" Frannie or Francie—there was a dark smear in the middle of her name tag—clucked sympathetically.

"Very."

"Coffee?" she asked, already reaching for the pot.

"Please." I must have sounded desperate, because she shot me a quizzical look over her shoulder. "Cream, no sugar."

Wondering if I looked as frazzled as I'd sounded, I stole a glance at the long mirror behind the counter. The black flecks in the ancient glass made my auburn hair look polka-dotted, while my face seemed to be showing early signs of bubonic plague. My gaze drifted over a framed photograph next to the mirror, then snapped back as I recognized the barn.

Frannie/Francie jerked her head toward it. "Yep. That's the Crossroads Theatre."

If you're looking for the crossroads . . .

Maybe that was why the barn had looked so familiar. I'd spent my first season in summer stock at the Southford Playhouse, a converted barn that seated about one hundred people uncomfortably. Bats made occasional appearances, drawing gasps from the audience and stealing focus from the performers. We made a hundred bucks a week, which included living quarters in a dilapidated rooming house nicknamed Anatevka after the village in *Fiddler on the Roof*. And performed in front of a mottled black-and-gray backdrop that we dubbed The Shroud.

Hands down, the best ten weeks of my life.

The mirror reflected back my smile. Quickly descending to earth again, I asked, "Is there a bed and breakfast in the area?"

Frannie/Francie sniffed. "There's one over to Hill calls itself that. Charge you an arm and a leg and give you toast in the morning. But the theatre folk all stay at the Bough."

As she plunked a plastic travel mug on the counter, I quickly said, "Cardboard is fine."

"This is better," she assured me as she poured. "Ten cents off each refill. Think of the savings." I was still doing the math when she added, "Be ready in a jiff. I know you don't want to be late."

"Late?"

"To see the cast lists."

"Cast lists?"

Frannie/Francie froze in the act of snapping the lid on my travel mug. "You mean you haven't auditioned yet?"

I shook my head. "I'm just up for a few—"

"Well, you better head right on over. Auditions close in ten minutes."

I may have inherited my father's love for acting, but that was more than offset by my mother's practicality. I'd given theatre a try, but when I turned thirty, I wrapped my acting dreams in mothballs and got a real job.

As I reached for my coffee, Frannie/Francie snatched up the travel mug and placed it under the counter. "I'll just keep this for you."

"You're holding my coffee hostage?"

"It'll taste even better after you audition."

"Oh, come on . . ."

When I ignored her shooing motions, she flung back the counter's bridge and marched toward me. I headed for the door, still complaining that I really wanted my coffee and I really, really didn't want to audition.

"Sure you do. It'll be fun."

No, it would only remind me that I'd failed as an actress. Just as I'd failed as a college admissions counselor, a tele-marketer, and a HelpLink representative.

"You'll do fine. Don't worry about your hair."

She followed me out of the café and stood at the curb

while I got into my car. As I eased into traffic, I heard her shout, "Break a leg, hon!"

"Break yours," I muttered.

A quick check of the rearview mirror at the roundabout proved she was still standing guard, ruining any chance of sneaking back to the Golden Bough. Resigned to searching for the overpriced B&B she had disdained, I headed north.

As soon as the barn came into view, my heart started racing. And—right on cue—my foot came off the gas pedal. Clearly, my body wanted me to stop, even if my mind was firmly against the idea.

What the hell. It couldn't hurt to look at the place.

I eased my car down the narrow lane, trying to avoid deep ruts that looked like they had been carved by the Conestoga wagons of Dale's original settlers. A white farmhouse sprawled atop a hill, overlooking the meadow and barn much the way the house in *Psycho* looms over the Bates Motel. As I drifted closer, I glimpsed a couple of outbuildings and what might be a small pond. Beyond that stretched the forest primeval.

There were close to two dozen cars in the gravel lot, sporting license plates from all over the Northeast; I even spotted a few from the South.

Even more astonishing were the hopefuls milling around the picnic tables. In addition to the motley crew I'd glimpsed leaving the Chatterbox, I saw a Rocky Balboa clone in a muscle shirt, Luca Brasi's twin brother, two Legally Blonde sorority chicks, a black Rasta dude, a white Rasta wannabe, and an elderly man in a walker serenading a mousy-looking woman with a quavering rendition of "Some Enchanted Evening." A few clutched sheet music, but most were empty-handed and looked as bewildered as I felt.

Up close, the theatre was as unimpressive as its prospective actors. The timbers of the barn were more of a sun-bleached gray than white. Ivy crept over its stone foundations to snake up the wood slats. Atop the cupola, a black weather vane in the shape of something vaguely mammalian creaked in the gusting breeze. Shivering, I slipped through the open front door.

Warmth enveloped me. Not merely the physical sensation

of walking into a heated building, but something more—like the embrace of an old friend. I shook my head impatiently; no use getting sentimental about the good old days of summer stock.

The small lobby was empty save for an elderly woman sitting in the box office. She looked up from her magazine and examined me over her reading glasses. Her patrician New England face—bone structure to die for—only added to the impression that she was looking down her nose at me. Then she smiled and morphed into the elegant but warm-hearted fairy godmother the Disney animators should have given Cinderella.

"Reinhard will be out in a moment."

I nodded politely and made a mental note to flee before then. There was still time to look around, though; beyond the two sets of double doors that led to the house, the current victim had just launched into a quavering a cappella version of "Born to Be Wild."

A flyer impaled to the wall with a thumbtack advertised next weekend's Memorial Day parade. Another flyer—bright pink—advertised the "Spring into Summer Sale" at Hallee's. All corsets twenty-five percent off.

A poster between the house doors revealed that Janet Mackenzie was the theatre's producer, while Rowan Mackenzie was its director. Doubtless some chirpy husband-and-wife team with pretensions of artistic brilliance. They clearly loved musicals because that was all they were doing: *Brigadoon*, *Carousel*—hoary chestnuts both—and an original show called *The Sea-Wife*. Book and lyrics by Rowan Mackenzie. He'd probably bombed in real theatre, but had enough money to start his own to soothe his wounded ego.

God only knew what *The Sea-Wife* was about; if there were mermaids involved, I was doomed. I'd be perfect for the comic lead in *Brigadoon*, but I'd always despised *Carousel*. Maybe because the story hit a little too close to home. Abusive ne'er-do-well woos small-town girl, who continues to adore him no matter what kind of crap he pulls. Returns to earth years after his death to square things with his wife and daughter. Misty-eyed finale with everyone singing some plodding anthem of hope and love.

To be fair, Daddy never hit us. And it was only during that last year that he began vanishing for weeks at a time. Then Mom kicked him out and he vanished for good.

A weight descended on my chest. I shrugged it off. I had no intention of wallowing in the past. Or spending the summer singing about bonnie Jean and real nice clambakes. Or auditioning for the Crossroads Theatre.

Belatedly, I realized that "Born to Be Wild" had concluded. Before I could beat a hasty retreat, one of the house doors opened. A middle-aged man clutching a clipboard strode toward me.

"Name?" he demanded, pen poised.

"No. Sorry. I'm not—"

"Name."

"No. See, I'm not here for the auditions."

"Name!"

The Teutonic bullying brought out my Scotch-Irish temper. "Dorothy Gale. From Kansas."

His deepening frown chiseled new lines into his forehead. "And I am Glinda, the Good Witch of the North."

"As if," a voice proclaimed behind me. "That's my role."

I turned to discover a plumpish young man posed dramatically in the entranceway. His pink shirt *was* roughly the color of Glinda's gown, but he wore ordinary blue jeans rather than a chiffon skirt and, in lieu of a wand, trailed a plum-colored sweater across the floor.

"Reinhard bullies everyone," he said as he breezed toward us. "But he's really a pussycat. I'm Hal. Welcome to the Crossroads."

"Maggie."

"Ha!" With a triumphant grin, Reinhard scribbled down my name.

"Hal as in Hallee's?" I ventured.

"Aren't you the little Miss Marple? Actually, I'm only half of Hallee's. My other half—"

"Better half," Reinhard muttered.

Hal stuck out his tongue. "Lee's closing up shop for me. I have to be here when the cast lists go up. So exciting."

His radiant smile dimmed as he studied me. In my black tunic and sweatpants, I resembled a lumpish ninja. Doubtless, Hal wished he'd brought along one of those twenty-five-percent-off corsets.

The smile returned with so little effort that it had to be genuine. "You'll be wonderful. I have a sixth sense about these things. Next week, after you're settled, you come into the shop. I have a green sarong that'll look fabulous with that hair."

Reinhard sighed heavily. "Last name."

"Graham. I bet you own the Mandarin Chalet."

"His wife does," Hal volunteered. "Reinhard is a pediatrician."

With that wonderful bedside manner, he probably terrified the local children into good health.

"Mei-Yin also does our choreography. I, of course, do costumes. And set design. Lee—"

"She will find all of this out later," Reinhard interrupted. "Now, she auditions."

I cast a despairing look at each of my fairy godmothers, but Hal just beamed and the lady in the box office waggled her fingers.

I knew I should turn around and walk out. But something—curiosity? instinct? my father's musical theatre genes?—impelled me to follow Reinhard into the house.

The doors whispered shut behind us, cutting off the light from the lobby. We stood motionless in the aisle, allowing our eyes to adjust to the dimness.

I'm a sucker for darkened theatres. There's an air of hushed anticipation, more patient and mysterious than the hush that descends before the curtain rises. As if the theatre holds secrets that it will reveal only to those who will surrender to its magic and allow it to carry them away to another place, another time, another world.

Beneath the odors of dust and old upholstery, I smelled paint and fresh-cut wood, as if the theatre had been erected that morning instead of decades ago. And something more elusive that made me think of warm summer earth and a thick mulch of pine needles.

A shiver crawled up my back. I rubbed my arms, firmly quelling my imagination and the emerging crop of goose bumps.

Mr. "Born to Be Wild" must have left via another door, for the stage was empty. Thick clouds of dust motes lent a Brigadoony mistiness to the pool of light center stage. The music director's head peeped over the rim of the orchestra pit, hair gleaming like a newly minted penny. In the center section of the house, I spotted the dark silhouette of the director.

My stomach went into freefall.

"Break a leg, sweetie."

I started at Hal's whisper, unaware that he'd slipped in behind us. As Reinhard edged past me, I whispered that I didn't have any material, that I hadn't brought a resume or headshot. He ignored my running monologue and marched down the aisle. And once again, I trotted after him like an obedient puppy.

I mounted the five steps to the stage with the alacrity of Marie Antoinette en route to the guillotine. Then I remembered that I was a New Yorker, for God's sake. And once upon a time, people had paid to see me perform. I straightened my slumping shoulders and strode onto the stage as if I owned it.

A shock of static electricity stopped me in my tracks. And with it, that weird sense of coming home that I had felt when I stepped inside the barn.

Get a grip, Graham.

I took a deep breath, let it out, and walked into the pool of light.

"Good afternoon. And welcome."

Although I knew the invisible director was just adopting the same soothing tone I used on HelpLink calls, my heartbeat slowed from rabbit speed to human.

"I'd like you to read a scene first. Something from *Brigadoon*."

I couldn't place his faint accent, but it was also strangely soothing.

"If you please, Reinhard."

Reinhard thrust a piece of paper at me. Meg and Jeff. Funny, secondary-lead stuff. No sweat. Hearing Jeff's lines delivered in a German accent reminded me how absurd this whole thing was.

"Very nice," Rowan Mackenzie said when I finished. He probably said that to everyone, but a warm glow blossomed in my stomach.

"What will you be singing for us today?"

Exit warm glow, stage left.

I shot a panicked glance at the music director, who just stared up expectantly from his piano in the pit. I couldn't think of anything. Neither the uptempo number nor the ballad I'd always used for auditions. I tried to remember the plodding anthem from *Carousel*, but all I came up with was "A Real Nice Clambake."

Then a title popped into my head. Before I could stop myself, I blurted it out.

I had to hand it to the music director; the guy didn't miss a beat. Never mind that it was a man's song. And a major cheese-fest. With a rippling arpeggio, he launched into the intro of "Some Enchanted Evening."

In spite of my horror, I noted that Penny Hair had chosen a good key for me. Silently blessing him, I dove in. The first verse was shaky, but by the second, I'd begun to enjoy mocking the sappy lyrics and over-ripe music.

But at the end of the bridge, something strange happened. I found myself remembering how I'd felt when I met Michael freshman year. And how Eric burst out laughing when I bumped into him at the Cineplex and drenched him with Diet Coke. That giddy, unexpected "Oh, my God" magic that warms you like single malt whisky and leaves you cold and shivering at the same time.

And just like that, I was singing my heart out. My voice soared during that final verse, only to drop to a choked whisper at the end. The last note was still hanging in the air when Hal shouted "Brava!" and began clapping. The silhouetted head turned, and the applause stopped.

Just as abruptly, my chick-flick sentimentality evaporated. Moisture prickled my armpits and forehead, that awful cold dampness that actors call flop sweat. I hung my head, desperately searching for a trap in the floor so I could plummet quietly to my death.

"Now as to your availability . . ."

"She came in late." Reinhard's disapproving voice boomed out of the darkness. "She did not fill out the form."

"Thank you, Reinhard. Rehearsals begin after Memorial Day. The season ends in mid-August. We hope our actors will be able to join us for the entire summer, but that's not always possible. I need to accommodate everyone's schedule when I make casting decisions, so if you could tell me your availability . . ."

"Oh, I'm available. Free as the wind. No job. No husband at home. Not even any home to speak of since the bathroom ceiling caved in."

Realizing that I sounded more pathetic than amusing, I shut my mouth. The ensuing silence brought on another wave of flop sweat.

He'd given me the perfect cue and I'd blown it. I should have politely but firmly told him that I wasn't looking for a job. Not here, anyway. I had to get back to Brooklyn. File for unemployment. Check out job sites.

As I opened my mouth to explain, he said, "Thank you. Would you please wait outside? The stage door is to your right."

I slunk into the wings where a work light guided me to the door. As I stepped into the real world, the little old man with the walker advanced carefully over the grass.

"Such a lovely song. Not so often you hear a girl sing it."

The familiar cadences of New York restored my spirits.

"We danced to it at our wedding, Rachel and me." As I glanced around, he added, "No, no. She passed away a few months ago."

"I'm so sorry."

"Fifty-two years we were married."

"Wow. That's terrific. Sometimes it feels like I've gone that long without a date."

"A nice young thing like you? You've got plenty of time to find Mr. Right. Who knows? Maybe here. Look at my granddaughter, Sarah." He jerked his head over his shoulder. "The one with the blue hair who's eating up whatever Jack Kerouac's dishing out."

I smothered a laugh; the kid his granddaughter was with did look like a young Jack Kerouac.

"The two of you drove all the way up from the city?" I asked.

"You're a New Yorker, too?" he exclaimed. Because of course, to New Yorkers, there is only one city.

"Transplanted," I admitted.

"Born and bred." He thumped his chest proudly and listed a little to starboard, but steadied himself before I had to leap to the rescue. "Prospect Park."

"Crown Heights."

"We're practically neighbors! Well. Would have been. I live with my daughter now. Over in Manchester."

"If you don't mind my asking . . ."

"Ask."

"Are you an actor?"

"Dentist. Retired. Bernie Cohen."

"Maggie Graham. But you auditioned?"

"Me and Sarah both."

"How did you even find this place?"

"Well, it's funny . . ." His gaze moved past me, and he whispered, "I'll tell you later. Here comes Hermann Goering with the cast lists."

It seemed impossible that Rowan Mackenzie had made his decisions so quickly; I'd known directors who spent days mulling over their choices. But Hal was tacking sheets of paper to the side of the barn.

The buzz of conversation died, replaced by a silence so profound I could hear the creak of the weather vane and the soft whistle of Dr. Cohen's breathing.

Reinhard surveyed us, frowning. "The cast lists are up. Three copies. So do not crowd."

We darted nervous glances at each other, uncertain if this was our cue to inspect the lists and reluctant to move without Reinhard's permission. He nodded, clearly pleased by our obedience, then said, "Now. You look."

In the general stampede that ensued, I stuck close to Dr. Cohen so he wouldn't be trampled. There were excited exclamations as people found their names. A few retreated in obvious elation. Most just looked confused. But clearly, everyone had gotten a role, because there were no tears or brave "It's an honor to be nominated" smiles.

After the first wave subsided, I edged forward with Dr. Cohen and his granddaughter. Once again, my heart was pounding like a demented bongo, but I tried to appear nonchalant as I scanned the list.

Brigadoon: Chorus. Chorus? I nailed that scene. And he put me in the chorus?

The Sea-Wife: Chorus. Again.

Carousel: Nettie. Who the hell was Nettie? The tough-talking carousel owner?

The ear-shattering squeal of a pig being slaughtered turned out to be Dr. Cohen's granddaughter. "Grandpa, I got Louise!"

"That's wonderful, sweetheart!" He angled away from her to mouth, "Who's Louise?"

"I think that's the daughter in *Carousel*," I whispered. "With the big ballet number."

"Ballet?" He glanced at Sarah who was jumping up and down, plump bosoms, belly, and thighs quivering like Jell-O. "Oy. So who's this Mr. Lundie? If he's got a ballet number, I don't want to know."

"You're safe. He's the village elder who explains the miracle of Brigadoon."

"What miracle?" Luca Brasi demanded, shouldering a geeky accountant type aside.

"Of why the town vanishes into the mists and returns for one day every hundred years."

"Cool." One of the Legally Blondes nodded solemnly.

"What about this Heavenly Friend in *Carousel*?" the shorter church lady asked.

"I think he . . . she's a sort of angel."

As the church lady preened, the straw hat of her taller companion loomed behind her shoulder. "And Mrs. Mullin?"

I suddenly remembered who Nettie was: not the tough-talking carousel owner but the salt-of-the-earth woman who sings the plodding anthem whose name had eluded me earlier: "You'll Never Walk Alone." As well as "June Is Bustin' Out All Over." And the fucking clambake song.

It wasn't the age thing I minded. Much. I was rarely cast

as the ingénue, even when I was the right age to play one. I'd played Mrs. Kendal in *The Elephant Man*, the Witch in *Into the Woods*. But those were sexy, witty, glamorous roles. Starring roles. Not well-meaning, anthem-singing, clambake-loving frumps.

"Does anybody know who Mrs. Mullin is?" the second church lady pleaded.

"I think she's the owner of the carousel," I replied.

"And Carrie?"

"Hey! *I'm* Harry."

"Not Harry. *Carrie*."

"What about this guy Charlie?"

In moments, I was surrounded, spitting out plot synopses and character snapshots. It was clear most of them knew nothing about these shows. What the hell were they doing here? More importantly, what the hell was I doing here? Chorus in some dreadful original musical. An anonymous villager in *Brigadoon*. And Our Lady of the Clambake.

Rowan Mackenzie must be blind. Or on crack. Why would he cast me as Nettie when he had his pick of not one, but two church ladies? Or cast the geeky accountant as sinister Jigger when he was clearly made to play the insufferable Mr. Snow? And what bonnie Jean in her right mind would go home with Luca Brasi?

What made it more confusing was that some of the casting was spot on. Dr. Cohen was perfect for wise old Mr. Lundie. And Jack Kerouac would be great as the brooding guy who nearly destroys Brigadoon. So how come some of Rowan Mackenzie's picks were so right and others so woefully wrong?

There was an onslaught of shushing as Reinhard waved his clipboard.

"Rehearsals start after Memorial Day. You will be paid one hundred dollars a week. You will live at the Golden Bough. No charge. You will have breakfast at the Chatterbox. No charge. All this is spelled out in the contract. But you do not sign now. Tonight, we celebrate. Dinner at the Mandarin Chalet. No charge. Rooms at the Golden Bough.

No charge. Tomorrow, ten o'clock, company meeting. Here.
You meet the director. You meet the staff. You make up your
minds. Any questions?"

Only about a thousand. But they could wait. I'd take the
free food and the free night's lodging. Hell, I'd even stick
around for the company meeting to get a look at the demented Rowan Mackenzie. After that, I would hit the road.

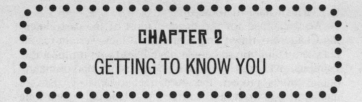

CHAPTER 2
GETTING TO KNOW YOU

THE NEXT MORNING FOUND ME AT THE CHAT-
TERBOX, surprisingly well-rested but no closer to understanding the method behind Mackenzie's casting madness.
My plan to pump Hal for information had failed miserably
when I ended up at a dinner table with six other bemused
cast members and Javier, captain of the stage crew, who was
long on charm but short on facts.

Later, I'd voiced my doubts to my roommate, the mousy-
looking woman who'd been on the receiving end of Bernie
Cohen's serenade. Nancy possessed either a high degree of
inner serenity or a low tolerance for late-night chat. All I
discovered was that she was a librarian who lived just over
the border in Massachusetts with her mother, that she had
learned about the auditions while visiting Javier's antique
store, and that she had been cast in what should have been
my role as Meg in *Brigadoon*. I crawled into bed, pulled the
patchwork quilt over my head, and tried to banish the image
of Reinhard chortling with unholy glee as he paired us up.

Breakfast proved equally unenlightening. I found allies
in Lou—the Luca Brasi look-alike—and Kevin—the Jack
Kerouac clone. Everyone else shrugged off my concerns.

Bernie Cohen patted my hand. "So we go to the theatre.
We listen to their spiel. What's the harm?"

Frannie (she'd cleaned her name tag) clucked and refilled
my coffee cup. "You gotta learn to relax, hon. Things are
different in Dale."

"That's what I'm afraid of."

We decamped for the theatre, most of the cast clutching Chatterbox travel mugs, proof that they were in for the duration. Didn't these people have lives to return to? Jobs? Families? Was the Crossroads Theatre some kind of bizarre public works project, the human equivalent of cash for clunkers? Was it a nest of cultists? Was I the only one asking these questions?

"You're not a clunker," Bernie assured me as we settled into our seats in the second row. "And as for cults . . . what cult would have Hermann Goering as its front man? For that, you want a face like *his*."

He could only mean Javier, who was strolling onto the stage with his arm around a young woman in overalls. That had to be his wife, Catherine, who was in charge of set construction. If Javier had been tight-lipped about Rowan Mackenzie, he'd had no such reservations about Catherine. In true newlywed fashion, he'd gushed about her artistic nature, her extraordinary handcrafted furniture, her business sense, her natural beauty.

Thanks to Javier, I also knew that the penny-haired music director was Catherine's father. Alex was the kind of man who epitomized nice: pleasant face, friendly smile. If I wanted a recruiting officer for my cult, I'd pick Alex, hands down.

Lee and Hal were clearly a case of opposites attracting. Where Hal talked nonstop, hands flying to punctuate his words, Lee was quiet. Hal wore another vivid shirt—this one buttercup yellow—Lee, a white T-shirt and jeans. And while Hal might be cute in a "pinch those Dutch boy cheeks" kind of way, Lee was drop-dead gorgeous, an impossible amalgam of Kanye West, Derek Jeter, and Beyoncé.

In terms of odd couples, however, Reinhard and Mei-Yin had them beat. She'd been in the kitchen last night, but given "Chinese-American choreographer" to work with, I had imagined an ethereal beauty whose haunted expression testified to Reinhard's bullying and their loveless marriage. The reality was a short, middle-aged barrel of a woman whose piercing voice silenced all conversation and produced a scramble onstage as the staff lined up. Even Reinhard jumped to obey, drill sergeant deferring to commanding officer.

Helen, my box-office fairy godmother, had to be related to the sandy-haired, middle-aged woman standing next to her. Mother and daughter? Aunt and niece? While they shared the same fabulous bone structure, the younger woman's hatchet face held none of Helen's sweetness. "Formidable" was one descriptor that came to mind. "Ball buster" was another.

Reinhard introduced her as Janet Mackenzie. Owner of the "Bates mansion," the Golden Bough, and the Crossroads Theatre. She was also in charge of hospitality. I studied that unsmiling face, tried to imagine her serving up cupcakes and punch, and felt a quick stab of pity for her husband.

As Reinhard launched into a dramatic reading of our contract, I leaned toward Bernie to whisper, "So where's our illustrious director?"

"Waiting to make a big entrance, maybe."

Reinhard paused and glared at us over his ubiquitous clipboard. "There is a question?"

"No. Sorry," I called out and turned my attention to our contract.

Ridiculous to call it that. The one-page document merely spelled out everything Reinhard had told us yesterday and listed our roles. No grounds for dismissal. Not even a line for a signature. Nothing, in fact, that made the "contract" enforceable as a legal document.

Why should I be surprised? Nothing about this place was normal.

Impatiently, I eyed the wings, willing Rowan Mackenzie to show up. I pictured a gaunt man dressed in black, with a melancholy expression, a tragic past, and some horrible deformity. A blend of Dracula, the Phantom of the Opera, and Quasimodo.

I was still debating the hump when Reinhard's stentorian voice faltered. The heads of every staff member jerked right. Murmurs rose from the company. One of the Legally Blondes squeaked. Ashley or Brittany. I still couldn't tell them apart.

A slender man walked onstage. No discernible hump. He wore black jeans, but the shirt was disappointingly beige.

His hair was black, too. He wore it loose and very Viggo Mortensen, which was fine for *The Lord of the Rings* but seemed affected for a resident of Vermont rather than Middle Earth. But at least it was clean. Was I the only woman in the world who had watched that movie and wondered why the dwarf always had clean hair while the king looked like he shampooed with lard?

Rowan's vampiric pallor fit nicely with my preconceived image. His stature did not; he was only an inch or so taller than fairy godmother Helen. But he radiated a quiet confidence that gave you the sense that he was in control of himself, the theatre, and everyone in it.

"If there are no questions, I will turn you over to your director, Rowan Mackenzie." With a flourish of his clipboard, Reinhard stepped back, allowing Rowan to assume center stage.

"Thank you, Reinhard. On behalf of the entire staff, I'd like to welcome you to the Crossroads Theatre."

That voice. Yesterday's nerves had kept me from fully appreciating it. Soft and intimate, as if he were speaking only to you, yet each word carried clearly. He augmented its power by allowing his gaze to roam slowly across the front rows, ensuring that each person felt embraced by his welcome.

"I had a chance to meet you briefly yesterday. In the weeks to come, I hope to get to know you better."

Forget about directing. He should have been a therapist. Or a hypnotist. Or a snake charmer.

You are getting sleepy . . . sleepy . . . you want to join our company . . . you want to turn your life savings over to me . . .

"Svengali," I whispered.

Bernie started as if emerging from a dream. "But lovely teeth."

"Your contract outlines the basic information about your stay with us."

Rowan's gaze lingered on me, as if he'd sensed my silent derision. I slumped a little lower in my seat.

"After this meeting, Reinhard will give you a tour of the theatre and our adjacent outbuildings. He'll also have you fill out a short information form—name, address, cell phone, that sort of thing—and hand out scripts and vocal books to those of you in *Brigadoon*. Be sure to refer to the pages outlining the changes and cuts I've made."

One demerit for dissing the shades of Lerner and Loewe.

"Alex will give you an audio recording of your vocal part. Please let him know which format you'd prefer—tape, CD, or MP3."

Okay. Bonus point for organization.

"Some of you will want to return home until rehearsals begin next Tuesday. However, if you cannot afford to do so or you've come from a great distance, you're welcome to stay at the Golden Bough this week as our guest."

Double bonus points for generosity.

"I've been part of this theatre for many years. The staff and I have mounted dozens of shows with actors who have little or no experience. I'm sure you're wondering how we manage that."

Well, the answer is simple. We take you into a subterranean room where we grow these giant pods . . .

"Well, the answer is simple."

I jerked erect in my seat.

"Hard work."

I wondered sourly if his little smile was directed at me.

"Learning the dances, the songs, the staging. Understanding the characters. Bringing them to life. Working as a team. There will be times when you'll want to quit. When you'll think it's not worth it. But . . ." A pause while that penetrating gaze swept over us again. "If you trust me and allow yourselves to believe that we can make the impossible happen on this stage, we'll have a summer to remember all our lives."

A self-deprecating shrug to undercut the rhetoric. A paternal smile to embrace the huddled masses. You could almost feel the entire cast heaving a collective sigh.

"Thank you for listening so patiently. I look forward to sharing our season at the Crossroads."

Cue curtain. Cue applause. Reinhard herded everyone stage left for the tour. I exited stage right in pursuit of Svengali. Seeing no one in the shadowy wings, I groped my way toward the stage door, flung it open, and bellowed, "Rowan!"

"Can I help you?" a soft voice inquired just behind me.

With an unfeminine screech, I spun around and promptly bashed my head into something. "Jesus, don't do that."

"I'm sorry . . . Maggie, isn't it?"

"Yes, I . . ." For some reason, I couldn't catch my breath. I was hyperventilating like mad and my ears were ringing. Brilliant gold sparks flashed before me like fireflies. A fog of black spots narrowed my field of vision to the pale oval of Rowan's face.

"Maggie?"

This was ridiculous. I hadn't hit my head that hard. I clutched the doorframe and tried to take deep, calming breaths, but my knees buckled.

Strong arms lifted me as if I were Legally Blonde weight instead of a size twelve if the pants were cut just right and had elastic in the waistband. I floated past the picnic tables and into the meadow beyond, silently assuring myself that I had never fainted in my life and was not about to start now.

My first sensation on regaining consciousness was breathing in a sweet, floral scent. My brain finally processed it as honeysuckle. Since it was far too early for honeysuckle to be blooming, it must be Rowan's cologne. What kind of a man wore honeysuckle cologne? He was either boldly confident about his masculinity or totally gay. Or both.

Sunlight warmed my left cheek. Something hard dug into my right. Rowan Mackenzie's heartbeat thudded in my ear. It seemed unusually slow, but maybe he was a Zen master as well as a weightlifter.

I kept my eyes closed while I considered how to repair my shattered dignity. Fingers probed the back of my head gently before brushing against my forehead. So cool, those fingers, and incredibly soothing. As was the voice that murmured my name. My body relaxed. Then tensed as other voices intruded on my pleasant stupor.

"Oh, my God. Is she all right? Should I call 911?"

Hal, of course.

"She fainted," Rowan replied. "I think she bumped her head."

"Oh, poor thing."

Fairy godmother Helen.

"Should I get Reinhard?" A man's voice. Lee, maybe?

"It's just a bump on the head." A woman's voice this time, sharp and authoritative. "Hal, stop hopping around and fetch a damp cloth and a glass of water. The rest of you, back to the theatre."

The thud of retreating footsteps and the murmur of worried voices. A silence broken only by the ecstatic warbling of a robin. And then: "Isn't it a bit early for you to start sweeping women off their feet, Rowan?"

The same female voice as before, but softer now. And venomous.

"I didn't sweep, Janet. Merely caught her before she fell."

I could feel her studying me and tried not to flinch.

"I wouldn't have picked her as the fainting type."

"The air was a little close backstage."

"The air is whatever you—"

"As Maggie can tell you since she regained consciousness several minutes ago."

Busted.

I considered a theatrical fluttering of my eyelashes, but contented myself with simply opening my eyes and staring up at Janet.

Her gaze traveled over me. "Well. At least this one can act."

As she walked toward the theatre, I sat up and gingerly felt the back of my head. No gaping wound. No blood. Just a small but painful lump.

"Is she really in charge of hospitality?" I asked.

"One of life's little ironies," Rowan replied. "But her charm wasn't directed at you."

"I imagine working together can be a strain on any marriage."

Rowan's smile betrayed creases at the corners of his eyes. "Good thing we're not married, then."

"Oh. I just assumed . . . because of the last name . . ."

"It's a common name in Dale."

"Fourth cousins or something."

The smile vanished. "Something."

He gazed up at the Bates mansion, absently stroking the braided silver chain around his throat. I took advantage of his momentary absorption to study him.

The boyishly smooth cheeks belonged with a softer face. His was all angles—long nose, jutting cheekbones, sharp chin, swooping black-winged eyebrows. Even his eyes were slightly slanted. From the house, they had looked hazel, but up close, they were definitely green. Cat eyes. Or a fox, maybe.

Abruptly, those cat-or-maybe-fox eyes shifted back to me. "You're sure you're all right? No dizziness?"

I shook my head and started to get up, but he forestalled me with a hand on my shoulder. "Wait a bit. Just to be sure."

I rubbed my cheek, fingertips probing a small indentation.

"You wanted to ask me something, I believe."

As I tried to remember what, I realized why I had a dented cheek. His shirt buttons were small but decidedly pointy.

"Are those made out of bone?" I blurted.

Startled, he stared down at his shirtfront, then nodded solemnly. "The bones of former cast members. Who proved . . . troublesome."

For a second—okay, maybe a few seconds—I just stared at him. Then I realized he was screwing with me. He leaned back on his hands, completely unperturbed by my scowl.

"Actually, they're antler tines. And no, I don't race after bucks and wrest their antlers from their heads with my bare hands."

"Of course not. You wait until they shed their antlers, then drag them to the scene shop and saw them up. Along with the bodies of cast members who proved troublesome."

"I'll have to try that next year. Meanwhile, I'll continue to order my shirts online."

"From Last-of-the-Mohicans-Menswear.com?"

The antler tines bounced as he laughed. "I assume you didn't follow me to discuss my taste in clothes."

I shifted uncomfortably, dug a pebble out from under my butt, and said, "It's about the theatre. It seems a bit . . . unconventional."

He nodded, waiting.

"I've done some acting before."

"I gathered that."

I resisted the urge to preen. This was not about my ego. At least, I didn't think it was.

"If you're concerned about your Equity status . . ." he began.

"I wish."

I'd never made it into the actors' union. Just four years in out-of-the-way non-Equity theatres, holding down a series of dead-end jobs to pay the bills. Any lingering urge to preen vanished.

"Look. Can I be blunt?"

"Please."

I scrambled to my feet. He rose with far more grace, one hand extended in case I showed signs of imminent collapse. I was struck again by his height. Or lack of it. Maybe an inch taller than me and I'm hardly statuesque.

Realizing I was staring again, I forced my mind back on track. "Most of the people in there have never been on a stage in their lives. They don't even know why they came here."

"Why did *you* come here?"

"I was looking for a B&B and Frannie held my coffee hostage . . ." I took a deep breath and tried again. "Some of your choices are a little hard to understand. I mean, casting Luca . . . Lou as Charlie, and Sarah as Louise—"

"And Nancy in the role you wanted."

"That's not what this is about," I said, silently vowing to slug him if he quoted that annoying theatre truism: "There are no small roles, only small actors."

"You could play Meg with your eyes shut. Why should I offer you that role?"

"Because that's what directors do!"

"I don't."

"Yeah. I got that. What I don't get is why."

His gaze moved skyward, then returned to me. "I cast people in the roles they need, not necessarily the ones they'd be good at."

I need *to be an anonymous Villager? And Our Lady of the Clambake?*

Those green eyes held mine. Flecks of gold danced in their depths, like the sparks I'd seen right before I fainted.

"You're right. This is not your typical summer stock theatre. We're here—I'm here—to serve the players as much as the players are here to serve the show. Ask the staff. Most of them wandered to the theatre the same way you did. And they were just as unsure why. But they found something here that had been . . . lacking in their lives. Something they didn't even know they were looking for. I know it sounds crazy, but it's worked for a very long time. Why not give it a chance? What have you got to lose?"

"Well, in no particular order of importance, my unemployment benefits, my apartment, my sanity . . ."

He laughed and held up his hands in surrender. "Rehearsals don't start for another week. Think about it. If you decide to join us, we'll be pleased to have you. If not . . ." He shrugged. "The theatre will always be here." His smile faded.

Before I could barrage him with more questions, the stage door banged open and Hal appeared, a cloth in one hand and a mug in the other. I was surprised to discover fairy godmother Helen leaning against the side of the barn. Hal raced past her, spilling most of the water en route.

"It's my coffee mug, but I don't have germs. Are you feeling better? You nearly gave me a heart attack." He held up the dripping cloth. "Do you want this? Or the water?"

"No. But thanks for bringing them."

He slapped the cloth on his forehead and gulped down the water. "So. Is she staying? Are you staying? You have to. You can't walk out after that dramatic beginning."

When I hesitated, Rowan replied, "She's thinking about it."

"What's to think about?" Hal hooked his arm in mine and led me toward the theatre. "I'm an artistic genius. Even when forced to design an entire season of happy villager drag." He shot a reproachful look over his shoulder at Rowan. "Alex is a love. Helen's an angel. She's feeling better," he called and received an appropriately angelic smile in response. "Mei-Yin's a terror, but you'll get used to her. And Reinhard. They're really both—"

"Pussycats?"

"Absolutely."

"Is Rowan a pussycat, too?" I inquired sweetly.

Hal burst out laughing.

"I'll take that as a no."

"Rowan is brilliant and insightful and deliciously mysterious."

"Yes, Hal. Thank you."

Rowan's tone would have squelched anyone else. "You have to see him in action to understand. But you will. Because you simply have to stay. Doesn't she, Helen?"

"Yes, I think she does." Helen's expression was thoughtful. "She made Rowan laugh."

"You made Rowan laugh?" Hal echoed in an awed whisper. "The very first day?"

I heard a sigh behind me. "The staff suffers from the illusion that I am . . . dour."

"It took me a whole season to get him to laugh," Hal said.

"How'd you do it?" I asked as he ushered me into the theatre.

"Showed up at the final cast party dressed as Titania, Queen of the Fairies."

My laughter faded when I spied Janet—Bitch Queen of Hospitality—watching us from the shadows. Then I laughed again. It seemed safer than thumbing my nose at her.

On my return to Brooklyn, I Googled "Crossroads Theatre" and discovered half a dozen throughout the country, but nothing other than a White Pages listing for the one I had stumbled upon.

I monitored the progress on my bathroom ceiling. Updated my resume. Wondered what Rowan Mackenzie thought was lacking in my life. Added a new folder to my Web favorites list with links to nonprofit job sites. Considered the benefits of a change of scene. Filled out the online application for unemployment. Made a list of pros and cons about spending the summer at the Crossroads. The cons took up an entire column. Under pros, I wrote three words: "I want to."

I threw the list away. Opened an online banking account where my unemployment checks could be directly deposited.

Notified the post office about forwarding my mail. Put an ad on Craigslist and found a normal-sounding college intern to sublet until August 15. Thanked God I no longer had a landline that could betray my absence to my mother.

Then I packed my bags and returned to Dale.

CHAPTER 3
LIFE UPON THE WICKED STAGE

AS I UNFOLDED MYSELF FROM MY CIVIC, a bass voice bellowed, "Yo! Brooklyn!"

Shading my eyes against the late afternoon sun, I discovered Lou and biker chick Bobbie on the third floor porch of the Golden Bough. The beefy guy who had been cast as carousel barker Billy Bigelow completed the trifecta of muscle shirts and tattoos.

"Yo, Joizey!" I bellowed back, feeling an absurd glow at his warm greeting.

"Need help with your stuff?"

"No, I'm—"

"We'll be right down."

As they stampeded toward the French doors, I winced, waiting for the porch to collapse under them. Their voices echoed like distant thunder from the bowels of the hotel, but returned to normal shouting volume as they reached the front doors.

While the guys wrestled over my two suitcases, Bobbie rolled her eyes and said, "You should've got here earlier. You missed the Memorial Day parade. Hal had a float."

"A float?"

"For that crazy shop of his," Lou said. "With guys posed like mannequins, wearing fishnet stockings and corsets and nighties and shit."

"Bunch of faggots," Nick muttered.

Bobbie jabbed her elbow in his ribs. "Hallee's caters to

37

men and women of discerning taste, including the tristate
gay, transgender, and cross-dressing communities."

"You sound like you're quoting from a promotional
brochure."

"She is," Lou said, earning an elbow in his ribs as well.

"Gay or straight," Bobbie said, "those drag queens were
hot. Lou thought so, didn't you, Lou?"

Lou punched her shoulder. She punched his harder. They
grinned at each other. I tried to picture them as the sweet
young lovers in *Brigadoon* and failed.

"What room you in?" Lou called over his shoulder as I
followed them into the hotel.

"I was in 304 the night after auditions."

"Right under Nick and me!"

Which explained the ominous thuds I'd heard overhead.
Thrusting aside visions of another ceiling cave-in, I managed a smile and said, "Just let me pick up my key . . ."

But they were already marching up the stairs, Bobbie
leading the men in a chorus of "I'll Go Home with Bonnie
Jean."

With its oak paneling, discreetly clustered sofas and
chairs, and pools of lamplight, the Golden Bough called to
mind a miniature version of New York's Algonquin Hotel.
It even had a resident house cat like the Algonquin, a gray
tabby I'd met on my previous stay with the improbable name
of Iolanthe. If the upholstery was a bit threadbare and the cat
a bit arthritic, it only added to the hotel's charm.

The air was thick with the contrary odors of dust and
lemon oil. Shadows drowsed in corners and curdled like
thunderclouds below the high ceiling. It was the kind of
place you'd expect to find uniformed bellhops darting up and
down the carved staircase, ladies with bustles and parasols
exchanging pleasantries with gentlemen in frock coats.

Instead, actors hunched over scripts and mouthed the lyrics of the songs flowing through their earbuds. In the adjacent lounge, someone pounded out chords on the piano
for a group of singers hesitantly crooning, "Brigadoon,
Brig-a-doo-oon."

Helen smiled as I approached the reception desk. Janet—

predictably—frowned. Iolanthe, lounging atop the counter, regarded me with sleepy eyes roughly the same green as Rowan's.

"So you're back," Janet said by way of greeting.

"I didn't want to break his heart," I replied with deliberate vagueness.

"I'm sure Hal will be delighted," she said dryly.

"We're all delighted." Helen shot a reproachful glance at her daughter/niece/second cousin.

"Has everyone come back?"

"Some of the younger ones like Sarah and Ronnie can't join us until school's out," Helen replied.

"But everyone accepted their parts?"

"Why, yes. Didn't you think they would?"

"Well, you know. Jobs, families . . ."

Helen waved those away. "Goodness, I can't remember the last time we had a no-show."

"Six years ago," Janet said. "Lee."

"That's right." Helen smiled fondly. "He refused twice, didn't he? But once he joined us, he never left."

"Kind of like a Roach Motel," Janet noted. "The actors come in, but they can't get out."

Helen looked mildly alarmed. "We certainly don't have roaches in Dale. Or bedbugs."

Janet snorted, then lifted a skeleton key from the board behind the reception desk and slapped it on the counter. Clearly, they didn't have much in the way of security in Dale, either.

Helen slid a manila envelope across the desk, her perfectly manicured nails at odds with knuckles that were thick and swollen with arthritis. "Your welcome packet. Plus a copy of your contract and information sheet. In case you forgot to bring yours. You can drop them off here." She patted the wooden inbox at her elbow, currently filled by Iolanthe. "Be sure to check the message board for schedule changes," she added, gesturing to a corkboard that sported the banner "Welcome, Crossroads cast!"

"Phones," Janet prompted.

"Oh, yes. On your last visit, you probably noticed there

were no phones in the rooms. And that cell phone reception
is a little . . . iffy. The best place for making calls is the third
floor porch. Or the road into town."

"Or the hill in the new cemetery," Janet said.

I must have looked appalled because Helen quickly
added, "You can always use the house phones. There's one
in the lobby and one on the second floor."

"For credit card, calling card, and local calls only." With
that gracious remark, Janet walked into the office and closed
the door behind her.

I decided I'd better shell out a few bucks for a Skype sub-
scription. I had to be able to talk to prospective employers in
private without fear of losing them in mid-conversation. And
I had to maintain the fiction that I was still in New York during my Sunday morning check-in call to my mother.

🌢🌢

The next morning, after breakfast at the Chatterbox, I
bundled Bernie and Nancy into my car and drove to the
theatre.

"I'll give you the cut-rate tour," Bernie volunteered as he
maneuvered cautiously along the uneven brick path. "Since
you were too busy knocking yourself out to go on the last
one. To our right, the Crossroads Theatre."

"That I remember."

"Over there is the rehearsal studio. Also known as the
Smokehouse."

"Because there used to be one on that site back in the
nineteenth century," Nancy explained.

"Back there's the Mill." Bernie nodded to a three-story
building of dark wood that resembled the House of the Seven
Gables without the gables. "Scene shop. Storage. And a loft
on the top floor where Catherine and Javier live. Very cozy,
Reinhard says. And speak of the devil . . ."

He shouted a greeting to Reinhard who was hurrying
along the covered breezeway that connected the theatre to
the Mill.

"Right on time," Reinhard called. "Good. I will see you
inside. Mind the step up, Bernie."

"Will do."

As Reinhard ducked into the Smokehouse, I asked, "Since when are you two so chummy?"

"Since I found out he's Swiss."

"Not . . . German."

"A bad habit," Bernie admitted. "Making assumptions. To hear that accent and start wondering what his family might have done to mine during the war." He shook his head impatiently. "Who needs sad thoughts on our first day? We have to . . . what's the saying? Break a hip?"

"Leg, Bernie. Break a leg."

"I thought you only said that before a performance," Nancy said.

"Morning, noon, and night, we should say it. We need all the luck we can get."

The rehearsal studio was utilitarian but cheerful with pale yellow walls and a bank of open windows. Like the stage, its hardwood floor was pegged rather than nailed; the architects who had restored the post-and-beam barn had brought the same eye for historical accuracy to this building, down to the wooden latches on the doors.

A dance barre was mounted on one wall, but there were no mirrors. Probably to spare us the horror of watching ourselves blunder through the choreography. A battered upright piano sat in a corner. The aroma of coffee wafted from the kitchenette along the back wall, but I was already jittery from three cups of Chatterbox coffee.

As I took a seat in the semicircle of folding chairs, Reinhard stalked toward me and brandished my vocal-chorus part. "Welcome back, Dorothy Gale."

Somehow, holding that booklet made everything real. I was in summer stock again. I was doing a show.

"What, no snappy comeback?"

My fingers caressed the black cover. "Tams-Witmark," I finally managed, whispering the name of the licensing company like a prayer.

An unexpected smile softened Reinhard's craggy features. "Welcome back," he repeated. Then he frowned. "No fainting today."

His frown deepened as the Legally Blondes darted into the studio. "The schedule said ten o'clock. Not 10:04."

As they slunk toward the two empty chairs, Rowan laid down his pen and folded his hands on the table. A breathless silence replaced the murmur of conversation.

"Welcome back, everyone. I know some of you have had a chance to get to know each other this past week, but for the benefit of those who just arrived, let's begin with introductions."

Given the mix of race and ethnicity among the cast, our Brigadoon was going to be a lot more diverse than your typical eighteenth-century Scottish village. The mix of occupations was pretty staggering, too: corporate execs and lawyers, teachers and chefs, computer wonks like the Rastas, auto mechanic Lou, and college dropout/aspiring writer/part-time musician Kevin.

I missed the mark on Nick (a bartender rather than a bouncer) and Bobbie (a home health aide), but I'd pegged many of my cast mates correctly. Church ladies Romaine and Albertha were members of an African Methodist Episcopal congregation in Baltimore. Maya the flower child worked in a New Age bookstore/crystal shop. The Legally Blondes had just finished their junior year of college and were members of Tri Delt sorority.

Top honors for the best introduction went to a twig-like Goth with purple hair who announced, "I have taken the name Kalma, in honor of the Finnish goddess of death whose name means Corpse Stench." Even Rowan blinked at that one.

I found myself wondering what he thought these people needed. Bernie might need to heal from his wife's recent death. Nick definitely needed to get over his homophobia. Caren, the yappy woman who went on and on about her husband the lawyer and their lovely condo on the golf course, just needed to shut up.

Introductions concluded, Rowan called for a read-through. When he explained that this meant reading the dialogue aloud, the principals had a collective panic attack.

"I don't expect a polished performance," he assured them. "But since many of you have never been in a show, it's better to tackle your nerves now rather than opening night."

A few chuckles. A couple of rueful smiles. And voila!

Panic gone. If I could bottle what the guy was selling, I'd be a billionaire.

The line readings ranged from leaden to overenthusiastic, but Rowan's benign expression never faltered. As we worked through the script, my respect for him grew. He'd made subtle changes in dialogue, removing references that were hopelessly outdated and altering lines to make Jeff less smarmy, Fiona a bit tougher, and Tommy less of a vacillating dickweed. Librettist Alan Jay Lerner might be spinning in his grave, but the net effect was to make the characters feel more like real people.

After Bernie read the last line, Rowan and Reinhard applauded. The principals grinned. Even I felt triumphant, and I'd just sat there for the last hour.

"Let's take a five-minute break," Rowan suggested. "The bathroom is next to the kitchen. To avoid lines, I suggest you avail yourselves of the ones in the Dungeon as well. When you return, I'll leave you in Reinhard's capable hands for a crash course in stage directions. Please stack your chairs against that wall before you go. And remember—five minutes only!"

"Smoke 'em if you got 'em!" Lou bellowed, prompting a general exodus.

As I rolled Bernie's walker up to his chair, I asked, "What's the Dungeon? Or don't I want to know?"

"You don't have to play nursemaid. Go. Mingle. Get to know the nice single men."

"You're a nice single man. And I'm not playing nursemaid. What's the Dungeon?"

"The basement. Dressing rooms, costume room, the what-do-you-call-it where you sit before the show . . ."

Before I could say, "Green room," the voice behind me did. At least this time I didn't screech. Or bash my head.

"You've got to stop doing that."

"The Dungeon green room is for the musicians," Rowan said, ignoring my comment. "It's next to the pit entrance. The actors' green room is backstage left."

Bernie groaned. "Pit entrance. Backstage left. You give me a headache with all that theatre lingo."

"Wait until Reinhard gets through with you."

"I heard that!" Reinhard called from across the room.

As Bernie pulled his walker closer, Rowan said, "You can sit this one out if you'd like."

Bernie shook his head and pushed himself up. "Long as you don't have me doing Highland flings, I'll be fine."

We spent our remaining three minutes studying the un-framed posters on the wall above the dance barre. Rowan had apparently gotten his start as a librettist by adapting Shakespearean plays. His taste in musicals was almost as old-fashioned; *Into the Woods* was the most contemporary of the bunch.

"Do they ever do shows from this century?" I whispered.

"It's Dale," Bernie whispered back. "They want Rodgers and Hammerstein, Lerner and Loewe . . ."

"Punch and Judy. Funny about the dates."

Bernie peered at the poster for *Once Upon a Mattress*. "What's so funny?"

"No years."

"Who needs years? You hang 'em in the lobby, you know what's playing."

Before I could reply, Reinhard shouted, "Back to work, everyone!" And I joined the returning horde for Theatre 101.

Reinhard lined us up facing the bank of windows. "We will now pretend that we are standing on the stage. The windows are the audience. The part of the stage nearest the audience is called downstage. The part farthest away from them is called upstage. So. When you move toward the audience, you are crossing . . .?" He glanced around and nodded as Legally Blonde Ashley raised a tentative hand.

"Downstage?" she ventured.

Reinhard beamed. "Correct! Now. Stage left is your left—when you are onstage facing the audience." He turned toward the windows and pointed left. "So. I am pointing . . .?"

"Stage left," we chorused.

Like the Scarecrow in *The Wizard of Oz*, his left arm came down and his right snapped up. "And now I am pointing . . .?"

"Stage right!"

"Of course, people do go both ways," I muttered.

"Is there a question? No? Moving on."

He marched us upstage and down, stage left and right.

Taught us about the wings located on either side of the stage and the apron that extended in front of the curtain. Pointed out the gaffer tape on the floor that outlined the dimensions of the performing area. Explained sight lines and cheating front instead of facing the actor you were talking to.

I should have been bored out of my skull. Instead, I marveled at how much fun I was having.

Half an hour later, he shooed us to the dressing rooms to change for dance class. On our return, Mei-Yin greeted us wearing a tracksuit and a scowl, shouted "LINE UP!" and stalked past us like a general inspecting her troops, all the while shaking her head and muttering to herself. Finally, she stabbed an accusatory forefinger at Legally Blonde Brittany. "YOU! BLONDE girl! You ever DANCE or you just know how to DRESS the part?"

Clad in black leotard and tights, Brittany had already drawn her fair share of envious stares from the women and admiring ones from the men. Her ponytail bobbed as she nodded.

"I studied ballet, ma'am. At the LouAlma School of Dance in—"

"I don't need your RESUME! What else?"

"Jazz and modern. In college. And one class of—"

"You're DANCE CAPTAIN. Warm them up!"

With that, Mei-Yin stamped out of the Smokehouse. Although she slammed the door behind her, we could still hear her shout, "Shoot me NOW, Rowan. Just put a GUN to my head and pull the TRIGGER!"

I joined a few of the braver cast members at the windows.

"What's she doing?" Brittany asked from the safety of the kitchenette.

"Beating her fist against the side of the barn," Kalma replied.

"Every year they get WORSE!"

"And her head," Kalma added.

"Reinhard's coming out the stage door." A guy named Gary picked up the play-by-play. "He's patting her shoulder, trying to calm her down . . ."

Mei-Yin's howl would have made a banshee quail.

"It doesn't seem to be working," Gary noted.

I caught a flash of movement high under the eaves of the barn. For the first time, I noticed the small balcony projecting out from the wall facing the Mill. Slatted wooden blinds jerked open, revealing a figure framed in the glass door.

"'But, soft! what light through yonder window breaks?'" Gary quoted.

"I think it's Rowan," Nick replied with a fine disregard for Shakespeare.

The glass door slid open. Rowan stepped outside, walked to the end of the balcony, and leaned over the railing.

Mei-Yin shook her fist at him. "What am I? A MIRACLE WORKER?"

"'O! speak again, bright angel.'"

"Now you're just showing off," I said.

Gary grinned. "Twelve years teaching high school English."

Whatever Rowan said made Mei-Yin throw up her hands and stomp into the meadow.

"'Good night, good night! parting is such sweet...' whoops, here comes Reinhard."

With commendable cool, Brittany shouted, "Stretch, everybody, stretch!"

The window brigade barely made it back in line before Reinhard burst through the door. He'd evidently been dragging his fingers through his short hair because it was standing on end like gray porcupine quills. Unless his wife's voice alone had produced that effect.

"Everything will be fine," he assured us in a hoarse whisper. "Always, she is like this the first day. It is her artistic nature. Not to worry." He shot a quick look over his shoulder. "But best to hide backpacks. And mugs. Any objects that can be thrown, yes?" With those comforting words, he scuttled out.

Before we could act on his advice, Mei-Yin stalked into the Smokehouse and stripped off her jacket. The leotard underneath revealed the arms and torso of a weightlifter. Several people surreptitiously nudged their vocal books toward the walls.

"All right, then." Mei-Yin favored us with an unexpectedly benign smile. "Let's begin!"

Compared to Mei-Yin, Reinhard was indeed a pussycat.
While Rowan worked with the principals, he herded the chorus into the theatre to stage our first number. I had to give
him major points for patience as he relayed Rowan's blocking. It's just hard to remain enthusiastic when you're being
moved around the stage like a chess piece.

Evening brought our first music rehearsal. When I walked
into the Smokehouse, Alex waved me over to the piano and
held out a flash drive. "I'm afraid your vocal lines are going
to be jumping all over the place. That'll teach you to have
a big range," he added with a grin. "You'll be singing alto
most of the time. But I need you on the second soprano line
at a couple of points. Better find a seat in the DMZ between
the two sections."

"No problem." I pocketed the flash drive. "Sorry for the
last-minute scramble."

"Oh, I created the files after auditions." He flashed that
mischievous grin again. "I'm good, aren't I?"

"You're . . . amazing. How did you know I'd be back?"

"Everybody comes back. I can't remember the last time
we had a no-show."

"Six years ago. Lee."

His ruddy eyebrows soared. "You're pretty amazing yourself."

"Janet."

"Ah. Janet."

Astonishing how he could convey respect, ruefulness,
and genuine affection in just three syllables.

"Janet's a tough cookie," he admitted. "But her heart's in
the right place."

"I'm just relieved to know she has one."

He laughed and turned to the milling crowd. "Okay, let's
get started." Several people groaned, and he shook his finger
at them. "Some of you probably think you can't sing. Well,
that's nonsense. If you can breathe, you can sing. And that's
what we're going to concentrate on tonight: breathing and
relaxing. Tomorrow, we'll get into the real work."

We breathed lying on our backs. We breathed standing up

straight. We hissed like snakes to practice breath control. We blew imaginary bubbles to relax our lips. We worked on diction by repeating tongue twisters like "fluffy, floppy puppy" and "red leather, yellow leather" and "unique New York."

Then he moved on to physical warm-ups: neck rolls and shoulder rolls, leg stretches and propeller arms, reaching for the ceiling and bending from the waist to touch the floor.

"Okay, shake it out. Arms, legs, heads. You can't sing with tension in your body. Now, open your mouths and yawn." His voice swooped up and down, and we imitated him, sounding like inmates of Bedlam on a bad day.

We chanted "Ah," staggering our breathing to create a wall of sound on every conceivable note known to man until I expected the monolith from *2001: A Space Odyssey* to appear. We climbed up the scale by half steps, intoning "Ah, A, E, Oh, Oo" like the caterpillar in *Alice in Wonderland*. In between chords, Alex shouted out instructions: "Drop those jaws! . . .Give me a nice, full sound! . . . Full does not mean loud, people. Listen to your neighbors. Blend. . . . Don't push. Drop out when it gets too high."

Two hours later, self-consciousness had given way to a strangely tribal sense of community. Every cast became a community, of course. But I'd never seen it happen the first day of rehearsal.

Only in the last few minutes did we open our vocal books. Like Rowan, Alex had no fear of editing. He'd cut reprises, chopped verses and choruses from some of the longer songs, trimmed dance numbers and the endless chase scene at the top of Act Two. A troupe of professionals might be able to pull the full show together in three weeks, but those cuts gave me a glimmer of hope that we could, too.

"As you can see from the list of cuts, the chorus will not be singing the 'Prologue.' I'm just using the music to bridge us into that opening scene." Alex raised one palm and gazed skyward before returning his attention to us. "When I do that, I'm asking the shades of Lerner and Loewe for forgiveness.

"Moving on to 'Brigadoon.' It's written for the full chorus, but we're going to add voices a few at a time." Hand and gaze moved heavenward again. "The practical reason is to prevent the chorus from drowning out the actors' lines. But there's another."

Alex's fingers softly sounded the opening chords of "Brigadoon" on the piano.

"We're trying to create a sense of mystery here. Of wonder."

His voice was gentle, like a father telling a bedtime story to his children.

"Listen to the music. A new day is dawning. The people of Brigadoon are starting to stir. Half-awake, half-asleep, caught between the otherworld and this one."

He fell silent, allowing us to appreciate a soaring high note.

"Slowly, the village emerges from the mist. And the villagers awaken from their dream."

His voice gained power with the music, building to Brigadoon's triumphant assertion of faith and hope.

"A hundred years slip by while they sleep. But they only age a single night. And wake as if it's the next morning. Because once again, the miracle has occurred!"

Music and words echoed in the sudden silence. For a moment, we all sat there. Then Alex rubbed his arms. "I get goose bumps just thinking about it."

So did I. Judging from the half-open mouths and dazed expressions around me, so did everyone else in the room.

"Okay, people. That's it for tonight. Practice those breathing exercises. Five minutes on the floor before bed. Five minutes standing in the morning."

🔻🔻

"Alex is a lot like Rowan," Nancy observed as we crawled into our beds after our five minutes on the floor. "The way he does things, I mean."

"How *does* Rowan do things?"

Nancy rolled toward me, the lace around the neck of her flannel nightgown peeking over the patchwork quilt. "Well, we didn't do any acting. Just exercises and games. Is that . . . typical?"

"Well, it helps to break the ice and build trust before you get into the scene work."

"But we've only got a couple weeks to put the show together."

"Don't remind me," I muttered.

"It's funny. The exercises seemed silly at first, but I felt good while I was doing them. Rowan makes you feel like you're a real actor. That by opening night, you'll be wonderful."

"That *is* just like Alex."

"But do you feel like that now?"

Reluctantly, I shook my head.

"I noticed it at our meal breaks," Nancy confided. "I left the Smokehouse feeling on top of the world, and by the time I got to town, all my doubts were back."

I frowned. The same thing had happened to me. I'd left the music rehearsal on a real high, flattered that Alex had asked me and Gary to work with the chorus an hour or two each week until he was finished teaching. Now, I found myself dreading the extra work and recalling everything that had gone wrong during rehearsal: how shrill the sopranos sounded, how the basses seemed incapable of blending with the rest of us, how yappy Caren giggled each time she stumbled over her "fluffy, floppy puppy."

"It's only natural to have doubts," I said, as much to reassure myself as Nancy.

"Of course. Don't mind me." She snapped off the lamp on the nightstand between our beds. "I'm just tired."

Footsteps thudded overhead. Springs screeched next door as someone bounded onto a bed. Toilets flushed in the hall. A door banged shut.

Long after silence had descended, I lay awake, puzzling over a director who cast actors in the roles they needed, a dictatorial stage manager who made me enjoy Theatre 101, a music director who cast a spell with his words. Wondering if I was making way too much out of their perfectly ordinary desire to build up our confidence and meld us into a company.

Maybe it was only natural that somewhere between the theatre and the hotel, their spells wore off and our giddy confidence waned. And like the villagers emerging from the mists of Brigadoon, we awoke to reality.

The thought coincided with the sound of muffled footsteps in the hallway. An oddly irregular rhythm. Five steps, then silence. Five more steps, then silence again. It didn't take a vivid imagination to picture someone pausing outside each room.

Like a good New Yorker, I'd locked our door and put the chain on before crawling into bed, but I still stiffened as the footsteps stopped outside our room.

I heard something brush across the wooden door. My knotted muscles relaxed. Warmth suffused my body. As if gentle arms had enfolded me, I felt embraced by a sense of comfort and safety and peace.

Too tired to question or doubt or do anything other than accept what I had been offered, I closed my eyes and surrendered to the Golden Bough.

CHAPTER 4
TENDER SHEPHERD

MY REHEARSAL DAYS QUICKLY ASSUMED A pat-
tern. Breakfast at the Chatterbox. Dance rehearsal with
Mei-Yin. A quick lunch picked up at the Chatterbox or the
roadside grill known as the Ptomaine Stand. Blocking with
Reinhard in the afternoon. Take-out pizza from Nonna Te-
resa's or take-out Chinese from the Mandarin Chalet or—
less frequently—an honest-to-God sit-down dinner at Duck
Inn or the Golden Bough. Then music rehearsal with Alex.

On the nights Alex worked with the principals, Gary led
the men into the Dungeon, while I pounded out the women's
vocal parts on the piano in the Smokehouse. The hour or two
a week Alex had requested quickly became an hour or two
a day.

After rehearsals ended, we adjourned to the lounge of the
Bough. Helen played bartender, providing a sympathetic ear
along with pints of Vermont microbrews. Promptly at midnight, Janet appeared in the doorway to announce that the
bar was closed. We learned to talk and drink fast.

Every afternoon, Helen arrived at the theatre with a
wicker basket over her arm like Little Red Riding Hood.
By day four, we concluded that she brought Rowan his
lunch. Nancy, our resident mole among the principals, lent
credence to this surmise by reporting that Rowan always
brought a strawberry milkshake with him to the Smokehouse
when rehearsals resumed. If he ate solid food as well, it was
consumed out of sight in his office under the eaves.

Helen's basket always contained a treat for the cast as well: oatmeal raisin cookies, corn muffins, cranberry nut bread. Her energy amazed me. She looked so delicate, almost frail, yet she managed to run the hotel, handle advance ticket sales, and bring us comfort food.

The rest of the staff was equally adept at multitasking. Reinhard still kept office hours several times a week. Hal had his lingerie shop, Javier his antique store. Mei-Yin managed the Chalet with Max, Reinhard's son from a previous marriage. Alex taught at Hillandale High. Lee had a small legal practice.

I gleaned those tidbits from Hal during a costume fitting squeezed into the brutal schedule. But even he had only the haziest information about Janet.

"She must be well-off to keep the theatre going all these years," I ventured.

"Her husbands were."

"Husbands? How many has she had?"

"Two, I think."

"What happened to them?" I asked, immediately casting her in the role of Black Widow.

"They died. Of natural causes," he added pointedly. "She's been a widow for years. Like Helen." Hal sighed. "Helen was only married a year, poor thing. And after her husband died, she never remarried."

When I wondered aloud how the Golden Bough managed to turn a profit with our non-paying cast as its only residents, Hal assured me that the hotel would be full once *Brigadoon* opened, and that it did a brisk business during fall foliage and ski seasons.

My cautious feelers revealed that a number of my cast mates had experienced the same extremes of giddy confidence and stomach-churning doubt that Nancy and I had discussed. Everyone simply assumed our doubts surfaced when the staff cheerleaders were absent. Or as Bobbie put it, "If they told us we sucked this early, who'd stick around for opening night?"

The phenomenon nagged at me, but I was too exhausted to obsess about it. I worked harder that first week than I ever had in my life. Which made our Act One run-through doubly painful.

Richard marched through the role of the conflicted Tommy with the pained determination of a boss eager to conclude an unpleasant performance review. Ashley did better with Fiona during the infrequent moments you could hear her. Nancy and Will lacked any semblance of comic timing, a serious drawback for the "funny" couple in the show.

On the plus side, Kevin delivered a strong performance as brooding Harry Beaton. And if Bernie stumbled over his speeches and delivered them in the accents of Brooklyn rather than Scotland, he perfectly captured the gentle humor and wisdom of Mr. Lundie.

I'd been wondering how Alex would coax a lyric tenor from Lou. Now I discovered that he'd dropped Lou's songs a fifth. While it was strange to hear "I'll Go Home with Bonnie Jean" sung in a booming bass, Lou's "hoisting a few with the boys" approach worked.

Even more amazing was his awkward yet sweetly sincere rendition of "Come to Me, Bend to Me." Although Bobbie was supposed to respond in dance, Mei-Yin had wisely cut much of the ballet and assigned the trickiest parts to Brittany and Maya. Yet with a few simple movements, Bobbie managed to convey the sensitive nature lurking beneath her tough exterior.

When the number ended, we broke into spontaneous applause. Lou and Bobbie clowned a bit, but as Rowan brought us back to order, a look passed between them, as sweet as those they had exchanged as Charlie and Jean.

Was that why they were here—to find each other? But how could Rowan Mackenzie have realized that at auditions?

After three interminable hours, Kevin shouted Harry's line about the end of the miracle. He raced offstage, the men raced after him, and the staff applauded; everyone had come that night to lend moral support. Relief turned to dread as Rowan mounted the steps to the stage.

"Well, I'm sure that felt more like a stagger-through than a run-through. Believe me, it's always like that the first time you put everything together."

As he reviewed our accomplishments, the collective tension gave way to renewed confidence. Sure, we were still stumbling over our choreography, flubbing our vocals, groping for lines and characters. But we had made it through Act One.

The only problem was, it shouldn't have been possible.

At Southford, we'd rehearsed an entire show in a week. But we were professionals. That encompassed far more than simply arriving with music and lines memorized. We had a common language. We knew upstage from down, a quarter note from a half. We could execute a plié or a grapevine or a step-ball-change without a lengthy demonstration.

True, Alex and Mei-Yin had simplified the music and choreography, but it should have taken weeks for our cast to reach this level. And although I had just seen the evidence of our success, I still couldn't understand how we had achieved it.

I watched as Rowan drew aside the principals for notes. When they returned to the group, they looked liked worshipers who had come face-to-face with their god of choice. Which might explain their confidence but did little to solve the mystery of how that translated into credible performances.

I was on the verge of broaching my questions to Nancy that night when she suddenly burst into tears. Stunned, I grabbed the box of Kleenex from the nightstand's lower shelf. Nancy plucked out a tissue, blew her nose, and declared, "I was awful."

"No, you weren't!" I protested, assuming my supportive HelpLink expression.

Nancy grimaced.

Wondering if I'd lost the knack of the supportive HelpLink expression, I added, "You had all your lines down cold."

Which is almost as bad as going backstage after a terrible performance and telling an actor that his costumes looked great.

I tried again. "What did Rowan say?"

"He told me I was off to a good start, but I needed to think more about Meg's character. And then he asked how I felt about her."

"How *do* you feel about her?"

Nancy ripped another tissue from the box. "I think she's pathetic! Throwing herself at Jeff. So desperate and grasping and needy. As if having a man—any man—is the most important thing in the world."

I took a moment to digest that, then asked, "Did you tell Rowan that?"

"I didn't have to tell him. He knew."

I was beginning to think Rowan Mackenzie knew way too much about way too many things. But I had a more immediate problem. I plopped down beside Nancy and squeezed her hand; she didn't seem like the hugging type.

"He asked me to find her strengths as well as her weaknesses. To look at the things I disliked about her and try to turn them into something positive."

It wasn't exactly Stanislavsky, but it was better than suggesting that the real reason Nancy disliked Meg so much was that the character possessed qualities that she lacked.

I jumped up and pulled a notebook and pencil from my carryall. "We'll make a list. Meg's strengths in one column and her weaknesses in another."

Ten minutes later, the qualities Nancy perceived as weaknesses filled the entire column. Under strengths, I'd scribbled "Tenacious." But at least she'd stopped crying.

"Now, let's look at the weaknesses and flip them so they're strengths."

Nancy stared at item #1: Pushy. Then looked up at me, wire-rimmed glasses shining in the lamplight. "Self-confident?" she ventured.

"Self-confident. Great! Item #2: Desperate."

"Maybe that should go with 'Tenacious.'"

I drew an arrow between them. We filled in "Flirt" opposite "Tramp," "Earthy" opposite "Obsessed with Sex," "Eternal Optimist" opposite "Completely Clueless about a Future with Jeff."

"This is great," I assured her. "Sure, Meg's been around the block, but she's held onto her hopes. And her sense of humor."

"Put 'Humor' under strengths. No. Make it . . . 'Rueful Self-Awareness.'"

"Maybe she realizes Jeff won't work out. But even if he isn't Mr. Right, someone else might come along. And until then, she'll manage just fine on her own."

"Ooh! 'Self-sufficient.' Write that under 'Strengths.'"
Nancy watched me scribble for a moment, then said, "Rowan
should have cast you as Meg. You're so much like her."

"Well, the string of failures with men is familiar."

The notebook shuddered as Nancy's forefinger stabbed
the phrase "Rueful Self-Awareness." Shuddered again as I
stabbed "Eternal Optimist" and said, "Not so much."

I couldn't even remember the last time I'd gone out with
a man, unless you counted the lunch when my boss fired
me. My two serious relationships were case studies in Mr.
Wrong. Michael—gay. Eric—commitment-phobe and asshole. Okay, only an asshole after he got salmonella poisoning from my deviled eggs and changed from The Guy Who
Might Be the One to The Guy Who Stopped Calling.

As far back as elementary school, I'd yearned for the
wrong boy, sighing over brooding Allan Parkinson and ignoring Tommy Barnett who nicknamed me Maggie Graham
Cracker Crust and made up this stupid song about me. How
was I supposed to know that "She's So Crusty" was a ten
year old's idea of a romantic serenade?

"Don't make the mistake I did," my mother told me in
one of our rare heart-to-hearts. "Don't fall for a man who's
forever chasing rainbows."

The thing was, I'd seen her photo albums. She looked
radiant in some of those pictures. Later, of course, the radi-
ance leached away, leaving the anxious, pinch-faced woman
I knew. I'd always wondered if it was my fault. If having a
kid strained their marriage. Or if it was because I was so
totally Daddy's little girl.

Add that guilt to my string of professional failures, my
appallingly small circle of friends, my "I look great as
long as I don't stand naked in front of a full-length mirror"
physique . . .

God. I was a total loser.

Nancy, however, looked quite cheerful. At least one of us
had been buoyed by our exercise.

"I know it's late, but would you mind running Jeff's lines
with me in Scene Three?"

I plastered a smile on my face. "Let's do it!"

◆━

No good deed goes unpunished. The next morning—our first day off—Nancy rushed into our room with Will in tow.

"I told him about your list," she announced, "and he wants to try it."

"That's great! Let me know how it goes."

As Will's eager expression faded, I realized I'd miss the key point: he wanted to try it with me.

"There's no trick," I assured him. "You just make two columns—"

"But you have to be there," Nancy said. "To ask the right questions." She held out my notebook and pencil like an acolyte offering the high priestess her tools for the mystical rite.

By midafternoon, "Craft Your Character with Maggie" had become the game of choice among the principals. Kevin's list took two hours to develop and involved an extensive backstory undreamed of by Alan Jay Lerner that included Harry Beaton's childhood trauma as a bed wetter, the recurring bouts of eczema that had prompted his aversion to weaving, and his penchant for masturbating in the heather on the hill.

At least Bernie was done in fifteen minutes. And brought his own paper and pencil.

"Now I get it," he said, folding his list into a neat square.

"You already had it. You know Mr. Lundie inside and—"

"Lundie, Schmundie. It's you I'm talking about. Miss Tough New Yorker. Ha! You're a pussycat. Just like Reinhard."

"Pussycat, schmussycat."

"What? It's so bad to help people? That's what you do for a living."

I considered telling him this was hardly the kind of work I performed—had performed—at HelpLink. For one thing, I was seldom on the front lines; I trained and supervised those who were. If answering the phone could be considered the front lines. We weren't social workers or counselors. We were middlemen, providing the information callers needed to *find* a social worker or counselor. Hence, the all-important "Link" in HelpLink. On the rare occasion

I covered the phones, I gave callers the information that would lead them on the next stage of their journey down the Yellow Brick Road to wellness and effected a speedy disconnect.

Helping once removed. That's what I specialized in. This hands-on thing was a lot harder. Sure, I'd always enjoyed picking apart characters to discover what made them tick. And I got a warm glow when a fellow cast member had that "Aha!" moment. But spending an entire day doing that was exhausting. Especially since I needed to do my laundry, answer my e-mails, and apply to any job in the five boroughs that looked remotely promising.

And I really needed to avoid pissing Rowan off by playing director behind his back.

"Do you know why you're here?" I asked Bernie.

The wrinkles on his face realigned as his smile morphed into a frown. "I auditioned. Same as you."

"But why?"

"It just felt like the right thing to do. Sarah and I were passing through town. We saw the barn." Bernie shrugged.

It was eerily reminiscent of my experience.

"How does it make you feel? Working here?"

"Again with the psychoanalysis?"

"No. Really."

Bernie cocked his head, considering. It increased his resemblance to a bright-eyed, balding sparrow.

"I feel . . . good. Tired, but good. I haven't slept so well since Rachel passed. I wake up in the morning excited. Instead of wondering how I'll fill the hours until bedtime. And the exercise must be good for me. These old hips haven't felt so strong in years." He leaned forward, bright sparrow eyes intent. "And what about you, Maggie Graham? Why are you here?"

"I'm still trying to work that out."

"Well, you keep working." Bernie pushed himself up from the table. "I'm going to grab a nap before movie night."

I groaned, wondering how I could have forgotten. Hal had started the tradition when he joined the staff. Every season began with a Judy Garland double feature: *A Star is Born* and *Summer Stock*. Hal provided the DVDs, Nonna's provided giant wedges, and Helen served some of her trademark desserts.

It had seemed like a fun idea when Hal mentioned it at my costume fitting. But I would gladly have traded movie night for a long walk. Or a long shower. Or even a solitary vigil in the laundry room. At least there I could ponder the mystery of Rowan Mackenzie undisturbed. And that of a seventy-four-year-old widower who had found an astonishing new lease on life.

❧❧

I was no closer to solving either mystery when I trudged up to my room that night, canvas bag of laundry slung over my shoulder. It was well after midnight and although I'd taken the fire stairs to avoid passing anywhere near the office, I eased the door open cautiously in case Janet was prowling around. When I saw the robed figure outside my room, I caught my breath.

Helen turned toward me, her lips parted in a round "O" of surprise, the fingers of her right hand splayed across my door.

That explained one mystery; clearly, Helen was the unseen visitor I'd heard that first night. Before I could ask why she was lurking outside my room, she started down the hall, beckoning me to follow. Her destination became apparent when she walked through the small sitting room and eased open the French doors to the porch.

"It's not too cold for you?" she asked, eyeing my T-shirt.

I leaned on the railing, breathing in the crisp air. "It feels wonderful. I've been trapped inside all day."

With its twin lines of streetlamps, Main Street resembled a landing strip. Hallee's glowed pinkly in the distance, but the other shops were dark. The curved sickle of the moon floated among a thousand stars that seemed much closer and brighter than they did in New York. But as always, it was the silence that struck me most. The first few nights, I'd found it unsettling, accustomed to the nighttime mix of sirens, car alarms, muted conversations from other apartments, the occasional not-so-muted argument on the street. Now, the quiet felt restful.

Which reminded me of Helen's visitations.

As if I had spoken, she asked, "You promise you won't laugh?"

I nodded.

"It's . . . a sort of ritual. I stop by each room at night and . . . bless those inside." She plucked nervously at the sash of her baby blue robe. "I suppose that sounds silly."

Actually, it sounded sweet. Just the sort of thing Helen would do.

"I heard you once. Just footsteps and something brushing against the door. I thought at first it was a burglar."

"In Dale? We don't even lock our doors at night."

"The thing is, after you . . . blessed us . . . I felt this amazing sense of . . . well, peace."

Helen clapped her hands like a delighted child. "Maybe it really works."

It certainly seemed to. I hadn't felt such peace since I was small enough to believe that my parents' presence would protect me from anything that went bump in the night.

Helen's bright smile faded as I stared at her. "This may sound stupid, but you're not some sort of . . . witch, are you?"

"Goodness, no. But I've always suspected my great-great grandmother was. A white witch," she added quickly.

"Like Glinda?"

Helen smiled. "Minus the puffy gown. I never knew her, of course, but her book was handed down to me."

"A book of . . . spells?"

Her smile grew. "Recipes. And herbals. Some are quite effective. I haven't had a deer in my garden for years. Of course, that might be due to the boys on staff."

My puzzlement must have shown because she laughed and quickly pressed her fingertips to her mouth. "They urinate around the perimeter of the garden. Lee started it, and men being what they are, it escalated into a . . ."

"Pissing contest?"

A giggle escaped Helen's fingertips. "Javier's mostly taken it over, since he lives so close. And has a weak bladder," she added in a whisper. "I'd just as soon use my garlic and Tabasco spray, but it's become something of a tradition."

I made a mental note to pump Hal for details, but couldn't resist asking, "Does Rowan . . . ?"

"Oh, no. That wouldn't work at all."

Before I could question that unusual statement, Helen said, "It's terribly late. And you have a busy week ahead."

Right on cue, I yawned.

"Oh, dear. I've kept you far too long." Helen's anxious frown deepened. "You won't tell anyone? About the blessing? It's really quite harmless, but . . ."

I crossed my heart. "They'll never hear it from me."

Helen's hug filled me with the same peace and contentment as her blessing. Maybe it was just the feel of her arms around me. Daddy had been the hugger in our family. After he left, my mother managed a few awkward ones when I left for college or came home for a visit.

"Do you have any children?" I blurted.

Helen's hands cupped my cheeks, but her gaze drifted past me to embrace the Golden Bough and its sleeping inhabitants.

"Dozens of them."

CHAPTER 5
BEWITCHED, BOTHERED, AND BEWILDERED

MY "DAY OFF" MADE ME REALIZE I could take only so much nonstop togetherness. I tried holing up in my room at lunch, but nibbling fruit, bread, and cheese on my bed was depressing. Plus I got crumbs everywhere. Walking through town meant inevitable encounters with other cast members, the friendly citizens of Dale, or the staff.

Except Rowan. I never saw him in town. I rarely even saw him on the grounds of the theatre. Once rehearsal was over, he hightailed it to his office. Clearly, he had a low tolerance for togetherness, too.

Finally, I took a brisk walk around the meadow during our lunch break. To my dismay, Caren tagged after me, chattering nonstop. When I informed her—politely—that I needed some time alone, her crestfallen look left me feeling guilty and pissed off about feeling guilty. I grimly trudged past the pond, resigned to crumb-filled bedding. Then I spotted a hand-painted sign describing a trail through the neighboring woodland.

The next day, I waited for everyone to head out to lunch, liberally sprayed myself with "Bug Away", and marched off in search of solitude.

I quickly discovered that the sign painter had used the term "trail" rather loosely. I wasn't expecting paved walkways, but I did assume there would be some sort of path. With signs along the way. And maybe a bench or two.

Instead, I found myself doing a Lewis and Clark through

the wilderness, hoping that the red splotches adorning the tree trunks were more than the random results of a local paintball battle. Fortunately, the trees were so enormous that only a few saplings and shrubs had managed to spring up on the forest floor, reducing my need for a machete. The dense canopy blocked most of the sunlight, so I had to tread cautiously. Still, it was wonderfully peaceful. The only things breaking the silence were the twittering of birds, the soft crunch of dead pine needles and leaves, and my occasional curses when I stumbled over an unseen hazard.

I was catching my breath after one such hazard when I heard the singing. A man's voice, faint but discernible. I was too far away to make out the words, but the unfamiliar tune was achingly beautiful.

I wasn't aware of leaving the trail. And by the time I realized there were no paint splotches to guide me, I no longer cared that I might be lost. Like a sailor out of legend, I had to follow that siren call.

My steps kept pace with the long, sustained notes of the melody. As it shifted into a variation, I found myself moving faster, only to slow again as the chorus returned. No longer a sailor, but a strand of seaweed, caught in the relentless ebb and flow of the music.

The language of the song was as unfamiliar as the tune, but the longing in that clear voice made my throat tighten. Its mingled blend of hope and despair, joy and melancholy were so palpable that I discovered my hands outstretched before me as if to grasp those emotions.

His voice soared again to that pure, high note, and my spirit soared with it. It faded to a whisper, and helpless tears welled in my eyes. It caught in his throat, emerging as a ragged cry, halfway between a sob and a growl, and I had to clutch at the trunk of a tree until the dizziness passed.

My chest ached with the effort to breathe. My pulse raced with the urgency to reach him. With every step, the inchoate yearning inside me grew stronger, a longing for something that remained just out of reach, just beyond conscious desire. And with it, the hope that if I found the source of that voice, I would understand my yearning and find what I was seeking.

I broke into a trot, weaving among the tree trunks. Some-

thing caught at my hair, and I clawed free, barely aware of
the twigs scratching my hands. Something snagged my foot,
and I stumbled, cursing the tangle of vines for slowing me
down.

Only when I felt water trickling down my shins did I realize I must have splashed through a small stream. Only when
I felt the ache in my legs and the burning rasp of my breath
did I discover I was running heedlessly fast.

A wall of stone suddenly loomed before me. As I veered
away, my feet skidded on some loose pebbles. I lurched sideways, arms flailing as I tried to regain my balance. I only
succeeded in scraping my hands on the rough bark of a pine
as I fell.

The singing stopped.

If I hadn't felt the cry tearing at my throat, I would have
thought a wounded animal had made it. And like a wounded
animal, I collapsed onto the pine needles and curled into a
ball.

I don't know how long I lay there. Minutes, probably, although it felt like hours. Slowly, I returned to myself, aware
of the painful throbbing in my left knee, the sharp stinging
when I flexed my hands, sweat cooling on my back, pine
needles tickling my cheek. If there was such a thing at the
end of days as the Rapture, this was how it would feel to be
left behind. Or worse, to be given a glimpse of heaven and
have it snatched away.

Dismissing that thought as overly dramatic, I pushed
myself to my feet and took a few cautious steps. Nothing
broken, thank God. But dancing would be hell for the next
couple of days.

I knew the road through Dale ran north to south. Which
meant the woods were west of the theatre. If I could figure
out which way east was, I might emerge from this little fiasco
intact. Unfortunately, the few shafts of sunlight penetrating
the canopy made it difficult to get any sense of direction.

As I searched for additional clues, I belatedly discovered
that the stone wall belonged to a small hut. I examined the
skid marks I'd left in the thick mulch of leaves and pine
needles, wishing I were more like Natty Bumppo. Or any
moderately adequate, modern-day Pathfinder.

Desperate to avoid calling Reinhard's emergency number, I made a slow circle, seeking consensus from skid marks and sun on the direction I should take. Then I froze, my brain finally registering what my eyes had just passed over.

A figure stood a few feet away. A man. A man who had crept toward me with Bumppo-esque stealth, blending so perfectly into the patchwork of sunlight and shadow that I'd neither seen nor heard him approach.

Then it all clicked and I snapped, "Do you always sneak up on people?"

"I could ask you the same thing," Rowan replied.

Hard to believe that mild voice was the same one I'd heard earlier. But it had to have been Rowan singing. He had cast a spell just talking about our contract.

In the two weeks I'd known him, I'd seen him in various modes: the polite acquaintance, the rueful hypnotist, the earnest teacher, the avuncular director. It was difficult to find any of them in the blank-faced stranger walking toward me.

Neither his manner nor his expression revealed anger, yet somehow, it filled the forest. The birds fell silent. A cold breeze buffeted my face. The shadows deepened under the trees. He even seemed to grow taller and more threatening with every slow, inexorable step.

Without conscious thought, I backed away. He drew up short, his head snapping back as if I'd slapped him.

The breeze died. The sun came out from behind a cloud. The birds resumed their twittering. And Rowan looked like Rowan again.

"Forgive me. I frightened you."

I shook my head, but the lines between those wild-winged brows deepened.

"Are you hurt?"

"I fell." I sounded like a six-year-old about to burst into tears because of the nasty boo-boos on her hands and knees.

He reached me in a few long strides and gently guided me toward a fallen tree. After easing me onto it, he went down on one knee. Like a courtier before a queen. Or a suitor asking for my hand in marriage.

When he actually asked for my hand, I nearly fell off the log.

"Your hands," he repeated patiently. "Are they badly scraped?"

When I continued to gawk at him, he simply took my right hand in his and turned it palm up. His fingertips glided across the abraded flesh, trailing cool relief in their wake.

He just has cold hands. Nothing weird about that.

He also had beautiful hands, the pale skin unusually smooth for a man. Each long tapering finger had a perfect little crescent moon at the tip of each nail. He and Helen had to go to the same manicurist.

So he's the human equivalent of a Mexican hairless. So what? Or maybe he's the original hairy ape and he waxes. And gets manicures. Nothing weird about that, either. Lots of men do it. I don't know any, but . . .

He turned his attention to my left hand, and I sighed, doubts subsiding along with the stinging in my palm. His hands descended to my sore knee. I closed my eyes, enjoying the gentleness of his massaging fingertips.

Then Nancy's words popped into my head: "I didn't have to tell him. He knew."

I flinched.

Rowan's hands fell still. "What is it?"

Not "Did I hurt you?" which would have been the logical question. Because he knew he wasn't hurting me. Just as he knew exactly where I was hurting before he did the whole laying-on-of-hands thing.

"Maggie?"

So he's a hands-on healer. Nothing . . . okay that is weird. But not impossibly weird.

Abruptly, he rose and stalked away, shoving his fists into the pockets of his jeans.

I'm alone in the forest with my director, that's all. A director who casts people according to need and happens to be a hairless hands-on healer who lives on strawberry milkshakes and only leaves the grounds of the theatre when he hikes into the forest to sing in tongues.

I examined my palms. They still looked red and raw, although they didn't hurt as much.

"I've frightened you again."

I shook my head.

"Come on, Maggie! You're shaking like a leaf and you're staring at me like I'm a . . . . ."

"What?" I whispered. "What are you?"

Just like that, the mask slipped over his features. Not the blank face of anger I'd seen moments ago, but the distant expression I'd noted the morning I'd bashed my head. As if he'd withdrawn into private memories or some secret place where no one could possibly reach him. And then it was gone, replaced so swiftly by an expression of ordinary frustration that I wondered if I was making all this shit up.

"I'm a good reader of faces and body language. A useful skill for a director. When I walked toward you, you held up your hands to stop me."

"I did?"

"That's when I noticed your palms. And when I saw your limp—yes, you were limping—I thought I should ascertain how badly you were hurt in case I had to carry you back to the theatre. Which I'm prepared to do. Although two miles is a long way to walk with a woman slung over your shoulders. Any other questions?"

Dozens flooded my overheated brain. But I was tired and sore and still too dazed to trust myself to frame them, never mind process the answers. When I shook my head, he walked back to me and extended his hands to help me to my feet.

A thick red weal creased each palm. Smaller ones marred his fingertips.

I took his hands without comment, but the tightening of his jaw proved that he'd noticed my slight hesitation and the direction of my gaze.

He drew my left arm around his waist and wrapped his right one around mine. Entwined like kids in a three-legged race, we hobbled through the woods for a bit. Then I eased free.

"I'm just a little stiff," I assured him. "I'll be fine if we go slow."

He stuck close to my side in case I needed help. At the steeper spots, his arm snaked around my waist to support me, the embrace as impersonal as any medic's. When the ground leveled off again, he stepped away. Once or twice, he nodded as if pleased by my progress. But the silence seemed to pulsate with my unspoken questions and his lingering resentment.

Finally, I stopped. As I struggled to find the right words, his expression hardened.

"They're burns."

"What?"

"The marks. On my hands. Burns."

"No . . . that wasn't . . . I just wanted to apologize. For disturbing you. I didn't mean to. Or to spy on you. I just . . ." I shrugged helplessly. "I heard you singing."

The tension had drained out of him during my fumbling explanation. He nodded, unsurprised. He'd probably encountered similar reactions so often that he'd learned to hide in the woods before allowing himself the pleasure—the release—of singing.

We walked on, the silence a little less forbidding now. Which gave me the courage to say, "Could I ask you one question?"

His chest rose and fell as he nodded. I wasn't sure if he was heaving a resigned sigh or bracing himself.

"The song. What's it called?"

From his short exhalation of breath, I decided he'd been bracing himself.

"It's usually translated as 'The Mist-Covered Mountains.'"

"Gaelic!" I exclaimed. "That was the language."

He nodded, grasping my elbow to guide me around a fallen birch.

"What's it about? Other than mist-covered mountains." At his sidelong look, I added, "Okay, that's two questions, but—"

"Home. It's about home. The places you once walked. The people you once knew. The welcome that awaits you when . . . if . . . you return."

"An exile's song."

His head snapped toward me. "Why would you say that?"

"It sounded like a lament. But not without hope."

Slowly, he nodded.

Had he been born in Scotland? That would explain the

trace of an accent I'd detected the first day. And the Gaelic. Had something happened to drive him from his native land? Or prevent him from returning?

"Ask." A small smile—more of a grimace—tugged at the corner of his mouth.

"I was just wondering if you were born in Scotland."

"Yes. And before that vivid imagination of yours runs wild, let me assure you that I am not a Scottish serial killer hiding out in the hinterlands of Vermont."

"Hey, you were the one who said you chopped up cast members for buttons."

"I was joking." The green eyes narrowed. "But the idea is growing on me."

"So I guess I shouldn't ask about the hut."

"You mean the *cottage*?"

From the way he emphasized the word, it was clear that he took exception to the term "hut." But a one-room building barely ten paces wide hardly qualified as a cottage. Unless it was located in Brigadoon.

"What's a cottage doing out in the middle of nowhere?"

"It was built a long time ago. Back in the 1700s, the Mackenzies received a land grant of two hundred acres. There are only twenty acres left, but that's more than enough for someone to get lost. Especially—"

"A city slicker like me?"

"Especially since they adjoin the Green Mountain National Forest."

I thought of reminding him that I would never have gotten lost in the first place if not for his singing, but common sense told me to avoid that sensitive subject.

"So the first Mackenzies lived in—"

"My turn. Why were you walking in the woods? You don't strike me as a nature lover."

"I like nature." I batted away a cloud of gnats and saw him turn his head to hide a smile. "I do! I just . . . this was the only quiet place I could find. Away from everything."

"You needed to get away?"

"Yes! We rehearse together. We eat together. We even sleep together. I needed some private time."

"You didn't find any on your day off?"

"Romaine called an extra chorus rehearsal. And then there was movie night. And—"

"And coaching the principals."

I stopped short. "Who told you?"

"I believe you just did."

My withering look had no effect whatsoever on him. "Okay, Columbo. You want to tell me how you figured that out?"

"Elementary, my dear Watson," he replied, blithely mixing detectives. "If a couple of the principals had improved in the space of a single day, I simply would have assumed they'd had time to process my comments. When all of them improved, I began to wonder if they had outside help. You were the natural suspect."

"It wasn't something I planned. Nancy was upset after the run-through and—"

"Upset?" he asked, his voice sharp.

"She was . . . well . . . crying."

I didn't understand the passionate explosion of Gaelic, but he was obviously swearing.

"She's fine now. Rowan! She's fine."

He stopped swearing, but his frown remained.

"She was just frustrated. So I asked her what you'd suggested. And then all I did—I swear to God—was draw a line down a piece of paper, and write 'Strengths' in one column and 'Weaknesses' in another."

"And ask a few questions."

He was smiling again, thank God.

"A few," I admitted. "But mostly, it came from her. And then she told Will, and Will told Ashley and Richard, and before I knew it . . ."

"The line was forming to the right."

"I wasn't coaching them. Or trying to play director. Or—"

"I'm not angry at you, Maggie. Only at myself. For letting Nancy down. I should have realized . . ." With an impatient wave, he dismissed whatever he'd started to say. "I'm glad you were there for her. For all of them."

"That's me. Maggie Graham. Helping Professional."

He regarded me gravely. "Did you dislike it so much?"

"No," I replied, surprising myself. "It was kind of fun,

actually. But by the end of the day, I was feeling a bit over-whelmed."

"It's important to have boundaries."

"Yeah. Well, next time Kevin launches into Harry Bea-ton's masturbatory fantasies, I'll send him straight to you."

Rowan's laughter startled the birds into momentary silence.

"Oh, to have been a fly on the wall," he mused. "You should be grateful he isn't singing 'Come to Me, Bend to Me.'"

"Or you."

"Me?"

"With your voice? Are you kidding? I'd come in a heart-beat."

I recognized the potential for double entendre at the exact moment that Rowan's eyebrows rose. A wave of heat flushed my body and traveled swiftly faceward.

"Come *to* you," I clarified. "And . . ."

"Bend?" he inquired with a polite smile.

"Oh, look. We're back on the trail. See? The red blotch?"

"Yes."

But he was gazing at my face, not the tree.

"We were talking about boundaries," I said firmly.

"Yes. Boundaries are . . . essential." For a moment, he withdrew into that other place again. Then his expression sharpened. "I'm glad you could help your cast mates, Mag-gie. But I don't want you to neglect your work."

"Actually, I was wondering if that *was* my work. If that's why you'd cast me."

He shook his head, but refused to say more.

"What? I have to learn it for myself? Like Dorothy in *The Wizard of Oz?*"

"Something like that. Ask me again at the end of the sea-son if you like."

"I will. But if you give me some crap about my heart's desire being in my own backyard and there's no place like home, I'm going to be pissed."

"Duly noted."

"Which, by the way, is a completely dumbass moral. Dorothy had already figured that out before the twister.

Glinda could have just told the poor kid to click her heels together while she was in Munchkinland. But no! She sends her traipsing off to Oz to learn what she already learned from Professor Marvel."

Rowan regarded me with mingled amusement and wariness. "I'll have to share your insights with the staff."

"Your staff is obsessed with *The Wizard of Oz*?"

He grimaced. "If I tell you a secret, will you swear not to tell anyone?"

"Is this another bones-of-the-cast-members secret?"

"No. A real one."

I crossed my heart and waited expectantly.

"Every summer, the staff puts on a performance for the cast. The Crossroads Follies, we call it. This year, it's *The Wizard of Oz*."

As he described the Follies, his face lit up like a kid's on Christmas morning, his body trembling with suppressed excitement. It was a side of him I'd never seen and I marveled at the transformation.

"A few days before the performance, we hand out ballots. The cast has to decide who's playing which part and write the name of the staff member next to the role. The person who gets the most right wins a week's salary. Of course, there's always a fair amount of side wagers, too."

Suddenly, the light snapped out. He scuffed at the leaf mold with the toe of his boot. No longer a kid at Christmas but an awkward adolescent whose voice had broken when he asked a girl out on a date.

"It's just silliness," he muttered.

"It sounds great."

Three little words and the light snapped back on.

"Helen would be perfect for Glinda," I continued, wanting to keep it shining. "But I suppose Hal will insist on playing her. You're obviously the Wizard." I paused to gauge his reaction, but he just shrugged. "The big question is who's playing the Wicked Witch." My palms moved through the air as if balancing weights. "Janet. Mei-Yin. Janet. Mei-Yin."

Without warning, the light died again. Following the direction of his gaze, I peered through the trees. What I'd thought was a clearing in the woods was actually the meadow by the theatre. I wondered if he shared my regret at arriving at our destination.

As we approached the edge of the woods, I saw a small knot of people in the picnic area. Two were pacing. The rest huddled together in what appeared to be a very serious conversation.

"Do you think there's been an accident?" I asked.

"Only yours. Come on."

We were still hidden in the trees when they all turned and gazed in our direction. Like bird dogs on point. Then they hurried toward us. It was the staff, I realized as our paths converged. Everybody except Alex. Even Javier and Hal who should be at their shops.

I glanced at my watch. "We're ten minutes late to rehearsal and they send out an all points bulletin?"

"I'm never late. I imagine they were concerned."

"But how did they—?"

"Let's not keep them waiting."

"Which means I've used up my quota of questions for the day."

"Which means you're not the only one who likes privacy."

I added mental telepathy to Rowan's growing list of skills and kept my mouth shut. He squeezed my shoulder, perhaps to apologize for his brusqueness. Then the pressure increased and I realized that, in spite of his words a moment ago, he wanted me to stop.

"Will you do something for me?"

Struck by his serious expression, I nodded.

"Don't mention the scars to the cast. The staff knows. But I wouldn't want the actors to feel . . . uncomfortable."

Again, I nodded.

"Thank you."

As he started walking, I blurted out, "You're all right now, though?"

His eyes widened. I was on the verge of yet another apology when he smiled. A smile so unexpectedly sweet that the breath caught in my throat.

"Maggie Graham. Helping Professional. Yes. I'm all right now."

The smile vanished. In a few purposeful strides, he slipped from confidant to director again.

I doubted I would ever understand the man. Or be able to anticipate his quicksilver changes of mood. Reason told me not to try. There were too many mysteries, too many secrets. But how could I think of him without hearing that song resonating inside of me, without seeing the scars on his body and imagining the others on his soul?

One thing I did know. It wasn't the burns on his hands that he wanted to keep secret, but the other scars. The ones I'd glimpsed when he had extended his hands to help me off the log. The ones that usually remained hidden beneath the cuffs of his long-sleeved shirt.

Jagged white scars. Created by a knife gouging deep through the flesh and arteries and veins of his wrists.

CHAPTER 6
EVERYBODY SAYS DON'T

FOR THE REST OF THE DAY, the speculative glances of the staff followed me. So I was less than receptive when Alex beckoned me toward the piano during a break in our music rehearsal.

"Don't start," I warned him before he could speak. "Catherine and Javier think I overreacted. Lee and Hal advised me to stay focused on the show. I've endured Reinhard's bullying, Helen's sighs, and Janet's innuendos. And an outpouring of sweetness from Mei-Yin that was far more disturbing than Rowan's singing."

Alex wiped an invisible streak of dust from the top of the piano and said, "Ah."

"I take it you've heard him sing?"

"Yes."

"Are you going to tell me I overreacted?"

"That's hard to say. What was he singing?"

I hesitated, knowing how Rowan valued his privacy. But if the staff knew about his scars, there seemed little harm in telling Alex the name of the song.

When I did, he just said, "Ah." Again.

"Is that bad?"

"No. Probably not important at all. Just the natural curiosity of a music director."

Which seemed way too pat.

Before I could pursue it, Alex said, "Rowan's fine. Right

now, the staff is more concerned about you. We don't want you to get hurt."

"I'm already hurt," I replied, holding up my palms.

Then I finally realized what he was getting at—what they'd all been getting at.

"My God. You're afraid I'm going to fall for him."

"It's happened before. Not for years," he added quickly. "Rowan takes his responsibility to the cast very seriously. That's why he keeps his distance. But you know what it's like during a summer stock season."

Passions blooming right and left, only to die a quick death as soon as you emerged from the hothouse of the theatre.

"Which is why I'm not likely to get caught up in that," I reminded him.

"Of course not." Alex waved his hand impatiently. "Look, forget I said anything. I worry too much. Catherine always says so. Maybe it's because I have a daughter. I have this alarming tendency to take up sword and shield in defense of every young woman who crosses my path, whether or not she needs protection. So when I go into my father act, just remind me that you're a strong woman who's fully capable of—Maggie? Honey, are you okay?"

It was the "honey" that did me in. I managed to control my voice long enough to say, "I'm just . . . I'm more tired than I thought. Would you mind if I skipped the rest of rehearsal?"

I bolted for the door before he could answer. Concerned faces turned toward me. Someone called my name. I yelled, "My knee's killing me," which was the best I could come up with on the spur of the moment.

As I hobbled down the brick path, I heard footsteps pounding after me. Then Gary shouting my name. I had almost made it to the parking lot when he grabbed my arm.

"Slow down. You'll only make it worse."

"I'm fine. Let me go."

"You're not fine." But he released my arm and stepped back. "Look, I don't know what happened in there—"

"Nothing happened! I've just had a really long day and I want to go back to the hotel."

"Fine. I'll drive you."

"I don't need you to drive me."

"You don't have to talk. And I won't ask questions. But you're too upset to drive."

"It's half a mile!"

"I don't care if it's half a block. I'm driving. Now give me the keys and get in the goddamn car!"

We both kept our parts of the bargain: I didn't talk and Gary didn't ask questions. By the time he pulled up in front of the hotel, I was calm. Calmer. Yelling at him had provided a viable alternative to tears.

He put the car in park and we sat there, staring through the windshield.

"Thank you," I said.

"Thank *you*. It's not often I get a chance to unleash my inner caveman."

My smile faded when I saw how tightly he was gripping the steering wheel.

"Look, I know I said I wouldn't ask questions. But I saw you coming out of the woods with him. And if he hurt you—"

"No! God. Nothing like that. I fell while I was walking. And Rowan helped me back."

His fingers relaxed. For the first time since leaving the theatre, he looked at me. "Then . . . ? Sorry."

"I just snapped, okay? The staff's been at me all afternoon. Making a huge deal out of nothing. And then Alex . . . he was just being kind and protective and . . ."

Fatherly.

". . . I had a meltdown. God. Poor Alex. He'll be frantic."

And probably sending out an APB to the entire staff that I'd gone 'round the bend.

"Look. Keep my car. Go back to rehearsal and tell him— tell everybody—that I'm fine."

"Are you?" Gary asked quietly.

His genuine concern deserved more than a quick brush-off. I took a deep breath, let it out, and said, "The thing is . . . I lost my father."

Strictly speaking, he had lost us. I saw him twice after Mom kicked him out. Got an occasional postcard after that—places like Sedona and Stonehenge and Machu Pichu. But we hadn't seen or heard from him in twenty years.

"Alex was all fatherly and it . . . brought up a lot of stuff."

It felt weird talking about it. Especially with someone I barely knew. Mom never mentioned him. We'd had the obligatory "Daddy still loves you and this isn't your fault" speech when he left—the kind of thing you say to an eight-year-old. I was in high school before she told me about the times he'd vanish for a week or a month, the repeated absences that cost him his teaching job, the series of part-time jobs he lost the same way, the drug use.

It did little to ease the pain of his absence, but at least I stopped blaming her for the divorce. And understood why she'd thrown out all the shit he'd collected over the years: the programs and photos and newspaper clippings from his "career" as an actor; the books on folklore and mythology and New Age mysticism. She threw out his old cast albums, too, but I found them stacked beside the garbage can and hid them under my bed. I'd carted them from apartment to apartment, even though I didn't own a turntable to play them on. Stupid. As stupid as my occasional Google searches for Jack Sinclair.

Another thing Mom had thrown out: Sinclair. She resumed her maiden name and after the divorce changed mine to Graham as well. A little bit of paperwork, a modest fee, and bam! I was somebody else. And he hadn't even objected.

I kept it simple for Gary. I'd had a lot of experience turning our family psychodrama into an ordinary tale of a marriage gone sour and a single mom raising her kid alone. Still, my calm delivery was pretty impressive when only minutes ago, I'd been on the verge of tears, childishly longing for a father like Alex.

I definitely needed a real day off.

When I finished, Gary sighed. "I lost my dad last year."

He meant that his father had died, of course. For all I knew, mine had, too. There were too many Jack Sinclairs in the world to find one via Google. When I narrowed the search parameters with our Wilmington address or his college or the few other personal tidbits I knew about him, no results came up. Like Mom, he'd been an only child, so there were no aunts or uncles to turn to. And by the time I started looking for him, my grandparents had passed away.

He might be using another name. He might have started

another family. He might be chanting mantras in Tibet or chewing coca leaves in Peru or drinking Sterno on skid row. In the end, death and a twenty-year absence amounted to pretty much the same thing.

"If you ever need to talk . . . or feel like you're on the verge of another meltdown . . ." Gary shrugged, suddenly awkward. "Feel free to call your friendly neighborhood caveman."

He waited until I was inside the hotel vestibule before driving off. I waved one last time and pulled open the door.

Helen stood in the lobby, staring anxiously at me. Clearly, Alex had broken a speed record getting out that APB. But it was Janet who asked, "What happened?"

I went through the whole spiel again. Janet eyed me like a lioness stalking a wounded gazelle. Helen gathered me in her arms. I gave her a quick, hard hug and pulled away.

"If you start being motherly, I'll have another meltdown."

"Why don't I make us some tea? Chamomile, skullcap, St. John's wort. Very calming."

Before I could beg off, she hurried toward the hotel office. Leaving me with the lioness.

Janet waved me toward an easy chair, then sat in the one opposite, leaving Iolanthe, sprawled on the settee, to referee. Ignoring the "No Smoking" sign on the wall behind her chair, she pulled a pack of Parliaments and a lighter from the pocket of her cardigan. With elaborate care, she removed a cigarette, lit it, and took a deep drag, all the while watching me.

"Do you want some advice?"

"No."

Her smile did little to dispel the image of a stalking lioness.

"I like you, Maggie."

I clamped my lips together to keep from gaping. If brittle sarcasm was her response to people she liked, I shuddered to think how she treated her enemies.

"You're not as tough as you'd like people to believe, but you say what you think and I like that. Please don't feel obligated to return the compliment."

"I won't."

Her smile widened as she leaned back and crossed her legs. "Are you the kind of woman who can enjoy sex without requiring romance?"

Didn't see that one coming.

"I'm flattered by your interest, Janet, but you're really not my type."

"Because if you are," she continued, ignoring my come-back, "you might consider sleeping with Rowan."

This time, I did gape. Then I got to my feet. "I am not having this conversation."

"Of course you are. You're fascinated."

I sat down.

"He needs a woman. Well, a man would suffice. It has in the past. But he seems to like you. And you seem to like him."

My head had snapped back against the cushion, like a bantamweight boxer who'd gotten sucker punched by the heavyweight champion of the world. I took a deep breath, gripping the arms of the chair to steady myself. I'd stood up to Reinhard that first day; I wasn't about to let Janet get the better of me.

I crossed my legs, deliberately imitating her. "I didn't realize a producer's responsibilities included pimping for the director. Or does this come under the general heading of hospitality?"

"You'd enjoy him."

"Are you speaking from personal experience?"

Janet laughed and flicked ash into the brass spittoon next to her chair. "God, no. I'd never sleep with Rowan. But he has a powerful effect on people. As you discovered this af-ternoon."

She was the first person on the staff to admit that. The others had either skirted the issue or tried to make me believe I had imagined the whole thing.

Janet was watching me with a satisfied smile. "What you experienced today was quite intense, wasn't it?"

"But not remotely sexual."

"Mmm. But just imagine experiencing that same

intensity—physical and emotional—during sex. I see from your blushes that you are. Oh, for God's sake, stop bobbing up and down like a jack-in-the-box."

I could feel the sheer force of her will urging me back into my chair. But this time, I stayed on my feet.

"Is this something you do every summer? Scope out the cast looking for someone to put into Rowan's bed?"

She shrugged. "Most of the women who come here are too vulnerable."

"And I'm not?"

"Not to romance. That's why I'm proposing this. But before you decide, you need to consider two things."

"Please. Enlighten me."

"Love has no role in this relationship. It's simply a sexual affair that ends when the season does. More importantly, you'll have to forgo your compulsion to play social worker."

"I don't—"

"You can't help Rowan. You cannot heal his wounds or grant him redemption or make him forget the past. Believe me, others have tried. And failed."

My legs were shaking. I would have given anything to sink into my chair—or at least grip the back for support—but I refused to give Janet that satisfaction.

"You'd never make this proposition unless you had a vested interest in the outcome. So what's in it for you?"

Janet's approving nod further infuriated me.

"You've worked in stock. You know how volatile the atmosphere can be. Well, that's more than usually true here."

"Because of Rowan."

She shrugged.

"If Rowan's happy, everybody's happy."

"Something like that."

"And all I have to do is spread my legs."

Janet took a long drag on her cigarette, blew the smoke toward the ceiling, and smiled. "With Rowan, you wouldn't even have to do that."

Before I could ask her what the hell that meant, she added, "Stop acting like some poor sacrificial lamb. If that's all I wanted, I could choose anyone. Sex with Rowan would probably do you a world of good."

"Probably? What happened to experiencing intensity beyond my wildest dreams?"

"Well, that's the risk, of course. That you would enter into this affair with the best intentions and still be unable to resist his . . ."

"Charms?"

"If you like. So a lot depends on how well you know yourself. And how much of a gambler you are." Her smile vanished as she leaned forward. "If you have any doubts, stay away from him. Or you'll be hurt. Deeply, terribly, irreparably hurt."

"By Rowan."

"By your inability to follow the rules I've just laid out. Rowan has little to do with it. He can't help what he is."

"And what exactly is he?"

"Rowan is incapable of love. And he is equally incapable of change."

As I absorbed that damning judgment, I heard a clatter behind me.

"That's not true."

God only knew how long Helen had been standing there or how much she'd heard. Enough to upset her; the cups and saucers were still rattling on the silver tea tray. But she sailed into the lobby like a queen and carefully lowered the tray onto the coffee table between Janet's chair and mine.

"Rowan *is* capable of love. And change."

"Helen, you see, is a romantic. She still cries when the village reappears at the end of *Brigadoon*, proving that true love can work miracles."

"While you don't believe in love at all."

"Oh, I believe in love. I've seen what it can do. The unhappiness it can cause. The lives it can ruin."

Helen was the calm one now. It was Janet whose voice shook with emotion, whose features were twisted with anger. I wasn't sure what lay behind this exchange, but clearly, they had been waging this battle for years. The funny thing was, although I disliked Janet, I pretty much shared her opinion about true love.

"You're wrong about Rowan," Helen said. "And about me. And it's very wrong of you to try and mold Maggie into the kind of woman you've become."

"What kind of woman is that?"

"Bitter. And lonely. If I've been unhappy—"

"If?"

". . . the joy I've known has more than made up for it."

Janet crushed out her cigarette on the rim of the spittoon and rose. "I'll leave you to your joy. Think about what I said, Maggie."

Neither Helen nor I moved until the office door closed behind her. I let out the breath I hadn't realized I was holding. Helen sank onto the settee.

For once, I had the sense to keep my mouth shut. Or maybe I was still too stunned by my conversation with Janet and the turn it had taken at the end.

Iolanthe butted Helen's hand. Absently, she stroked the fur beneath the cat's left ear. "You must forgive Janet. Sometimes, she's . . . overzealous."

"Ya think?"

Helen sighed. "You must find all of this very strange."

"Very."

"The staff really does try to do its best for the cast."

"Even Janet?"

"Whatever she told you was the truth. As she sees it. But don't be guided by her. Or by me, either. Trust your own instincts, Maggie."

"If I did that, I'd be on the road to New York now."

"Have some tea instead."

"I don't suppose you have anything stronger?"

"Why, yes. Lagavulin. Single malt. Would you like a glass?"

"I'd like a bottle. I think I need to get drunk."

Helen nodded solemnly. "That's a marvelous idea."

As she gently dislodged Iolanthe from her lap, I took a deep breath. "What I felt today in the forest was real, Helen. As real as the scars on Rowan's wrists."

Caught in the act of rising, Helen sank back onto the settee. After a long moment, she said, "That was a bad time for Rowan. As you can imagine. But it was many years ago." Then she asked, "Which song was he singing?"

The question was beginning to take on a surreal quality.

When I told her, she sighed. "Yes, of course. He's always nostalgic for home at this time of year." With a determined nod, she rose. "I'm going to fetch the Lagavulin. And you and I are going to forget about the theatre's oddities and Janet's scheming and Rowan's . . ."

"And Rowan."

"Yes. And get gloriously, wonderfully tipsy."

CHAPTER 7
PUTTING IT TOGETHER

THE ONLY PROBLEM WITH GETTING gloriously, wonderfully tipsy was waking up miserably, horribly hung over.

When I crawled into the Chatterbox the next morning, Lou gave a low whistle and said, "Man. You look like shit." Nick suggested a breakfast of raw eggs and Worcestershire sauce, then hastily retreated when I threatened to vomit on him. Romaine clucked. Brittany offered me her under-eye concealer. Nancy—God bless her—silently passed me a bottle of Tylenol.

I had little dancing in Act Two, so it was easy to obey Reinhard's stern instructions to take it easy during rehearsal. Singing proved more painful, thanks to the proverbial twelve drummers drumming in my head.

I had no contact with Rowan until our lunch break. When I lingered to clarify a bit of blocking, he replied, "Check with Reinhard," and strode away.

I stared after him, torn between surprise and resentment. I hardly expected yesterday's encounter to render us Best Friends Forever, but I did expect the same courtesy he extended to everyone else in the cast. Maybe he was self-conscious in the face of the staff's less-than-surreptitious surveillance. Or uncomfortable because I'd seen his scars. I just hoped to God he hadn't ascribed my meltdown to some burgeoning passion.

Our first full run-through on the set did little to restore my spirits. The malevolent fog machine churned out so much mist that the actors were invisible. The small footbridge I had to cross during "Vendors' Calls" lurched so alarmingly that I feared I would tumble into the orchestra pit. Wheeled carts collided in MacConnachy Square. Dancers stumbling through their steps during the wedding sequence gave new meaning to the term Highland reel.

The highlight was when Kevin's kilt slipped off during the chase. Like the dedicated method actor he had become, he wore what every eighteenth-century Scotsman wore under his kilt—nothing. So the last we saw of Harry Beaton before he plunged to his death was the gleam of his pale but muscular buttocks.

That was Sunday, the first day of Hell Week. Hell Week was really only three days. It just seemed much, much longer.

Farewell to our day off Monday. We worked Act One in the morning, Act Two in the afternoon, and then moved on to tech rehearsal at night. Four hours of Reinhard calling cue lines so we could shuffle to our next position while Javier and the stage crew practiced set changes and Lee punched up the proper lighting or sound effect on his console.

Tuesday afternoon, we worked the problem scenes in the Smokehouse, while the crew made frantic final adjustments to the set.

Dress rehearsal Tuesday night. No calling for lines. No stopping unless disaster struck.

Last chance to put music and lyrics together while wheeling carts or hefting kegs of ale or holding up bolts of woolen cloth. Last chance to master singing and dancing in bulky skirts and petticoats. Last chance to achieve some sort of balance between the musicians in the pit and the singers onstage. Last chance to make the set changes smooth, the costume changes quick, the special effects brilliant.

Last chance to get it right.

Or not.

"Bad dress rehearsal, great opening night," Hal assured me the next afternoon as he slid another pin into the hem of my forest green gown.

"Yeah. I know the saying."

After Helen finished her crash course on applying

theatrical makeup, I'd gone to the costume shop for a final fitting. In my case, it was more of a salvage job. During dress rehearsal, I'd managed to rip my hem not once but twice during my mad dash out the stage door, around the barn, and into the lobby for my breathless entrance through the back of the house for "Vendors' Calls."

Hal put down his pincushion and gazed up at me. Yet another man kneeling at my feet. "Relax. In eight hours, it'll all be over. Now walk for me."

I grimly marched between the costume racks and his cluttered sewing table.

"Turn. Slowly!" He scrutinized the bottom of my skirt and grimaced. "Is one of your legs shorter than the other?"

"That must be it. God knows the hem couldn't be uneven."

Hal pursed his lips. "Someone's a little bitchy."

"God. Yes. Sorry. I'm just . . ."

"Exhausted? Nervous? Still recovering from your tryst in the forest?"

I snatched up a pair of scissors and brandished them.

Hal rolled his eyes. "What? Death by pinking shears?"

"Very slow. Very painful."

"Well, put them down and stand still. I can't possibly adjust for your withered leg when you're flouncing around."

I obeyed, impatient to get back to the hotel. I needed to check my e-mail to see if I'd gotten any response to the resumes I'd sent out. I needed to go through a week's worth of forwarded mail and pay bills. I needed to squeeze in a nap, get a shower, and eat dinner before heading back here for opening night.

My stomach executed a nauseating flip-flop; it better be a light dinner.

Still brooding, my gaze was caught by a sketch on Hal's sewing table. I unearthed it from the detritus and studied it in disbelief.

"This is the program?"

Hal glanced up, then nodded and returned to his work.

"This. Is the program."

A single 8½ x 11 page folded in half. A drawing of the barn on the cover with *Brigadoon* written below it. Cast list on the left-hand page. Scenes and songs on the right. Names of the production staff on the back.

Where were the ads from local vendors? The listing of the "Angels" whose donations helped to support the theatre? The "Who's Who in the Cast?" The notification about the next production and the time-honored director's notes on this one? My middle school had created better programs.

"You're always bitching about not having enough money for new costumes," I reminded him. "Why don't you solicit ads? Or hit up the wealthy folk of Dale for donations?"

"They're not that wealthy. And they help out."

That was true. I'd seen familiar faces among the stage crew, including Beatrix, Reinhard's daughter by his first marriage and owner of Bea's Hive of Beauty. Frannie and her Chatterbox cronies ushered. And the all-volunteer pit band included some of Alex's students as well as folks from town. But still . . .

"I don't know how you people stay in business."

"Stop fidgeting."

"How tough is it to turn out a program that looks professional?"

"Take it up with Helen. She does the programs."

"God. What am I doing here?"

Hal sat back on his heels. "Right now, you're getting your hem fixed. After that, you're going to relax. Tonight, you'll be utterly brilliant—"

"If I don't tumble off the Bridge of Doom."

"And then you'll have a fabulous time at the cast party."

"That's another thing! Who throws a cast party on opening night? It's supposed to be closing night of the show."

"We have one then, too," Hal replied calmly. "But after all the hard work everyone's put in, we deserve a celebration tonight."

"I'm too tired to celebrate."

"Everyone says that. And everyone ends up dancing the night away."

"Even Rowan?"

Hal returned his attention to my hem. "Rowan's not much for dancing."

"Or mingling. Or leaving the grounds of the theatre. I think he actually lives here."

Expecting Hal to laugh, his silence was revelatory.

"My God. He does live here. That's not just his office under the eaves. It's his . . . lair."

"You make him sound like the Phantom of the Opera. It's a lovely loft apartment with exposed beams, hardwood floors—"

"A giant organ."

"I know nothing about the size of Rowan's organ." Hal managed to wink, leer, and waggle his eyebrows suggestively all at the same time. "Perhaps you could fill me in."

"Perhaps I could slap you silly."

"I'm not into S&M. Although I do look fabulous in black. Makes my fair hair and complexion pop. Still, I'm not sure I should go that route tonight. It might play funereal rather than elegant. Maybe just a spot of color. A violet tie, say . . ."

As Hal nattered on about clothing options, I turned over the latest piece of the Rowan Mackenzie puzzle. So far it resembled an early Picasso, all dislocated features and oddly angled limbs.

But we had the morning off tomorrow. That would give me time to Google phobias. And "The Mist-Covered Mountains." And see if I could fill in a few more pieces of the puzzle.

CHAPTER 8
THERE'S NO BUSINESS LIKE SHOW BUSINESS

AT 7:45, WE FILED INTO THE GREEN ROOM. It looked like all the others I'd been in, except it was actually painted green. This one had the usual dilapidated couches, two easy chairs with stuffing creeping out of the arms like fluffy caterpillars, a coffee table with a book under one broken leg to keep it level, a card table with four folding chairs, and a kitchenette with one working burner.

Someone—probably Helen—had hung crepe paper garlands and filled the table with lemonade, a plate of orange slices, a bowl of herb tea bags, and one of those plastic honey bears. The homey touches failed to alleviate the tension in the room. Not just the nervous anticipation that always precedes an opening, but the sweaty, barely suppressed sense of imminent doom.

Only Bernie seemed immune. He'd been depressed since Rowan assigned Hector, one of the tenors in the chorus, to guide him on and off the stage for each entrance and exit. But tonight, his gnomish face was alight with barely suppressed excitement.

"So. Give," I whispered.

"Rowan's going to let me walk on alone for the ending. I practiced all afternoon." He thumped the floor with the heavy cane he was using for the show. "Just had to get my sea legs."

"But with the mist . . . and the dark . . ."

"I'll be fine."

I hoped he was right. Still, his determination cheered me;

after Rowan's decision, he'd seemed to dwindle, becoming a tired old man before my eyes.

"Nervous?" he asked.

"A little," I admitted.

"You're a pro. Nothing to worry about. Them, I'm not so sure."

I glanced around the sea of plaid. Nancy was mouthing the words to one of her songs. Bobbie was twisting the lace at the neck of her gown. Kevin checked the clasps on his kilt for the hundredth time. Lou was nowhere in sight; he'd probably ducked out for a cigarette.

I was surprised to see Richard's dark head bent to Ashley's blonde one. Unlike Will and Nancy, their relationship had been awkward onstage and off. Maybe it was the fifteen-year age gap. Or the wider gap in background and personality. Or the never-to-be-spoken-about-but-potentially-uncomfortable issue of race that separated a black executive from Massachusetts and a white sorority girl from Virginia. Probably a combination of all those factors.

But they had apparently surmounted their differences. Just getting to know each other better or yet another example of Rowan Mackenzie's casting magic?

Right on cue, the door to the green room opened and he stepped inside. Immediately, all conversation ceased.

"Hello, everyone. I just wanted . . . where's Lou?"

"Right here, boss." Lou edged past Rowan, trailing the aromas of cigarette smoke and Old Spice aftershave.

"I just wanted to thank you all for your hard work. I know it hasn't been easy. And I know you've all had your doubts about whether we could pull this off. Well, tonight, we'll prove that we can."

His intent gaze swept across every face, just as it had the morning of our first company meeting. Then he said, "Take the hands of the people standing next to you. Close your eyes. And just breathe. Slow and deep."

A few weeks ago, there would have been a lot of eye rolling and grimaces. But we had shared a lot since then, including dozens of group exercises that helped us to relax and focus and connect with each other.

His soft voice urged us to feel the hands we were holding,

to notice the energy passing through them. And as he spoke, I felt it. A strange tingling sensation that followed the path Rowan described. Up through my arms and down through my torso. Warming my belly like whisky. Flushing my body with heat as it reached my groin. Flowing down through my legs and into my toes, only to circle back again to fill my belly, my lungs, my throat, my head.

Faster now, as if the energy moving through me was feeding on the energy of the others. A stream surging through us and between us, racing around our circle, gaining power with every breath, every heartbeat, pulsing through every body, every mind, leaping from cell to cell, too strong to contain a moment longer.

"Let it go!"

The energy burst free on a wave of sighs and groans. I opened my eyes to find Rowan watching us, his lips parted, his eyes heavy-lidded. Almost as if he had just climaxed. Which, I suddenly realized, was exactly how I felt. Drained and exhilarated, relaxed and keyed up all at the same time.

For a long moment, we savored the release and the silence. Then Rowan straightened.

"I want you to step onto that stage with confidence. To trust yourself. To trust each other. And believe that you're ready. Because you are. Tonight, we will create magic in this theatre."

His smile embraced us. Then he slipped out the door.

It opened again a moment later to admit Reinhard, wearing black pants and a black shirt like everyone on the crew. Reinhard had dressed for the occasion, though, adding a black tie to his ensemble.

He examined us critically and nodded. "You will be wonderful." It sounded more like a command than a prediction, but it made us smile, dispelling the lingering effects of the dream-state Rowan had conjured.

"Places, please, for the top of Act One."

Richard kissed Ashley on the cheek. Lou kissed Bobbie on the mouth. Will hugged Nancy. Brittany hugged me. Kevin glowered, already in character.

We silently filed to our positions accompanied by Reinhard's taped announcement forbidding the taking of photographs and reminding the audience to turn off all cell phones. Not that anyone would get reception inside the theatre.

I joined the members of the chorus onstage. Listened to the faint sounds from the unseen audience: the rustling of programs, the creak of the old seats, the murmur of conversation. As the house lights dimmed, the sounds faded, replaced by a hushed anticipation.

The drone of horns issued from the pit. Then woodwinds and violins broke into a wild skirling that made my heart pound.

The work light that had guided us onstage went dark. The overture segued into the slower, softer music of the "Prologue." The fog machine hummed. The red velvet curtain slid open. The lights slowly came up.

A murmured "Ahh" rose from the house as the audience got its first glimpse of the stage. Because of Lee's lighting design, we remained invisible behind the painted scrim. The audience saw only Hal's shadowy maze of tree branches and the deep, swirling blues of the nighttime sky.

Richard and Will clumped onstage, and the music ended. The audience chuckled at Will's zingers and warmed to Richard as he tried to puzzle out what was missing in his current relationship. Their delivery was so natural you could almost believe their conversation was spontaneous rather than scripted.

As our cue approached, an electric current rippled through me, similar to the energy Rowan had conjured backstage, but far stronger. Like we were being charged by some giant battery. Each time the charge passed through us, the current grew stronger, not only feeding us, but feeding on us, gaining power from our collective energy.

A shiver slid down my spine. My fingertips tingled. My nipples grew hard.

Hector's fingers dug into my shoulder. Brittany squeezed my hand so hard it hurt. I wanted to laugh or scream or fling out my arms, but I couldn't. We had to contain the energy, just as we had during Rowan's meditation.

Was he doing this? Were we? I only knew I'd never experienced this on any opening night. It was as if I was truly alive, truly aware for the first time in my life. As if we were

all awakening like the villagers of Brigadoon, realizing that
something impossible and wonderful was happening.

The furor raging through me slowly began to fade until it
was just a comfortable glow. Allowing me to breathe again,
to remember where I was, to hear our cue.

Kalma hummed the opening notes of "Brigadoon." Three
of us joined in, then four more. Then Kalma began to sing.
The first time we heard her clear soprano, we'd all marveled
that such a sound could come out of the throat of a girl
whose name meant Corpse Stench. But tonight, it was so
sweetly ethereal that it seemed to come from another world.

The rest of the chorus added their voices to hers. For
once, we didn't have to fight to keep the sound soft so that
the men's dialogue could be heard. We simply allowed the
hushed expectancy of Brigadoon's dawn to fill our minds
and our spirits before emerging from our lips.

At the height of the song, the chorus dropped out, leaving
the orchestra to finish the number. For a moment, we stood
there, still ensnared by the strange connection between us.
Then it just . . . snapped off.

Kalma nudged me toward the stage door. We raced around
the side of the barn and bolted through the front door of the
theatre, panting. Helen handed us our market baskets. Janet flicked off the lobby lights. Then she and Helen cracked
open the doors so we could slip inside.

Seeing the packed house gave me a jolt. Either Janet had
papered it with complimentary tickets or everyone in Dale
had shown up. After that first glimpse, I was too caught by
the spectacle onstage to think about it.

The lights changed and the thatched roofs of Brigadoon
became visible through the gauzy scrim. As it rose, ghostly
figures emerged from the dissipating mist, shaking off the
effects of their hundred-year sleep as they wandered into the
square for market day.

I came out of my daze in time to echo Kalma's line, drawing a startled "Oh!" from an elderly woman sitting in one of
the aisle seats. Still singing, I sauntered down the aisle.

As the tempo quickened, I walked faster, heart and feet
keeping rhythm with the growing urgency of the music. I
skipped across the shaky footbridge over the pit, sure-footed

as a mule, nimble as a gazelle, and stepped onto the stage just as early morning sunlight flooded Brigadoon, and chorus and orchestra burst into the bustle and excitement "Down on MacConnachy Square."

⊰⊱

Most of that night was a dizzying blur, but some moments were etched clearly in my memory. Ashley's shining face as she allowed Richard to coax her into walking through "The Heather on the Hill." The audience laughter punctuating Nancy's comic lament "The Love of My Life"; Lou and Bobbie, touchingly solemn at the wedding. Kevin's terrifying explosion of motion and emotion in the sword dance. And Bernie's triumphant grin as he slowly walked through the town square to welcome Richard back to Brigadoon.

And it wasn't just the performers who rose to the occasion. The mist curdled obediently around our ankles. Lee's lighting captured every shift in emotion. Catherine's promontory was as solid as if it were actually made of rock. The decades-old kilts swung as jauntily as if they had come off the weaver's loom that morning, while the costumes Hal had constructed looked like perfectly preserved clothing from the eighteenth century.

Sure, there were mistakes—harmonies that were off, lines that were flubbed, dance steps that were clumsy—but we recovered and we went on. And by the time our voices blended in the final, majestic chorus and Richard swept Ashley up in his arms, the mistakes had faded to insignificance.

Rowan was right. We did create magic.

CHAPTER 9
SUNNY SIDE TO EVERY SITUATION

MOST OF THE MEN OPTED TO SHOWER at the theatre. The women piled into cars and raced back to the hotel to change for the cast party.

When you're twenty and gorgeous like Brittany, you can blow dry your hair, throw on a tank top and jeans, and look spectacular. When you're thirty-two and not gorgeous, you have to blow dry your hair, coax the tangles into submission, apply mousse for a casually tousled look, artfully create cheekbones with two shades of blusher, go for a sensuous, smoky-eyed look and abandon it after realizing you look like an exhausted raccoon, try on three outfits, discard them all, and finally settle on a kicky sundress that shows off your best features (cleavage) and hides your worst (hips).

My car was the last to arrive.

"Oh, look!" Nancy exclaimed as we pulled into the theatre parking lot. "Isn't it pretty?"

In addition to the pale amber of solar lights, two rows of luminarias snaked up the hill. There were dozens of them, candles glowing softly in their brown paper bags. Lights blazed from the house, dimming now and then as shadowy groups of people passed by the windows on the ground floor. As we approached, the faint strains of recorded music grew louder, as did the hum of conversation and occasional bursts of laughter.

All resemblance to the Bates mansion vanished as I stepped inside. From the crystal chandelier to the decorative moldings to the marble floor, the foyer radiated the same wealth and elegance as its owner. Absently greeting staff and cast, I drifted through the house, gawking.

The parlor, a symphony of soothing golds and browns and greens with silk upholstery on the settees and Persian rugs on the floors. The dining room, where people crowded around a table large enough to conduct surgery on Paul Bunyan to sample the array of hot and cold dishes. The living room, lit by a crackling fire and filled with people sprawled in leather armchairs and sofas.

The sunroom was empty; clearly, everyone who'd come this far had moved right out onto the patio. Through the windows, I could see groups of people chatting, their faces aglow in the illumination of the paper lanterns strung through the trees.

"Are you finished sightseeing?"

I turned at the sound of Hal's voice. "Oh. My. God."

"Yes, it's pretty fabulous. And speaking of . . ." He seized my hands and held me at arms' length. "Hello, gorgeous. I always knew you'd clean up nice. Great tits, by the way. The men will be far too busy staring at them to notice your withered leg. Oh, thank God," he added as Lee approached carrying a small china plate. "I'm starving."

He opened his mouth like a baby bird demanding to be fed, and Lee obediently popped a caviar-topped crostino into his mouth.

"Ain't it great to have rich friends?" Lee observed

"I wouldn't exactly call Janet a friend, but . . . yeah."

"She pulls out all the stops for these affairs. You noticed the buckets of champagne in the dining room, I hope?"

"I was too blinded by the silver serving trays."

Hal hooked his arm through mine and led me toward the feast. "If you're very good, I'll stand guard while you sneak upstairs and peek in all the bedrooms."

"Doesn't she get lonely? Rattling around this enormous house?"

"Janet's pretty self-sufficient," Lee said dryly.

"And Helen's here most of the year," Hal added.

"Helen? Helen lives with Janet?"

Hal glanced uncertainly at Lee. "Well . . . yeah. She only stays at the Bough during the season."

"They *are* mother and daughter, aren't they?"

Again, Hal glanced at Lee who said, "You didn't know that?"

"I guessed. God. Poor Helen. I mean, it's not *Mommie Dearest*, but still . . ."

"There you are!" Gary exclaimed, elbowing through the crowd. "I was wondering when you were going to show."

"You think all this beauty just happens? It takes hours of hard work."

"Well, it was worth it. You look terrific."

I am a liberated woman. I believe in inner beauty and have never thought you need a runway model's body to be attractive. That said, being the object of masculine admiration—straight and gay—is a major ego booster.

"No one's said a word about how I look," Hal complained.

"You look fabulous," Lee said. "Now stop fishing for compliments." When Hal began to protest, he popped a scallop into his mouth.

"This is why I'm fat," Hal moaned.

"Tell him he's not fat," Lee said. "I'm getting more champagne."

"That's right! Run away!" As Lee made his way toward the sideboard, Hal dropped his mock outrage and smiled. "He adores me."

"You're a lucky man," Gary said.

"Luck had nothing to do with it. I worked on him a whole season before he finally succumbed." Hal sighed. "We had one glorious night together before I went back to California. We e-mailed all winter, but I despaired of ever seeing him again. Then Helen called and told me that the man who'd been doing costume and set design—this dreadful queen with absolutely no taste—well, anyway, he resigned. And guess who got the job? Everyone kept mum about it until I appeared at the first staff meeting. You should have seen Lee's face!"

"What about my face?" Lee asked, miraculously balancing four brimming champagne flutes in his upraised hands and hugging a bottle under his arm.

"The day I returned to the theatre," Hal said, plucking two flutes from Lee and handing one to me. "When you devoured me with your eyes."

Lee handed the third flute to Gary and raised his own in a toast. "Here's to finding the true loves of our lives."

I laughed at the reference to Nancy's song. Then I noticed Gary's expression. So did Lee, apparently, for he asked, "What? Don't believe in true love?"

"Not so much since my wife dumped me."

After a brief moment of shocked silence, Lee said, "Shit. I'm sorry, man."

"Oh, God, I feel like an idiot!" Hal exclaimed. "Babbling on and on about us when all the time, you were dying inside."

"Look, guys. It's okay. Really. I'm the one who should apologize for spoiling the party."

"Don't be silly," I said. "Friends are supposed to help each other." Before I could do more than squeeze Gary's arm, I heard Lou's familiar bellow.

"Brooklyn! When did you get here?"

"Just a few minutes ago."

"Some spread, huh? But where the hell's Rowan?"

"Got me." I turned to Lee and Hal. "Have you guys seen him?"

Hal glanced at Lee who just shrugged. "Rowan's not much for parties."

"Yeah, but it's the cast party," Lou said. "He's gotta come for that, right?"

Their silence spoke volumes.

"You're kidding me," I said. "He can't even show up for five minutes? Just to say 'Great job, everybody?'"

"He said that when he stopped into the green room after the show," Lee reminded us.

"But—"

"Let it go, Maggie."

I subsided before the quiet warning in Lee's voice.

Lou shook his head. "That sucks. I mean, that totally sucks."

"What totally sucks?" Bobbie inquired, squeezing between Gary and Lou.

"Rowan. He's not coming."

"At all?" She bit her lip and glanced from Lee to Hal. "He's disappointed, isn't he?"

"Of course not!" Lee exclaimed.

Bobbie looked so forlorn that I wanted to put my arm around her. Lou beat me to it. "See?" he demanded, voice and color rising. "See what you've done? She's upset!"

"Lower your voice," Lee said. "Before the whole room hears you."

Instead, Lou lowered his head, looking like a bull about to charge. "I don't care who hears me! He's got no right to go and upset Bobbie. She worked her ass off tonight. We all did!"

All conversation in the immediate vicinity had stopped. Now, it started up again, a dozen voices clamoring to know what Lou was shouting about, who had upset Bobbie, what was that about Rowan, and on and on until Lee shouted, "Will everybody please shut up?"

Everybody shut up.

"Here's the deal. Rowan doesn't like parties. Not even cast parties. He's never attended one. It's one of his little quirks."

"Phobias," Hal interjected. "A phobia. About crowds."

"He came to the green room," Lou pointed out. "Before and after the show."

"Look, he's just weird," Lee said, wisely avoiding the issue of the on-again, off-again phobia. "But it's got nothing to do with you guys."

Alex chimed in to reaffirm Rowan's pride in us. Reinhard ordered us to enjoy ourselves. Helen added her calming voice, Mel-Yin her hectoring one. Heads nodded in agreement, but I could feel the energy drain out of the party and see disappointment on every face.

As I edged out of the dining room, I bumped into Janet.

"What's the problem?" she asked in her usual cut-to-the-chase manner.

"We just found out Rowan isn't coming."

"Did you expect him to?"

"Well . . . yes."

She gave a snort. "Pigs will fly before Rowan Mackenzie darkens this doorstep."

"You mean you didn't invite him?"

"Of course I invited him. It's a game we play. I politely invite him. He politely declines."

"Maybe if he really felt welcome—"

"It's very rude to lecture the hostess, dear. Trust me. Nothing will convince Rowan Mackenzie to attend this party."

Later, I wondered if she'd said that to goad me. Or if I harbored some lingering resentment about Rowan's brusqueness since our walk in the woods. At that moment, I was too pissed off to consider Janet's motives or mine.

I charged down the hill, brimming with righteous indignation. The front doors of the theatre were locked, but the stage door opened easily.

I was momentarily blinded by the ghost light. Ours had been cobbled together by clamping the light bulb's metal cage to a battered mic stand. Superstition claimed it would ward off specters. Its more practical purpose was to prevent accidents when non-spectral personnel entered a darkened theatre. While I appreciated the tradition, it took nearly a minute before the afterimage of the megawatt bulb faded enough for me to mount the stairs to Rowan's apartment.

The muffled sound of music grew louder as I approached. Fiddle, flute, and squeezebox combined in a spirited reel, accompanied by the softer patter of a bodhran. Rowan was either following his Celtic muse or preserving the spirit of *Brigadoon* offstage.

I knocked softly and received no answer. Knocked again. Still nothing. Finally, I reached for the wooden latch. The door cracked open and I cautiously poked my head inside.

There was just enough light to make out a tall wooden file cabinet, an old-fashioned rolltop desk, and the bookcases lining the walls. Clearly, Rowan's office. The lack of windows struck me as odd until I looked up. Beyond the heavy exposed beams, four skylights had been set into the sloping roof. A cool breeze wafted through the apartment, so they must admit air as well as light. Unless the sliding doors to the balcony were open. It was hard to tell; the lamplight in the bedroom to the left illuminated little more than an armoire and the slatted wooden blinds screening the balcony.

As I opened my mouth to announce my presence, Rowan strode into the bedroom doorway.

He was barefoot and wore a long silk dressing gown that looked like something out of a Victorian melodrama. His hair hung in loose, damp waves around his shoulders. It didn't take a rocket scientist to figure out he'd just emerged from the shower. Or that he'd known someone had invaded his privacy before he saw me. Or that he was furious.

"I knocked. Twice. And when I didn't get an answer—"

"Get out."

I swallowed hard. "I wanted to—"

"I don't care what you wanted. This is my home!"

"I know. And I'm—"

"No one walks into someone's home unannounced. And no one walks into mine uninvited. Do you understand?"

"I just—"

"Do you understand?"

He was absolutely right. If he'd sauntered into my apartment in Brooklyn, I would have raised holy hell. But I never responded well to bullying, however justified.

I gave him glare for glare and calmly said, "Fuck you." And had the enormous satisfaction of seeing those green eyes widen with shock.

"I'm sorry I walked in on you. It was completely inappropriate and it'll never happen again. But before I go, you should know that you've let down the entire cast."

I waited a moment, hoping for a response. When none was forthcoming, I took a step back and reached for the door.

"What do you mean?"

"I mean they expected you to come to the cast party."

"I never—"

"I know. We all know. The staff spent ten minutes explaining how you never attend parties. Look, nobody expects you to come to movie night or hang out after rehearsal. But we did expect you'd show up for a few minutes tonight. To celebrate with us."

"I came backstage—"

"It's not enough," I said flatly. "And you should know that."

"I'm sure they will enjoy themselves without my presence," he said stiffly.

"But they won't! They're not! That's what I'm trying to tell you. If you could have seen their faces . . . I thought Bobbie was going to cry."

His mouth tightened. Even from across the room, I could see the muscle twitching in his jaw. A blast of cold air gusted through the apartment. Then he slammed his fist against the doorframe so hard I could feel the reverberation through the floor.

"Am I always to be held hostage to this place?"

The raw anguish in his voice shocked me even more than his words. As I tried to summon a response, his hand rose to grope at his neck. That's when I noticed the thick red weal. The same sort of burn mark I'd seen on his hands. Circling his throat like the silver chain he wore every day to hide it.

The frenetic music had segued into something quiet. I sought the same level of calm for my voice.

"The morning after auditions, you told me you were here to serve the players."

The hand at his throat knotted into a fist.

"You said that everyone who came here was searching for something they needed. Well right now, everyone at that cast party needs you. Maybe it's silly. And childish. Or just the typical insecurity of actors who never tire of hearing how wonderful they are. But they need to hear that. And they need to hear it from you."

He'd turned while I was speaking, bracing himself against the doorframe. As he bowed his head, the long hair drifted across his face, shielding it from my view. Instead of feeling pleased at my victory, I felt miserable. And ashamed.

"Look. I'll tell them I spoke to you. That you told me how proud you were. And how much you wished you could make an exception and come to the party. But you couldn't. Because of your phobia about crowds. Or something. I'll think of something. A feud with Janet, maybe. They'd believe that. I'll make them believe it. It'll be okay."

When he failed to move or acknowledge my words, I whispered, "Forgive me."

The last thing I saw before I pulled the door closed was Rowan lowering his head onto his forearm.

The Janet thing worked like a charm. People were still disappointed, but everyone believed that a long-standing feud prevented Rowan from entering her house.

It took Hal all of three minutes to corner me in the foyer. Instead of demanding the juicy details, he observed me carefully, led me into a sumptuous powder room, and closed the door behind us.

"You really did talk with him."

I nodded.

"Was it awful?"

I nodded again.

"Oh, sweetie." He hugged me hard. "Don't worry. It'll be okay."

"No. It won't."

"Maybe Helen should talk with him. She can always—"

"No! Just let it go, Hal."

I tried to enjoy the party, but I kept hearing Rowan's anguished cry. Finally, I gave up the pretense and headed for the front door.

A buzz of excited conversation made me hesitate. Curious, I followed the crowd hurrying toward the back of the house. I heard startled exclamations, soft cries of pleasure. The words rippled back to me:

"He's here."

"He's outside."

"On the patio."

I couldn't get any closer than the sunroom. Peering through a window, I saw the entire cast huddled close to the house. A good ten feet separated those in front from the shadowy figure standing under the big maple. Obviously, they were still unsure whether there was any truth to the phobia explanation. I almost smiled, but I was having too much trouble breathing.

The staff clustered together at the far end of the patio.

Hal's mouth hung open, but the rest did a better job of concealing their shock.

Rowan wore his usual linen shirt and black jeans. The silver necklace was around his throat. He'd tied his damp hair back. A paper lantern hanging from the lower branches of the maple lent a rosy glow to his pallid features. He looked tired, but very calm and completely in control of his emotions.

It was so quiet you could hear the dull chirp of crickets and the faint tinkle of wind chimes as a breeze touched them. Rowan stepped out from under the tree, but stopped just beyond the slates of the patio. Given Janet's comment about Rowan never darkening her doorstep, the feud had seemed a plausible invention, but now I wondered if her words were true. If so, he would find my behavior even more unforgivable.

"I was reminded recently that a director's responsibility to his cast does not end when the curtain comes down."

Janet's head snapped toward my window, and I resisted the urge to shrink back.

"As you know, I am not someone who normally attends parties. But I wanted to come here to thank you again for your hard work. I asked more of you than you probably thought you could give, but sitting in that theatre tonight, I watched each of you dig deep and bring something fresh and wonderful and . . . magical . . . to that stage. And it seemed only right to celebrate that accomplishment together."

His smile was slow to form, but as sweet as I had seen it that day in the woods.

"I'm proud of you," he said quietly. "So very proud."

I heard a muffled sob. A few sniffles.

"This does not mean I shall begin attending movie night," he added with mock severity. "Even for the Barbra Streisand double feature."

After the laughter subsided, Rowan spread his hands. "That is quite enough speechmaking. Please. Return to the party and enjoy yourselves."

For an awkward moment, everyone just stood there. Then Lou strode forward and engulfed poor Rowan in a bearlike embrace.

I expected that to be the signal for the entire cast to converge on him. Instead, they exercised admirable restraint, approaching singly and in pairs like courtiers paying homage to their king. A possibly phobic but nevertheless gracious king who put the welfare of his subjects before his personal desires. And seeing the warmth with which he greeted each person, I felt renewed shame at the way I'd behaved.

I considered slinking away, but disdained that as cowardly—and unfair to Rowan who deserved at least a word of thanks for breaking his policy.

The staff was staring toward the sunroom in the familiar bird-dog-on-point attitude. If they'd made a fuss after our walk in the woods, I could only imagine what I was in for now.

I was reconsidering my decision to remain when Reinhard detached himself from the group and started toward the house. Obviously, the others had elected him as their delegate. I'd have chosen Helen or Hal or Alex, but given my tendency toward meltdowns with both Alex and Helen, and Hal's tendency toward drama, perhaps Reinhard was a better choice.

He closed the sunroom door behind him and glanced around to ensure that we were alone.

"I see you lost the coin toss," I said.

He heaved an impatient sigh. "I said to leave you alone. But do they listen? No! Just talk to her, they say. Make sure she is all right. And don't make her cry."

"Poor Alex."

"Poor Alex is outside drinking champagne. Poor Reinhard is here. So. You are all right?"

I hesitated, wondering if I should tell him what had happened or if that would be a further violation of Rowan's privacy. But someone on staff had to know what he was feeling.

"I'm okay," I finally said. "But he's not."

In a few terse sentences, I described our confrontation. Reinhard scrubbed the top of his head, sending his hair into porcupine mode. Then he sank onto the love seat near the windows.

"He actually said that? About being held hostage?"

"Yes."

"That is not good."

"That is not good," I agreed.

"He has not spoken that way in many years."

"That doesn't mean he wasn't feeling that way."

"I am aware of that!" His scowl faded, and he sighed. "Forgive me. I bark. Mei-Yin always tells me this."

Mei-Yin was a more than adequate barker herself, but I decided this was not the time to mention that. Instead, I sat down beside him and said, "I deserved it for stating the obvious."

Reinhard patted my hand. "Poor Maggie. Always, you are the one in the middle. Why is that?"

"Because I'm nosy and pushy and can't let well enough alone."

"Yes. That is true."

I smiled at that, but he had swiveled around on the love-seat to gaze out the window.

"Such a strange man," he mused. "I have known him a long time and sometimes, I think I do not know him at all. Helen, she knows him best. And Alex. Because they write the shows together. And now you come here. Shaking things up."

Reinhard fixed me with an unnerving stare. I hoped to God he wasn't going to suggest I go to bed with Rowan, too.

"Maybe a little shaking up is good. For Rowan. For the theatre. For everyone. No one on staff talks back. Well, Janet. The rest of us wheedle and suggest and encourage. But you! You confront him. You make him talk about things he does not wish to talk about."

"That's definitely not good."

"But . . ." Reinhard held up his forefinger. "You also make him laugh. You make him think. You make him . . . change."

"That's good. Right?"

"That, Dorothy Gale, is astonishing."

So much for Janet's assessment of Rowan. I preferred to think Reinhard's was more accurate.

"So what do we do now?" I asked.

"You want my advice? Say no and I am not offended."

"Yes," I replied, surprising myself.

"Have you ever fished? Not worms on a hook, but real fishing with a fly rod."

I saw my six-year-old self standing on the banks of the Brandywine, holding up a long stick so my father could tie an imaginary lure on the imaginary string. Felt my father's hands guiding my arm as I cast. Heard his patient voice telling me not to hurl the line like a Wiffle ball, but to flick it like you were swatting a fly.

His excited whisper as he predicted that the Giant Brandywine Fish could never resist the lure of the twenty-winged blue dragonfly. His delighted laugh as he described the string snaking through the air and landing in a perfect line atop the tumbling waters. His shout of triumph as he pulled me back into his arms, both of us straining to reel in the mighty fish. And his bellow of disappointment as it sprouted twenty giant dragonfly wings and sailed skyward, cleverly eluding the mere mortals who sought to capture it.

"No, I've never done much fishing."

"Well, maybe it will make sense anyway. Rowan is like a trout. He cannot be hauled into a boat like a crab in a pot. He has to be played. For that you need patience and skill. Give him too much line, he will slip away. Pull too hard, you will hurt him. And yourself."

"I am *not* trying to land Rowan."

"God forbid! That kind of heartache you don't want. But friendship, maybe, is not such a bad thing."

"If he'd allow it."

"Pooh! He is not God Almighty. Although he acts like it most of the time."

"But he's no ordinary man, either."

Reinhard studied me silently. "No. He is not. And that is all I will say about that. Rowan is entitled to his privacy. Just as you are."

"Me?"

"I ask about fishing and the expressions fly across your face. Happy, bitter, angry, determined. All in ten seconds. And I know there is a story there. But do I ask you to share it? No! It is your story. Your past. To share or not."

I stared at the intertwined flowers on the rug at my feet. "You're very observant."

"Yes. But you are also very bad at hiding your feelings."

I sighed. "That is not good."

"Maybe not for you. But it is refreshing to find someone so . . ."

"Transparent?"

"Honest."

I looked up at him. "Ditto."

Reinhard nodded briskly and rose. "So. We are done talking. You are all right. I will tell the others. They will not pester you." He paused at the door and jerked his head toward Rowan who was chatting with Ashley and Richard. "Talk with him. Tonight."

"I was going to! Jeez. Talk about pushy."

"Little girl, you know nothing of pushy until you have lived with Mei-Yin for twenty years." He glanced at the patio, where Mei-Yin was shaking a meaty forefinger in Hal's face. Then he sighed happily. "Such a woman."

As he marched across the patio to give his report, the cast began drifting back into the house. Caren grabbed my arm, babbling excitedly about Rowan's unexpected arrival. I nodded politely and excused myself as soon as she paused for breath.

He was alone now and watching me. My heart went into rabbit beat as I approached. Before I could speak, he said, "I'd like to apologize for my rudeness."

"Please. Don't. When it comes to rudeness, I've got you beat by a mile." His brief smile encouraged me to add, "I just wanted to thank you. For coming tonight. You don't know how much it meant to everybody."

"Of course I do." His smile was just as brief and just as cool. "I've always known that my cast—all my casts—wanted me to share this night with them. I chose not to. I simply . . . drew a line and refused to cross it."

Without thinking, I looked at his feet, still firmly planted in the grass just inches from the edge of the patio.

"Yes," he remarked. "I suppose I'm still drawing a line."

"But you came. That's the important thing. I know how hard that must have been."

"No, Maggie. You don't."

Although his voice was quiet and free of accusation, I winced.

"It's not your fault. You couldn't possibly understand . . . the history."

"Between you and Janet?"

"It goes back far longer than that. To the people who originally owned this land. And my folk."

He made it sound like the Hatfields and the McCoys, the sort of blood feud that went on for generations. Of course, some of the Scottish clans were notorious for their long-standing enmity, but that was centuries ago.

I recalled the audience cheers during the "Entrance of the Clans," each group trying to outshout the others to support its . . . folk. But it was one thing to indulge in some friendly rivalry during a performance of *Brigadoon*. Quite another to refuse to cross the threshold of a long-dead enemy who had committed some crime against your equally moldering ancestor.

"You won't come inside, will you?"

"Never."

His quiet finality was more disturbing than if he had shouted.

"Why don't you leave?" I asked. "If you're so unhappy. Get out of here and start over someplace new."

The silence stretched for so long that I assumed he would refuse to answer. But finally he said, "My home is here. My work. And in spite of that display of self-pity you witnessed tonight, I am not unhappy."

I didn't believe him. And since he was skilled at reading faces, he probably knew that. But instead of disputing his statement or pressing him further, I asked, "So we're okay?"

"Of course."

Again, I didn't believe him. He'd been avoiding me all week and what I'd witnessed tonight had only made him more uncomfortable.

"I am . . . it's hard for me. To break old habits. Including my habit of retreating from people." He cocked his head, observing me as if I were some interesting new strain of bacteria that he'd discovered under his microscope. "What do you want from me, Maggie?"

I wanted to know how he had transformed a bunch of

non-actors into the troupe that had just brought off an incredible opening night. I wanted to know how his singing
had created such longing inside me. I wanted to know how
any man could soothe doubts and ease fears and create that
mesmerizing current of power I'd felt backstage.

    But he was not about to reveal those secrets to me. So I
simply said, "I want us to be able to work together. And be
comfortable around each other. I don't expect us to become
best friends. Or sip champagne by candlelight and share our
deepest, darkest secrets."

    "That's good," he said with a thoughtful nod. "I don't re-
ally like champagne."

    A slow smile blossomed on his face. Mischievous as a
little boy who had scored a point. And like a temperamental little girl who knew she'd gotten zinged, I stuck out my
tongue. That made him laugh, which sealed the victory for
me. Making Rowan laugh seemed the greatest contribution I
could make to this weird company.

    "It's a deal, then," he said. "No champagne. No candlelit
confessions."

    He stuck out his hand. I shook it firmly, the ridge of his
scar bumpy under my fingertips.

    As he walked away, I reflected that the pact was about
as ironclad as my contract. Its two prohibitions left the
door wide open for me to pursue all those questions I had
refrained from asking. Which raised yet another question
about this strange theatre and the man who ran it: what did
Rowan Mackenzie want from me?

ENTR'ACTE
THE JOURNAL OF ROWAN MACKENZIE

Sleepless. Again.

Reread Act One of *By Iron, Bound.* And finally realize what has been nagging at me.

She reminds me of Jamie.

Her stubbornness. Her sense of humor. Her kindness, too, though she tries hard to keep that hidden. Like Jamie, she heard me singing "The Mist-Covered Mountains." Like Jamie, she was shaken to the core. She even fell outside the cottage he helped me build. The hut, as she called it.

I do not believe in fate. Or ghosts. But when she appeared in my apartment tonight, I could almost hear their voices: the old Mackenzie witch and Jamie.

I taunted the witch and was punished by the iron collar and her curse. I rejected Jamie's offer of friendship with a blatant display of power that shamed and humiliated him. Yet later, he was able to joke about it. Another trait they share. As well as a boundless capacity to beat against the barriers I take such care to erect.

She's pushed for a few weeks. Jamie pushed for nearly sixty years. Dragging me to that first ceilidh in the barn. Encouraging me to use my powers to help those who had lost loved ones in the war. Refusing to let me do it from the shadows, but insisting that I mingle with them. Become part of their community.

Even the theatre was his idea. I merely brought the vision to life by calling to the Mackenzie descendants each spring.

And it all began with his simple gift of milk and strawberries, offered with the innocence and courage and curiosity only a child possesses. A gift for me. The nameless specter in the forest. The accursed one. Little more than an animal after so many years of isolation.

I ate the food he brought. Drank the whisky. Wore the clothes. All gone now. But the cottage still stands. And in it, the furniture we built and the earthenware jug that held the whisky. I am surrounded by Jamie there.

And here. I've only to walk into the next room to see the melodeon he taught me to play, the books he brought me, the battered copy of his schoolboy primer from which I learned to read and write.

So many gifts, the greatest of which I can only preserve in memory: his trust, his friendship, his love. In return, I gave him the necklace. It was just a bitter reminder of the mistakes I had made, the home I had lost. An easy gift to bestow and a selfish one; I was saving my home as well as his. But the greater gift of a true and loving friendship? That, I withheld. I allowed him close, but not too close. I never even told him what his friendship meant to me.

On nights like this, I wonder what would have happened if I had risked more. Would I have broken the curse? Or destroyed him? Both, I think. Too easy to let friendship slip into another sort of closeness. With the others, sex was merely a pleasurable release. Except Helen, of course. And look how that turned out. If I had exercised the same caution with her that I did with Jamie, she, too, might have found a loving partner, raised a family, known real happiness.

Useless to speculate. And foolish to conjure memories that can only fuel my emotions. When will I learn? But if I still struggle to control my power after more than two centuries, why should I be surprised that I cannot master my emotions, either?

In spite of all she has seen, she seems intrigued rather than enthralled. Unwilling to venture too close, to risk too much. In that, she is like me rather than Jamie. But while that wariness will protect her now, it will make it harder for her as the season progresses.

If she is to discover what I hoped for when I cast her, she'll have to let down her guard and look into the dark places of her spirit. And then she will be vulnerable. Which makes it even more imperative that I avoid another misstep, another reckless loss of control. This next week will be difficult, but once Midsummer has passed, I will be calmer. I must be calmer.

Only she can decide how much to risk, how far to travel. My job is to keep her safe on the journey. To let her choose her own path, but remain close enough to support her. Just as I did on that long walk back to the theatre.

It is my responsibility to establish the boundaries and adhere to them. However unsettling the parallels between her and the man who was my best, my truest friend in this world, she is not Jamie. I must remember that.

And accept that even Maggie Graham, Helping Professional, cannot help me.

ACT TWO

THINGS ARE SELDOM
WHAT THEY SEEM

CHAPTER 10

MUSIC OF THE NIGHT

IN THE WAKE OF *BRIGADOON*'S OPENING, the Bough was bursting at the seams with visitors and the company members joining us for *The Sea-Wife*. Bernie's granddaughter Sarah was back. And the Asian street gang, although I knew by now that they were really members of a church youth group.

Their arrival coincided with the first departures, including Nancy's. She had used up all her vacation time and would have to commute to the theater for weekday performances. A week ago, I'd complained to Rowan about the lack of privacy, but now I realized how much I would miss our late-night chats and our endless speculations about all the weirdness here. Having her stay over on the weekends just wasn't the same as sharing the day-to-day craziness.

And rehearsing one show during the day and turning in a dazzling performance on another at night was bound to push us to the brink of insanity. Thank God, *The Sea-Wife* had fewer musical numbers and a lot less choreography.

It took place in the Orkney Islands during the mid-nineteenth century and was based on the legend of the selkies, the mythical creatures who were seals in the sea, but could shed their skins on land to become human. In some ways, the story reminded me of *Brigadoon*, but there was no "true love makes miracles happen" ending. Selkie-woman loves schoolteacher, but longs for her true home. Schoolteacher loves selkie, but refuses to hold her prisoner. She goes back to the sea. He mourns. Curtain. Okay, maybe the

changes he undergoes will help him find love again, but by
the end of the read-through, I'd concluded that Rowan's
view of true love was even bleaker than mine.

One aspect of the story intrigued me, though: the selkie-
woman who is trapped on land, unable to return to her home.
For about five seconds, I congratulated myself on discovering Rowan's secret: the guy was a seal. Then logic kicked in
and I knew he'd simply been drawn to the legend because it
somehow paralleled his mysterious past.

Maya was the perfect choice to play the selkie; she always
seemed to have one foot in another world. Sweet-natured
Hector would have to go to the dark side to portray James,
the fisherman who steals her skin. Caren was playing Hector's jealous wife. If she had exaggerated the challenges of
playing a nameless villager in *Brigadoon*, I dreaded to think
what she'd be like now that she had a leading role.

But I was far more worried about Gary. He'd shrugged off
our concern at the cast party, but playing the schoolteacher
was bound to dredge up a lot of painful issues about his
failed marriage. No matter how much support we offered,
the next few weeks would be difficult for him.

And daunting for all of us. If we butchered *Brigadoon*,
Lerner and Loewe were unlikely to rise from their graves to
berate us. But Rowan and Alex had created this show, and
we all felt the added pressure of bringing their vision to life.

Rowan was obviously nervous about our ability to do so.
We'd gotten used to his preternatural calm, his "everything
will be wonderful" vibe. Now, the Smokehouse crackled
with his pent-up energy, leaving everyone unsettled.

His mania peaked the morning he broke us into family
groups and asked us to come up with our personal storylines
and relationships to the other island families. Then he had us
share our stories and improvise scenes based on what was said.

I was playing Bernie's daughter. Kalma and Sarah were
my younger sisters. All we knew about our family was our
professions: Bernie was a pauper, his daughters were straw
plaiters. Apparently, straw plaiting was big business in the
Orkney Islands way back when. Another useful skill to add
to my resume. Too bad I wasn't applying for a job in Colo-
nial Williamsburg.

Still, we all got into the role-play—especially Rowan, who paced back and forth, unable to keep still as our families revealed long-standing grudges, secret romances, and personal tragedies. In spite of his mania—or maybe because of it—we ended the rehearsal totally stoked. No longer anonymous villagers, but living, breathing people.

As everyone raced off to grab lunch, I watched him stalking restlessly around the Smokehouse. As I hesitated, Reinhard's head came up. He shot me a warning look, then sighed and waved me forward.

After telling Rowan how much I'd enjoyed our improvs, I said, "You know, you and Alex might consider doing your next musical as a staged reading first. That way you could get feedback from the cast. And the audience. Then rewrite over the winter and present the full show the following summer."

Rowan galloped toward me. "That's exactly what we should do. I don't know why I didn't think of it."

For the last week, he'd barely spoken to me. Now, he hugged me so hard the breath whooshed out of me. Tremors coursed through his body, like the purring of a giant cat. The aroma of honeysuckle was so overpowering I had to turn my head away.

Caught by my movement, he pulled back to peer at me. Golden light flashed in his eyes. Sweat beaded his upper lip. His tongue flicked out to taste it. I clung to his arms, dizzy and breathless and a little bit terrified.

"Rowan."

Reinhard's voice, close to my ear. I hadn't even realized he'd left his chair.

Rowan dropped his hands and stepped back. "Heady stuff, the creative process," he said with a rueful smile. "Imagine what poor Alex had to put up with during our collaboration."

I nodded, still caught up in whatever had just happened.

"Lunch," Reinhard prompted.

When I just stood there, his hand descended on my shoulder.

"Right. Lunch."

At the doorway, I glanced back. Rowan was sitting at the table, studying the script. The pages shook in his hands.

Although he seemed a little calmer in the afternoon, we were all glad that the theatre was dark that night; his mania was so infectious that *Brigadoon* would have been a train wreck. We were happier still that Mei-Yin had invited us all to the Chalet for a free dinner.

I was hurrying toward the parking lot when I spotted Helen at one of the picnic tables. She waved me over and smiled as I slid onto the bench opposite her.

"How was rehearsal?" she asked.

"Rowan's driving us crazy."

"He's always a little nervous when he begins rehearsals for his new show. He'll settle down in a day or two." She pushed a small pile of papers toward me. "Hal mentioned that you might like to help with the program."

Some were yellowed with age, the paper stiff between my fingers, but each program was a single sheet of paper folded in half.

Choosing my words carefully so I wouldn't offend her, I said, "I know Rowan's adapted plays in the past, but *The Sea-Wife* is his first original script. Let's make this opening really special. Expand the program. Send out press releases. Invite critics to review the show."

"Oh, my . . ."

"That's what theatres do, Helen. A world premiere will bring in lots of new business. That's got to be a good thing."

Or not, judging from Helen's expression.

"I'll mention your ideas at our staff meeting."

As she pushed herself up from the picnic bench, I noticed how tired she looked and cursed myself for shoving more work on her shoulders.

"I didn't mean you had to do it. Just give me a flash drive with the *Brigadoon* program and I'll draft something for *The Sea-Wife* that you can . . . Helen? Are you okay?"

She cocked her head, her expression faintly quizzical, as if she were listening to something I couldn't hear. Then her gaze focused and she smiled.

"Just a little tired."

"Let me drive you up to the house."

"Don't be silly. It's . . ." She glanced at the hill, and her smile faltered. "Well, if it's not too much trouble."

I dashed around the table and took her arm, but she gently freed herself and glanced around to see if anyone had noticed.

"Oh, dear," she murmured.

I followed the direction of her gaze and grimaced when I saw Caren hurrying toward us.

"Helen, you look dreadful!" she announced with a breath-taking lack of tact. "Should I get Reinhard?"

"No!" Helen and I exclaimed. Hoping to speed Caren on her way, I added, "I'm just going to drive Helen up to the house."

Caren latched onto Helen's arm. "I'll help! I'm dying to get another peek inside. Did Janet do the decorating or was that you? I redecorated my condo last year. I thought of hiring someone, but I just couldn't see spending the money. Especially since I knew exactly what I wanted and everyone says I have marvelous taste. Not to brag or anything. It's a sort of gift."

Short of ripping Helen's arm off at the shoulder, I saw no way of prying Caren loose. It took less than a minute to follow the gravel road around the back of the hill to the house, but Caren's running monologue about her fabulous new furnishings made it seem much longer. When I stopped the car under the portico, she scrambled out of the backseat to help Helen into the house, cooing soothing banalities like "There we are" and "Just one more step up" as if Helen suffered from dementia instead of weariness.

We walked through a little mudroom and into an enormous country kitchen that could have graced an interior design magazine: stainless steel appliances, miles of cabinets, marble countertops, terra-cotta floor. As we headed toward the foyer, Helen paused. "I would love a glass of lemonade. Caren, dear, would you mind? I think there's a pitcher in the fridge."

Caren cannonaded back down the hallway, and Helen and I let out simultaneous sighs.

"She's very nice," Helen whispered, "but just a bit . . . taxing."

I followed her up the stairs and into a bedroom that was . . . well . . . Helen. All soft blues and pinks. Ruffled pillows on the flowered bedspread. Ruffled canopy over the bed. Ruffled curtains at the windows. Even a ruffled skirt around the dressing table. It was the kind of bedroom a furniture catalog would describe as a young girl's dream. Well, some young girls. I went directly from my "all-things-unicorn" phase to plastering my walls with posters of R.E.M., Nirvana, and Broadway musicals.

Helen sank into the rocking chair and leaned her head back. "I do love this room. Such a wonderful view, don't you think?"

The open window next to the bed overlooked the patio. Patios. The one next to the house where we had greeted Rowan and a larger one at the bottom of a flight of stone steps. Beyond it, a series of walled terraces led to Helen's beloved garden. The boys must be pissing up a storm because it was filled with bright splashes of color. A cobblestone path wound through low green hedges to a small pond. The faint sound of splashing water vied with the tinkle of wind chimes and the more strident chorus of birds saluting the sunset.

Beyond the garden, an open field stretched toward the woods like Walt Whitman's sea of grass. The evening sky was a glory of pinks and purples and blues, as if special-ordered to complement Helen's garden.

"My mother would be so jealous."

"Is she a gardener, too?"

"Well, our backyard's about the size of your bedroom. But she grows roses. And has a little herb garden. When I was a kid, I used to cut lavender and make sachets out of old pantyhose."

"I still do that! You'll have to help me this year. It'll be such fun."

"What will be fun?"

Enter Caren with lemonade pitcher and glasses on a silver tray.

"Harvesting herbs. Thank you, dear. Just set that on the dressing table. And—oh, would it be dreadful of me to ask another favor?"

"Of course not!"

"I meant to cut some fresh flowers, but . . ."

"I'll do it! I love flowers. We have a beautiful garden at home . . ."

After she described it in excruciating detail, Helen directed her to the gardening shed. "You'll find everything you need there. The good vases are in the sideboard in the dining room. The everyday ones are in the hutch in the kitchen."

As Caren raced down the stairs, I poured two glasses of lemonade and sank into the easy chair near the window. "If I hear about her rich husband or her fabulous vacations or her marvelous condo one more time . . ."

"Poor thing. She's so insecure."

"*She's* insecure? I've got no job. No man. And an apartment the size of your kitchen."

"Yes, dear," Helen said, completely unfazed by my confession. "But what Caren sees is your sense of humor and your confidence and your strength. That's why she's drawn to you. Why she follows you around like a puppy."

Guilt warred with annoyance at Helen's assessment. Guilt won. I silently vowed to be a little nicer to Caren—or a lot more adept at avoiding her.

Helen turned the conversation to *The Sea-Wife*. Her admiration for Rowan's talent was obvious. But as she described his work, her voice grew soft, her expression tender. As if she were talking about a beloved son. Or simply, her beloved.

Helen and Rowan? She was at least twenty years his senior. It was just too kinky.

I breathed a little easier when she began talking about the other staff members.

"Reinhard got involved with the theatre after his first wife died. He played Captain von Trapp in *The Sound of Music*."

"Talk about perfect casting."

"And guess who his Maria was?"

"No."

Helen giggled. "Mei-Yin was a good forty pounds lighter in those days, but just as bossy. My, she looked stunning in that nun's habit. No wonder Reinhard fell in love with her. By the end of the summer, everyone knew they would spend the rest of their lives together."

"Sort of like Lee and Hal."

"You've heard all about them, I suppose? Yes, Hal loves to tell that story. He's such a romantic. Now, Javier's big role was Sky Masterson in *Guys and Dolls*."

"The Slick Charmer."

"Of course, he's not like that at all. Well, he *is* charming. But underneath, he's quite shy."

It seemed a stretch to call Javier shy. Maybe he was just good at putting up a front. Like me.

"I suppose Catherine played Sarah."

"No, Catherine built the set. She'd assisted on other shows, but that was her first as our construction chief. She and Javier started talking at one of the cast parties and discovered a mutual love of antique furniture . . ."

"And the rest is history." I shook my head, smiling. "You make this place sound like Match.com."

For a moment, Helen looked blank. Then she laughed. "Oh, yes. I've seen that advertised on TV. It sounds so . . . modern. Have you ever tried it?"

"No. But it's got to be better than chatting up some guy in a bar. Or hoping to meet Mr. Right during summer stock."

"Well, you never know. Look at Lou and Bobbie."

"I suppose you knew they'd be perfect together."

"Why, of course. Didn't you?"

"Actually . . . yes. They seemed like best buds from the moment they met."

"That's important, I think. Sexual attraction . . . well, it's all very exciting. But you need to be friends as well as lovers."

Ten years after college graduation, Michael and I were still friends, albeit long-distance ones. We'd never made it to lover status, of course. But there had been that instant spark when we met. For me, anyway. Same with Eric. But when the spark fizzled with him, there was nothing left to hold us together.

Helen idly smoothed her skirt. "Anyone on the horizon now?"

"Not unless it's a very distant horizon."

There were plenty of sparks with Rowan, but everyone felt those. Who could help it? The soft voice that seemed to speak to you alone. The penetrating gaze that made you feel like you were the most important person in the world.

And today, when he hugged me . . .

Sparks. Big-time. Along with the potential for big-time third-degree burns.

Eager to abandon the depressing topic of my nonexistent love life, I asked, "Did you ever tread the proverbial boards?"

Helen smiled. "Just once. I played Mabel in *The Pirates of Penzance.*" She closed her eyes, humming softly to herself. *Pirates* was one of the few Gilbert and Sullivan shows I knew, so I recognized "Poor Wandering One."

"I was just sixteen that summer. And I had the most beautiful costume. A white lace gown with four layers of ruffles on the skirt and mother-of-pearl beads on the bodice. A pink satin sash. And sweet little white kid slippers. Rowan said I looked like a princess."

"I bet you . . . wait. I'm confused. If you were sixteen, how could Rowan have seen you?"

Helen's eyes flew open. "In a cast photo, of course. We *did* have photography back then. Daguerreotypes," she added, her mouth curving in a mischievous smile.

"Okay, okay." I hesitated a moment, then plunged in. "How about Rowan? Did he ever do any acting?"

"He prefers to work behind the scenes."

With that singing voice, he'd have to. Otherwise, he'd start a riot in the theatre.

"How long has he been directing here?"

"Oh, quite a while." Helen's nose crinkled in thought. "At least twenty years."

Which made him closer to fifty than the forty I'd suspected he was. Although a wunderkind like Rowan could have leaped right into the director's job after college.

"What was he like back then?"

"Much the same as he is now. A bit more aloof, perhaps."

"Is that possible?"

"He's made great strides," Helen said firmly. "Especially during these last few weeks."

None of the staff had said anything about my bullying him into attending the cast party, but I knew they had to be talking about it. My cheeks grew warm under Helen's penetrating gaze. For the millionth time, I wished I could control my stupid blushes. Maybe if I got out in the sun more, my freckles would multiply and provide some protective coloration.

In lieu of camouflage, I rose and gazed out the window again. The brilliant colors of the sky were fading, the chorus of birdsong reduced to a few halfhearted chirps. Post lanterns near the house and along the drive created creamy pools of light, but I could barely make out Caren's shadowy figure darting around the garden like a demented bumblebee.

The wispy clouds faded from rose to violet, the deep blue of the sky to the softer blue-gray of a Prospect Park pigeon. I tried to remember the last time I had watched a sunset. In the winter, it was always dark by the time I left the office. And the rest of the year, I just jumped on the subway, then hurried down the street with the other worker bees buzzing back to their hives.

I did a lot of racing around here, too. It was nice to slow down, to allow myself to surrender to the calming hush of twilight. Or to the spell of Midsummer.

My stomach growled, reminding me of our dinner. I turned back and discovered that Helen had fallen asleep. Her color looked better, but maybe that was just the light filtering through the pink lampshade. As I debated whether to wake her or simply tiptoe out, I heard Caren's footsteps on the stairs.

"Here we are!" she sang as she waltzed through the doorway.

Helen jolted awake. "Oh! I must have drifted off."

Her gaze slowly focused on the Delft vase Caren cradled. Okay, maybe she did have marvelous taste; the tall spikes of iris and foxgloves were perfect for Helen's room.

As Caren set the vase on a chest of drawers, Helen gasped. "It's nearly dusk!"

"I'm sorry it took me so long," Caren said. "But I don't suppose anyone will mind if we're a little late for dinner."

Helen clearly minded. She jumped to her feet and shooed us into the hall. As we reached the top of the stairs, the front door banged shut.

"Helen? Are you home?"

"Up here, Janet."

"Have you seen—? Good Lord. Why did you cut so many flowers? It looks like a goddamn funeral parlor in here."

Caren's soft exclamation fell somewhere between a squeak and a moan.

"Don't mind her," Helen whispered. "I'm sure they look lovely."

Janet stopped short when she saw us. "What are you doing here? You're supposed to be at the Chalet."

Before I could reply, Caren said, "Helen wasn't feeling well, so Maggie and I—"

"What do you mean? What's the matter?"

"Nothing's the matter," Helen said. "I was feeling a little tired and—"

"Did you call Dr. Hearn?"

"There's no need to call Dr. Hearn," Helen replied, her voice as sharp as Janet's. "I had a lovely visit with the girls. But they have to leave now. It's very late."

"Yes. You're right." Janet strode to the front door and flung it open.

"Umm . . . we drove," I mumbled.

"From the theatre?" Janet's gaze snapped back to Helen. She choked back whatever remark she wanted to make and marched toward the back of the house. I scampered after her, calling farewells to Helen and stealing a glance at my watch. We were going to be *really* late for dinner. It was so hard to judge time around Midsummer; the uncertain gray of twilight seemed to linger for hours.

As we pulled away, I looked in the rearview mirror and saw Janet slump against one of the pillars supporting the portico. For the first time, I wondered if Helen had a serious health problem. No one rushes to call a doctor simply because her mother feels tired.

The house had barely disappeared from view when Caren said, "Could you stop the car?"

I braked next to one of the post lanterns. Caren looked so queasy that I pressed the button on the armrest to lower her window.

"If I ask you something, will you be completely honest with me?"

Praying it was not going to be a "Why can't we be friends?" conversation, I said, "Sure."

"Did you think the house looked like a funeral parlor?"

I might have laughed, but Caren seemed to be on the verge of tears.

"The house looked beautiful."

Which was true. It looked like a beautiful funeral parlor. Or a thriving florist's shop. Where else would you find three giant vases of flowers in the foyer alone?

"I think I overdid it. Danny always says I overdo. That I try too hard. Do you think I try too hard?"

"Janet was just busting your chops. You know how she is."

"But do you think—?"

"I think you need to take a deep breath and let this go."

"I can feel it happening. When I overdo it, I mean."

"Deep breath."

"But I just can't seem to stop myself."

"You can if you take a deep breath!"

Caren took a deep, shuddering breath and let it out. So did I. The lovely calm that had descended upon me while I watched the sunset had vanished.

"Better?" I asked.

"No."

"Well . . . keep breathing."

In terms of interventions, this one was the equivalent of "Shut up and stop bothering me." Further proof that my HelpLink skills were eroding at an alarming rate. By the time I found a new job, I'd probably be advising callers to get a fucking life.

As we started downhill again, Caren shouted, "Stop!"

I slammed on the brakes. "Shit! Was it a deer?"

"No. Down there. In the meadow."

All I could see were the dark silhouettes of trees. And Caren with her head stuck out the window like a dog.

"Go down a little more," she ordered. "Then turn off your lights."

I heaved a gusty sigh and let the car drift around the curve of the hill. As we cleared the trees, the barn came into view, a pale rectangle amid the varying shades of gray in the meadow. I braked yet again, shoved the gearshift to park, and switched off the headlights.

It took a moment for my eyes to adjust to the dimness. Then I caught my breath.

Fireflies drifted through the meadow. Hundreds of them. Or perhaps the flash of their golden reflections in the pond created that illusion. Mesmerized, I watched them blink on and off like the "twinkie" lights my mother hung on the Christmas tree every year.

"Have you ever seen so many?" Caren whispered, gazing raptly through the windshield.

"No," I whispered back.

Not even during those picnics in Brandywine Park. I closed my eyes, summoning the smoke and smell of grilling meat hanging in the air along the river. My mother chiding me for gobbling my hot dog too fast, my father waving away her objections, just as eager as I was for twilight.

Climbing up Monkey Hill, past Brandywine Zoo's small brick primate house to the abandoned pavillon near the summit. My delighted laughter mingling with Daddy's when the first fireflies appeared. Grass tickling our bare feet as we stalked them. His soft voice warning me to be gentle as I captured one between my cupped palms. The light flashing through my fingers, turning them rosy, then pale.

I pretended they were fairies. And I, of course, was their princess, trapped in mortal form. Had I dreamed that up or was it one of my father's stories? He had a million of them.

"Isn't it awful early for fireflies?" Caren whispered.

"What? Oh. I don't know."

They blinked faster now. Pheromones—or whatever insects had—kicking into high gear at the proximity of so many potential mates. One thing was certain: there would be one helluva love fest in the meadow tonight.

Suddenly, Caren leaned forward. "Do you hear that?"

I heard the drone of the idling motor. The harsh ratchet of night insects. The whispers of leaves and pine needles as the breeze shifted. And Caren's sudden intake of breath.

I glanced over and discovered her straining against her seat belt, hands gripping the dashboard. When I returned my gaze to the meadow, I gasped, too.

The fireflies had abandoned their stately dance. A single glowing ball of light raced toward the trees. I glimpsed something dark at its center. Heard a faint burst of laughter, wild and exuberant. And something barely audible in response—high-pitched and silvery, like the rippling glissando of a harp.

In spite of the warmth of the evening, I shivered. My fingers ached and my chest felt constricted. Belatedly, I realized I was clutching the steering wheel in a death grip and straining against my seat belt just like Caren.

The music—the sound, whatever it was—had already faded. I slumped back and took a deep, steadying breath. Then jerked erect as Caren flung open the car door. She raced across the drive, but by the time I switched on the headlights, she was gone.

I scrambled out of the car and shouted her name. Off to the left, I heard a loud crashing in the underbrush. I shouted again, but the crashing just grew fainter.

Shit.

I yanked open the glove compartment. Fumbled for the flashlight. Flicked it on and was rewarded by a gleam of light with the total wattage of one firefly.

Shit!

I leaned on the horn. Three long, nasal blasts. But I knew no amount of calling or cursing or honking would bring her back. Any more than they would have restrained me the afternoon I'd heard Rowan singing.

Frantically, I dug my phone out of my carryall and pressed it on. While I waited for the Verizon Wireless logo to morph into my display, I fished out my packet of Kleenex and stuck a tissue in my right ear. If the harp music came back, I'd be prepared.

I pressed Reinhard's speed dial and waited impatiently for him to pick up. When he didn't, I glanced at the display. No service available.

Shit, shit, shit!

Helplessly, I watched the fireflies move deeper into the woods, no longer a single glowing ball but a dozen clusters of golden light bobbing among the trees. I'd tripped over my feet in broad daylight. Caren could easily break her leg in that dark forest. Or her neck.

"Caren, God damn it, get your ass back here now!"

The roar of an engine answered. Twin white lights blinded me. The SUV jerked to a halt. Four doors flew open. Reinhard leaped out of the driver's side. I was so glad to see his frowning face I could have kissed it.

I raced toward him, babbling about Caren and the fireflies and the harp music. Reinhard grasped my shoulders, murmuring, "Slower, Maggie, slower." My stress level plummeted from incipient hysteria to "this is still bad, but I don't have to cope with it alone."

"Catherine, drive Maggie back to the house. Hal, go with them. Lee, Javier, Alex. Come with me."

I wondered how they'd all managed to squeeze into one vehicle. Then I realized there was another behind Reinhard's. The cavalry galloping to the rescue. But how had they known we needed rescuing? Had they seen my headlights from the theatre?

Reinhard had already plunged into the woods with the others, their flashlights an eerie coda to the earlier brilliance of the fireflies. Shaking, I let Catherine and Hal bundle me into my car. Catherine maneuvered the Civic around and drove us slowly back to the house.

Helen and Janet were waiting at the top of the drive.

"What happened?" Janet demanded.

While Catherine explained, Hal gently plucked the tissue from my right ear and pressed it into my hand.

"This is all my fault," Helen said. "If I hadn't fallen asleep—"

"It's not your fault," Janet snapped. "She left fifteen minutes ago." Her furious gaze returned to me. "What were you doing?"

"Caren was afraid she'd gone overboard on the flowers."

"It took you fifteen minutes to agree?"

"No! It took me five minutes to assure her that you were a ball buster and she wasn't a total loser. Then she spotted the fireflies and things went . . . downhill."

I was almost grateful to Janet for being her usual

combative self. It allowed me to unleash my anger rather than dissolve into tears.

"Why don't we all go inside?" Helen suggested. "I'll make tea."

Before anyone could respond, the lights flashing in the woods winked out.

We all froze, Helen still gesturing toward the house, Hal reaching for my arm. Like we were posing for a diorama at the Museum of Natural History. I'd just begun to breathe again when I heard a low rumble like distant thunder that crescendoed to a shocking howl.

It was Janet—naturally—who broke the silence that followed.

"Well. I think we can safely assume that's the end of Rowan's Midsummer celebration. The next few days should be ever so jolly." She sighed and shook her head. "You couldn't have kept driving while you explained she wasn't a total loser?"

"If I'd known Rowan was going to perform the Dance of the Fucking Fireflies, I would have."

Janet snorted. "Well, I've heard our local Wiccans described many ways before, but never as fireflies."

"Wiccans?"

"They hold their Midsummer ritual in the woods."

"Those weren't Wiccans. They were fireflies. Swarming around Rowan."

"I'm sure there *were* fireflies," Janet replied in the soothing tone of a psychiatrist talking to a delusional patient. "The meadow's thick with them this time of year. But they don't swarm."

Catherine's arm snaked around my shoulder. "The light's tricky around dusk. Maybe you saw lanterns."

Helen squeezed my hand. "I suppose you heard music, too?"

"Well . . . sort of. Like . . . harps."

"Usually it's drums," Janet remarked. "Harps make for a pleasant change."

Before I could argue, Reinhard's SUV thundered up the drive. Javier held the door while Lee helped Caren out of the car. She looked dazed but unhurt except for a rip in the right knee of her jeans. Then she saw us all standing there and burst into tears.

"Just what we need," Janet muttered. "More drama."

"Cut her a break!" I whispered as Helen hurried over to Caren.

"Where's Dad?" Catherine asked.

For the first time, I realized Alex wasn't with them.

"He stayed behind," Lee said. "To look for Rowan."

Janet rolled her eyes. "Well, that's a waste of time."

"Maybe it is," Lee replied, an edge to his voice. "But Alex wanted to try."

"Argue about it later," Reinhard said. "Let's get these girls into the house."

Everyone was too busy fussing over Caren to respond to my continued protestations about what I had witnessed. They guided us to the living room and sat us down on one of the sofas. Janet sloshed whisky into two glasses and shoved them at us. I gulped mine gratefully. Caren took a small sip and made a face.

"Sorry," Janet said. "Would you prefer an amusing chardonnay?"

Reinhard shot her a look, and she subsided.

They clustered around us like so many fireflies: Reinhard perched on the coffee table, examining Caren's knee; Helen sitting on Caren's left, holding her hand; Catherine on my right, patting my forearm; Lee and Javier behind the sofa, their hands on our shoulders.

Janet stood next to Reinhard and stared down at Caren. "You've had a little shock, that's all. From wandering around the woods at night."

A soft litany of voices joined hers.

"We always have fireflies at Midsummer."

"But the ball of light? That came from the lanterns."

"The lanterns that the Wiccans carry."

I didn't believe a word of it. Yet I could feel my head nodding obediently.

"Rowan celebrates with them every year."

"They meet in the meadow."

"And sing. And play instruments."

"And march into the woods for their ritual."

I lifted my glass and discovered someone had refilled it. I drained it and shuddered as the whisky's heat settled in my belly.

"You decided to follow them, Caren."

"And got lost."

"But you're fine now."

"No need to be frightened."

"No need to think about it at all."

The tension had left my body. Maybe that was the whisky. I glanced over at Caren and found her gazing up at Janet, her head bobbing in agreement.

Just like mine.

I shifted uneasily. The watchful eyes and soothing voices made me as uncomfortable as the hands pressing down on my shoulders. Equally disturbing was Hal's odd expression. When he caught me watching him, he turned away.

"Maggie."

My head jerked toward Janet.

"You and Caren should go now. Enjoy your dinner. Get a good night's sleep."

She and Reinhard escorted us out. I glanced back as I left the living room. Lee had his arms around Hal whose face was crumpled up like a kid about to cry.

All the way to the car, Caren babbled apologies. I kept thinking about Hal's unhappy face and Rowan's terrifying howl, wondering what the hell had happened tonight.

"Will Rowan be okay?" I asked Reinhard.

"Yes, of course. There will be other Midsummers."

I couldn't understand why he had to forgo this one. Wiccans wouldn't have gone ballistic if Caren had interrupted their ritual. It wasn't like they sacrificed babies or anything.

Reinhard's smile was warm and reassuring. So why didn't I feel reassured? Yet when he patted my shoulder and opened the car door, I obediently slid inside.

As we started down the hill, Caren exclaimed, "I don't know what possessed me to go running after those Wiccans. I'm a Presbyterian!"

I let her chatter on until we reached the hotel. As she unbuckled her seat belt, I grabbed her arm. "Caren. What did you really see in the meadow?"

"You mean the Wiccans?"

"No. Before." When she just stared at me, I prompted, "The fireflies?"

"Oh. Right. They were something."

"And the ball of light?"

"The lanterns? Yeah, I saw them, too."

I tried again. "And the music?"

"I heard . . . something. Just for a moment. Then it went away." She glanced down and moaned. "Just look at that hole! My favorite jeans, too. Well, it serves me right. I'm starving. I hope there's some food left."

I got out of the car, but just stood there, frowning.

"Maggie?"

"I think I'll skip dinner."

"Oh, but you have to come. It just won't be—"

"I really don't feel like it."

"Are you sick? Should I call—?"

"No! Just a killer headache. I'll be fine if I lie down for awhile."

I sent her on her way, then climbed the stairs to my room and flung myself on the bed.

Everything Caren had said—everything the staff had told us—sounded reasonable. The light *was* tricky at dusk. Fireflies *didn't* swarm. Could I swear in a court of law that they had surrounded Rowan? Or that I'd seen a glowing ball of light and not the glow of a couple dozen lanterns?

I'd experienced the mesmerizing effect of Alex's voice at that first music rehearsal. And the urgency to obey Janet when she ordered me back to my chair during our memorable chat in the lobby of the Bough. At the cast party, Reinhard had discerned each disquieting emotion evoked by the memories of my father. And with a hug or a blessing, Helen could fill me with peace.

I'd chalked it up to charm or insight or simply strength of will. Now, I wondered if it was something more, if they had actually reshaped our perceptions as they calmed us.

The thought made me shake my head. This wasn't *The Manchurian Candidate*, for God's sake. And if they had brainwashed us, why had it only worked on Caren? Was she simply more susceptible?

I opened my laptop, clicked on the Skype icon, and pulled on my headphones. My breath blew out in a sigh of pure relief when Nancy picked up.

"Hey. It's me. Maggie."

"What's the matter?"

"Nothing."

"You sound funny."

"I just . . . I need to talk to someone normal."

Silence. Then: "Let me get my glass of wine."

"Better get the bottle, Nancy. This might take a while."

CHAPTER 11

PUT ON A HAPPY FACE

DISCUSSING THE EVENING'S BIZARRE EVENTS with Nancy helped calm me down, but brought me no closer to understanding what had actually happened. Only the staff could provide those answers. And none of them would break ranks. Except—maybe—Hal.

Moments after I hung up with Nancy, someone knocked at the door. As I opened it, Lou and Bobbie thrust out six-packs of beer, Brittany and Kalma, pints of the Chatterbox's hand-packed ice cream. Gary cradled fortune cookies in his palms.

Caren shyly held up a carton of takeout. "Shrimp and snow peas."

My favorite.

I hugged her. I hugged all of them. We crammed into my room and sat up for hours, talking and laughing and groaning over the vague fortunes our cookies contained. Maybe it was just another example of the summer stock law of fast-blooming friendships, but I felt closer to them after a month than I had to my colleagues at HelpLink after two years. And their cheerfully normal company kept me from obsessing about the Midsummer madness.

My questions resurfaced during the company meeting the next morning. Reinhard brusquely announced that Rowan was "under the weather" and declared the woods off limits to avoid "unfortunate accidents."

"You think I am treating you like children, yes? Well,

139

until I can rely upon certain members of this cast to exercise common sense, this is how it must be for all."

Caren wilted under his glare. I fumed. Neither of us had wanted to go blundering through the woods, but in order to conceal that little fact, we had to be cast as the village idiots.

Reinhard blocked two of the company scenes in Act One, snapping out stage directions like a drill sergeant. At our lunch break, I decided to brave another wave of Teutonic wrath and attempt a frontal assault. He gave me the opening I needed by asking how I was feeling.

"I don't know which was more unsettling: what I saw in the meadow or what happened at Janet's."

Reinhard didn't bat an eye. "What do you mean?"

"The brainwashing."

"Is that what you call it?"

"What would you call it?"

"Calming two young women on the verge of hysterics."

"Then explain to me why one young woman's memories of last night differ so drastically from the other's."

Reinhard's frosty expression shifted to exasperation. "Because you are as stubborn as a rock." Then he sighed and pinched the bridge of his nose, looking so tired that my anger faded.

"You were honest with me at the cast party," I reminded him. "When you said Rowan wasn't . . . ordinary."

"And I also said that was all I intended to say on the subject. About last night, I can only tell you it was not anything bad."

"Maybe I should just ask Rowan."

Reinhard sighed again. "You can't. He is not in his apartment."

"He hasn't come back?"

Reinhard shook his head.

"Should we call the police?"

"No!"

"But he might be hurt! He could have fallen or—"

"Rowan knows every inch of those woods. He'll be back. We must give him a little time."

A somber Alex awaited us at our afternoon music rehearsal. Everyone else probably attributed his mood to the

folk songs we were learning; lost love and grief featured
prominently in both "The Great Selkie of Sule Skerry"
and "The Water is Wide." Judging from his haggard face, I
guessed he'd spent the night combing the woods in vain for
Rowan.

After rehearsal, I made my way to Hallee's. The latest
window display featured scantily clad mannequins frolicking in a forest glade, their corsets, panties, and bras like so
many brightly colored flowers. The single male mannequin
sported a scarlet thong and a donkey's head that rested in
the lap of a female mannequin in a shimmering negligee of
green silk. Hal's tribute to *A Midsummer Night's Dream*.

If only our Midsummer had been so dreamy.

Although it was after 6:00, the door opened when I turned
the knob. As I stepped inside, the bell chimed the opening
notes of "People" from *Funny Girl*. From somewhere in the
back, Hal called, "Sorry, we're closed."

He slipped through the pink velveteen curtains, wrestling
with a mound of fabric, and stopped dead when he saw me.

"Oh, sweetie, are you okay?"

I meant to demand explanations. But one look at his worried face and I was fluttering my hands like a fledgling bird
and fighting back tears. I hardly ever cried, but lately, one
kind word and I sprang a leak.

He hurried toward me, enfolding me in a fierce hug
and yards of green tulle. I babbled an apology, but he just
shushed me. Finally, he stepped back, wiping first my eyes
then his with the tulle.

"Sorry," I managed. "I'm still kind of shaky after last
night. And now Rowan's disappeared—"

"That's not your fault."

"We ruined his Midsummer."

"Caren ruined it. Stupid cow."

"That's not fair."

"No. But saying it makes me feel better. Stupid, stupid
cow. There."

I hesitated, then said, "What happened . . . at Janet's . . ."

"They meant well. Really."

Hal's eyes pleaded with me to believe him. And part
of me did. Hurting a cast member violated the code of the

Crossroads. But the code had to be pretty flexible if it included brainwashing.

"They're like Rowan, aren't they? The same power. Only not as strong."

His gaze slid away, and I realized how foolish I'd been to hope that he would tell me the truth. How could he? Lee was part of it and Lee was the center of his world.

"It's okay, Hal. It's not your fault. It's not anybody's fault, I guess. But that doesn't change the fact that Rowan's vanished."

"He'll be back."

"That's what Reinhard said."

"Because it's true."

"This has happened before?"

"The Midsummer thing? No. But there have been other times . . ." Hal shrugged. "Rowan's moody. Like all artistic geniuses. But he'll be back before the curtain goes up."

Curtain time rolled around. Still no Rowan.

"You don't suppose something awful happened?" Nancy, back for the Wednesday night performance of *Brigadoon*, looked as worried as I felt.

I shrugged helplessly.

Janet surprised us by showing up in the green room. One look at her face told me Rowan was still MIA. Reinhard glanced at the wall clock for the tenth time in ten minutes. By 8:05, he had yet to call places. Standard operating procedure at other theatres, but the Crossroads observed its 8:00 curtain time with relentless punctuality.

Suddenly, Janet and Reinhard went into bird dog mode. The green room door swung open. Rowan entered, looking so drawn and pale that I could almost believe he *was* sick. His regulation linen shirt and black jeans were stained and wrinkled, but his hair was neatly tied back with a leather thong.

Ignoring his supposed phobia about crowds, the cast clustered around, exclaiming with relief and making sympathetic noises. Caren hung back, watching Rowan like a nervous schoolgirl expecting a reprimand from her favorite teacher. His quick smile brought her rushing forward to join the others.

"I apologize for my tardiness. And for missing rehearsal today."

His voice was hoarse. I imagined that awful howl tearing at his throat and shuddered.

"I appreciate your concern. But now, let's focus on the show."

As we formed our customary circle, Reinhard leaned forward to whisper something. When Rowan shook his head, Reinhard stepped back, but continued to watch him anxiously.

We closed our eyes and clasped hands, breathing together in silence. Instead of soothing me, the ritual brought back disturbing images of the previous night, the gentle pressure of Brittany's hand and Nancy's an unpleasant reminder of the staff touching me.

I told myself that Rowan had not been part of that, that the energy he summoned could never hurt me, that we needed this strange connection in order to turn in the best possible performance. But my body remained tense, my mind churning, my emotions a jumble of resentment and confusion and lingering concern about Rowan.

"We all have concerns."

My eyes flew open at this deviation from the script.

"We might be missing our families. Worrying about our jobs. Questioning why we're here. Questioning what this theatre is all about."

His words were clearly directed at me. Had someone on the staff told him what had happened last night? Or did he just know?

"This is not the time for those concerns. Tonight, we have only one purpose: to present this show."

Nancy squeezed my hand. Could she feel my separateness? Could everyone sense it?

"Some members of our audience probably know *Brigadoon* by heart. Others will be watching it for the first time. They all deserve the best performance we can give."

As the quiet words washed over me, I studied Rowan. The drooping shoulders that belied the confident voice. The deep lines bracketing his mouth. The two grooves etched between his brows.

I wanted to tell him that everything would be all right, just as he had reassured us so many times. I wanted to promise that he would rediscover the joy that had been snatched away from him last night. Mostly, I wanted to put my arms around him and urge him to let go of his disappointment, of his responsibilities, of the bonds that held him hostage to this place.

His voice trailed off. The smile that curved his mouth was so sweet and tender it made me ache.

"Don't worry," he said, his voice little more than a whisper. "Just acknowledge your concerns as you breathe in."

I closed my eyes and took a shaky breath, filling my lungs with the confusion and doubts of the last twenty-four hours.

"And let them go as you breathe out."

Around the circle, people exhaled in a long, collective sigh. I released my breath and felt the tension drain away.

All of my questions would be there in the morning. For now, I was just relieved to feel the connection between us once more. For a few minutes, I'd felt like Tommy, standing forlornly on the hilltop, scanning the empty valley where the village had once stood. For better or worse, I was back in Brigadoon.

CHAPTER 12

ICE CREAM

THE ENSUING DAYS PROVED that Brigadoon's foundations were still shaky.

"Maybe we're just tired," Brittany said as we trudged into the women's dressing room after another lackluster performance.

"Or maybe," Romaine said, "we all got a little too cocky after opening night. We should thank the good Lord for our success instead of taking the credit ourselves."

I suspected Rowan had more to do with it than God, but I hated to think the credit—or blame—was entirely his. That reduced us to marionettes, dancing on the strings he pulled. Which was uncomfortably reminiscent of how I had felt during the staff's brainwashing.

I slumped into my chair at one of the makeup tables. The mirrors on the wall reflected multiple images of cast mates grimly hanging up costumes and packing up their gear.

Nancy slid into the chair next to mine. Our gazes met in the mirror.

"Do you think we're in this funk because of what happened to Rowan?" she whispered.

"I don't know."

If we had been swept up in his pre-Midsummer mania, we could easily catch his post-Midsummer depression. But his mania had been obvious; the only evidence I could find of his depression was how *we* were feeling. And how the staff tiptoed around him, observing his behavior as intently as they studied Caren's and mine.

Rehearsals of *The Sea-Wife* were just as dispirited. I played what had now become known as "the list thing" with the principals. Caren was wildly excited, but Hector and Maya just went through the motions. Gary refused to participate at all, saying, "Trust me, I know way more about this character than I want to."

I quizzed Maya about Wicca and got a crash course in Reiki healing and chakra alignment as well. The way practitioners moved energy around sounded similar to what Rowan did, but nothing like the staff's brainwashing.

I researched hypnosis on the Web. And energy healing. And firefly behavior. Two hours later, I shut down my laptop. Just what I needed. Another "like father, like daughter" moment. During that last year, he'd spent countless hours doing "research," too. Shut away in the basement when I left for school. Still closeted there when I came home. Sometimes, I'd hear him muttering to himself or strumming the same chord over and over on his guitar.

The Saturday matinee of *Brigadoon* went a little better. And the free dinner afterward—catered by the Mandarin Chalet—helped everyone relax. Rowan showed up long enough to fill his paper plate with chicken and bean sprouts. Then he retreated to his apartment. The previous week, he had surprised everyone by eating with us, putting to rest the rumor that he existed exclusively on strawberry milkshakes.

Spurred by that memory, I made an impulsive trip to town. When I returned, the cast was buzzing excitedly about Reinhard's announcement of the Crossroads Follies. In light of their renewed spirits, I considered stowing my purchases in the green room fridge. My idea—which had initially seemed as fun and foolish as the Follies—just seemed stupid now. But maybe it would make Rowan smile.

As I mounted the stairs to his apartment, my courage evaporated. I left the bags outside his door, knocked firmly, and turned tail.

I'd made it halfway down the stairs when I heard the door open. I froze, hoping the shadows would conceal me.

Rowan's puzzled "Maggie?" proved the futility of that strategy.

I turned to find him silhouetted in the doorway. He bent down and picked up the two small bags. Paper rustled as he examined the contents.

"By way of apology," I said. "For wrecking your Midsummer." When he just stared at me, I babbled, "It was supposed to make you laugh. Because you always drink strawberry milkshakes at lunch."

The silence from the top of the stairs lengthened. Sweat broke out under my arms.

"But obviously, it's not funny. So I'll go now."

"You brought me milk and strawberries?"

His voice sounded odd. Strained.

"Ice cream and strawberries." Had he even looked in the second bag? How do you mistake a pint of vanilla ice cream for a milk carton? "It was a joke. A coals-to-Newcastle thing. Because you drink—"

"Yes. I see."

Slowly, he descended the stairs, the bags dangling from his fingertips like they contained dead rats. He stopped two steps above me. The small light on the stage manager's desk revealed little of his expression, but I thought he was frowning.

"Look, I'm sorry I bothered you."

"Don't apologize. It was very . . . neighborly."

"Neighborly?"

"Kind. Thoughtful." He cleared his throat and descended another step. He was definitely frowning. "Unexpected. An unexpected gift."

"It's just ice cream and strawberries."

"Yes. Still. Thank you."

We lapsed into silence. His stare was becoming really unnerving.

"Okay. Well. I'd better get ready for the show."

I glanced back as I reached the stage. He was still standing there, watching me.

Rowan's strange reaction made me wonder if I'd made matters worse, but he seemed perfectly at ease when he led warm-ups. Even better, our performance bounced back to pre-Midsummer standards.

After the Sunday matinee, laughter filled the dressing room, a refreshing change from the morose silence of the last few days. Women dashed from costume racks to makeup tables, eager to vacate the theatre and enjoy their evening off.

As the dressing room emptied, Nancy whispered, "So everything's back to normal."

"I guess."

"And all it took was ice cream and strawberries?"

"Or the prospect of the Follies," I replied, still uncertain what had effected the change.

"'Ours is not to reason why,'" she quoted. "Any plans for your day off?"

"The usual. Laundry. E-mail. Job hunting."

And I really needed to start work on *Carousel*. Or at least read it without flinging the script across the room. Maybe that was why Rowan thought I needed to play Nettie—to learn self-control.

I examined my reflection critically. The heavy stage makeup congealing in every line on my face made me resemble a saddlebag that had been left out in the sun for a few centuries. I made a mental note to remember the look; it would be perfect for good ol' Nettie.

As I reached for my jar of cold cream, I heard Nancy's quick intake of breath and looked up to find Rowan reflected in the mirror.

Nancy's head swiveled back and forth like she was watching a tennis match. Finally, she announced, "I've got to be going. See you both Wednesday."

Rowan stepped into the dressing room to allow Nancy to exit. From behind his shoulder, she jabbed her thumb at him, raised an imaginary telephone to her ear, and mouthed, "Call me." I glared at her and heard her chuckle as she retreated down the hallway.

Rowan cleared his throat. "I just wanted to thank you again for your thoughtfulness. And to apologize if I seemed ungrateful."

"No. Just . . . confused."

"Yes. Well." His gaze swept the costume racks, the mirrors, the floor—pretty much everything except me. "Helen tells me you're working on a new program design."

"Nothing too different," I assured him. "Or expensive."

"Perhaps we could discuss it tomorrow."

"Tomorrow?"

"I realize it's your day off, but I thought we might have lunch."

"Lunch?"

"A working lunch. My treat."

"Your . . . ?" I stopped myself before I parroted his words again.

"Treat. Yes."

Lunch with Rowan. His treat. Strawberry milkshakes for two and whatever solid food he usually consumed.

"Okay."

His wandering gaze finally settled on me. "Shall we say noon?"

"Noon, it is."

He turned to go, then hesitated. "Dress for walking."

"Walking?" I asked, reverting to parrot mode.

"There's something I'd like to show you. In the woods."

I couldn't help myself. "Boy, if I had a nickel for every time a guy's used *that* line."

For a moment, his face went blank. Then he smiled. And all the weirdness of the last few days evaporated. Rowan was happy. I was happy. God's in his heaven, all's right with the world.

Still smiling, he shook his head. "What I want to show you is a wonder of nature."

"Yeah. That's what they all say."

His laughter made me giddy.

When I reminded him that the woods were off limits, he just shrugged and said, "Not if you're with me." I was a little skeptical, though, when he revealed that the wonder of nature was a beach. I'd never imagined there was a lake hidden in the depths of the woods. He refused to give me any details, just pointed his finger at me and said, "High noon. At the picnic area."

After he left, I swiveled back to the mirror and told my reflection that this was a business meeting. I would treat it with the same professionalism that I would treat any business meeting.

The woman in the mirror nodded gravely. Then a goofy smile blossomed on her face. When I shook my finger at her, she laughed.

CHAPTER 13
CANTATA FOR A FIRST DATE

I COULDN'T VERY WELL GO TO HALLEE'S and have Hal pepper me with questions about my sudden need for a bathing suit. After my frantic search of the Internet revealed zero malls in the vicinity of Dale, I drove to the JC Penney in Bennington.

At 10:30, I raced into a dressing room with an armful of possibilities. I tugged on one suit after another before choosing a one-piece black suit with a little gold clip cinching the draping at the waist. The deep V of the bodice revealed some nice cleavage. I could always wrap a towel around my hips and rip it off right before I plunged into the water.

11:30: Back at the hotel for another shower; wriggling in and out of swimsuits had left me drenched.

11:50: Bathing suit on under canvas pants and T-shirt. "Bug Away" sprayed over exposed areas. Water bottle and bath towel in carryall.

11:52: Out the door and into the car.

11:53: Out of the car and back up to my room to grab the mock-up of the program and my notebook and pen in case I needed to jot down Rowan's suggestions. And a bra and panties so I wouldn't have to wear my damp bathing suit all afternoon.

At 11:58, I pulled into the theatre parking lot. I was surprised to find another car parked next to Catherine's Prius and tried to recall which staff member drove a Lexus. Hidden behind the open door of my car, I tugged at the crotch of my swimsuit. The prospect of a long hike on a warm day while swaddled in polyester grew less appealing as I walked to the picnic area.

I was still debating whether to change when I spied Janet and Rowan leaving the theatre accompanied by a man and a woman in business suits. I used their momentary distraction to race to the Dungeon. Five minutes later, I emerged, blissfully unencumbered by the swimsuit, and found Rowan sitting on a picnic table. Janet—thank God—was nowhere in sight.

He hopped off the table as I approached.

"Who were the suits?" I asked.

He shrugged. "Bankers."

Recalling my mother's early struggles to meet the mortgage payments on our row house, their presence signaled only one thing. "Is the theatre in trouble?"

"Of course not. I thought we'd picnic in the woods if that's all right with you."

"Look, I've had a little experience with fundraising. If there's anything I can do—"

"You can stop worrying about the theatre and enjoy yourself."

He bent down and slid a bulging knapsack out from under the bench. As he hefted it onto his shoulders, I exclaimed, "My God! What have you got in there?"

"Lunch."

"For all of Dale?"

"I wasn't sure what you liked. So I brought a little of everything. Shall we go?"

I tried to turn the conversation back to the bankers, but his monosyllabic responses made it clear he had no desire to talk about them. The oblique approach of mentioning that increased publicity might bring in additional revenue proved as unsuccessful as the frontal assault. Finally, I shut up.

A mile passed in silence. Rowan tramped along the trail with the enthusiasm of a soldier on the Bataan death march. Sweat beaded his forehead and upper lip. Every few minutes, he grimaced and shifted the weight of his forty-ton knapsack. When I caught him rubbing his chest, I finally re-

alized what was happening. Controlling my panic, I quietly
ordered him to lie down.

His head jerked toward me. "What?"

"I think you're having a heart attack. I want you to lie
down and try to remain calm."

"Maggie . . ."

"Lie down and remain calm, damn it!"

As I dropped to my knees and rummaged in my carryall
for my cell phone, Rowan said, "Maggie. I am not having a
heart attack."

I searched his face for any evidence of pain and found
only faint amusement.

"It's hot. The knapsack is heavy. And I'm a bit . . ."

"Preoccupied? Unsettled? Upset?"

"Something like that."

"Those damn bankers."

His mouth curved in a rueful smile. "You're as tenacious
as a pit bull."

"It's one of my best qualities. You're sure you're not having a heart attack?"

"Quite sure."

"So. The bankers."

As we walked, he explained that Janet's investments had
taken a nosedive. And Janet's investments supported the theatre. In good years, it usually managed to break even, but the
last few years hadn't been good. And while she was in no
danger of losing the property, it had become clear to everyone on the staff that something had to change.

"We've discussed various options. Taking out a second
mortgage. Refinancing the current one. Selling off some
acreage." He grimaced.

"What about incorporating as a nonprofit?"

"I don't want a board of directors telling me how to run
my theatre."

"So choose board members who believe in your theatre!
Which includes everyone in Dale. Call up some of the other
nonprofit theatres in the state. Pick their executive directors'
brains. If Lee doesn't know about this stuff, find a lawyer
who does. Someone who'll sit down for an initial question
and answer session without soaking you. And do it soon. It

might take a year to incorporate. Longer still for grants . . . what?"

Rowan had stopped walking and was watching me. "You're very passionate about this."

"Aren't you?"

"Yes. But the theatre . . . it's my life. It's just one summer in yours."

"I'd still hate to see it go under. It's special. Weird but special."

"I wasn't sure you felt that way. After Midsummer."

And there it was—the proverbial six-hundred-pound gorilla in the room. Or woods, in this case. I waited for him to say more, but he just shifted the weight of his knapsack and started walking again.

Instead of inundating him with questions about Midsummer, I returned to the subject of publicity. He was clearly uneasy, but I expected that; raising the theatre's profile might bring unwelcome scrutiny into his mysterious past—and his equally mysterious powers. But at least he seemed willing to consider my suggestions.

When I brought up salary freezes, though, he shook his head.

"Helen and Janet don't even accept a salary. As for the others . . . you know how much they make? A hundred dollars a week. Same as the cast."

And they didn't even get a free room.

"Alex and Reinhard and Mei-Yin make a good living, but they deserve salaries for all the hours they put in. And the younger members of the staff need the extra money."

"Lee's a lawyer," I ventured.

"Half his practice is pro bono work. Hal's business is just starting to make a profit. Same with Catherine and Javier. And in spite of that, they all volunteered to forgo their salaries this summer. That's how dedicated they are. But I'll be damned if I let them work for nothing! We've survived bad times before and we will now."

He took a deep breath, shook his head, and said, "Forgive me. I'm ruining the afternoon."

"My fault. I shouldn't have beat you over the head about the bankers."

"Let's make an addendum to our pact—no wallowing in guilt."

We shook hands and moved on. Occasionally, Rowan would point out something in the woods—a deep indentation in a bank of ferns where a deer had lain, the tracks of fox and opossum imprinted on a muddy stream bank. I found it wonderfully exotic, but part of my enthusiasm stemmed from his obvious love for these wild places. When the conversation faltered, the silence felt companionable rather than grim, both of us content to listen to the scolding of squirrels, the throaty purrs of wood pigeons, and the intermittent rat-a-tat-tat of a woodpecker.

Typical city girl, I failed to recognize where he was leading me until we entered the little clearing where I had fallen.

"I didn't know the beach was near here."

"Yes."

"Thank God. I'm starving. And hot." I nodded toward the hut and added, "You never did tell me who lived there."

"I did. I still do. From time to time."

I glanced at him to see if he was joking, but his expression was perfectly serious.

"That's where you were at Midsummer."

He nodded.

"And nobody thought to look for you there?"

"I made a point of being elsewhere when they did. Come on. It's just over this rise."

As we crested the top, I temporarily forgot about the beach and simply stared at the enormous tree straddling the next hill. Five men with their arms outstretched might have managed to circle the thick trunk. Dozens of branches sprouted from it, reaching out and up to create a leafy canopy so dense that nothing grew in its shade. Part of the slope had fallen away, carving out a hollow space among the roots. Perfect for pirate treasure or a family of gnomes. Daddy would have loved it.

"It must be ancient," I whispered.

"Nearly two hundred years old," Rowan replied just as softly.

As I started down the slope, he gently took my arm. Maybe he knew I wouldn't be able to take my eyes off the tree. With every step, my head tilted farther back until my neck ached as I craned to see the top. Crisp leaves whispered underfoot like mothers shushing their children in church, reinforcing the sense that this was a sacred place.

Up close, the twisted roots looked fantastical, spilling down and over and into the soil like tangled tendrils of hair. I ducked under a low-hanging branch and knelt to brush off the leaves, surprised that the roots were narrow enough to cup in my hand. How could something so thin hold up such an incredible weight?

I stroked the tree, savoring the contrast between the smooth bark and the strange gullies coursing through it. It was as easy to imagine a dryad emerging from that trunk as it was to picture a family of gnomes living in the cavern under its roots.

And it was a cavern, not merely the small hollow I had thought. A wonderful playhouse for a child—or a hiding place for a man who didn't want to be found by his staff.

The leaves crackled as I stretched out full-length on the ground. I stared up into the latticework of branches, wishing my climbing skills were half as good as they had been in my youth. But another part of me shrank from such an act; somehow, it seemed sacrilegious.

Rowan crouched beside me, smiling. "You didn't believe me. When I told you it was a wonder of nature."

"I thought that was the beach."

He frowned. "It was. It is."

"So there are two wonders of nature out here?"

"Maggie." Rowan rested his palm against the tree's trunk. "*This* is the beech."

For a long moment, I simply stared at him. "It's . . . a beech . . . tree."

He nodded, his expression wary.

I burst into helpless laughter. Rowan stared at me like I had lost my mind. Finally I managed to wheeze out, "I thought you meant . . . a beach. With sand. And water."

"In the middle of the woods?"

"That's what I said when you told me!"

He shook his head, a smile tugging at his mouth.

"I thought there was a lake. Or a river. Something." I convulsed helplessly, hands holding my aching stomach. "I even went out . . . and bought . . . a bathing suit!"

I'd read books where people yelped with laughter. Or barked. Or brayed. The sound that emerged from Rowan's mouth was more of a bellow that tailed off into a series of high-pitched yips. He laughed so hard, he lost his balance and sat down hard on the roots. That elicited a genuine yelp, which set me off again. We fell back into the leaves, our laughter slowly easing to a duet of moans and sighs.

"I brought bottled water," Rowan said. "If you change into your bathing suit, I'll pour it over you."

With a supreme effort, I rolled onto my side so I could treat him to the full effect of my glare. He grinned at me, unrepentant, then scrambled to his feet, brushed off the leaves and twigs, and hefted his knapsack.

I groaned. "Can't we eat here?"

"We're not going far. And it'll be worth it."

"Another wonder of nature?"

"Actually, yes."

I allowed him to help me to my feet and clung to his hand as we sidestepped down the beech's hill and marched up the next. As I stumbled over the top, a cool breeze caressed my face. My hand tightened on Rowan's as I gazed out at the limitless expanse of earth and sky before us.

Round-backed hills rolled west in undulating waves of green that faded to a misty blue in the distance. Fat-bellied clouds drifted over them, their shadows chasing each other across the nearest hillside. Farther west, storm clouds curdled in the sky, gray and purple and cream.

I tottered through the sparse grass. The pressure of Rowan's fingers warned me to stop before I reached the edge of our little plateau, but I could see the silver thread of a river at the bottom of the gorge and hear the faint thunder of its water as it tumbled over rocks and boulders.

The sun emerged from behind a cloud as if to bless us, and my eyes closed against its sudden brilliance. When I opened them, I found Rowan watching me.

"You're right," I said. "It was definitely worth it."

I knew this was the place where he sang. He must have stood here countless times, enjoying the play of sunlight and shadow on the hills, watching storm clouds roll in to veil the mountaintops in mist. Sharing this with me was a gift even greater than the magnificent beech.

"Thank you," I whispered.

He just smiled and plucked a leaf from my hair.

I felt strangely shy, as if our relationship had shifted and there could be no going back to the give-and-take we usually shared. As I helped him spread a faded quilt on the grass, I kept stealing glances at him for any hint that he shared those feelings, but he seemed perfectly at ease.

My shyness receded as he began unpacking lunch. Or rather, unveiling it. Linen napkins swaddled bottles of lemonade, white wine, and spring water. Linen placemats and dishtowels protected china plates, crystal goblets, silver utensils. My mouth hung open as he arranged them on the quilt. When he presented the food, I nearly dislocated my jaw.

Poached salmon on a bed of fennel fronds. Cold grilled quail with mustard vinaigrette. Wild rice salad with pecans and dried apricots. Haricots verts and new potatoes with walnuts and Stilton. A French baguette and a tiny cup of sweet butter. A selection of cheeses. A china bowl of strawberries to accompany the lemon curd tart.

When he placed my plate in front of me, I simply stared at it. Then stared at him.

His shoulders moved awkwardly, as if his shirt had suddenly shrunk two sizes. "I just wanted it to be nice."

"Nice? Nice is cold cuts and beer. This is . . ." I waved my hand helplessly. "It's . . . I'm . . ."

"Speechless?"

"Well. I'm rarely speechless."

"I've noticed."

I ripped off a chunk of baguette and threw it at him. Grinning, he snatched it out of the air and took a bite.

"You and Janet must have the same caterer."

He shook his head and mumbled something unintelligible.

"You don't mean to tell me Helen made all this."

"No, I did."

I laughed.

"I *did*!" he protested.

"You. Made all this."

"Catherine was kind enough to help with the shopping. I couldn't get everything delivered on such short notice. And I don't usually keep a side of salmon around the apartment."

"Or a covey of quail?"

"Actually, I made that for supper the other night. I just refrigerated the leftovers and—"

"Okay, now you're scaring me."

He laughed. "With everything you've seen and heard this summer, what scares you is the fact that I can cook?"

"I bet you're kind to animals, too."

"Yes, but I beat my staff regularly." He shook his head, still smiling. "I just like to cook, Maggie. It relaxes me. Now what would you like to drink?"

I eyed the wine longingly and decided I'd better stick with lemonade. As he filled my glass, I ventured, "So if you're a gourmet chef, why does Helen bring you lunch every day?"

He sighed. "She likes bringing me lunch. Just as she likes baking for the cast. She's one of those people who's happiest caring for others."

"Yeah, I've heard of them."

"And it makes my life easier. I'm lucky if I have fifteen minutes to eat. There's always a cast problem or a set problem or some other problem." Suddenly, he stiffened. "Helen doesn't pay for lunch. I've set up accounts with the shops in town. My salary doesn't allow me many luxuries, but it does put clothes on my back and food on my table."

Guilt swamped me as I realized this spread must have cost him a week's salary. "You really shouldn't have, Rowan."

"Shouldn't have what?"

"Done all . . . this."

"It was fun. I can't remember the last time I cooked for someone." He raised his glass. "No wallowing. Remember?"

Our glasses clinked with the musicality of fine crystal.

"So how did you manage to create this feast in that little apartment of yours?"

"It's not so little. Nearly two thousand square feet."

I choked on my lemonade. "You're kidding."

"Ah, that's right. You didn't see much of it that night. It runs pretty much the length of the theatre."

"My God. Do you have any idea what you'd pay for that kind of space in New York?"

"I shudder to think. So what's your apartment like?"

"A hovel. Okay, not a hovel. But not much bigger than your office. Still, the park's pretty close. Prospect Park. The site of my last picnic."

I regaled him with the deviled egg debacle, expecting him to smile like everyone else who'd heard the story. Instead, he frowned and said, "He should have laughed it off."

"Maybe when he quit vomiting, he did. But it was a little late by then."

"That should be the story you told your grandchildren. How Grandma gave Grandpa salmonella poisoning and he fell in love with her anyway."

"You have a strange sense of romance."

"Maybe. But I would have laughed."

The quiet intensity of his voice sent a wave of heat surging into my cheeks. Another settled a good deal lower in my body. I dug into my food, grateful when he turned the conversation to my life in New York.

The more I talked, though, the less interesting that life sounded. My discouragement increased when he asked about some of my previous jobs. I tried to dredge up funny stories, but somehow each ended with me getting fired or quitting or drifting to another job as unfulfilling as the last.

Maybe that was why I switched to wine. After the second glass, I could joke about my lackluster career and pretend I didn't notice how brittle my laughter sounded.

I was relieved when he asked about my previous summer stock experience. On safer ground, I soon had him laughing with my description of our quarters in rundown Anatevka, the mottled black and gray shroud that served as our backdrop, and the romantic foibles of my cast mates, including the guy who left his wife for one of the musicians, the woman who came out as a lesbian after sleeping with a townie, and the gay guys who formed a ménage-a-trois with our female stage manager.

"All in one summer?" he asked.

"All in one show."

That prompted him to pour a glass of wine for himself. "Where did you fit into all that?"

"Mother confessor. People were always showing up at my door to share their woes."

"A Helping Professional even then."

"No. Just a telemarketer. But my mother still had a fit when I quit my job and ran away to the theatre."

"Life upon the wicked stage," he mused.

"That and the fact that my father—"

After a short silence, Rowan quietly prompted, "Your father?"

"He was an actor, too. For awhile." I shrugged. "Not much to tell."

"Then why has all the light left your face?"

"Because I don't want to bore you with the story of my parents' divorce, okay?"

"Okay."

"I'm surprised Janet didn't fill you in on all the gory details."

"She did. So did Alex. He was worried about you."

"The whole thing was stupid. I don't know what's the matter with me. It's been ages since I've thought about my father. But these last few weeks . . ." I glared at Rowan. "I suppose that's your doing. Somehow."

"Maybe it's just being back in summer stock."

"Yeah, Right. And those were Wiccans in the woods at Midsummer."

He folded his napkin neatly and laid it beside his plate. "You're very good at that. Using anger or humor to turn aside questions that are too personal."

"And you're not?"

"Yes. We've both developed similar methods of coping with the circumstances of our lives. I'm not sure whether they've helped us or hurt us. But we *have* learned to cope."

"Lunch and psychoanalysis. It's my lucky day."

I wanted to take back the words as soon as I spat them out. Not only did they sound hateful, but they proved his point.

I wasn't stupid. I knew all about using anger to hide fear. Making fun of myself before someone else could. Slipping into whatever role would work best for the moment. Maybe that's why acting came so naturally. I'd spent most of my life doing it. It just got so damn exhausting sometimes.

And it was really annoying that Rowan saw right through my game and called me on it.

Striving for a calm I didn't feel, I asked, "Would you like to look at my mock-up of the program?"

"Maybe later. Would you care for some lemon tart?"

"I'd love some."

The sticky-sweetness of my tone evoked a very small smile. He sliced the tart and sprinkled a few strawberries atop my piece. I waited in polite but turbulent silence for him to serve himself. Then I lifted a forkful to my mouth.

It was delicious. I could hardly get it down without choking.

After two bites, I flung my fork down and demanded, "Why do you have to push so hard?"

"Because I think you're worth it. And because I want you to be happy and I don't think you are."

I bit down hard on my lower lip.

"Why do *you* push so hard?"

I stared at my plate. "Mostly . . . because I'm scared."

The words hung there for a long moment. Then he asked, "Of me?"

"No. Sometimes. But mostly, just . . . scared. That the things I love about this place are an illusion. That after I leave, my life will go back to the way it was."

That the friendships I've made here will peter out like all the others. That I'll always be alone.

"That I'm just going to drift through life . . ."

Like my father.

The aroma of honeysuckle sweetened the air. A crow cawed, a hoarse, mocking jeer. The sun drifted in and out of the clouds, alternately dulling the silver and burnishing it to a high sheen. Rowan's long-fingered hands rested quietly on his knees. Mine were fisted in my lap.

"You don't have to be afraid of me, Maggie. Or fear that everything at the Crossroads is an illusion. I know it's hard not to worry about the future, but maybe by the end of the summer, you'll have a better sense of what you want."

I nodded mechanically; I'd told myself the same things a dozen times since I'd arrived here.

"One thing I do know—you're not a drifter. You're too strong, too stubborn. But what's the harm of allowing yourself to drift for the next two months? Drift and play and dream. Theatre speaks to the child in all of us. The part that still believes in magic. That wants to inhabit other lives, other places. That can burst into laughter or dance or song because we're filled with joy."

My head jerked up. "And believe a painted set is an enchanted village. And fireflies are fairies. And gnomes live under tree roots." I didn't bother disguising the bitterness in my voice. "I believed that kind of crap when I was a kid. And then . . ."

"Then your father left. And took the magic with him."

"There was never any magic. Just make believe."

"You're wrong, Maggie. There is magic in the world. Maybe that's why you're here. To rediscover it."

"And you're here to make the magic happen?"

His gaze slid away as he studied the clouds. "I can't offer you a scientific explanation. Any more than I can explain how a psychic works. Or a faith healer. You probably don't believe their powers are genuine."

It seemed more likely that those who claimed to possess them were just preying on gullible people. But I'd felt Rowan's power before every performance and it sure as hell felt real.

"I'm not pulling any strings, Maggie. I'm more like . . . the catalyst. The battery that charges the cast. And is charged *by* them. The power flows both ways. And I can only describe that as magical."

Although his description perfectly captured what I felt at the beginning of every performance, I was still astonished that he would admit so much to me.

"You can't always control it, can you?"

He took a deep breath and let it out slowly. "When I'm under the sway of some strong emotion—anger, grief, joy— yes, it's more difficult then. That's what happened at Midsummer. When I left the theatre and saw the fireflies . . . I was so happy, you see. And they were so beautiful. The power just . . . burst free. And they flocked to me. Surrounding me in light, their wings beating faster than my heart, their spirits singing with mine . . ."

His voice trailed off, his face suffused with longing. Then he shrugged. "I suppose that sounds ridiculous."

I shook my head. "It sounds like . . . what I saw. What I thought I saw. Before the staff fed me that crap about Wiccans and their lanterns."

"They were trying to protect me. And calm Caren. She's not as . . . resilient . . . as you."

I felt anything but resilient. The things he was telling me were incredible, impossible. And yet they were the only explanations that made any sense.

"They have the same sort of power you do."

With obvious reluctance, he nodded.

"But . . . how? Where does it come from?"

"Maybe every person possesses it to some degree. But few tap into it. I haven't always used my gift well. Especially when I was young. I was foolish and arrogant. Enthralled by my abilities. Disdainful of those I considered ordinary. I made mistakes. I . . . hurt people. But I'm older now and wiser, I hope. And I hope you'll believe that I would never deliberately hurt a member of my company. Neither would the staff."

I groped for an answer that would be honest. The power that helped us during performances could just as easily hurt us if he became angry. And while the staff might have been protecting him, their manipulation still felt wrong.

When I told him that, he sighed. "Maybe it was. We're only . . . we all make mistakes. But we're committed to the cast. To your welfare. That's why I told you so much. Maybe that was a mistake, too. But I know you've been troubled. And it was starting to drive a wedge between you and the staff. Between you and me. I want you to be able to trust me. To trust the good things that we're doing here."

"And so . . . the picnic."

I should have known it was just an excuse to allay my suspicions. But the bitter twisting of my stomach still surprised me.

"This was just supposed to be fun. I didn't plan on . . ."

His thumb absently traced the scars on his fingertips. Then he frowned and folded his hands. "It's been a long time since I've talked with anyone. About myself."

It sounded like the truth. If he was using his power to convince me, I couldn't detect it. And he seemed as genuinely uncomfortable as I did.

"I'm not exactly a whiz at sharing, either," I admitted. "In case you hadn't noticed. It's a whole lot easier to tell other people how to fix their lives than it is to fix your own."

"You don't need fixing, Maggie."

"Just a tune-up."

"We all need that. From time to time."

Our eyes met, held. Goose bumps popped up on my arms. Warmth flooded my loins. My flesh tingled as if his fingertips were running lightly over my body. I closed my eyes, dizzy and unmoored, wondering whether it was the intimacy of his gaze or further evidence of his power. Or just too much wine in the middle of the afternoon.

"Eat your tart," Rowan said. "I slaved over it. Afterward, we'll talk about the program."

The spell dissipated, but his eyes still warmed me, and the golden light dancing in their depths made me shiver with pleasure.

No wonder I forgot to ask about the strange music I'd heard at Midsummer.

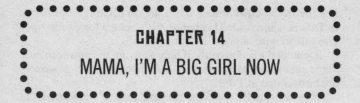

CHAPTER 14

MAMA, I'M A BIG GIRL NOW

FOR THE NEXT FEW DAYS, I was like a child torn between savoring her secret and chanting, "I know something you don't know." The mere sight of Rowan left me giddy, excited, and a little scared. Thankfully, he behaved like a grown-up, treating me with an easy combination of friendliness and professionalism, and the fever abated.

Although Rowan refused to invite any theatre critics, he did let me send out press releases. And create a nicer program. He insisted Ashley and Bernie come with me to solicit underwriting because people would recognize them from *Brigadoon*. I suspected he wanted her Southern charm and his Brooklyn folksiness to offset my pit bull aggressiveness.

We only had to make one stop. The owner of Dale's General Store—my Good Samaritan in the John Deere cap—agreed to print it in return for an ad on the back cover.

Although it was only two double-sided pages, I loved my program. I loved the stylized waves I used as a graphic motif. I loved the fact that working on it allowed me to shrug off the thundering silence that continued to greet my job queries. And I loved that it gave me an excuse to avoid working on Nettie.

I'd memorized the few dozen lines I had. And the lyrics to my songs. But ever since my heart-to-heart with Rowan, I'd shied away from looking too deeply into her character. This from the woman who urged everyone else to play the "list thing." My avoidance was starting to verge on the pathologi-cal and it was a lot easier to distract myself with the program than to seek an explanation.

Like a proud parent, I showed my program to everyone. I brought the final draft to rehearsal, hugged it to my breast, and whispered, "My precious" in my best Gollum voice. Even *The Lord of the Rings* fans eyed me with misgiving.

Helen proved more receptive. "Oh, it's lovely, dear. What pretty curlicues."

"They're waves."

"Of course they are."

"You know. *The Sea-Wife*. Waves."

"We'll get it printed on blue paper," Helen declared. "Like the sea."

Janet's derisive snort failed to puncture my excitement. I was in the zone, seizing the day, drifting happily in the world of make believe.

Then my mother called.

When I saw the voice mail icon, I prayed it was a prospec-tive employer. When I heard her voice, I panicked, fearing something awful had happened to her or—equally awful—that she'd discovered what had happened to me.

Although our seven o'clock call at the theatre was only minutes away, I Skyped her immediately. She picked up on the second ring.

"What's wrong?" I demanded by way of greeting.

"Nothing's wrong. Why should anything be wrong?"

"You never call during the week."

We'd never had a Hallmark card relationship. Or the kind found in ads for feminine hygiene products where mother and daughter sit in a flower-strewn meadow and the daughter asks about "feeling fresh." I spent Thanksgiving and Christ-mas in Delaware and usually got down there for a week in the summer. In between, I called every Sunday for a five-minute "touching base" conversation.

"Sue's rented a condo at Rehoboth again. She's invited me down the last week of August. I thought you might want to join us. Get away from the city for awhile."

Vacationing with two sixtyish divorcées whose shared passions included board games and Masterpiece Theater

sagas like *I, Claudius*. Not exactly thrilling. But it was still
a free week at the beach. The theatre's season would be over
by then. The only obstacle I could foresee was the possibility that I might have a job. Administrators tended to frown
on employees asking for a week off seconds after they were
hired. No one was clamoring for my services now, but—
please God—that would change before August.

To buy some time, I said, "I'll have to check vacation
schedules at work. Let me get back to you."

"Is everything all right? You sound tense."

"Oh, you know. Everyone's a little on edge. Because of
the merger. Trying to impress the new bosses."

"Well, go the extra mile, Maggie. Show them you're a
team player. Even if it means skipping Rehoboth."

"Mom . . ."

"But don't get caught flat-footed if they make deeper
cuts. Make sure your resume is up to date. And put out some
discreet feelers to your friends in the industry."

I forced patience into my voice. "I'm already doing that,
Mom." When I wasn't rehearsing one show and performing
in another. "There's just not a whole lot out there."

"I'll keep an eye out down here and let you know if I see
anything."

I envisioned waking up in my childhood bedroom every
morning. Sitting across the dinner table from my mother every night. Playing Scrabble with her and Sue every Saturday.

"That'd be great."

"Oh, and I meant to tell you . . ."

She launched into a story about some upcoming program
she was helping to organize for the Delaware Nature Society.
Between her job at Barclays, the neighborhood association,
Thursday night book club, and volunteering with DNS, it
was a wonder she still found time to hound me. When she
started talking about another volunteer named Chris, I finally
interrupted.

"I'm really sorry, but I have to run." I was already ten
minutes late; Reinhard would be on the warpath.

"Oh! Do you have a date?"

"No. Just . . . a picnic. With a couple that moved into the
building a few weeks ago."

"A picnic? Isn't it raining in New York? It's pouring buckets here."

My heart rate quadrupled. "It stopped. A little while ago. But we may end up going to a restaurant for dinner instead."

"I should hope so. Sitting in a soggy park? You'll catch pneumonia."

My mother was a firm believer that dampness—outside of a bathtub—inevitably resulted in a life-threatening illness. How she ever became a volunteer guide at the Nature Society was beyond me. Try as I might, I could not envision her leading screaming schoolchildren through the marshlands.

"I'll let you go," she said. "Just . . . watch yourself. At work."

"What?"

"You know how you can be."

"No. How?"

"Just be careful what you say to people. Especially in e-mails."

"Mother . . ."

"And don't use the F-word every two minutes."

"Jesus, Mom . . ."

"See? There you go. I try to be helpful—"

"I appreciate that. What I don't appreciate is that you seem to think I'm a complete idiot."

"I don't think—" Her sigh blew through the phone like a sirocco. "Have a good time tonight. I'll talk to you Sunday."

I said the F-word about forty times in the three minutes it took me to drive to the theatre. So I'd had a string of jobs. But I'd done well at HelpLink. Until they fired me. Would it have killed her to acknowledge that?

And why was it I could teach other people all about active listening skills and telephone etiquette, but as soon as I got on the phone with my mother, I reverted to a whiny teenager?

CHAPTER 15

AS WE STUMBLE ALONG

ALTHOUGH I FAILED TO RECAPTURE THE JOY of drifting, I succeeded in banishing my mother by closing night of *Brigadoon*. Twenty minutes after basking in the glow of a standing ovation, we were back on stage in work clothes to strike the set, deafened by hammering instead of the cheers and applause of the audience. After little more than an hour, all that remained of our enchanted village was a pile of lumber.

Rowan stopped by the cast party and—standing at the edge of the patio—thanked us for our hard work. He also took the time to speak privately with everyone leaving the company.

The staff left shortly after he did; they had to be at the theatre first thing in the morning to load in the set of *The Sea-Wife*. Their departure was the signal for the drinking to begin in earnest. By one A.M., everyone was sloppily sentimental, hugging those who were leaving and swearing eternal friendship.

Nancy and I escaped to the sunroom where I asked, "So what have you learned, Dorothy?"

"Maybe just that my life needed a little shaking up. I'd gotten into a rut. Work. Eat dinner with my mother. Play with the cat. Don't get me wrong. I love my mother. And my cat. But I was starting to live out the Marian the Librarian stereotype." She smiled. "Do I get bonus points for that musical theatre reference?"

"Triple bonus points."

"I'll be back next weekend," Nancy promised. "For *The Sea-Wife* and the Follies."

We stared mournfully at each other. When I first met Nancy, I'd dismissed her as dull, failing to perceive her quiet strength and common sense. A bad habit, making assumptions. It had taken Bernie only a few days to realize that. I'd needed weeks. Maybe that was the lesson Rowan wanted me to learn this summer.

From the living room, we heard Lou bellowing the lyrics to "I'll Go Home with Bonnie Jean."

Others joined in. A moment later, a very un-Scottish conga line danced past the doorway.

Nancy nudged me. I smiled. Tears averted, we hurried out of the sunroom to join them.

Early the next afternoon, the cast straggled back to the theatre. I was nursing a small hangover, but some of the others looked like they were auditioning for *Night of the Living Dead*.

"How late were you up?" I whispered to Lou.

He groaned and shook his head.

"I think we saw the sunrise," Bobbie said, her voice ragged. "But maybe that was just the rosy glow of Hallee's."

Most of our new village was painted on the backdrop, but the theatre had scraped together sufficient funds for two real buildings. Well, part of two real buildings. The corner of the Craigie cottage jutted from the stage right wings, the schoolhouse from stage left. Both sets had been built atop wheeled platforms that could be turned by the stage crew for the interior scenes. It would have been a lot simpler with revolves, but the theatre's technology was mired in the last century.

Unlike the stylized set of *Brigadoon*, this one was starkly realistic, a symphony of grays and whites and browns. Only the beach scenes offered hints of the fantastic, courtesy of Lee's lighting design that included a blazing sunset, a ghostly dawn, and a star-studded night sky dominated by an enormous golden moon.

"Which cottage do you suppose is ours?" Sarah asked as she studied Hal's backdrop.

"Probably the one with the hole in the roof," I said.

"I'm a pauper," Bernie protested. "What do you want?"

"I vote we move to that ruined fortress on the hill," Kalma said.

Brittany grimaced. "It's in worse shape than our cottage."

"Yeah, but at least we can look down our noses at everyone."

Buoyed by indignation and family spirit, we joined the others drifting onto the stage to receive Reinhard's marching orders.

Having survived one Hell Week, I expected the run-through to be a little ragged. I failed to anticipate just how deadly the combination of too little sleep, too much partying, and a new set could be.

Our first number was a train wreck. Cast members tripped over the cottage sets. Gary's suitcase—roughly the size of a steamer trunk—became a lethal battering ram. Fishing nets ensnared anything and anyone that came within reach.

Janet fetched another suitcase from storage. Hal hung and rehung the nets. Rowan joked that he should simply give us tridents and turn the opening number into a gladiatorial contest. After an hour, the jokes ceased.

We soldiered grimly on. It took three minutes and ten guys to turn the Craigie set. The schoolhouse set refused to turn at all. Catherine was practically in tears. Reinhard's hair stood on end. Finally, Rowan shot to his feet and yelled, "Stop!"

We all froze.

"Take ten minutes."

Silence descended as he strode out of the house. A few cast members exchanged nervous jokes about the sheer magnitude of our awfulness, but most of us just shot each other guilty glances. Then Reinhard walked onto the stage, footsteps thudding ominously in the silence.

"I do not even know what to say. You stay up half the night partying. And this show, you treat like an afterthought."

We shifted uneasily at his accurate assessment. Maybe—as Romaine claimed—success had made us cocky.

Or perhaps the entire cast unconsciously expected Rowan to pull everything together. The "magic" went both ways, he had told me. Clearly, today, we had failed to hold up our end of the bargain.

Reinhard shook his head, his expression more sorrowful than angry. "Those two men spent a year of their lives on this show. They poured their hearts and their souls and their talent into it. If that were not enough, they have spent these last weeks nurturing *your* talents, *your* souls. And you repay them with . . . I will not even call that a performance. And to laugh about it afterward . . ." His reproachful gaze traveled around the stage. "Shame on you." With that, he plodded into the wings.

Lou broke the silence with a heartfelt "Jesus." For once, Romaine and Albertha didn't chide him for taking the Lord's name in vain.

Bernie thumped his cane on the floor. "You heard the man. Ten minutes."

"And when we come back," Kalma added, "let's get our heads out of our asses."

Maya slipped off stage left. Catherine crawled around the schoolhouse set, adjusting wheels. Gary slumped onto the Craigie platform, head between his hands. As the rest continued to mill around in various states of shock, I made my way over to Gary and sat beside him.

"Well, maybe you were slumming," he said, "but I just sucked. And no. I don't need to make a list of my strengths and weaknesses. They're all too apparent."

"The character's strengths and weaknesses. Not yours."

"They're pretty much the same. That's the trouble."

Many directors would urge him to let his personal pain inform his performance. While that sounded good on paper, it just felt too cold-blooded. Like his troubled marriage was merely fodder for his acting.

"You could be over-thinking it," I suggested.

"My life or my role?"

"I don't know. But Rowan said something the other day. About pushing too hard. He told me I should just drift. Or as we actors like to say, be in the moment." I nudged Gary with my shoulder and got a bleak smile in response.

It faded as a rectangle of light appeared at the back of the house. The staff filed into the theatre. Instead of taking his seat, Rowan continued down the aisle and mounted the steps to the stage. His expression was serious, but I found no hint of anger or disappointment, although he had to be feeling both after watching us mangle his creation.

"You all earned the right to celebrate last night. But now I need you to focus on this show. Remember the passion you brought to your role-play. Feel the emotion behind the words. The emotion of Alex's beautiful music. And above all, listen to each other."

We picked it up at the scene where the schoolteacher and selkie-woman finally connect. As Reinhard called, "Places!" I gave Gary a thumbs-up and hurried into the house to watch.

"Always the Sea" was Maya's only musical number in Act One, the first time the audience hears her voice. During last week's run-through, she'd been as nervous and tentative as Gary, neither able to get past their awkwardness to capture the potential power of the scene.

But from the moment Maya drifted onstage, she was the selkie-woman. Maybe wearing her costume—a loose-flowing shift—helped her make the transformation. Her movements were slow and a little uncertain, as if she was still adjusting to her new body, her voice soft and husky, as if she seldom used it.

The verses of the song expressed the loneliness of her captivity, the chorus her longing for the sea. Alex's music—slow and rhythmic and melancholy—captured the ebb and flow of the tide. The gentle swaying of Maya's body conjured seaweed floating on the waves, foam dissolving on a rocky shore.

She began to dance—a love ballet with the sea as her partner. She splashed through the shallows with childlike joy. Cupped imaginary water in her hands and let it trickle over her face. Then, as if she could not bear the restriction of her shift, she pulled it over her head and flung it away.

For one jaw-dropping moment, I thought she was naked. Judging from the collective gasp that filled the theatre, so did everyone else. Then I realized she was wearing a unitard so sheer I could see the outline of her ribs, the taut swell of her nipples, even the faint triangle of dark hair between her legs.

The music became more passionate, her movements that of a wild creature making love to wind and water and sky. My breath came faster, as if I were the one engaged in that elemental lovemaking. When the music slowed again, I could feel my body relaxing into the languor that follows climax, relishing both the release and the strange sadness that accompanies it.

She sang the last verse on her knees, a prisoner of the land again. On the final note, her arms reached toward us, toward her lost home. That was Gary's cue to leave his hiding place where he had been spying on her. But Gary seemed as spellbound as we were. When he finally picked up her discarded shift, he clutched it to his chest instead of draping it around Maya's shoulders, as if afraid to come too close to her.

Maya's head came up, tangled hair falling back from her face. Her smile was both wary and tender. She plucked the shift from Gary's fingers and let it fall over her body. Then she led him into the dance, guiding first his steps, then his hands, drawing them down over her hips, then up to cup her waist, her breasts, her face.

Her fingertips brushed Gary's cheek. He closed his eyes and drew a long, shuddering breath. Their expressions conveyed both wonder and profound sorrow, both characters realizing that their happiness would be as fleeting as the kiss they shared.

When the scene ended, there was utter silence in the theatre. Then we all leaped to our feet, cheering and applauding. Rowan and Mei-Yin hurried onstage. I saw Gary shake his head as he addressed Mei-Yin. Probably apologizing for blowing the choreography. When she swatted him across the shoulder, his grimace became a grin. Rowan cupped the back of Gary's neck with his right hand and kissed Maya's cheek. The smile he bestowed on them was as tender as the one they had exchanged during their scene.

"I think we all need to catch our breath after that," he said. "Let's take five minutes."

I joined the rush onstage to congratulate Gary and Maya. Then I noticed Rowan leaning against the proscenium arch, watching the proceedings with a strange smile.

When I walked over, he asked, "Do you know how extraordinary that was?"

I nodded. That kind of chemistry was hard to achieve during a performance, never mind a rehearsal.

"It was perfect," he said. "One of those rare moments when everything comes together to create . . ."

"Magic?"

"Can you think of a better word?"

I shook my head.

"And the extraordinary part is . . . I didn't do anything. I just watched it happen. Like everyone else."

Another man might have felt jealousy or resentment. Or pointed out that his direction had allowed the moment to occur. Rowan's expression held only wonderment and pride.

This was what he was trying to do at the theatre. Guide us into the forest, but allow us to choose the path through it, always nearby to help us if we stumbled, but never insisting that the path he saw was the only one worth traveling.

"Perfect," he repeated softly. "Two people completely attuned to each other, completely caught up in the magic. Have you ever felt that?"

"Not onstage."

"But off?"

I replayed the usual moments with Michael during college. Reluctantly added a few from my childhood involving my father. And even more reluctantly acknowledged the quiet communion I'd shared with Rowan as we watched the clouds drift over the hills and the helpless laughter that had left us rolling in the leaves under the beech.

"Yeah. I've felt it." I hesitated a moment, then asked, "Have you?"

"Oh, yes," he replied, still watching Gary and Maya. "But only a few times. A few precious times."

His wistful expression made me wish that one of those times had been with me.

That extraordinary performance launched us into a gloriously trouble-free Hell Week. We even got time off to enjoy Dale's Fourth of July parade. So I was surprised to catch Rowan's worried expression as he dismissed us after dress rehearsal.

Instead of heading to the parking lot, I slipped up the stairs to his apartment. After knocking a few times and getting no answer, I figured he wanted to be alone. I retraced my steps, ignoring Reinhard's curious look, and hurried out the stage door.

The air was still thick and heavy from the thunderstorm that had blown through, but the sky was clearing and the haze-shrouded moon was full and fat and mysterious. As I murmured a brief prayer for good weather on opening night, I glimpsed something moving down by the pond.

I had to wait for the moon to emerge from behind a cloud to determine it was Rowan. I watched him circle the pond, moving in and out of moonlight and shadow. Then I dropped my bag and picked my way carefully over the uneven ground of the meadow, guided only by the mercurial moon.

The night chorus of insects ebbed and flowed with my passage. Damp grass brushed my bare legs, sending delicious shivers through my body. Another coursed through me when I discovered that Rowan was standing quite still, staring in my direction.

I promptly skidded on a wet patch of grass and fell on my ass. By the time I recovered from the shock, he was reaching down to pull me to my feet.

"Are you all right?" he asked.

"I feel like an oaf, but otherwise, I'm fine. You must think I'm the clumsiest woman in the world."

"Not at all," he replied gallantly.

The moon slipped behind a cloud. I took advantage of its absence to rub my butt. Then I asked, "Are *you* all right? You looked weird when you left the theatre."

"Did I?"

"I thought the show went really well."

"Yes," he replied with a noticeable lack of enthusiasm.

"Oh, come on. Just because the old superstition says a bad dress rehearsal predicts a good show doesn't mean the reverse is true."

I attempted to pat him on the forearm, but the darkness threw off my aim. His stomach muscles quivered, and I quickly withdrew my hand.

"I just don't want people to get overconfident," he said.

"They won't."

"Or sloppy."

"They won't!"

My second attempt was more successful. Having smacked one shoulder, I groped for the other and shook him. "It's going to be great. You're not the only one with powers, you know. I can see the future."

"Really?" His voice hinted at a smile. The emerging moon confirmed it.

"I see crowds thronging the theatre. Women sniffling and dabbing their eyes. Men pretending to have head colds so they can sniffle, too."

"Sounds like an awful lot of sniffling."

"And laughter. In all the right places. And at the end . . ." I stepped back and threw out my arms. "Tumultuous applause and cries of 'Author! Author!'"

"At which point, I will quickly vacate the premises."

"And in your wake, the critics will acclaim you—"

"Critics?" he demanded in a panicked voice. "There are critics coming?"

"Nah, I was just fucking with you."

His fingers found my throat and squeezed gently. "Maggie Graham . . ."

"Strangle away. I hope they do come. Did I mention that the show's going to be great?"

"I believe you said something to that effect."

His fingers slid down my throat to my shoulders, trailing warmth and a little shiver of excitement in their wake. Then he guided my hand to the crook of his elbow.

"I'm escorting you back to civilization. Lest you end up in the grass again."

His words conjured a very different image of me in the grass—one that involved him lying with me. I kept up a stream of inconsequential chatter to distract me, but I was far too aware of the muscularity of his forearm and the warmth of his hand atop mine.

When we reached the walkway, he gently eased away. "Well. It's late."

I clasped my hands behind my back. "Yeah."

"Thanks for talking."

"Sure. See you tomorrow."

I retrieved my carryall, but as I was heading toward the parking lot, I glanced back. He was still standing on the walkway, watching me. The light of the wrought iron lamps revealed his troubled expression. Clearly, he was still worrying about the show.

"It's a great script, Rowan."

My words seemed to startle him. As I walked toward him, I saw him stiffen.

"I mean it. It breaks your heart. You keep hoping for a happy ending, even though you know there can't be one. She has to return to her home. And he has to let her go. When I first listened to it at the read-through, I thought the ending was kind of . . . bleak. But now . . . even though the ending is sad, it's not depressing. Because he's changed. He's learned to believe in the impossible. To hope again. And to love. And even though he's lost her, you know that—now that his heart and his mind are open—he'll find someone else. Someday."

Emotions flitted across his face as I spoke. Wariness. Doubt. A pained sort of longing.

"That's what I hoped for. What I tried to accomplish. I just wasn't sure I managed it." A smile pulled up one corner of his mouth. "Ever the neurotic artist."

"Well, as long as you don't cut off an ear or anything."

He chuckled. "You always make me laugh. More than anyone I've ever known."

"That's me. Your favorite comic relief."

His smile vanished. "You're much more than that." His hand cupped my left cheek. His lips brushed my right. "Good night, Maggie. And thank you again. For everything."

On the drive back to the hotel, I puzzled over that kiss, mostly because of what didn't happen. I didn't get all goosey with excitement. Or feel any dizzying blast of power that indicated Rowan was particularly goosey, either.

Maybe we were becoming friends. And maybe, as Reinhard had suggested, that was a good thing. The fact that I was leaving in six weeks gave him the freedom to confide in me. And it afforded me the same freedom. I was too smart to get involved with my director. He was too conscientious to allow it to happen. Those boundaries would protect us both.

I went to bed, congratulating myself on my maturity and wisdom.

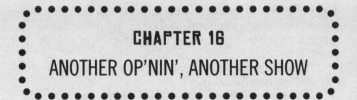

CHAPTER 16
ANOTHER OP'NIN', ANOTHER SHOW

THE NEXT MORNING, WE REHEARSED the opening number one last time. Then Rowan announced that he was giving us the rest of the day off. He interrupted the cheering to remind us about the dangers of overconfidence and insisted that we use our time to relax.

I had no intention of relaxing until I ensured that "Operation Sea-Wife" was on target. Helen had called a secret luncheon meeting at the Bates mansion. The plan was for her to distract Rowan so I could sneak up the hill undetected.

I loitered in the dressing room until everyone took off for the hotel, then crept up to the lobby. I nearly had a heart attack when Helen flew out of the box office, her expression so wild that I feared Rowan had discovered everything.

"Oh, Maggie, Maggie, Maggie!" She waved the newspaper she was clutching.

"What is it? What's happened?"

"I just got off the phone. A critic from *The Bennington Banner* is coming tonight!"

"Oh, my God!"

We hugged each other, hopping up and down like demented bunnies. Then I seized Helen's shoulders. "You can't tell Rowan."

"Are you mad?" Helen demanded, breathless. "When he's already so nervous? Oh, I never dreamed that a big city critic would come."

I suppressed a smile at the description of Bennington as

181

a big city. But it *was* the home of Bennington College, renowned for its arts programs, as well as an Equity theatre. So any entertainment critic would bring a wealth of experience to the job.

"Thank God we went ahead with the reception," I said. "That'll impress the critic."

"The show will impress the critic," Helen said firmly.

"Yeah. But free food and liquor can't hurt."

"Oh, and look!" She brandished her copy of *The Hillandale Bee.* " 'Local Playwright and Composer Debut Original Musical.' " Helen read the words slowly, savoring each one. Then her head jerked up and she spun around.

Rowan stopped short as he came through the house door, then hurried toward us. "Helen? Are you all right?"

"Of course, I'm all right. Look!" She thrust the newspaper in Rowan's face.

Rowan glanced at the headline and nodded. "*The Bee* usually puts in something."

"A few lines," Helen said scornfully. "Not a big long article. They printed every word of Maggie's press release. Isn't that wonderful?"

Rowan studied Helen. Then his gaze snapped to me. I tried to look excited and happy and very, very innocent.

"What's going on?"

"Nothing!" I protested.

He rounded on Helen. "There's more to it than this press release. Out with it."

"Well . . ." Helen bit her lip. "We . . . the staff . . . and Maggie, of course . . ."

"Of course." That narrow-eyed gaze shifted back to me, and I smiled brightly.

"We're planning a little reception."

Rowan's breath huffed out in a pained exhalation. "A reception?"

"After the show. We're serving traditional Scottish fare. Smoked salmon and cold lobster salad and—"

"Helen! We can't afford—"

"I'm paying for it. And I don't want to hear another word about it. We've already bought the food. And told the cast. It's all settled."

Rowan's frown deepened. "So everyone knew. Except me."

"It was supposed to be a surprise."

"I hate surprises!"

Helen slapped the rolled-up newspaper against her thigh. I sincerely hoped she would whack him over the head with it.

Rowan took a deep breath and slowly let it out. "I'm sorry. I didn't mean to sound . . ."

"Ungracious?" Helen prompted.

"Unkind?" I suggested.

Rowan glared at me. "You keep quiet! This is all your fault. Putting these publicity ideas in Helen's head."

Helen swatted his arm with the newspaper. "So I'm too simpleminded to think up a publicity idea on my own. Is that it?"

"You know I didn't mean . . ." Rowan scowled. "You've been spending entirely too much time with Maggie. You're starting to act like her."

"Good! I was getting tired of being Little Mary Sunshine."

Rowan shoved his fists into his pockets. "I liked Little Mary Sunshine."

"Oh! I almost forgot." Helen darted into the box office and emerged with blue papers in her hands.

"My program!" I exclaimed, snatching one away from her.

"Isn't it lovely, Rowan?"

"It's blue."

"To symbolize the sea," Helen explained. "The little curlicues are waves."

"Ah." When Helen nudged him, he quickly added, "Very nice." Then he winced.

"What?" I demanded. "Is it a typo?"

"No. It's the director's notes."

I skimmed the paragraph quickly. "It's the same text I showed you."

"It's different seeing it in black and white. Black and blue. I sound like a pretentious ass."

"You sound warm and lovely." Helen flashed a mischievous smile. "No doubt that was Maggie's doing."

"See? You're even starting to talk like her."

"Nonsense. I've been putting you in your place for years." Helen patted his cheek. "Now. Maggie and I have some business to attend to."

"More plotting?"

"Yes. A secret meeting to discuss the surprise reception. Tell Maggie how lovely her program looks so we can go."

"The program's lovely, Maggie. Really. I appreciate all your hard work. But if you have any more surprises up your sleeve—"

"Gotta run! See you tonight!"

Helen and I made it to the parking lot before we began giggling like naughty schoolgirls. "What do you think he'll do when he sees the banner?" I asked.

"We'll just tell Javier not to hang it until 7:00. By then, it'll be too late to do anything."

"And when do we tell him about the critic?"

"After the curtain comes down."

"Doesn't give him much time to prepare."

"Rowan's very good at thinking on his feet. And with so many people around, he'll have to be charming."

I grinned. "Then we're sure to get a five-star review."

❦

When I pointed out the banner on our way to the theatre that evening, everyone in my car burst into simultaneous exclamations of pleasure. It was very gratifying.

The dark blue banner hung on the central gable, right below the star. White letters proclaimed, "World Premiere: *The Sea-Wife*." The two lines underneath gave the show's dates and the phone number to call for tickets. I'd wanted to include Rowan's name and Alex's, but Hal said it would look too cluttered. He did include my stylized waves, though, under the show's title.

"It's beautiful," Brittany said.

"Just like a real theatre," Sarah added.

"Did Rowan approve it?" Bernie asked.

"He will," I said, forcing confidence into my voice. "When he sees it."

The usual pre-opening frenzy reigned in both dressing rooms. Unlike our *Brigadoon* opening, however, everyone was more excited than nervous.

Hal popped into the women's dressing room, garbed in a turquoise shirt, and told us to break a leg. Alex wore his usual tuxedo, but he had tucked a midnight blue handkerchief in the breast pocket. Even Reinhard had added a navy pocket square to his usual black ensemble. Janet eclipsed them all in an aquamarine cocktail dress. Clearly, the entire staff had taken our sea motif to heart.

"You look terrific," I told Janet.

"My new fundraising strategy. I'm going to flash my cleavage at wealthy widowers."

"Let's hope they don't keel over."

Janet shrugged. "That's one way of culling the herd."

The door to the green room creaked open. All conversation ceased as Rowan stepped inside. He was dressed in his usual beige and black, but the shirt was silk and the pants were leather. In addition to the chain he always wore, he sported a pair of silver cufflinks.

"Looking hot, boss!" Lou bellowed.

To my amazement, color flooded Rowan's face. The enthusiastic cheers from the rest of the cast made it deepen.

"Yes. Well. Let's settle down and form our circle, please."

I quickly discovered why Janet and Reinhard joined our pre-show ritual. Although Rowan's voice was as quiet as ever, the energy zinging around our circle testified to his nervousness. I heard Sarah gasp and squeezed her hand. This was the first time she had ever stood in our circle and it was nothing like I had promised her.

My nerves were still jangling when I took my place onstage. I tried to focus during Janet's announcement about the reception, but I gripped my basket so tightly that errant strands of braided straw dug painfully into my palms.

The lights went down. The curtain rustled open. Ocean waves sighed over the loudspeakers. A seagull cried. Then the seals began to call, their voices sampled by Alex and augmented by strings to create an otherworldly effect that made me shiver.

As the recorded sounds faded, a pale blue wash came up on the scrim. A single violin sounded the opening notes of "Always the Sea." A second offered a wistful counterpoint.

The lights changed, revealing the chorus in still life behind the scrim: women carrying market baskets and hanging out laundry, men repairing fishing nets. A bodhran tapped out an impatient rhythm. Flutes and fiddles joined in. As the band launched into "Stranger from the Sea," the scrim rose and we came to life.

The number was supposed to offer a musical snapshot of the village: the envy arising from the Craigie's newfound prosperity, the speculation surrounding the strange woman who had joined their household, and the gossip about the schoolteacher who was arriving from the mainland. But our tentative voices undermined the tension of the music and the situation.

A jolt of energy made me catch my breath. A moment later, Hector swaggered onstage and began to sing. His boastfulness and disdain fed us as surely as Rowan's power. Lou pushed past Hector with deliberate brusqueness. Romaine turned her back on him in the middle of a lyric. Kevin pretended to spit in his direction, then quickly lowered his head over his fishing net.

I was exhilarated and terrified. None of this had ever happened in rehearsal. The improvisation fueled my performance, but I recognized that this could get out of hand if Rowan's power continued to rage so fiercely.

Just as my anxiety peaked, the energy receded. Maggie the character shrugged off her resentment, recognizing that the changeable winds of fortune might bless her family next. Maggie the actress realized that Rowan had timed his intervention perfectly. By the end of the number, the community had united to welcome the schoolteacher and the cast had come together to perform.

⧟

When the finale ended and the lights faded to black, there was a terrifying silence. Then the applause began. The chorus quickly assembled for our bow. The applause surged as the curtains parted. When Maya and Gary came out, the audience rose to its feet.

We all did the standard "hand to the music director" bit. I heard a man shout, "Author!" and wondered if it was Hal. Gary gestured toward the center section aisle seat where Rowan always sat. One of Lee's crew members swiveled the spotlight in that direction. Rowan rose, lifted one hand in acknowledgment, and quickly sat again.

Lou bellowed, "Speech!" The cast took up the cry, then the audience. Helen nudged Rowan, who shook his head, but when the commotion continued, he rose again and started down the aisle.

I thought his expression seemed strained, but maybe the harsh glare of the spotlight created that illusion. Certainly, he was smiling as he stepped onto the stage, although he shook his fist at Lou in mock anger.

A hush fell as he turned to the audience.

"I see a lot of familiar faces tonight. It's good to know that the friends and neighbors who have supported us for so long enjoyed the show tonight."

He paused to clear his throat. "This might have been my first original script, but Alex Ross has written and arranged the music for our adaptations for many years. He's a gifted musician and a lovely man and I am honored to work with him."

For a moment, Alex stared up at Rowan. Then his face crumpled and he ducked his head.

After thanking the rest of the staff, Rowan acknowledged the cast, adding, "As most of you know, they are not professional actors. They've left homes and families and jobs to come here. To learn about theatre, about acting, and about themselves. If you want to cheer someone, cheer them. They're the ones who create the magic night after night."

He retreated to the far side of the stage, his arm sweeping across us, his gaze embracing us. As the applause diminished, he said, "Forgive me for talking so long. I know most of you have to work tomorrow. But don't even think of slipping away without stopping by our reception. Helen's spent a fortune on the food and she's even put out the good china." He blew a kiss to Helen, waved to the audience, and strode offstage amid laughter and applause.

After the curtain closed, the cast indulged in a lot of hugging and kissing, then raced to the dressing rooms to change. I donned my kicky sundress and joined the others streaming toward the breezeway, but kept a wary eye out for Rowan; I didn't want to be anywhere in the vicinity when he met the critic.

Luminarias glowed along the walkway. Paper lanterns hanging from the breezeway's ceiling shed pools of colored light on the faces of the crowd. Lace tablecloths covered the buffet tables. Helen had raided the Bates mansion for serving trays, ice buckets, and candlesticks as well as the good china. The silver gleamed softly in the flickering light of the pale blue candles.

By the time I managed to snag a glass of champagne, I realized Rowan was conspicuously absent. Spying Helen in earnest conversation with a teenaged boy, I made my way over to her.

"Maggie!" she exclaimed. "You have to meet Tom Anderson, the critic from *The Bennington Banner*."

I glanced around before I realized Helen was referring to the teenager.

Tom grinned. "I know. Not exactly Addison DeWitt."

Points for knowing *All About Eve*, the all-time greatest movie about the theatre.

"I'm a summer intern. When I read your press release, I volunteered to review the show."

"What school do you go to?"

"Amherst." The grin returned. "Everybody says I look young for my age."

"But you live in Bennington?"

"All my life. And I never even knew there was a theatre in Dale." He scanned his program quickly. "Now you played . . . ?"

"Nobody important. You should talk with Maya and Gary."

"Already did. And Alex Ross. I was really hoping to get a chance to talk with the director, but . . ."

Helen managed a bright smile. "Let's see if we can find him."

As they made their way toward the buffet tables, I scanned

the crowd again. When I spotted Lee and Hal, I began edging toward them, hoping they might have seen Rowan. Before I could reach them, a man with a mane of white hair blocked my way.

"Why, hello there. And who are you?"

His voice sounded too deep and mellifluous to be genuine.

"Maggie Graham."

"Longford Martindale. Most people call me Long."

He just managed to avoid leering. His face was as unnatural as his voice, so conspicuously unlined that he had to be either a prematurely white-haired jerk or a generously Botoxed one.

"I don't remember seeing you around town," I said.

"I live in Hill. I'm the owner and editor of *The Bee*."

I quickly plastered an admiring smile on my face. "Really!"

"Among other things."

"Such as . . ."

"Real estate. Banking. The Board of Selectmen."

"My! What a busy life."

"Never too busy to while away the evening with a beautiful woman."

Who said things like that outside of cheesy movies?

"Are you enjoying your stay in Vermont?" he asked.

"It's lovely. Such a change from New York City."

"You're from New York!" He moved closer, allowing his arm to brush against my breast as if by accident. "Well." With one word, he managed to convey approval, lust, and the impression that all women from New York were nymphomaniacs. "You must come over to Hill. I'd be delighted to take you to lunch. Show you the sights."

I took a step back and bumped into someone. My eyes widened when I discovered it was Rowan.

Long appeared surprised as well. "Ah, the elusive Mr. Mackenzie. Longford Martindale. Owner and editor of *The Bee*. Astonishing that both of us have lived here so long without ever meeting."

"Astonishing," Rowan agreed.

"I was just urging Maggie to visit my little town."

"Alas, I lock up my actors when they're not performing.

Keeps them out of mischief. Isn't that right, Maggie?" Rowan's arm settled casually across my shoulders.

The touch of his warm fingers on my bare skin brought a flush to my face. Hoping both men would believe it came from the rose-colored lantern hanging overhead, I said, "He's a slave driver, Long. You have no idea."

"Long! There you are!"

Janet sailed toward us. Well, as much as her tight-fitting sheath would allow. She favored Long with a brilliant smile, but he was more interested in her cleavage.

"I was hoping you'd come," she said.

"Well," he drawled as his gaze rose slowly to her face, "the night is still young."

Janet chucked him under the chin. "You old rogue. Come on. I'll let you ply me with champagne and practice some of your other pickup lines."

Long's astonished laugh was the first genuine thing about him. "Ah, Janet. Why do you always take the wind of my sails? When you know I'm devoted to you."

"Like a fox is devoted to hens."

He laughed again and allowed her to guide him toward the bar. "A pleasure to finally meet you, Mr. Mackenzie," he called over his shoulder. "And you, Maggie. That invitation to lunch is always open."

I waggled my fingers in farewell. Rowan removed his arm from my shoulders.

"Old lecher," he growled.

"He's harmless."

"Show you the sights, indeed. I know exactly what sight he wants to show you."

"Another natural wonder of Vermont?"

Rowan glared at me. "It might be natural, but I doubt it's a wonder. No matter what his nickname is. And you encouraged him!"

"Oh, come on. I just flirted with him. I flirt with a lot of guys. It doesn't mean anything."

Just like that, the mask slipped over his face. "Of course. Forgive me."

I watched in astonishment as he strode off, then scampered after him, lurching a bit in my heels.

"Wait a minute," I said, grabbing his arm. "You're really pissed."

"Don't be ridiculous."

"Jeez, Rowan, you're acting like—"

"Like what?" he demanded.

He was acting like a jealous lover. But I stopped myself from blurting that out and said, "You're acting like an over-protective father."

"A father!"

"Director," I substituted, aghast at his reaction.

"Just because I'm concerned about the welfare of my cast—"

"I did it for you, damn it! For the theatre. So he'd give us a good review."

The mask slowly slipped off. "Yes. Well. You've done quite enough for one night. I suppose that banner was your idea."

I nodded.

"And that cub reporter?"

"He called Helen out of the blue," I protested.

Rowan muttered something under his breath.

"Come on. All this publicity will be great."

"I hope so."

His expression was so serious that I touched his arm lightly. "Hey. You're supposed to be celebrating. You can start worrying tomorrow."

"When we begin *Carousel* rehearsals." A slow smile curved his mouth. "And then, Maggie Graham—Helping Professional, Publicity Hound, and Outrageous Flirt—then, I'll give *you* something to worry about."

CHAPTER 17
I'M THE GREATEST STAR

*C*AROUSEL.

A seriously dysfunctional romance. A too-little, too-late redemption for its "hero," who dies in the middle of Act Two, leaving me to cheer up his pregnant wife by reminding her that "You'll Never Walk Alone." Plus a scene in heaven. And a real nice clambake.

As Bernie would say, "Oy."

Even the glowing review in *The Bennington Banner* ("New Musical Hits All the Right Notes") and a favorable one in *The Hillandale Bee* ("Crossroads Theatre Reaches High") failed to avert my sense of imminent doom. Nor did Rowan's speech at our read-through.

"Some of you may have seen the movie version of *Carousel*. You might have heard the song 'You'll Never Walk Alone' and found it naïve and sentimental."

His gaze lingered on me, stern teacher lecturing his most recalcitrant pupil.

"*Carousel* is neither naïve nor sentimental. It is a story of haves and have-nots. Of conformity vs. disobedience, Puritan values vs. the primal forces of sex and violence. At its heart is the carousel—this marvelous, almost otherworldly creation that brings color and light and glamour into a hard-scrabble world of black and white and gray."

Not a schoolmaster, but a preacher. Or a labor organizer uniting the workers.

"Julie is not a dewy-eyed virgin, nor is Billy a soulless

192

lout. At its best, their love exalts them. As opposed to Carrie whose exuberance drains away under the yoke of a man who begins as ambitious and colorful, and ends as a hypocrite and a bigot."

The four leads reacted in distinctly different ways to those capsule characterizations. Kalma looked relieved, Nick, wary, and Brittany, a little scared. J.T. merely nodded thoughtfully and jotted down Rowan's comments about Enoch Snow.

"These are not trite, sentimental issues, but universal ones about the human condition. I ask you to remember that as we begin exploring this show together."

I felt a little ashamed of my refusal to look more deeply into the characters. I was even more ashamed of my lousy performance during the read-through. Too hearty at some moments, artificially warm in others.

During our first chorus rehearsal, I fell back on all my old theatre tricks to get through "June Is Bustin' Out All Over." So far, the only good thing I'd discovered about Nettie was that she never had to dance. Still, these were early days, and as I joined Rowan in the Smokehouse for our first private meeting, I felt sure he would acknowledge that.

He scrutinized me in silence, then said, "Take out your notebook."

I unearthed it from my carryall.

"Turn to a blank page."

Once again, I obeyed, pencil poised to scribble down his brilliant suggestions.

"Draw a line down the middle of the page."

Without waiting for further direction, I wrote "Strengths" at the head of the left-hand column and "Weaknesses" atop the right one.

"Fill it out. We'll talk tomorrow."

After my next lackluster rehearsal, he signaled me to remain. As I slumped onto my chair, he held out his hand. Reluctantly, I gave him my list.

Under "Strengths," I'd written "Strong" and "People like her." I had a somewhat longer list of "Weaknesses" that included "Bossy cow" and "Mouths platitudes to comfort Julie seconds after Billy dies."

Rowan read the list silently and handed it back to me. "You have the day off Monday. That should give you plenty of time to write Nettie's life story."

"Oh, come on."

He regarded me coolly. "Is there a problem?"

"It's like some assignment from first-year acting class."

"Did you ever take an acting class?"

"No, but—"

"Then you should find this useful."

"You don't give anyone else homework," I grumbled.

"How do you know?"

"Because we talk about you behind your back!" Which was true, but not the best possible response. "Just about show stuff," I added, lest he think I had blabbed about some of our private conversations. "Nobody else mentioned homework."

"Nobody else requires homework."

Which was pretty damn cold. And insulting. I was the only member of the cast who'd ever acted professionally. And I got homework.

To cap my humiliation, he added, "Ask Kevin to help you. He's very good at inventing backstory."

"Great. So you have no objection if I quietly masturbate among the lobster traps during 'June Is Bustin' Out All Over.'"

"Try it and see."

I picked up my bag, but paused at the doorway of the Smokehouse to ask, "Are you doing this because you're still pissed about me flirting with Long?"

Rowan slowly closed his script. "Whatever disagreements we have had, whatever confidences we have shared, in this room I am your director. And I will do whatever is necessary to drag a good performance out of you."

"What about helping me discover what I need to learn? And guiding me on my journey?"

His expression softened. "When you start digging deeper, Maggie, I'll be right beside you."

"And until then, you'll be standing behind me, kicking me in the ass."

His silence was eloquent.

Nancy was waiting in our room. She'd come down the

night before to see *The Sea-Wife* and was staying over for the Follies. I slammed the door behind me, flung my bag on the bed, and declared, "I think you made up all that stuff about how warm and supportive Rowan is."

Nancy calmly looked up from her book and said, "He *was* warm and supportive."

"With you, maybe."

"Because he knew I needed reassurance. If he's tough on you, it just proves that he respects your acting abilities." Nancy hesitated, then added, "And he knows you sometimes need a push instead of a hug."

Recognizing the truth of her words—and his—didn't make them any easier to accept. This was only Act One. If I couldn't make June bust out believably, how could I convince an audience it was a real nice clambake? Or comfort anyone with "You'll Never Walk Alone?"

I'd never liked the song. The music was nice, very soaring and goose bumpy when the company sang the reprise at the end of the show. It was the sentiment that stuck in my craw. And the high G.

"I'll never hit it," I moaned during my first rehearsal with Alex.

I might have had a chance if I was singing a nice open vowel like "ah" or "oh." But no. I had to sing a high G on "nev." As in "never walk alone." Or never hit the note.

"Not with that attitude," Alex replied. "Let's try it from the top."

We tried it. Halfway through, he stopped me.

"I know. I sound awful."

"It's not the sound that concerns me. You don't believe a word you're singing. And you look about as hopeful as a woman heading to her execution."

I attacked the last half of the song, but broke off when I heard the unearthly wail emanating from my throat.

"Oh, my God, I sound like a dying seagull."

Alex laughed. "You do not sound like a dying seagull." At my skeptical look, he added, "A wounded one, maybe."

I offered my most winning smile. "You took Lou's songs down a fifth."

"You'll sound like you're singing 'Ol' Man River.'"

"Better than sounding like a dying seagull. Please, Alex. Couldn't you drop it a third?"

"I could." He raised eyes and hand to heaven to placate the shade of Richard Rodgers. "But we're not going to surrender just yet."

At that moment, surrender would have felt like victory.

"Have you been doing the exercises I gave you?"

I nodded miserably, envisioning more late-night vocal sessions in the laundry room. The first time, I'd heard Iolanthe yowling from the floor above. By the time we opened, all the cats in Dale would be caroling outside the Bough.

"Don't strain. Sing from your diaphragm. Not your throat."

"I know, I know."

I did know. But it was hard to resist the panicked urge to throw back my head and screech out that high G.

"Now that you've got the notes—"

"All except one."

"Let's talk about the spirit of the song."

The spirit of the song was obvious: if you soldier on through the dark times and never lose hope, you'll never walk alone. As a philosophy of life, it was right up there with "every cloud has a silver lining" and "always look on the bright side." Sure, you'll never walk alone. You'll be surrounded by other misguided fools, all with hope in their hearts and the same stupid smiles on their faces.

I just couldn't buy it. But that's what being an actress was all about. Making sure the audience buys it even if you didn't.

Maybe I could channel the nun from *The Sound of Music*. "Climb Every Mountain." "You'll Never Walk Alone." Same difference. I could ask Hal if he had a copy of the film. And a set of rosary beads.

"Maggie?"

"Spirit of the song. Yep. Got it."

But of course, I didn't.

CHAPTER 18
SO YOU WANTED TO SEE THE WIZARD

THANK GOD FOR THE FOLLIES. We all needed a break after Hell Week, the opening of *The Sea-Wife*, and the start of *Carousel* rehearsals. And I definitely needed a break from Nettie.

The weather had been unsettled all day and ominous clouds scudded overhead when we arrived at the theatre. A painted backdrop of an austerely sepia Kansas hung from the two maple trees that flanked the Smokehouse. Lee had cobbled together rudimentary lighting trees by lashing lights to two A-frame ladders. As we ventured closer to inspect them, the black-clad crew members securing the cables waved us away and sternly warned us that anyone caught lurking around the Smokehouse would be summarily ejected.

After chowing down on pizza, we spread blankets and quilts on the grass and waited impatiently for the show to begin. Frannie and Bea made a final pass through the audience to collect ballots and last-minute bets. A few minutes later, the lights came up on the backdrop and the brooding music of the movie's overture crackled through the unseen speakers. We all joined the recorded chorus for that eerie "Oooo-oww-ohh," then burst into spontaneous applause.

A new wave erupted when we spotted gingham-clad Catherine running down the walkway. She cooed endearments to her stuffed Toto, then unceremoniously dumped the doll on the ground and dragged it after her on its leash. The sight of the poor thing rolling head over paws evoked the first laugh of the evening.

Helen's entrance as Auntie Em drew applause, but I heard worried whispers when Alex appeared as Uncle Henry. We knew the staff had to double up in roles, but when the show skipped over the farmhands' scene and segued right into "Somewhere Over the Rainbow," we realized we'd have to wait a little longer to discover whether Alex would play the Tin Man as most of us predicted.

Tension mounted as we heard the familiar Miss Gulch theme. The entire cast had been waiting nearly two weeks to find out whether Janet or Mei-Yin would play the role.

A long-skirted figure on a bicycle careened down the walkway. My spirits sank as it approached; surely only Mei-Yin could pedal that maniacally. Then the bicycle rider zoomed into the lights and the entire audience erupted into screams of laughter.

Rowan had to circle the picnic area twice before the up-roar subsided. He'd augmented his angular features with a jutting nose and long chin, making the resemblance to Margaret Hamilton positively uncanny. And he captured her screechy voice so perfectly that it set us all off again.

Reinhard's avuncular Professor Marvel was eclipsed by Hal's entrance in full Glinda drag. But the staff's performances as Munchkins left us gaping. Mei-Yin tiptoed on to represent the Lullabye League, then somehow managed a lightning-fast change to return as the Mayor. Lollipop Guild members Javier and Lee twitched like they had St. Vitus' dance. Helen showed up again as the Coroner, Reinhard and Alex as soldiers. And all of them—except Mei-Yin—played their roles on their knees, wearing boots and floppy shoes and—I hoped—a lot of padding.

We all gasped when a flash pot went off and smoke obscured the acting area. Then gasped again when it cleared to reveal a green-faced Rowan in black gown and pointy hat.

We alternately booed and applauded during his shameless hamming and sang along as Catherine skipped down the yellow brick road. When the stage crew flipped over the cornfield backdrop and pushed on Alex—crucified on his

scarecrow pole—I tore up my ballot and just sat back to enjoy the spectacle.

Alex revealed some impressive dance moves as the
Scarecrow, Lee camped it up as a terrifically gay Tin Man,
and Javier hammed even more shamelessly than Rowan as
the Cowardly Lion. Mei-Yin continued to astonish us in the
roles of flying monkey, Oz resident, and guard in the witch's
castle. Janet filled the latter two roles as well, but enjoyed
playing the grumpy tree far more, lobbing apples at cast and
audience alike with murderous accuracy.

The most incredible moment came when Catherine threw
the bucket of water on Rowan. The lights went out. A strobe
flashed, its stop-motion effect made even eerier by the sickly
green gel Lee must have taped over the light. As Rowan
writhed in his death throes, he really seemed to be melting
into the grass. Then the strobe went out. I was still marveling
at his incredible contortions when the lights came up again
to reveal his pointy hat atop a puddled black dress.

There was stunned silence. Then a wild explosion of
cheers. Of course, Rowan must have slipped behind the
backdrop in that brief moment of darkness while a crew
member placed his hat atop a heap of black fabric. Even he
couldn't just vanish before our eyes.

The farewells in Oz brought another surprise. When Hal
asked Catherine what she had learned, she delivered pretty
much the same rant I had made to Rowan during our walk
in the woods. Everyone onstage looked nonplussed; clearly,
Rowan and Catherine had cooked this up without telling
the rest of the staff. Hal twiddled his wand and finally demanded, "Look, sweetie, do you want to go home or not?"
When Catherine meekly nodded, he said, "Then click your
heels together and let's get on with it."

When the lights went out on the final tableau, we all
leaped to our feet. They saved Rowan's curtain call for last.
He raced out from behind the backdrop, pulled his long dress
up to his knees, and executed a sprightly jig. Then he swept
off his witch's hat and sketched a bow worthy of a Renaissance courtier.

I'd seen glimmers of his childlike side before, but it was

hard to believe this was the same man who had lectured us
so sternly about *Carousel* and sung in the woods with such
passionate longing. He was a prism with so many facets that
I'd never discover them all. Yet each time a new one was
revealed, it left me eager to try.

Unlike the rest of the audience, I knew we were responding as much to the power he could not quite contain as to the
joy that caused it. But I cheered and applauded as wildly as
the rest, caught up in the contagious excitement.

We were all in love with him. And for once, he permitted
it. But only for a moment. Then he motioned the stage crew
forward to accept our applause. By the time the entire company bowed, the untamed joy had leached away, leaving us
with a breathless but far more ordinary happiness.

❧

While the staff retired to the dressing rooms to change, we
gathered in the breezeway to exclaim over the desserts Frannie and Bea set out. Helen had baked two enormous cakes,
one in the shape of a broomstick with *The Wizard of Oz* em-
blazoned on the handle in green icing, and the other, a red-
frosted ruby slipper complete with iridescent sprinkles.

Hal returned, still wearing his enormous Glinda crown,
and acknowledged the applause and laughter with a regal
wave. When I made my way over to him, he demanded,
"Was I to die for or was I to die for?"

"You were incredibly to die for. And so were you," I assured Lee. "Although poor Jack Haley must be rolling in his
grave."

"If there's a bigger queen than Jack Haley, I'd like to see
him," Lee replied, prompting Hal's hand to shoot up in the
air.

"I totally lost out on the pool. But it was worth it to see
the many faces of Mei-Yin."

"And Alex dancing up a storm," Lee said.

"And Rowan," we exclaimed in unison.

We simply had to look for the largest cluster of people to
discover him at its center. His head turned, as if he felt our
gazes, and he smiled.

"He was on fire this year," Lee said.

"And what about this naughty girl?" Hal snagged Catherine's arm as she passed by. "Little Miss Ad Lib."

"Totally scripted," she assured him.

Again, we turned toward Rowan. This time, he excused himself from his swarm of admirers and began making his way toward us.

"Why the big secret?" Lee asked.

Catherine shrugged. "That's what he wanted."

"This from the man who doesn't like surprises." I deliberately raised my voice so Rowan would hear. He just smiled, looking like the proverbial cat that had lapped up a bowl of cream.

"You know," I ventured, "I've always thought that looking for your heart's desire in your own backyard is overrated."

"But sometimes," Rowan replied, "that's where you find it."

In the silence that followed his quiet pronouncement, I became aware that everyone in our little group was watching us with avid interest.

I flashed a quick smile at Hal. "Good thing, you didn't try that. You'd still be in California. And Lee would be a lonely tech director."

"Maybe. Maybe not." Lee skipped aside, laughing, as Hal tried to swat him.

"Settle down," Rowan warned. "Janet's about to announce the winner of the pool."

As the hubbub on the breezeway faded to excited whispers, Janet said, "Yes, it's that time. As I added up the votes, I couldn't help noting how many people lost because they predicted that either Mei-Yin or I would play the Wicked Witch. Imagine."

"THAT'LL teach 'em!" the erstwhile Mayor of Munchkin City crowed.

"But we do have a winner. And that person will receive a grand total of . . . $520." Amid the astonished cries, she called out, "Rowan! This is your cast. And your Follies. Why don't you present the prize?"

Rowan looked so startled that I knew he hadn't been expecting it. Janet handed him a folded slip of paper and graciously stepped aside. He opened it and smiled.

"By virtue of a highly superior brain, our winner is . . . Nancy!"

The initial groans gave way to good-natured applause as Nancy edged forward to accept her winnings.

"That's a sizable chunk of money," Janet observed. "What will you do with it?"

Nancy stared at the bulging envelope in Rowan's hand. Then she closed his fingers around it and announced, "I'd like to donate it to the theatre."

If Rowan had been startled by Janet's gesture, he was clearly stunned by Nancy's. As a new wave of cheers and applause erupted, he whispered something to her. When she nodded, he leaned forward and kissed her firmly on the mouth.

Nancy's face had been glowing. When Rowan stepped back, it was scarlet.

"I'd like to donate to the theatre, too!" Bobbie shouted.

"Me, too!" Brittany exclaimed.

"Me, three!" Hal said.

Laughing, Rowan waved them away.

"Now there's a fundraising idea," I said. "Twenty dollars a kiss!"

"Is that all?" Rowan demanded.

"You can get a hundred easy," Nancy said, sparking more laughter and winning an affectionate hug from Rowan.

A gust of wind eddied through the breezeway, scattering napkins and paper plates and eliciting cries of "It's a twister! A twister!"

"Not a twister," Rowan said, "but definitely a storm. Those of you who are driving any distance might want to make a quick getaway. The rest of you better collect your things. Lee . . ."

"I'm on it," Lee replied and raced toward the meadow.

I lingered long enough to congratulate Nancy and tease her about the kiss. Then I joined the cast members snatching up their belongings and helping the crew move set pieces and lights into the Smokehouse. By the time we returned, the rest of the staff had opened the back doors of the barn and moved the tables inside. People groaned when they spotted Bea and Frannie packing up the food, but Helen assured them the party was simply moving to the Bough.

"Why not the green room?" I asked.

"It was Rowan's suggestion." Helen pursed her lips in obvious disapproval.

"He should be with us," I protested. "Not sitting up in his apartment all alone."

Helen went still, her gaze moving past me.

"He's right behind me, isn't he?"

"Listening to every word," Rowan replied.

He took my arm and maneuvered me away from the stream of cast members hurrying toward the parking lot with supplies.

I batted a paper lantern in disgust. "We could squeeze into the green room."

"Not with the crew. And mountains of food. Stop fretting, Maggie. I've had a wonderful evening. And two parties in one week is more than I'm used to."

Before I could argue, I heard Janet calling my name.

"Good," she said as she strode out of the theatre. "You're still here. You can drive Helen back to the Bough. She insists on going to the party. Just make sure she goes to bed early," she added quietly. "She's had enough excitement for one night. And so have I," she said in her usual strident tone. "I've got to get home before the storm hits. I left every window up in the house."

A rumble of thunder punctuated her exit. The rest of the staff wandered out of the theatre, looking tired but happy.

"A magnificent success," Reinhard said.

"Naturally." Alex wriggled as he scratched his thigh and back simultaneously. "But I'm going to be picking straw out of my pants for the next week."

"At least you didn't have to lug around a hundred pounds of fur," Javier said. "No wonder everyone was so excited when I volunteered to play the Cowardly Lion."

"I must have sweated off ten pounds in my tin can," Lee said.

"If I hear one more complaint about my costumes . . ."

Lee slung his arm around Hal's waist. "I'm just saying that I can't wait for a nice, cool shower."

"For two," Hal replied with a leer.

"But you're coming to the Bough later?" When Lee

shrugged, I glanced at the others. Mei-Yin said she was leaving for Saratoga Springs to visit an old friend. The rest just shook their heads.

"What a bunch of party poopers," I complained. "Good thing I've got Helen. Where is she, anyway?"

"She wanted to tidy up," Hal said.

Rowan sighed, then cocked his head, listening to another rumble of thunder. "Go home—all of you—and get some well-deserved rest. I'll take down the lanterns while Maggie rousts Helen out."

I found her in the green room, washing out the punch bowl. As I picked up a towel, she smiled. "Oh, Maggie. Wasn't it fun?"

"Even more fun than I imagined."

"I love the Follies. They make me feel like a girl again. I was the very first Dorothy, you know."

"No, I didn't. That must have been . . ."

"A long, long time ago."

I lifted the punch bowl out of the sink, grunting with the effort. "This thing weighs a ton. You shouldn't have been carrying it."

"Now, don't you start. It's bad enough Janet treats me like an invalid." She wiped her hands on the end of my towel and surveyed the small pile of dishes on the drying rack. "There. Everything is spick and span. We'll take the punch bowl with us and leave the rest to dry."

I hefted the bowl and followed her to the barn doors. When Rowan saw me, he hopped off the ladder, took the punch bowl from me, and set it down on one of the tables.

"We can't leave it there," Helen protested.

"It'll be fine for one night. Javier can bring it up to the house tomorrow."

A violent gust of wind sent two lanterns careening around the breezeway. Rowan and I chased after them and stowed them inside the theatre. I snatched up my bag from under one of the tables and hurried back outside. Without seeming to strain, Rowan slid the huge doors closed.

"Come on," he urged. "Let's get you two to the car."

As we rounded the corner of the barn, the wind's fury stopped us in our tracks. A jagged bolt of lightning lit up the meadow. A moment later, a loud crack of thunder made me jump.

"Isn't it glorious!" Helen exclaimed. "I love thunder-storms."

She skipped down the walkway singing, "Follow the red brick path." Rowan and I hurried after her, took her arms, and slowed her pace to a brisk walk.

The first raindrops pattered onto us as we reached the parking lot. I got Helen into the car and raced around to slide into my seat. Damp and breathless, I turned the ignition and rolled down my window.

"You better get inside," I warned Rowan.

"You haven't said a word about the show."

"I loved the show! I told everyone a hundred—"

"Everyone except me."

Although his manner was as easy as his smile, I felt an immediate stab of guilt.

"The show was incredible. I don't think I've ever laughed so much in my life."

The rain was coming down harder now, but he merely stepped closer. Shoving his hands in his pockets, he bent down to peer at me. A drop of water rolled down his nose and splattered on my arm.

"You better tell him how wonderful he was," Helen said. "Because he's going to stay there until you do."

"Oh, good grief! You were impossibly wonderful, okay? And a shameless scene stealer."

"Ouch."

"I don't know how you did that whole melting thing . . ."

"Trade secret."

"But when you came zooming down the path on that bicycle . . ."

"Yes?"

"I very nearly peed my panties."

His breath huffed out in a soft chuckle. I breathed in the faint aroma of fruit punch.

"Now that kind of compliment is worth waiting for."

"Get inside, you idiot!"

He grinned and darted down the walkway. A bolt of lightning illuminated him as he paused by the stage door to lift his hand in farewell. By the time I flicked on my headlights, he was gone.

"He's such a child," Helen mused fondly.

"An exceedingly wet child."

I turned the wipers on high, but they barely managed to clear the water before the downpour obscured the windshield again.

"You'd better wait until it lets up a bit."

The violent tattoo of rain on the roof made conversation impossible, so we just watched the brilliant light show. After five minutes, the storm was as wild as ever, and I grumbled aloud that we were going to be stuck here all night. When Helen didn't reply, I glanced over at her.

"Helen? Are you okay?"

"Just tired. Maybe I *should* skip the party."

"Do you want me to drive you up to the house?"

"No, no. The hotel."

Without waiting for the rain to slacken, I backed the car out and eased cautiously up the lane. Helen gasped as the car jolted into a rut. I muttered an apology and turned my high beams on, but they merely reflected back the fury of the rain.

When Helen gasped again, I said, "Hang on. We're almost at the road." Then I realized that her gasps were too regular, almost as if she were panting.

"Helen?"

I stopped the car.

"Helen!"

"Call Reinhard," she whispered.

I shoved the car into park, punched the release on my seat belt, and twisted around, groping for my bag.

"Use my phone."

I tugged her purse off her arm and snapped it open. Feeling nothing that resembled a cell phone, I cursed and snapped on the overhead light. Helen's eyes were closed, her jaw clenched in a rictus of pain.

Frantically, I dug through her purse. Wallet, Kleenex, datebook, brush. Finally, I found her cell phone in a side pocket. I was still fumbling for the on button when Helen's door flew open.

Rowan fell to his knees beside the car. Rain streamed

down his face and plastered his unbuttoned shirt against his body. He folded his left hand around Helen's fist and pressed his right under her breasts.

"Breathe with me, sweetheart."

He shook his wet hair out of his face. Droplets of water spangled Helen's silk dress and dripped down her cheeks like tears.

"Call Reinhard," Rowan said.

"I'm calling 911!"

"Call Reinhard, Maggie."

My hands shook so badly, it took me three tries before I managed to turn the phone on. I scrolled through Helen's contact list, found Reinhard's name, and punched send.

No fucking signal.

I leaped out of the car, stumbled to the head of the lane, and bit back a sob when the call went through and Reinhard picked up. I tried to mimic Rowan's calm, but I could hear the incipient hysteria in my voice.

"Is Rowan there?" Reinhard demanded.

"Yes."

"Good. He knows what to do. Try to stay calm. I'll call 911 and be there in less than five minutes."

"What should I do?"

Receiving no answer, I peered at the display and realized Reinhard had already disconnected. Shoving my dripping hair out of my face, I hurried back to the car. As I slid inside, Rowan said, "Everything will be all right."

I wasn't sure if he was talking to me or to Helen. I tried to control my desperate desire to do something, anything, and simply took a deep breath and slowly let it out. For the first time, Rowan glanced at me and gave a quick, approving nod.

After that, I just breathed in unison with them and listened to the ebb and flow of Rowan's voice. Although the rain had begun to slacken, he spoke so softly that I caught only occasional words of that gentle litany. But my breathing grew as slow and regular as Helen's, my fears easing along with the tension in her face.

Her eyes fluttered open. As they focused on Rowan, she smiled. "You're always here when I need you."

His answering smile was as tender as hers. "No talking," he scolded. "Just nice, deep breaths. That's my girl."

Her hand stirred beneath his. He raised it to his lips, then laced his fingers between hers and returned their joined hands to her lap. Then he stiffened and cocked his head.

Helen sighed. "Oh, dear."

"Hush."

"She'll make a fuss."

"I'll handle her."

Only then did I hear someone screaming Helen's name. If I hadn't realized by then that they must be talking about Janet, I would never have recognized her voice.

There was a blur of movement behind Rowan, hands clawing at him, pulling his shirt off his shoulder.

"Janet! You're not helping matters!"

The scrabbling fingers froze, still clenched in the fabric of Rowan's shirt. Keeping his right hand firmly atop Helen's rib cage, he eased back against the doorframe, wincing as Janet squeezed in beside him.

She slid awkwardly to her knees, sodden negligee clinging to her body. Without her customary makeup, she looked old and unbearably fragile.

Helen's hand came up to stroke her cheek, and Janet's breath caught on a ragged sob. She seized Helen's hand and kissed it.

"Hush, dear," Helen whispered. "Everything's all right."

"You always do too much. You never listen to me."

"Not now," Rowan warned.

"You should never have let her perform tonight. I told you she wasn't up to it."

"Not now!"

Janet's head snapped back and thudded into the closed car window. I flung open my door and ran around the front of the car, stumbling twice on the slick gravel. As I bent over Janet, she flung out her arm wildly, striking Rowan across the face.

"Janet! Come around to the driver's side and sit with Helen."

I had to repeat the words before they finally registered. Then she allowed me to help her to her feet and guide her around the car.

"I know you're frightened," I told her, "but you have to be calm. For Helen's sake."

I waited long enough to ensure that she would follow my advice, then hurried back to check on Rowan. Before I reached him, the white glare of headlights blinded me.

The SUV careened onto the grass next to my car. Reinhard leaped out, his face invisible under the hood of his rain jacket. He paused long enough to squeeze my shoulder, then strode toward Rowan, a small black bag clutched in his hand. I hung back, afraid I would only get in the way.

For a long while, the two men knelt together beside the car. Thunder grumbled off to the east and the rain subsided to a drizzle, but I shivered uncontrollably, chilled by the faint breeze and even more by shock.

Suddenly, Rowan lurched to his feet and bent over, retching. I started toward him, but he waved me away. His head jerked up. A moment later, I heard the faint wail of a siren.

It seemed like an hour before the ambulance arrived, but it was probably less than a minute. The paramedics quickly lifted Helen onto a stretcher. I heard her call my name and rushed over.

"Stay with Rowan," she said.

"Don't be ridiculous!" Janet snapped.

Helen's hand groped for mine. "Please, Maggie . . ."

"Of course," I said, squeezing her hand hard. "Whatever you want."

"Promise me."

"I promise. Please, Helen. Don't worry."

"Ma'am," one of the paramedics interrupted. "We need to go."

I stumbled back as they slid her stretcher into the back of the ambulance. Janet tried to scramble in after it, but Reinhard seized her arm. As the paramedics slammed the doors, I turned, searching for Rowan, and spied Javier helping a sobbing Catherine into Reinhard's SUV. As Janet climbed in after her, Reinhard threw back his rain hood and slowly turned toward me.

"Is Helen going to be all right?" I asked.

"Yes. I think so."

"Was is—is it her heart?"

"Rheumatic fever. As a child. The damage was not detected until years later." With an obvious effort, he dragged his gaze from the ambulance and forced a smile. "You did everything right."

"I didn't do anything." Again, I searched for Rowan. In the twin beams of my headlights, I saw him leaning over the stone wall, watching the ambulance pull into the road.

"Go back to the hotel." Reinhard raised his voice to be heard over the siren's wail. "Get out of those wet clothes."

"I have to stay with Rowan."

"What?"

"I promised Helen."

Reinhard grabbed my shoulders. "You cannot stay with him! Not tonight!"

His ferocious expression made me quail. He must have noticed because he relaxed his punishing grip. "Rowan is too upset."

"He seemed . . . okay. Considering."

"That was for Helen. Trust me when I tell you that he is very upset."

"All the more reason I should stay, then."

"You don't understand! When he's like this, he can become . . . unpredictable."

"His power, you mean."

Reinhard's hands slid off my shoulders.

"He told me about it. How it sometimes . . . gets away from him."

"Then you should realize—"

"I promised Helen!"

Reinhard glared at me. "All right! You will stay. But not alone." He paced restlessly, muttering to himself. "Alex will already be on the way to the hospital. And Mei-Yin is halfway to Saratoga Springs by now. But Lee, maybe. Yes. Lee."

"You think Rowan might . . . hurt me?" I asked in a small voice.

Reinhard's head jerked toward me. "Never! But all the same, I will call Lee. And until he gets here, you will wait in your car."

"Reinhard!" Javier called. "Can we go? Catherine's a wreck and Janet's even—"

"Coming!" Reinhard seized my shoulders again. "You will wait in the car, yes?"

"Yes."

His stern expression softened. "Try not to worry. Helen is in good hands. I will call as soon as I have news."

I watched him carefully turn his SUV, then thunder back up the lane. The red glow of his taillights receded, then disappeared as he turned into the road. His headlights raked the stone wall, but Rowan was gone.

The rain had stopped, but drops of water slid off my car and spattered onto the gravel. It was about as soothing as Chinese water torture.

I got in the car and drove to the top of the lane where I poked my head out the window and called Rowan's name. Getting no response, I made a slow U-turn, scanning the grounds for any sign of him, then drove back to the parking lot.

The stage door hung ajar. Either he'd left it open in his headlong flight to Helen's side or on his despondent return. Clearly, he'd sensed something was wrong. And just as clearly, Janet shared that uncanny knack. Maybe they all did. That would explain why they had been waiting in the meadow after my tumble in the woods, why they had arrived so quickly at Midsummer.

I thrust aside those speculations and tried to do the same with my fears for Helen. As Reinhard had said, she was in good hands. But God only knew how long it would take to get to a hospital. Could the paramedics do more for her than Rowan? Obviously, his power wasn't strong enough to heal her or he would have done so years ago. But just calming her wasn't enough to avert a heart attack. Or maybe it was. Maybe that's why he'd gotten sick.

I shook my head impatiently. There was nothing I could do for Helen now except honor the promise I'd made. Even if it meant breaking the implicit one I had given Reinhard.

I opened the glove compartment, took out the pack of batteries I'd bought after Midsummer, and popped them into my flashlight. Then I set off in search of Rowan.

CHAPTER 19
IT'S A CHEMICAL REACTION, THAT'S ALL

WHEN I REACHED THE APARTMENT, I understood Reinhard's reluctance to let me stay behind. Rowan had flung the door open with such force that the hinges were nearly ripped out of the doorframe. Papers were strewn across the floor of the office. His wooden desk chair lay on its side amid a jumbled heap of books.

I hesitated on the landing and called Rowan's name. Then I cautiously went inside.

The bedroom was empty. So was the enormous living area I discovered through the other door in the office. At another time, I might have lingered to admire it. Instead, I headed back down the stairs.

I made a quick inspection of the theatre, although I doubted I would find him there. At Midsummer, he had sought the comfort of the woods. Likely, he had done so again. But I searched the outbuildings and the grounds, calling his name as I crisscrossed the meadow and circled the pond.

I hesitated at the trailhead before reluctantly admitting that I'd never be able to find my way to the cottage. I shouted his name once more; the only answer I received was the plaintive sigh of the wind through the trees.

Soaked and shivering, I trudged back toward the theatre. I kept recalling my last glimpse of him, straining against the stone wall as if he wanted to leap over it and race after the ambulance.

I froze, then started to run.

I was breathless by the time I reached the big maple at the corner of the property. Panting, I swept the flashlight's beam across the wall. A soft whimper escaped me. I'd been so certain I would find him here, as close to Helen as he could manage.

I edged closer, wincing as wet stones scraped my thigh. The flashlight picked up something pale. Half-hidden by the tree. Bracing my left hand on the maple's trunk, I peered behind it.

Rowan had wedged himself into the small space between the roots of the maple and the corner of the wall. His back rested against the tree, knees pulled tight against his chest. Torn between relief and anger, I opened my mouth to berate him for refusing to answer my calls. I closed it again when I saw that he was rocking back and forth, his expression utterly blank.

"Rowan?"

I crouched by the tree, squeezed my hand past the trunk, and touched his arm. No reaction. He didn't even blink when I shone the beam of the flashlight in his eyes.

I curled my fingers around his and flinched when I felt their chill. I pleaded with him to respond. Assured him that Helen was going to be all right. Begged him to come back with me to the theatre. Threatened to smack him if he didn't.

His blank expression terrified me. This wasn't the controlled mask I had seen before. It was the face of madness.

My breath caught on a sob. "Please, Rowan. Don't do this. You're scaring me."

The incessant rocking stopped for just a moment, then resumed.

Was that the way to reach him? By reminding him of his responsibility to a member of his cast? It had brought him back to us after Midsummer. Maybe it could bring him back to me now.

"Rowan. Please. I need you."

Again, the rocking stopped. Slowly, his head turned toward me. I dropped the flashlight and seized his face, trapping it before he could turn away again.

"I need you to come back to the theatre with me."

Without waiting for a response, I grabbed his hand, then the flashlight, and tugged him to his feet. He lurched forward, knocking me against the wall, and I bit back a cry.

I pulled his arm around my waist and draped mine around his. Just as he had that day in the woods. Reeling like two drunks coming home from a bender, we staggered toward the theatre.

The chill from his body radiated through mine. I was shivering so hard I could barely keep up my stream of soothing chatter. When I realized I was babbling the same sort of platitudes I sang about in "You'll Never Walk Alone," I shut up.

I considered retrieving my bag from my car, but decided it was more important to get Rowan warm. I could always use his phone to call Reinhard. By now, I was pretty sure I needed backup. Short of repeating my mantra about needing him, I had no idea how to reach Rowan.

Only when we arrived at his apartment did I realize he was barefoot. I winced, imagining the gravel lacerating his feet. I picked a path through the papers strewn across the floor. He just marched across them, leaving what I hoped were mud stains on the pages.

I poked my head into the bathroom. It was surprisingly large with a stall shower in one corner and a claw-footed tub tucked under the eaves. While a shower might be easier, a bath would be more soothing. I turned the water on, making it as hot as I dared, and turned to fetch Rowan.

He was gone. Before I could panic, I found him sinking onto the bed.

"Rowan. You need to get out of those wet clothes."

He looked up without a glimmer of recognition.

"Please, Rowan. I need you to get up."

Obediently, he rose. By dint of a lot of tugging, I managed to remove his sodden shirt. His skin was as white as a marble statue and almost as cold.

I fumbled with the buttons on his jeans. The material was so heavy and wet that I had to slip my fingers inside his pants and use both hands to work the buttons free. Each time the back of my hand brushed the bare flesh of his belly, he flinched. By the time I finally managed to shove his pants down around his ankles, a constant shudder rippled through his body.

I left on his white boxers. He'd just have to deal with those himself. But I couldn't help noting that his legs were as smooth and hairless as his chest and arms.

I rushed to the bathroom to avert a flood. As I turned off the water, I heard knocking and raced out again, desperately glad that Lee and Hal had finally arrived. Instead, I found Rowan curled up on the bed, his shivers so violent that the wooden headboard beat a steady tattoo against the wall.

I cried out when I saw the soles of his feet, scraped raw by the gravel and still oozing blood. I seized the lamb's wool throw hanging on the footboard and threw it over him. Then I hurried through the office, averting my gaze from the bloody Rorschach blotches on the papers.

I pulled open cabinets in the kitchen and grabbed the first pot I could find, a porcelain enamel saucepan. When I spotted a bottle of whisky on the sideboard, I grabbed that, too.

Back to the bathroom to fill the pan with water and gather additional supplies: a box of Band-Aids, a tube of Neosporin ointment, towels. As gently as I could, I washed and dried his feet. He might have flinched as I bandaged the worst cuts, but his shivering made it hard to tell.

In the armoire next to the sliding glass doors, I found soft lamb's wool socks. In the chest tucked under the eaves, a heavy wool blanket. I took out a cashmere sweater, too, but doubting I could wrestle him into it, I stripped off my wet T-shirt and pulled on the sweater.

I paused long enough to yank the stopper out of the bottle of Laphroaig and take a deep swig. Then I sat down on the bed and held out the bottle.

Rowan made a sound deep in his throat. His hand darted out and wrenched the bottle from my grasp. The suddenness of the movement startled me, but mostly, I was relieved that he had responded. God bless Laphroaig.

I leaned toward him to help him sit up, but he just tilted the bottle toward his mouth. Whisky slopped over his chin and neck to drip onto the quilt. When I tried to steady the bottle, he scrambled over the pillows to crouch against the headboard. Clutching the bottle in both hands, he drained the whisky in a few deep gulps.

A shudder coursed through him. The empty bottle slipped from his fingers. I gasped when I saw his right hand, the scars on his palm and fingers bright red, as if he'd burned them today instead of years ago.

"Rowan, I'm going to put the bottle on the nightstand. Okay?"

I kept my eyes on him in case he made another sudden move, but he simply watched me.

"Now I'm going to put some ointment on those burns."

He snatched his hand away and cradled it protectively against his chest.

"Okay. No ointment. But at least, let me clean you off."

I retrieved a towel from the pile beside the bed. Moving very slowly, I leaned forward and wiped the dregs of the whisky from his face and chest. As I sat back, two small furrows appeared between his brows. His lips moved, but no sound emerged. He squeezed his eyes shut, then opened them.

"Maggie?"

I was so happy I flung out my arms. He shrank back against the headboard.

"I'm sorry. I won't touch you," I said.

A new wave of shivering overcame him. He fumbled for the blankets that lay in a tangled heap at the foot of the bed. As I reached out to help him, he shook his head wildly.

"Go," he grated between clenched teeth.

"I just want to—"

"Go!"

"I promised Helen I'd stay with you."

He moaned, a soft, terrible sound. The temperature in the apartment suddenly plummeted, and I glanced at the sliding glass doors to see if they were open.

A wave of nausea made my stomach clench. Bile rose in my throat. Gagging, I slid off the bed and stumbled toward the bathroom, only to draw up short as rage flooded my body. I gripped the doorframe, fighting the urge to beat my fist against it, but I couldn't contain the furious scream that tore free from my throat. I was still standing there, panting, when grief overcame me. A sense of loss and despair so profound that I slid to the floor and huddled there, whimpering.

By then I realized that Rowan's power had burst free, that I was being inundated by his emotions, but all I could do was crouch there like a terrified animal. Even more terrifying were the answering emotions his power summoned from the hidden corners of my spirit where shame and guilt crouched, where childish anger yearned to leap into rage, where confusion and doubt and despair lurked just beneath the thin veneer of confidence.

Fear engulfed me. An icicle that seared flesh and bone, mind and spirit. A remorseless knife that shredded my pitiful barriers. A merciless fire that illuminated the shadowy places of memory.

I no longer knew where his pain ended and mine began. I was the boy, helplessly clawing at the cold fire burning his neck. I was the child, battering her fists against the windowpane as her father drove away. The young man, howling his despair to the forest. The young girl, muffling hers in a pillow.

Pain gripped my throat, choking off hope as well as breath. And then strong arms encircled me, lifted me, cradled me. Gentle hands smoothed my hair. A soft voice whispered my name, calling me back.

The mindless fear ebbed. The pain receded to a dull throb that shuddered inside of me with each breath. He soothed me with the calming tones I knew so well, but his voice shook as helplessly as his body and his teeth chattered as he told me not to cry.

His damp hair brushed my forehead. His racing heartbeat thudded under my hand. Goose bumps crawled up my legs. Dully, I noted that I was sitting on his lap, the chill of his thighs seeping into mine. Yet the fingers that wiped away my tears were warm. He must be making them warm. Drawing on his power to chase away the cold as surely as he had used it to drive the demons back to their dark places.

As I groped feebly for the blankets, he seized the lamb's wool throw and wrapped it around my shoulders. For a moment, I simply basked in the warmth and softness. Then I reached for the wool blanket. He tried to wrap that around me, too, but I batted his hands away. Together, we managed to drag it over our legs.

I leaned back into the curve of his shoulder and he rocked me gently, murmuring words too soft to understand. His hand stroked my back, up and down, up and down, the rhythm as soothing as the soft flow of words. Then he fell silent and I just rested against him, breathing in the sweet aroma of honeysuckle and the rain-washed scent of his flesh.

"I'm sorry," he whispered. "I never meant—"

I pressed my fingertips to his lips and felt him catch his breath. Then he let it out in a shaky sigh.

I cupped my hand against the curve of his jaw and traced the outline of his mouth with my thumb. His lips parted. He captured my thumb between his teeth and bit down just hard enough to still its movement.

Molten heat coiled between my legs. Delicate pinpricks of desire tightened my nipples.

Suddenly, the room was stifling. Sweat beaded my forehead and trickled down my sides. I kicked the blankets off, but if anything, the air grew hotter.

Rowan groaned. His tongue scraped against my thumb, sandpaper-rough like a cat's. Before I could do more than register the sensation, another wave of heat seared me. I pressed my thighs together, seeking to contain it, control it, and moaned when I felt the hard ridge of his erection. The waves came faster as I rocked against it, a relentless crescendo of desire I could neither contain nor control.

Rowan shifted beneath me. I dug my fingers into his shoulders, clinging to him. Iron bands closed around my wrists. And then I was tumbling off of him, falling back onto the mattress, my hands still reaching for him, my voice crying out his name as I climaxed.

As my cry dwindled to hoarse pants, another wave shook me, arching my body upward, then slamming me back onto the mattress as it peaked. I clawed at the blanket, seeking something, anything to anchor me.

Strong hands grasped mine. I gripped them hard as another spasm shook me. For a moment I hung there, suspended, every muscle quivering and taut. Then the relentless wave began to ebb, echoes of desire shooting through me like minnows darting through a pool. The minnows grew smaller and slower until there was only the liquid warmth between my legs and an incredible languor suffusing my body that made me slump, exhausted, onto the bed.

Rowan's hands wrenched free. I didn't have the strength to cling to them. I didn't even have the strength to open my eyes. I heard him moving around the bedroom. Drawers opening and closing. The soft slide of fabric against flesh. The rattle of wooden blinds.

A cool breeze wafted over me. I opened my eyes to discover Rowan staring out into the night. He was fully dressed, his hands clasped behind his back. His head moved as I struggled to sit up, then turned back to survey the darkness.

"I'm sorry," he said.

The same words he had spoken earlier. Only now his tone was stiff, almost curt.

Shame flushed my body with damp heat. All I could think of was how ridiculous I must have looked, thrashing about on his bed like a landed fish. Then anger replaced the shame. Yes, I had initiated it by touching him. But that was to comfort him, to demonstrate that I didn't blame him for his earlier loss of control.

Okay, maybe there had been a moment when desire intruded on the tenderness. But it was his arousal that had propelled me into the world's fastest orgasm. Too bad it wasn't an Olympic event; I'd have won a gold medal.

Maybe he sensed my anger. At any rate, he faced me. He'd obviously had time to control whatever he was feeling and plaster the blank mask on his face. He probably kept a supply in his armoire for uncomfortable occasions like this.

I scanned the floor for my T-shirt. When I found it folded neatly atop the low chest, I shoved myself to the edge of the bed. My legs felt as boneless as amoebas. Willpower alone kept me on my feet as I wobbled forward, snatched up my shirt, and headed to the bathroom. I wasn't about to strip off his sweater under his No-Need-to-Thank-Me-You-Know-Your-Way-Out gaze.

"Maggie . . ."

I slammed the bathroom door behind me, ripped off his sweater, and flung it onto the tiles. Then I picked it up, folded it just as carefully as he had folded my shirt, and set it on the toilet seat. Fitting somehow.

As I wriggled into my damp shirt, he called my name again. I took a moment to gaze into the mirror over the sink, relieved that I looked perfectly normal except for the tangled hair, red-rimmed eyes, smudged mascara, and swollen lower lip. I touched it lightly with my tongue and winced; I must have bitten it during my Olympic orgasm.

I smoothed my hair, then muttered, "Fuck it" and flung open the door. I marched past Rowan without looking at him.

"Maggie, wait."

I kept walking.

"Maggie!"

His shout echoed through the room. Then I realized it wasn't an echo. Someone else was calling my name. Lee.

"Sweetie? Are you here?"

And Hal. The cavalry had finally arrived.

"What are they doing here?" Rowan demanded.

"Reinhard called them. He said . . ."

"What?"

"He didn't want me to be alone with you."

Rowan's mouth tightened into a hard line. "We have to talk."

"There's no—"

He crossed the length of the office in a blur of movement. His fingers bit cruelly into my biceps, and I gasped. He relaxed his hands, but refused to let me go.

"Listen to me," he said, his voice soft but urgent. "It was an accident. I was upset."

Footsteps pounded up the stairs.

"I didn't mean to hurt you. You've got to believe that."

"You're hurting me now!"

And that—naturally—was how Lee and Hal found us. Rowan shaking me, me struggling to break free.

Rowan backed away, the mask slipping into place. Lee stared at him through narrowed eyes. Hal peeked over Lee's shoulder, his gaze darting from the damaged door to the bloodstained papers to me.

Lee stepped into the office, as wary as a man approaching a dangerous animal. "What happened here?"

"Nothing," I said. "Nothing happened."

"The door's off its fucking hinges." His voice was very quiet, but his eyes were hard, his body taut with tension.

"That happened earlier. When Rowan ran out to help Helen."

"Did you hurt her?"

Rowan made the fatal mistake of hesitating. When I saw Lee's hands clench into fists, I quickly stepped between them.

"I'm fine, Lee."

For the first time, he looked at me. "You're shaking, Maggie. And you've been crying." His accusing gaze shot back to Rowan. "What did you do to her?"

"He was upset. And his emotions got . . . out of hand." I grabbed Lee's arm to keep him from pushing past me. "It was a little scary, okay? But everything's all right now."

I flashed what I hoped was a reassuring smile, but I could have murdered Rowan for leaving me to leap to his defense.

"I think we should go," Hal said.

As I babbled agreement, Rowan said, "I need to speak with Maggie."

"I don't care what you need," Lee replied. "We're taking Maggie back to the hotel. Now."

"I warn you, Lee—"

"For God's sake!" I exclaimed. "Would you both dial down the fucking testosterone?"

For a guy who claimed to know exactly which part an actor needed, Rowan was astonishingly clueless about how to handle this situation. Or maybe, after everything that had happened this evening, his control was simply shot. The air in the office curdled with tension, as thick and unsettled as if another thunderstorm approached. That had to be Rowan's power leaking through once again. And once again, it was Maggie Graham, Helping Professional, who had to defuse the crisis before a fistfight erupted.

"Lee. Hal. Would you wait for me downstairs?"

"I'm not leaving you—"

"Lee! Please."

He hesitated, then nodded brusquely. "Two minutes."

With that, he stomped off. Hal lingered long enough to shoot me an anxious glance before following him.

"Okay," I said. "You've got two minutes."

"I don't like ultimatums. From Lee or from you."

"I don't give a shit. You said you wanted to talk. If you've changed your mind, I'll go."

"I can't talk with you when you're like this."

As I turned away, he strode past me and blocked the doorway. "I'm trying to explain."

"What's to explain? You lost control. I came."

He grimaced. His fingers slipped under the silver necklace to knead the scar around his throat. "You have every right to be angry. I can only tell you again how sorry I am. I didn't mean it to happen. Any of it. I was just . . ." He looked away, his fingers obsessively rubbing his throat. "I was upset. Over Helen. And you were so kind . . . afterward . . ."

"You thought you'd return the favor?"

He glared at me. "I told you to go!"

"So now it's my fault?"

"No!" He stalked away, kicking papers out of his way. His shoulders rose and fell as he took a deep breath. "It's been a long time. Since I've held a woman. Any woman."

I took a moment to digest that, then muttered, "Gee, thanks."

He turned back to me. His puzzled frown only fed my shame and anger.

"What?" he asked. "I just told you that—"

"You just told me it didn't matter who was with you. My grandmother could have given you a hard-on!"

"That's not—damn it, Maggie, stop twisting my words!"

"Maggie?" Lee shouted.

"I'm coming!" I called. Then winced at that infelicitous choice of words.

As I headed to the door, Rowan said, "I wanted *you*. Not any woman. You."

I paused and gripped the doorframe.

"Blame me for losing control. For failing to shield you from my emotions. For letting you feel things you should never have felt. But don't blame me for wanting you."

I slowly turned to him. "I don't blame you for any of those things."

The taut lines of his face relaxed and his fingers slipped away from his neck.

"I blame you for turning your back on me. You left me lying there on the bed, trying to make sense of what had just happened. And when you looked at me . . ." I bit my lip and winced. "You made me feel stupid and ugly and ashamed."

His hand had risen to his throat again as I spoke, his expression changing from guilt to shock to pain.

Lee shouted up to me. The urgency in his voice made me obey. I heard Rowan call my name, but I just bolted down the stairs and let the boys hustle me out to the parking lot.

CHAPTER 20
STRONG WOMAN NUMBER

LEE INSISTED I SPEND THE NIGHT WITH THEM. I was too tired to argue.

Hal drove my car back to the hotel, while I rode with Lee in his pickup. Other than asking me if I was all right, we made the drive in silence.

That was easier to deal with than Hal's nervous stream of conversation. While I threw a few clothes into my carryall, he apologized for the length of their shower and their failure to check messages as soon as they emerged, voiced his concern for Helen, and described their anxious drive to the theatre.

"When we saw the door hanging off its hinges . . . and Rowan shaking you . . . and your scared little face . . ."

"I wasn't scared."

Then. But now I was shaking.

"Lee's got this protective thing. And you do not want to fuck with him when it clicks on. He gets quiet. Scary quiet. And when he got scary quiet tonight, I was sure he and Rowan were going to kill each other. I'm awful in those situations. I just stand there like a deer in the headlights. But you! My God. You were like . . . Bette Davis. Or Susan Hayward. Or—is that all you're taking?"

"It's only one night, Hal."

When I followed them into their small bungalow a few miles out of town, I almost smiled. The simple but elegant furnishings of the living room reflected Lee's tastes. The

mink stole draped atop one of the bookcases clearly reflected
Hal's—as did the curio cabinet crammed with personal photographs, candles, small vases of dried flowers, music boxes,
two silver goblets, and assorted figurines of naked male
gods.

I excused myself to take a shower, explaining that I
wanted to get out of my damp clothes. The dampness that
bothered me most was the one in my panties. I didn't need
that little memento of the evening.

Yet in spite of my Olympic orgasm, I was more troubled
by the Vulcan mind meld that had preceded it and Rowan's
Spock-like coldness afterward. The roller coaster of emotions had left me numb, but whenever I recalled that awful flood of memories, I started shaking again. Anger might
have provided a safe refuge, but it required too much energy.

So did the effort to keep up a good front for the boys. Hal
plied me with food and wine and more nervous conversation.
Lee just watched me. It was hard to say which was more unnerving. After a half hour, I pleaded exhaustion and escaped
into the spare room. I'd just crawled into bed when I heard a
soft knock at the door.

Stifling a groan, I called out, "Come in."

Lee walked in, one hand covering the mouthpiece of his
portable phone. "It's Reinhard. For you."

I shrank deeper into the bedding.

"Just let him know you're okay."

Reluctantly, I accepted the phone. Lee walked out, closing the door behind him.

"Reinhard? How's Helen?"

"Stable. She's sleeping now."

"Are they going to operate or . . .?"

"Her cardiologist wants to see how she responds to the
medication first. What happened with Rowan?"

"Nothing."

Silence. Then: "I'll be there in half an hour."

"Reinhard, I'm fine. Just really tired. And I know you
must be, too. Can't the post mortem wait until tomorrow?"

Another silence, longer than the first. "All right." After a
brief hesitation, Reinhard added, "How is he?"

I had to take a deep breath before I trusted my voice.

"Hc's okay. Now. But he was practically catatonic at first. He wouldn't talk. He didn't even recognize me. And then . . ."

I broke off, damning my shaking voice.

"He did not hurt you?" Reinhard demanded. "The door, yes. But Lee said—"

"He didn't hurt me." I touched my arm and winced; I'd have bruises tomorrow.

"I should have known better than to leave you there. To expect you to stay in your car. I am a foolish old man. And you! You are a foolish, stubborn, softhearted young woman." He sighed. "But. It is done. Are you really all right?"

"I'm really all right."

"I have office hours in the morning. I will meet you at the hotel at one o'clock. And if you are not there—"

"You'll hunt me down and kill me."

"Kill you, no. But a tongue-lashing? Yes! That I will give you."

I shivered, recalling the rough scrape of Rowan's tongue against my thumb. Or had I imagined that?

"Maggie?"

"How's Janet?" I asked quickly.

"I gave her enough sedatives to knock out an elephant. Alex is staying with her tonight. Are you sure you don't want me to come over?"

"I'm sure."

"Then sleep, *liebchen*. Things will look brighter tomorrow."

My throat closed. I made some inarticulate sound of agreement and hurriedly ended the call.

Moments later, there was another soft knock at the door. I opened it, handed the phone to Lee, and said, "I'm meeting him for lunch tomorrow."

Lee smiled for the first time since taking me under his wing. He was too nice a guy to be relieved at the prospect of passing me off to someone else. Likely, he was convinced that Reinhard would get the whole story out of me and ensure that I was as fine as I claimed to be.

I crawled back into bed. Listened to the low murmur of conversation from the other room. Heard Hal shuffle off to bed. Waited for Lee to follow. The narrow rectangle of light beneath my door told me he was still sitting in the living room. I wondered if he was sleepless, too, or keeping vigil until he was certain I had drifted off.

I'd never had so many men looking after me. Reinhard. Hal. Lee.

And then there was Rowan. But I wasn't going to think about him.

Yeah. Right.

Hal prepared an enormous breakfast and urged me to spend the morning with him, but I begged off. I'd been restless and edgy from the moment I had awakened and doubted I'd be very good company. Besides, I had a million chores to do.

But once Lee dropped me off at the hotel, I couldn't seem to concentrate on any of them. Instead of responding to online job postings, I played around with the *Carousel* program. Instead of pondering Nettie's strengths and weaknesses, I helped Brittany and J.T. create lists for Carrie and Mr. Snow. I started drafting a press release and put it aside. I even jogged up and down the stairs of the hotel, which left me with aching muscles, but failed to alleviate my restlessness.

By the time I headed downstairs to meet Reinhard, I had little more to show for my morning than a pile of clean laundry and the suspicion that I was using hands-on helping as a way to avoid my problems both onstage and off.

I was still feeling a little antsy when we reached our destination, a rambling, ski lodgey-type inn in Hill. Reinhard must have noticed because he ordered a bottle of white wine to go with lunch. The first glass helped dispel the lingering restlessness. Reinhard had the grace to wait until I polished off another, along with my salad, before folding his hands atop the tablecloth.

"So."

I gave him the edited version of last night's events. He probably suspected that I was holding something back, but I knew he would not press me.

When I finished, he sighed. "I'm sorry, Maggie. Sorry you had to cope with that alone and sorry that you had to feel Rowan's grief and fear. It is a measure of his love for

Helen that he lost control that way. And a measure of your forbearance that you do not seem to blame him."

I shook my head, eyes on my plate.

"He must trust you very much. To tell you about his power. Can you still trust him? After last night?"

I reached for my wine glass, then let my hand fall to my lap. "I trust him as my director. I trust him to try and keep his feelings under lock and key. But if he gets upset, it could happen again. To me or someone else."

"To you, perhaps. But to another cast member? I don't think so. For better or worse, you have a special relationship with Rowan."

"It's not a *relationship* relationship," I protested.

"It's not strictly professional, either," he replied. "And has not been since you went on that picnic."

Had Janet seen us going into the woods together? Or maybe Catherine had spilled the beans; she'd picked up the food and had to realize it couldn't all be for Rowan.

"Nothing happened. We just talked. And ate. He showed me the beech. And the view from the plateau where he . . ."

Reinhard paused in the act of refilling his wine glass and slowly lowered the bottle.

". . . sings," I concluded lamely. "He's never taken anyone else there, has he?"

"Not since I've worked at the theatre."

I felt my face flush and tried to convince myself it was the wine.

"And that, I think, settles the issue of whether or not you have a special relationship," Reinhard said dryly. Any hint of humor vanished as he leaned forward. "The particulars of that relationship are none of my business. But the theatre is. And your welfare as a member of my cast. You'll have to work closely with Rowan during *Carousel*. Can you do that?"

"I think so."

"Do you *want* to?"

Unexpected emotion tightened my throat. Whether I wanted to work with Rowan or simply dreaded the idea of failing at yet another job, I knew I couldn't leave the Crossroads yet.

I raised my gaze from the glassy eyes of my grilled trout and met Reinhard's keen blue ones. "I want to stay, Reinhard. I want to make it work."

He studied me for a long moment, then nodded. "All right. Enough talking. Eat. You're as thin as a rail."

On our way back to Dale, the now-familiar antsiness returned. It was so strong that I squirmed in my seat, hands clenched in my lap.

Reinhard's head snapped toward me. "What's wrong?"

"I don't know. I've been restless all day. Maybe I'm just feeling the aftereffects of last night. Or I'm nervous about seeing Rowan tomorrow."

Reinhard gave a noncommittal grunt, but he stepped on the gas and only slowed when we reached the outskirts of town.

As we walked into the hotel, Bobbie hurried toward me and exclaimed, "There you are."

"What?"

She rolled her eyes. " 'Bustin' Out' rehearsal? Three o'clock?" When I continued to stare at her blankly, she pointed toward the message board. "I posted it this morning."

"Sorry. I totally forgot to check. I'll be there in a minute." As Bobbie marched to the lounge, I turned to Reinhard. "Thank you for lunch. And for talking. And . . . everything."

"You can always talk to me, Maggie. Any time. Day or night."

Before I could thank him again, he strode briskly out of the hotel.

I ran upstairs, grabbed my vocal book, and hurried to the lounge. For once, playing Nettie had an up side. As I launched into the introduction of "June Is Bustin' Out All Over," the antsiness that had plagued me all day abruptly vanished.

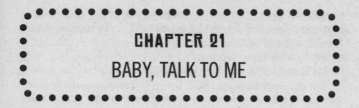

CHAPTER 21
BABY, TALK TO ME

REINHARD BROKE THE NEWS ABOUT HELEN at our company meeting and quickly allayed everyone's fears by assuring them she was doing fine and should return home on Thursday. For the next few days, his daughter Bea would hold down the fort. The relieved smiles faded when he announced that Janet would assume charge of the hotel after that.

The schedule called for Reinhard to work with the chorus that morning, so it was easy to avoid Rowan. But when we broke for lunch, I found him waiting by the stage door. As soon as he caught sight of me, the mask slid smoothly into place.

"May I speak with you, please?"

Reluctantly, I nodded.

Rowan suddenly scowled and snapped, "In private."

I glanced over my shoulder and found Reinhard hovering behind me.

"You can talk in the Smokehouse," Reinhard said. "I'll wait outside."

"We'll talk by the pond," Rowan retorted. "That way, you can watch."

As he strode off, I muttered, "Well, this oughta go well."

"Maybe now is not the best time for this conversation," Reinhard said.

"Better to get it over with."

I walked slowly after Rowan. That gave me a precious

minute to take some very deep breaths. Halfway to the pond, he glanced back, frowned, and waited for me to catch up. As I drew abreast of him, he started walking again, but this time, he matched his pace to mine.

"I wanted to have this conversation yesterday," he said. "Before rehearsals began again. Unfortunately, that didn't happen."

My steps slowed. Stopped.

"It was you. Yesterday. Your power that I felt."

Rowan opened his mouth, closed it, and finally said, "Yes."

Recalling its abrupt cessation, I realized something else. "Reinhard told you to stop."

He nodded brusquely. A muscle jumped in his jaw.

"I should have realized . . ." And then the full implications of what he had done hit me. "You tried to force me to come to the theatre."

"If I'd forced you, you would have come." He grimaced. "To the theatre."

His clumsiness only fed my anger. "Couldn't you sense that I didn't want to?"

"Yes, but—"

"And you deliberately used your power to try and make me do it anyway?"

"We needed to talk. I thought that was important enough to warrant my . . . interference."

"Interference? Jesus. You went ballistic when I poked my head inside your door. But when you spend half the day poking at me with your power, that's just interference?"

"It was a mistake."

"It was more than a mistake, Rowan. It was an abuse of your power. Don't you see that?"

"Fine! It was wrong. I apologize. What do you want me to do, Maggie? Grovel?"

I turned on my heel and strode back toward the theatre. I half-expected him to use his power to stop me. If he had, I would have walked away from the Crossroads and never returned.

"Maggie. Wait."

I kept walking. I heard him curse as he hurried after me.

"What I did was wrong. I admit that. But I kept thinking about what you said. How I'd made you feel stupid and ugly and ashamed. I couldn't bear . . . I couldn't let you feel that way. Or believe that I had deliberately tried to hurt you."

I stopped, but kept my gaze on Reinhard, standing guard by the Smokehouse.

"I thought I was doing the right thing after . . . afterward. If I had touched you or comforted you or even spoken to you . . . I was afraid! All right? Afraid of losing what little control I had left. So I . . . retreated."

I heard him sigh and dared a glance at him. He was staring off toward the pond, the fingers of his right hand kneading the scar around his neck.

"I thought I was helping you. Protecting you. Instead, I made things worse. But I never meant to hurt you. If that counts for anything."

"Yes," I finally said. "It counts."

His shoulders rose and fell. "I'll understand if you can't forgive me."

His manner was stiff and formal again, the mask firmly in place. I'd felt only the briefest flash of emotion from him during his speech, a hot wash of shame and anxiety that convinced me that he was telling the truth.

"But if you can't trust me . . . if you want to go home . . ."

"I don't have anything to go home to."

"That's not a good enough reason to stay."

"No. But I've failed at pretty much every job I've ever had. I don't want to fail at this one, too. And I still haven't learned what I'm supposed to. About myself." I hesitated a moment before asking, "Do you want me to stay?"

"Yes! Yes. But we have to be able to work together. If we let the events of the last two days interfere with that, we won't be able to accomplish anything."

"Well, we *are* grown-ups," I reminded him with some asperity. "And professionals." Then I realized what he was really concerned about. "Don't worry. I'm not going to start trailing after you, all moony-eyed."

Instead of looking relieved, the mask slipped back into place. "Of course not." He stared at the barn, clearly eager to end the conversation.

"Okay, then," I said. "We'll behave like grown-ups and make this work. Yet another addendum to our pact."

I thrust out my hand. He stared down at it, hesitating, and I tried to decipher his expression. Finally, his hand rose to clasp mine very lightly. As his fingers started to slide free, I tightened my grip, and felt him start.

"You have to promise me something."

He gave a wary nod.

"I want your word that you'll never deliberately use your power to make me do something I don't want to do."

He gripped my hand hard. "You have it."

Everyone loves a fresh start. This one made me believe that there might be something to those sappy lyrics of "You'll Never Walk Alone." My life had been storm-tossed these last two days. But I'd kept my chin up. I'd warded off fear. And as Rowan and I walked back to the theatre, I felt almost hopeful.

That lasted about a day.

CHAPTER 22
PICK YOURSELF UP

EXPECTED TO FEEL UNCOMFORTABLE during our pre-show circle. I didn't expect a full-blown panic attack.

As soon as Rowan's power touched me, my body was gripped by the same paralyzing fear I had felt in his apartment. My heart rate tripled. My mouth went dry. My hand gripped Sarah's so convulsively that she squeaked.

Reinhard finally eased me out of the circle, guided my tottering steps down the hall, and steered me into the cluttered production office. I collapsed on the swivel chair behind the desk and put my head between my knees.

The black dots swarming my vision melted away. The roaring in my ears subsided. My racing heartbeat slowed.

I felt something pressing against my wrist and sat up to discover Reinhard silently assessing my pulse rate. "Better now, yes?"

I nodded and started to get up. Reinhard firmly pressed me back into the chair.

"The curtain's going up any minute," I protested.

"It does not go up until I say so."

He suddenly glanced over his shoulder. A moment later, Rowan appeared in the doorway.

"I'm sorry," I said. "That was stupid. I knew nothing bad was going to happen, but—"

"My fault. I should have anticipated how you might react. Are you all right now?"

"I think she should lie down," Reinhard said.

"You mean . . . miss the show?" I asked.

"Do you really think you can perform?"

A minute ago, I would have said, "No." But I refused to screw up the show for everyone. "I may not be the greatest straw plaiter that ever came down the pike, but I'll be okay."

Rowan studied me for a long moment before nodding to Reinhard. "It's Maggie's call."

As predicted, I wasn't the greatest straw plaiter that night. Nor was it the best show we had ever put on. The rest of the cast attributed their disappointing performances to their concern about Helen and the usual bumps that followed a break in the schedule. I knew Rowan had deliberately refrained from using his power to help us, no doubt fearing my reaction.

My pre-show panic attacks abated as the week wore on, but I never completely relaxed into the energy connecting us. As a result, I felt anxious and adrift during performances.

Helen's return from the hospital cheered everyone up, but without her nighttime blessings, I tossed and turned until exhaustion finally claimed me. Instead of escape, sleep brought troubled dreams I could not remember in the morning or sex dreams about Rowan that I recalled with alarming clarity.

Worse still—if that were possible—I found myself resenting Rowan's easy give-and-take with other cast members. I'd watch him laugh at something Brittany said or joke with Bernie or offer gentle encouragement to Sarah, and I'd bristle like an indignant cat.

It was ridiculous. And appalling. I was behaving like a jealous teenager in the throes of her first crush.

Janet had warned me about the dangers. Foolishly, I had considered myself immune. Knowing I'd be safely back in Brooklyn in a month should have reassured me. Instead, the prospect made me alternately depressed and irritable.

Although I did my best to hide my turmoil, the discreet inquiries of my cast mates made it clear I was failing miserably. I was letting everyone down by my inability to master my emotions and my role. After a particularly wooden performance in our Act One run-through of *Carousel*, Rowan took me aside and scheduled our long overdue discussion of Nettie's life history for Sunday morning.

With everything else that had happened in the last week, I'd completely forgotten about the assignment and had to throw something together. Her father, the hard-working foreman at Bascombe's Mill who died tragically in a fire. Her mother who scraped together a living by opening a luncheon shack on the wharf—the precursor of the Spa that Nettie runs in *Carousel*. I decided that Nettie had taken take over the Spa after her mother's untimely death in a baking accident. And although she never married, she enjoyed the universal love and admiration of her neighbors.

I perched nervously on my chair in the Smokehouse and watched Rowan's expression as he read. His head remained bent over the page for much longer than the three paragraphs demanded.

Finally, I said, "I know it's not there yet . . ."

"It's a good start."

My initial relief quickly faded. It was a mediocre start. We both knew that. At the very least, he should have chastised me for the blatant steal from *Into the Woods*.

"The luncheon shack is a nice touch."

I'd thought so, too. But for Rowan to single that out was nearly as bad as my attempt to bolster Nancy's confidence by praising her for knowing her lines.

A small part of me was angry that he was treating me like an emotional cripple. A much, much bigger part was relieved. We had never discussed those shared glimpses into each other's pain. When I tried to recall the images that had flooded my mind, they slipped away, as impossible to grasp as mist. I could no longer say with certainty what memories I had dredged up from my past. Only the pain they evoked remained real. If turning in a fabulous performance as Nettie required me to revisit that pain, I was more than happy to be coddled.

Even more unprofessional was my response to being alone with him. I watched those long fingers smoothing the paper and remembered them stroking my back. I studied the sharp angles of his face and recalled how desire had softened them. When his tongue flicked out to wet his lips, it was all I could do to keep from dragging him off his chair, shoving him onto the floor, and riding him like a bucking bronco.

Rowan cleared his throat. "I think you can do better."

For one horrifying moment, I thought he was referring to the bucking bronc scenario. Then I realized he was critiquing what I had written. I babbled agreement and fled.

As I reached the top of the lane, my cell phone erupted into the screeching strings of the *Psycho* ringtone. Groaning, I dug it out of my bag.

"Hey, Mom. I meant to call you earlier, but—"

"What's wrong?"

"Nothing's wrong. Why should anything be wrong?"

"You sound strange."

"It must be the phone. It's been conking out a lot lately. What's up?"

"I was wondering if you'd had a chance to check on those dates." As I sat there in clueless bewilderment, she added, "Maggie? Are you still there?"

"Yeah."

"You're breaking up."

In more ways than one.

As I got out of the car, she said, "Oh, that's better. Anyway. About the beach . . ."

I silently cursed. "I'm working on it."

"If you don't want to go . . ."

"I do! It's just hard working around everybody's schedules."

"Because if you don't, you can just say so."

"I'll pin them down this week."

"I wouldn't pester you except Sue's daughter—Leila? The flaky one? She just told Sue she's getting married. And naturally, she's chosen the week we're at Rehoboth. So Sue won't be able to come down at all now."

"Leila's getting married in a month and she springs it on her mother now?"

"It gets better. She met her fiancé in June."

I'd met Rowan in May. It seemed like two years ago instead of two months.

"At this retreat center near Seattle. Or Sedona. I forget."

Not that we were getting married. We weren't even lovers. Technically. The Olympic orgasm didn't really count.

"They were there for some wacky Midsummer ritual."

Leila and I should compare notes. I was pretty sure the Dance of the Fireflies trumped anything in Seattle. Or Sedona.

"And get this: she's decided to become a shaman. Can you imagine?"

Actually, I could. Since coming to the Crossroads, my concept of what was possible had changed a lot.

"They're holding the wedding in a field. A three-day celebration. With everyone camping out in tents. Naturally, Sue's booked a room at the Hyatt."

Weren't shamans supposed to be able to summon elemental energy? I wasn't sure about summoning free-floating orgasms, but Leila might have some insights into Rowan's power and my reaction to it. Maybe that's all that had been going on this week—the residue of his power niggling at me. That would be a relief.

"Do you have Leila's e-mail address?" I asked.

"I could get it from Sue. Why?"

"I just thought I'd write and congratulate her."

"You don't even like Leila."

"Well. It would be a nice gesture."

There was a long silence. I could practically see the wheels turning in my mother's head.

"Maggie. You haven't gotten caught up in that New Agey stuff, have you?"

"No, I just want to—"

"Because a lot of those groups are practically cults."

"I'm not joining a cult, Mom."

"That's what those Manson Family girls probably said."

"Mother . . ."

"And the ones who drank the poisoned Kool-Aid."

"I am not—"

"That's what they do. Those cult leaders. Prey on susceptible people and fill their heads with nonsense and shovel drugs into them. And then . . ."

And then I realized what was behind this.

"I'm not Daddy."

Another long silence greeted my pronouncement. Then a sigh gusted over the phone. "I know. You've always been level-headed. Except for the theatre thing."

I winced.

"Which—thank God—you got over."

"Right. So. I'll let you know about the beach, but I've got to run now."

"Do you have a date?"

"No, Mom. Still no date. Just meeting some friends for brunch. I'll talk to you soon."

When I got back to the hotel and booted up my laptop, I found an e-mail from her with Leila's contact information. I added a fresh load of guilt to the ever-accumulating pile, shot off a quick thank you, and crafted a message to Leila that I immediately deleted. Whatever had happened with Rowan, flaky Leila wasn't the one to help me make sense of it.

I spent Monday morning working on Nettie's life history. When I went out onto the porch to check my phone for messages, I discovered two, both from New York area codes. One turned out to be from the United Way, the other from a victims' assistance center in the Bronx where I'd applied as supervisor of their hotline.

Stunned by the sudden change in my employment prospects, I Skyped them both and tried to sound professional and intelligent and not completely desperate. Then I discovered they were scheduling interviews the following week. Hell Week and the opening of *Carousel*.

I pleaded a family emergency to one, an out-of-town conference to the other. No dice. It was next week or never. In two months, these were the only places that had shown a glimmer of interest. I couldn't blow them off.

I tentatively scheduled interviews for Monday, then called Reinhard. He was less than thrilled that I'd miss part of Sunday's rehearsal and most of Monday's, but he agreed that I had to take the interviews. Since I couldn't very well oust the woman subletting my apartment, I called a HelpLink colleague who lived in Riverdale and arranged to stay with her Sunday night.

I gave up any attempt at figuring out Nettie's life and concentrated on mine. I did some additional research on both organizations and worked up a set of questions to ask during my interviews. Then, flash drive in hand, I hurried downstairs to ask Bea to let me into the office to use the printer. My steps slowed when I saw Janet behind the front desk.

I hadn't seen her since Helen's heart attack. She was as impeccably dressed as ever, but the dark circles under her eyes testified to the stress of the last week.

I hadn't seen Helen, either. Janet had left firm instructions that she was to have no visits or calls until next week, so I'd made do with handing get well cards to Helen's home health aide. The staff was clearly exempt from Janet's restrictions; at every lunch and dinner break, they made pilgrimages up the hill. Except Rowan. I hated to think he would allow that ancient feud to keep him from seeing Helen. Maybe he just preferred visiting when no one was around.

I put on a bright smile as I approached the desk and asked, "How's Helen?"

"She had breakfast on the patio this morning."

"That's great!"

"She'll be as weak as a kitten for the rest of the day. If she cajoles that goddamn aide into letting her walk in the garden, I'll kill them both."

Janet lifted one end of the inbox, unceremoniously dumping Iolanthe onto the desk. The cat shot her an irritable green-eyed glare and began repairing her ruffled dignity. As I watched the small pink tongue lapping against her fur, unwelcome heat suffused my body.

Finding Janet's gaze on me, I quickly asked, "So how are you holding up?"

"I always hold up. That's my role in life."

Abandoning any further attempt to play Helping Professional, I said, "I wrote up a press release for *Carousel*. And drafted a program. I still need Rowan's director's notes, though."

"I'll remind him at our staff meeting."

"Thanks. I'll print out the current draft for you. And if you wouldn't mind, I wondered if I could print out some personal stuff. I've got two interviews next week—"

"You're going on interviews during Hell Week?"

"I couldn't put them off."

"Have you told Rowan?"

"I told Reinhard."

Janet studied me, then brusquely beckoned me into the office. To my dismay, she followed me inside and closed the door.

The small office was filled with little Helen touches: the flowered wallpaper, the botanical prints, the bulletin board littered with cards and photos and cheerful sayings. Janet seated herself on the wooden Windsor chair in front of the file cabinet and lit a cigarette. I worked as fast as I could, conscious of her eyes watching me through the haze of smoke.

"I hear you had an eventful week, too," she remarked. As I babbled something about rehearsals, she added, "I was referring to Sunday night."

I took a deep breath. "Well, Rowan was in bad shape when I found him. But I got him inside and he came out of his daze and then—"

"You had sex with him."

My jaws closed and opened and closed again like a broken nutcracker. I stared up at a little card on the bulletin board that read, "Though time be fleet and I and thou are half a life asunder, Thy loving smile will surely hail the love-gift of a fairy tale." At that moment, I felt as thunderstruck as poor Alice after her little trip through the looking glass.

I forced myself to meet Janet's gaze. To my surprise, I found sympathy there instead of scornful satisfaction.

" 'Lord, what fools these mortals be.' "

"You were the one who tried to shove me into his bed!"

"And I was the one who warned you to keep out of it unless you could avoid emotional entanglements."

"Yes. You did."

"And you didn't."

"It's . . . complicated."

"I bet. So? Now what?"

"I'll get a grip."

"Pick yourself up, dust yourself off—"

"Do you have a better suggestion?"

"If it's just a sexual itch, you could go on sleeping with him."

"I told him we should behave like professionals."

Janet snorted. "Professionals sleep with each other all the time. And it might—"

"Do me good?"

"Calm you down, anyway. You're as jumpy as the proverbial cat on a hot tin roof."

"Sleeping with him would only make the roof hotter."

"Possibly." She took a deep drag on her cigarette and blew a plume of smoke toward the ceiling. "You didn't tell Reinhard about that part of the evening, did you?"

I shook my head. "Do you think he knows?"

"Probably. Reinhard's very perceptive. But he'll keep his mouth shut. And so will I. Just don't tell Helen."

"God, no! I wouldn't dream of upsetting her."

"She'd probably be pleased. You know what a hopeless romantic she is. But she doesn't need any added excitement right now."

"Neither do I," I muttered.

Janet stabbed out her cigarette and rose. "Forget about that 'road not taken' crap. Make a choice, stick to it, and don't look back. The longer you dither, the harder you'll make it for yourself. And him."

❧❧

I presented Nettie's revised life history to Rowan the next morning. He studied this version even longer than the first. Then he folded the paper in half and handed it back to me.

"Try again. And lose the baking accident."

"You thought it was implausible?"

"I thought it was a direct steal from *Into the Woods*."

I waited for the smile. Instead, he rose, obviously dismissing me.

That was the day he blocked the clambake scene in Act Two. Thankfully, Alex had cut my first solo, which consisted of listing the ingredients in the codfish chowder. So other than a brief recitation about lobsters, I had little to do except lounge onstage and remind the audience over and over again that it had been a real nice clambake.

And Rowan wondered why I didn't connect to the character.

On Wednesday, he staged Act Two, Scene 2: the bungled robbery, Billy's death, and "You'll Never Walk Alone." I didn't have much in the way of blocking in that number, either. Hug Julie. Gaze at her with determination. Face front and sing. Kalma did her best to act comforted, but when I screeched out the high G, she winced.

Rowan called a break. Then called me over to the edge of the stage. Alex gazed up mournfully from the pit. Rowan gazed at the floor.

"The song's too high for me," I said.

"You think that's the problem with the number?" Rowan asked quietly. "That it's too high?"

"Not the only problem. But if I can't sing it—"

"Why can't you sing it?"

"How could anyone mouth platitudes about keeping your chin up to a woman whose husband just died in her arms?"

Rowan's head came up. "Did it ever occur to you that she's using the only vocabulary a working class woman of that time possesses? That by investing the words with genuine emotion you could lift them above what you insist on calling platitudes? How can Julie believe anything Nettie says if you don't? How can an audience? On paper, you fill this woman's life with tragedy, but none of it shows onstage."

That stung me into defensiveness. "I worked hard on those life histories."

"A baking accident?" Rowan demanded.

"Okay, that was silly, but—"

"You need to consider how events have shaped her, how she developed the strength to go on, the strength that she shares at this crisis in Julie's life. You can't keep skimming the surface, Maggie. That's partially my fault. I allowed you to get away with it. But that ends now. You asked me to be professional and I will. *Carousel* opens one week from today. And if I have to push and pull and drag a meaningful performance out of you, I will."

Clearly, the happy coddling phase was over. And so was our special relationship. Grimly, I recalled Janet's Robert Frost reference. While I hesitated at the fork in the road, Rowan had chosen the safer route for us to follow. Only time would tell whether that would make all the difference.

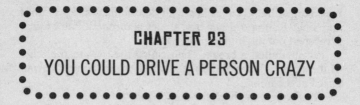

FOR TWO DAYS, HE PUSHED AND I PULLED. He told me to connect with my feelings. I avoided them like the plague. He claimed I wanted to learn about myself, but only if it was easy. I told him nothing about this was easy. He called me a coward. I called him an arrogant prick with a God complex.

That startled him into momentary silence. "You think I'm enjoying this?" he demanded.

"You sure as hell seem to be!"

A hot blast of air eddied around me as he shoved back his chair. I was terrified and delighted that I had broken his iron control.

"Is that what you really think of me?"

He looked so genuinely distressed that I shook my head. "No. I was just mad."

Rowan sighed. "Sometimes, I forget how young you are."

"You're not exactly Methuselah."

"Not quite. Although some days . . ." He shook his head. "What do you want from me, Maggie?"

He'd asked me that at the *Brigadoon* cast party, too. And I still didn't have a good answer. I wanted a breakthrough on Nettie without putting in the effort required to achieve it. I wanted the special relationship we had built up over the last month without any of the risks that might entail. I wanted the indescribable pleasure he had given me without the terror his power evoked. I wanted him to be warm and caring.

I wanted him to keep his distance. I wanted to prove I could succeed at something. I wanted to drive away from this place and never return.

"I don't know."

He nodded as if I'd confirmed what he already knew. "How can I help you?"

Tell me I'm getting there. Tell me to stop making excuses. Treat me like a professional. Take me to bed. Coddle me. Demand the best from me. Do it all. Do the impossible.

"I don't know," I repeated.

"Neither do I."

🙜🙙

Once Janet permitted the cast to visit Helen, I started going up to the house almost every day. We chatted in the sunroom or strolled through the garden. She never pushed or pried and rarely even brought up Rowan's name. I always came away calm and refreshed, but those feelings evaporated by the time I reached the bottom of the hill.

Knowing Friday was my last chance for a quiet chat before I headed to New York, I bolted a quick dinner and headed over to the house. The front door was open. Peering through the screen, I could make out little, but the house was quiet. Had her aide left early? If so, she'd be looking for another position by morning. Janet would fire her for leaving Helen alone.

No one on the patio. Or in the garden. I told myself Helen was probably napping, but my anxiety spiked as I crept into the house. I was halfway up the stairs when I heard the muffled sound of a man's voice coming from Helen's bedroom. Relieved that she was simply entertaining another visitor, I hesitated, wondering if I should wait on the porch.

The door to her room banged open. Rowan strode to the top of the stairs, his eyes wild.

"Oh, my God!" I cried. "What's happened?"

I raced up the stairs and flew into Helen's bedroom. She smiled calmly at me from her rocking chair.

"Are you okay?" I demanded.

"Yes, of course."

I whirled around and stalked toward the doorway, only to stop short when Rowan's figure loomed in front of me.

"You nearly gave me a heart attack!" I winced at my choice of words and muttered an apology to Helen. Then punched Rowan in the chest. "Don't scare me like that!" I raised my fist to punch him again, then slowly lowered it. "You came into the house."

"Of course," Helen said. "He's visited every day since I came home."

I was instantly ashamed of my earlier suspicions that his ridiculous vow meant more to him than her welfare. The wildness had left his eyes, but he looked distinctly uncomfortable. Maybe he had hoped to keep his visits secret.

"That's a really big deal," I said.

"I just wanted to see Helen," he mumbled.

"But . . . are you okay? I mean . . . before . . . you looked—"

"I'm fine. Helen, I have to go."

She leaned forward, gripping the arms of the rocker. "I wish you'd stay."

"I can't. I can't! Forgive me."

And with that, he bolted.

Mystified, I turned to Helen. "What the hell was that all about?"

She patted the stool next to her rocker. Rowan must have dragged it over; usually, it sat in front of her dressing table. The ruffled cushion was still warm from his body. I tried not to squirm at that unexpected intimacy.

"Things haven't been going too well, have they?"

"Oh, God. He was talking about me." My head drooped, then jerked up again. "What exactly did he tell you?"

"Nothing more than you told Reinhard," Helen replied. "Who was the first to tell me what happened the night of my heart attack. Then Hal came by . . . . and Lee . . ."

I groaned.

"Today was the first time Rowan spoke of it. And everything that's happened since."

"No wonder he couldn't wait to escape."

She held out her hand, and I clasped it. "I was the one who asked you to look after him that night. And now I'm going to ask for another favor. Be patient with him. He's used to being able to handle every situation that confronts him. And he doesn't know how to handle this one."

"Handle me, you mean. If anyone needs patience, it's Rowan. I'm a disaster. This fuck—sorry—this stupid role . . . I just can't get it. He called me a coward the other day."

"Yes, he told me that. He mentioned your response as well." Her mouth quirked in an unexpected smile. "People rarely talk to him like that."

"It was completely unprofessional. And childish. I don't know what—"

"Can I ask you something, Maggie? And feel free to tell me it's none of my business."

I nodded warily.

"Are you in love with Rowan?"

"No! God. Please. I don't even know Rowan! I'm just . . . confused. By his moods. And all his damn secrets. And his power."

I slid off the stool and began pacing. "I can't think straight. About him. Or the show. Or stupid Nettie. I'm afraid of this role and I don't know why and Rowan doesn't know how to help me. He can't even stand to be in the same room with me! And now I've got these interviews and my mind's in a million places and I'm supposed to be a helping professional and the one person I can't help is me! I just want . . ."

"What, dear?"

"To get out of here! To get some perspective. I can't eat. I can't sleep. I can't concentrate. It's exhausting."

I slumped into the armchair by the window and closed my eyes. That outburst had been exhausting, too. If cathartic. But the last thing I should have done was pour out my woes to Helen. Janet would kill me.

Fingertips brushed my hand, and I started; I hadn't even heard Helen approach. To my relief, she didn't seem upset. Just as Janet had predicted, she looked pleased.

She opened her arms, and I leaped to my feet. Her embrace enfolded me with warmth and calm. When she released me, I stepped back and forced a smile.

"See? That's the problem. You haven't been around to

bless me at night or give me hugs on demand. No wonder I'm a wreck."

"You're too hard on yourself," she scolded. "And on Rowan. This isn't easy for him, either."

"You won't tell him what I said? He already thinks I'm a basket case. I don't want him to think I'm turning into a stalker, too."

"Maybe the two of you need to go on another picnic."

"Oh, God! Did Reinhard tell you?"

"Goodness, no. I knew as soon as Catherine told me about all the food he'd ordered." Helen gazed out the window, her expression tender, almost wistful.

"He's taken you there, too," I said slowly. "To the beech."

"A long time ago."

Why had Reinhard lied? No. He hadn't lied. He'd just said that Rowan had never taken anyone there since he had joined the staff.

I hesitated, then decided to take the plunge. "Can I ask you something, Helen? And feel free to tell me it's none of my business."

Helen's smile embraced me. "Yes, Maggie. I was once in love with Rowan. And many years ago, we had a very sweet, very brief love affair."

When I'd first considered the possibility that they might have been lovers, the gap in their ages had made me squirm. It was easy to imagine any woman falling under Rowan's spell, but knowing Helen's sweet, caring nature—and imagining how beautiful she must have been when she and Rowan first met—I could understand how he might have fallen under hers as well.

"Isn't it hard? Being around him every day? And not being . . . with him?"

"We're much happier as loving friends. We each hold a special place in the other's heart, but we discovered very quickly that I wasn't the right woman for him."

"I'm not sure there is a right woman for Rowan."

"Of course there is. I don't know if it's you, Maggie, but if you could make each other happy—even for the few short weeks left in the season—that would be something."

"Yeah. A miracle."

"Miracles can happen," Helen said firmly. "Just look at *Brigadoon*."

"That's a musical, Helen. Miracles always happen in musicals."

"Because they're a reflection of life. With all its impossible possibilities."

CHAPTER 24
FRIENDSHIP

MISERY LOVES COMPANY. FOR the last week, Kalma and I had ended every evening sitting together in the lounge, bitching about the show. That night was no exception.

"Look at him." Kalma glared at Nick who was bellowing with laughter at something Lou had just said and slopping beer over Maya in the process. "Asshole."

That pretty much summed up my impression of Nick, too. Which made it hard for me to play Helping Professional and suggest she search for his wounded inner child. Ashley and Richard might have been able to overcome their differences, but for Kalma and Nick, working together had only deepened their mutual dislike.

"Did you know he has a kid?" Kalma demanded.

"I didn't even know he was married."

"He's not. But he has a baby daughter. Bobbie told me. You can guess what kind of a father he is."

And why Rowan had cast him as Billy.

"I keep telling myself to forget Nick and sing to Billy," Kalma continued. "Julie recognizes that all the macho crap is just a defense mechanism. But then I start singing 'If I Loved You' and there's Nick smirking at me and I just want to puke."

"Please tell me it's not that bad when I sing 'You'll Never Walk Alone.'"

"God, no!" Kalma exclaimed. "But I'm just so glad he's dead that I'm probably not a good judge."

"Maybe that's how we should play the scene. You laughing gleefully, me singing a cheery version of 'You'll Never Walk Alone' . . ."

"And we skip off arm in arm into the sunset." Kalma grinned. "It'd be worth it to see Rowan's face."

"He'd kill us."

Her grin vanished. "He might kill me anyway. During rehearsals, I'll nod and smile when Sarah asks whether someone can hit you and not hurt you, but I will not do it on opening night." She leaned closer and whispered, "I've written something else."

"I don't want to know about it. I'm already on Rowan's shit list."

"How many life histories are you up to now?"

"Don't ask. At least, he's stopped suggesting I get Kevin to help me."

Kalma glowered. "As if you need a man to help you understand Nettie. All you have to do is look at the two pairs of women. There's Julie and Carrie, who both need a man to feel complete. And Mrs. Mullin and Nettie who are managing just fine without one."

"Mrs. Mullin still wants Billy," I pointed out.

"Because he's good for business."

"And in bed."

"Okay, maybe. But she'll find another guy to fill her bed. Whereas Nettie—"

"Probably snuggles up to a lobster pot at night."

"Whereas Nettie," Kalma repeated sternly, "is independent. An Athena."

"So now I'm a Greek goddess?"

Kalma rolled her eyes. "It's an archetype, Maggie."

"And that helps me create her life story . . . how?"

Kalma's mug thudded onto the bar. "Because she's seen enough bad marriages that she chooses to remain single."

Her vehemence made me wonder if she was talking about Nettie's life or hers.

"Of course," Kalma continued, "a woman usually has the qualities of several archetypes. If Nettie has a strong strain of Aphrodite, there's always the chance that she chose to go for love like Julie and it blew up in her face. Or maybe she let the guy go and regretted it later."

I slowly lowered my mug of ale.

"Either of those scenarios could work," Kalma said. "It might be cool. That way, when Nettie sings 'You'll Never Walk Alone,' she's speaking from experience. Trying to help Julie survive like she has. I mean, it's pretty obvious when you think about it."

"It should have been," I replied.

Inspired by Kalma, I decided to have another go at Nettie's life history. I even took the Goddess Wheel quiz in one of the books she insisted on giving me. Once for Nettie and once for me.

It was profoundly depressing to discover that a fictional character's life was more in balance than mine. With a twenty-point spread between my top and bottom scores, my Goddess Wheel was decidedly wobbly.

My self-esteem took a second hit as I flipped through another of Kalma's books. My Goddess Wheel score suggested I had issues surrounding motherhood and my place in the community. Now it seemed I also had trust issues, a fear of rejection, and an inability to form meaningful relationships with women. The Aphrodite in me sought men who were complex, creative, and emotional; the Athena chose companions, heroes, or father figures.

I slammed the book shut. Told myself it was all bullshit. Reluctantly admitted that I did have trust issues, no female friends until I came here, and a string of personal and professional rejections. And I was currently attracted to a man who was complex, creative, emotional, often companionable, occasionally heroic, and intermittently fatherly. And a good cook.

"Shit."

I studied my responses again, lingering over my low Demeter score. My stomach lurched as I realized that I'd never called my mother back about the beach. It was far too late to call her now, but I hurried onto the porch to check for messages.

Her first just asked me to call. Her second reminded me that I'd promised her an answer this week and the week was nearly over. Her third had come in at 4:30. All she said was, "Maggie. Call me. We need to talk." Her voice sounded strained rather than angry. As if she were holding back some unwanted emotion. That was nothing new, but it didn't bode well for our conversation, especially since I couldn't give her a definite answer until I learned the results of my interviews.

I turned off the phone and the clamor of my inner goddesses. As I walked out of the sitting room, I nearly collided with Sarah. I let out a startled gasp and chuckled at our mishap. Then I took in her swollen eyes and red nose. Before I could say anything, she burst into tears.

I hustled her to my room. Eyeing the mess of papers and books on my bed, I pulled her down onto Nancy's and hugged her hard, murmuring the kind of soothing inanities people always murmur at such moments: "Let it all out. I'm right here. Don't be afraid. Everything will be all right."

Abruptly, I realized that I was mouthing Nettie-ish platitudes, just as I had that night with Rowan. To my astonishment, though, Sarah's sobs dwindled. I released her long enough to retrieve the trusty Kleenex box. She blew her nose and stared miserably at the floor.

"Is this about the ballet?" I asked.

She got out the words "I'm so awful" before succumbing to tears once more.

"No, you're not," I assured her.

But I understood why she felt that way. After stumbling over a bit of choreography during today's run-through, Sarah had gotten flustered and the ballet went rapidly downhill. As soon as it was over, she fled the theatre with Rowan in hot pursuit.

They returned ten minutes later. Sarah was calm by then. It was Rowan who looked upset. Maybe that was the reason for his odd behavior at Helen's. I wasn't the only performer who was struggling or the only one that Rowan was struggling to help. But I'd made it all about me and babbled that wild confession to Helen.

Thrusting aside that embarrassing memory, I flung my arm around Sarah's shoulders and said, "You did fine the other afternoon. When you and Ronnie were rehearsing in the Smokehouse with Mei-Yin."

"You watched us?"

"Bernie and I peeked through the windows. The ballet looked good."

"You're just saying that."

"No, I'm not. You were nervous today. Performing in front of everybody for the first time."

"If I can't dance in front of the cast, I'll never be able to perform in front of an audience."

"You've been performing *The Sea-Wife* for three weeks."

"I don't have to do anything in that. But the ballet . . . everyone will be watching *me*. And if I make a fool of myself—"

"Rowan would never let that happen."

Sarah's head came up. "That's what he said."

"See?"

"I didn't believe him."

"Well, you should. God knows I'm counting on him to help me hit that damn high G."

That wrested a tiny smile from her. It quickly faded. "I've watched the movie about a hundred times and—"

"Well, there's your problem. You can't compare yourself to a professionally trained dancer. Besides, I hate that Louise. She's so fakey dramatic. You're a much better actress."

Sarah's smile transformed her face. She looked luminous, almost beautiful.

"Stay just like that," I commanded.

I dragged her off the bed to the full-length mirror on the back of the door. "See how your face shines? How sweet and hopeful you look? That's Louise. Right there."

For an instant, I thought she saw it, too. Then she frowned and wiped her wet cheeks. "I'm just shiny because I've been crying."

"Trust me. I saw it." As she flopped back on the bed, I added, "You're miles ahead of me. I don't believe half the stuff Nettie says. And it shows. But in your ballet and your scene with Julie, every emotion feels real. You *are* Louise."

"Rowan said that, too." She peered at me suspiciously. "Did he talk to you about me?"

"Rowan barely talks to me about me."

"Because he knows you'll come through."

"From your lips to God's ears," I said in my broadest Bernie accent.

Sarah giggled, then sighed. "Poor Grandpa. He was so worried today."

I nodded. While Rowan was outside with Sarah, I'd sat in the green room with Bernie. He'd questioned his decision to let Sarah audition, blamed himself for failing her—and invoked Rowan's name like a mantra: Rowan will know what to do, Rowan will help her, Rowan will convince her she can be wonderful.

For a little while, Rowan had. Then—as Nancy and I had discovered that first week—Sarah's newfound confidence had leached away.

I wished Helen were here; Sarah could use a blessing. Instead, I offered a poor substitute.

"We're going to make a pact," I told her. "If one of us sees the other getting down on herself, she has to say, 'Knock it off. Believe what you're doing and you're going to be great.' Okay?"

"Okay."

We bumped fists. As I walked her to her room, I whispered, "Things will be better tomorrow. We just have to keep plugging away. And—"

"Keep our chins up?"

God, I was doing it again.

"It sounds stupid, but it's true," Sarah assured me solemnly. "Things *will* look better in the morning. And if we don't lose heart and keep our chins up and trust Rowan—"

"And ourselves."

Sarah struck a pose and softly sang, "We'll never walk alone."

"Out of the mouths of fucking babes," I muttered.

Sarah did a little shimmy, breasts and booty shaking. "No one's ever called me a babe before."

I cuffed her across the back of the head. "Go to bed, Babe."

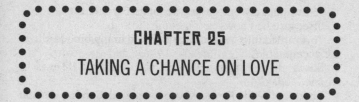

CHAPTER 25
TAKING A CHANCE ON LOVE

AFTER A BLISSFULLY DREAMLESS NIGHT, I awoke refreshed and clearheaded. I ate breakfast with the gang, all of whom commented on my newfound cheerfulness. I called my mother, carefully choosing the hour when I knew she'd be grocery shopping, and left a message on the home phone, apologizing for not calling sooner, offering the interviews as an excuse, and promising to call Monday to let her know how they went. Then I returned to my room and started scribbling Nettie's life history. Again.

I trimmed twenty years off her age. Decided that men enjoyed her humor and women admired her common sense. I made her father a whaler who left on a voyage and never returned, and concluded that his stories of faraway places fueled Nettie's imagination and dreams of a better life. I kept the luncheon shack, added a ne'er-do-well boyfriend who dumped her for a rich girl, and killed off her mother with a bout of pneumonia that forced Nettie to pick up the reins of the business at sixteen.

Before I could second-guess myself, I drove to the theatre, slid the pages under Rowan's door, and raced back to the hotel. Almost immediately, I succumbed to a fit of nerves, wondering what he'd think of my efforts. I distracted myself by ironing my business suit and tidying up the room in anticipation of Nancy's arrival for the closing night of *The Sea-Wife*. I tried to review Nettie's scenes with fresh eyes, but realizing I'd never be able to concentrate until I'd talked with Rowan, I slung my gear into the car and drove to the theatre.

As I pulled into the parking lot, I saw him sitting at one of the picnic tables. He immediately rose and strode down the walkway, my life history fluttering in his hand.

I slid out of the car and started toward him, feeling like a Death Row inmate walking the green mile to the electric chair. I told myself I was acting ridiculous, but when I saw his serious expression, my heart sank.

"You hated it." My voice sounded as forlorn as a little kid's whose crayon drawing was about to be consigned to the garbage can instead of proudly displayed on the refrigerator.

"What did *you* think of it?" Rowan asked.

"It's more me than Nettie," I admitted.

"Possibly." A slow smile blossomed on his face. "But it was real. And it was good."

The wave of relief left me giddy. Then I swung my carryall at him and shouted, "You big faker!"

He scampered backward, laughing. I pursued him, still swinging my bag. He danced out of the way of one blow, ducked under another, and neatly snatched the bag from my hands. When he lifted it over his head, I charged in for the kill. He backpedaled, using the bag to deflect my punches. Not that they would have done much damage; I was laughing too hard at his gyrations. He looked like an absurd combination of Rocky Balboa and the Lucky Charms leprechaun.

He backed into the wall of the barn with a sudden "oof" that choked off his laughter. It was still in his eyes, though, and in the smile that replaced his momentary look of surprise. I smacked my palms on his shoulders, pinning him against the barn, and demanded, "Give up?"

His smile fled. He clutched my bag to his chest. His tongue flicked out to wet his lips.

"Maggie . . ."

I leaned forward and pressed my mouth to his.

I felt his quick intake of breath, the rise and fall of the bag trapped between our bodies. But he remained utterly still, his lips unresponsive.

I stepped back, stunned by my impulsive act and by his reaction. Tiny sparks flashed in his eyes, like sunbeams dancing off damp leaves. I watched them, mesmerized, wondering if he was as unsure as I was about the wisdom of taking this any further. Maybe he was angry that it had taken me so long to act. Maybe he didn't want me any more.

His chest rose and fell with his quickened breathing. The heavy canvas of my carryall shuddered in his trembling hands. He was fighting for control, I realized, struggling to keep his power leashed. Honoring his promise never to use it to force me to do something I didn't want.

"Yes," I whispered.

He tossed my carryall to the ground and pulled me into his arms. His mouth was as hard as the fingers knotted in my hair. Then it softened, clinging to mine, demanding more. His tongue slipped between my lips, smooth as satin one moment, and the next, rough as sandpaper. When I let mine tease against it, his power burst free, flooding me with a desire so intense that my knees buckled.

His hands slid over my bottom, and he lifted me. I tried to wrap my legs around him, but after one feeble attempt, I just hung there, dangling in the air like a rag doll.

Suddenly, his body stiffened and his head jerked toward the parking lot. Frustration stabbed me; I couldn't tell if it was his or mine or both.

Very carefully, he set me on my feet. For a moment, his hands lingered on my waist, steadying me. Then he stepped back, a grimace twisting his mouth.

"The crew."

Seconds later, I heard the faint crunch of gravel. Reinhard's SUV pulled into the lot, followed moments later by Lee's pickup.

I fought the urge to seize his hand and drag him up the stairs to his apartment. Unsatisfied desire warred with the realization that the staff would sense our lovemaking, that Rowan's power could fill the entire theatre with his passion—and the very practical consideration that I wasn't on any form of birth control and had no condoms.

I managed a shaky smile. "Bad timing."

"Very."

"Rain check?"

A dizzying wave of desire washed over me. "Tonight," he whispered. "After strike."

I nodded.

"After all this time, what's another . . . eleven hours?"

"An eternity."

He cocked his head. "There's always the dinner break."

"With everyone at the picnic tables listening to my screams of pleasure wafting through the skylights?"

"I could stuff a sock in your mouth," he volunteered.

"It's sweet of you to offer."

We grinned at each other. As he pressed my bag into my hands, his fingertips caressed mine, a teasing promise of future pleasure. Then he shook his finger with mock severity.

"We leave the cast party at the stroke of midnight. Understood?"

"Yes, Cinderella."

CHAPTER 26
THE PARTY'S OVER

I DIDN'T REMEMBER MUCH OF THAT MATINEE; I probably floated through it with a goofy smile on my face. After I changed, I gobbled a few mouthfuls of Chinese food and hurried to the parking lot, fending off questions by explaining I had a quick errand to run.

Dale's only pharmacy carried a surprising variety of condoms, considering the town's size. Nothing like New York, of course, where I would have had a choice of flavors, colors, and graphic designs. I grabbed an assortment of Trojans: ribbed, lubricated, non, ultra thin, extra large. Faced with the prospect of presenting all those boxes to a cashier who looked about twelve, I put them back on the shelf and purchased a convenient pleasure pack instead. And the box of Magnums. Hope springs eternal.

On the way back to the theatre, I stopped in at the hotel to ensure that my mother had received my earlier message. She had. And left three increasingly terse ones for me. The last simply said, "Maggie. Call me. Today."

I found it incredible—and incredibly annoying—that she could turn a proposed week at the beach into a crisis. I checked the time and reluctantly booted up my laptop to Skype her.

I barely got out, "Hey, Mom," before she said, "I called you yesterday."

"Yeah, I know. I'm sorry I—"

"At HelpLink."

My stomach churned, a sickening whirl of chicken with snow peas and bile.

"Oh."

"That's it? 'Oh?'"

"Look, I—"

"A strange woman picked up your extension. She didn't even recognize your name."

"Probably new," I mumbled.

"She put me on hold, and I sat there for ages. Ages! Not knowing whether she was just an idiot or whether something had happened to you."

"I was going to—"

"And when the supervisor finally picked up, she told me that you'd been fired in—"

"Let go," I corrected.

"In May! When were you going to tell me? Were you *ever* going to tell me?"

"I didn't want to worry you."

"I was already worried! You've been acting strange all summer. Nervous and evasive. I'm not an idiot, Maggie."

No, I was. I should have foreseen this possibility. She'd never called me at HelpLink before, but then, she'd never needed to. If I'd just agreed to go to the beach when she'd first suggested it, I could have avoided this debacle.

As I started to apologize, she said, "You're not even in New York, are you?"

For just a second, I hesitated. But that was enough.

"Oh, God. I was right. You've joined some New Age cult. Like Leila."

"I have not joined a cult, I swear."

Another silence. Clearly, she was waiting for me to tell her what I *was* doing. As I frantically debated coming clean or concocting another lie, she said, "No. Of course not." Her voice sounded flat now, and weary. "You're doing theatre again."

I mustered my courage and said, "Yes."

"Where?"

"Up in Vermont. At this little theatre—"

"Not the Crossroads?"

For a moment, I was too shocked to respond.

"The Crossroads?" I repeated to buy myself time. Time to think, to make sense of the impossibility that my mother had heard of a theatre few people in southern Vermont knew existed—and sounded terrified by the prospect that I was working there.

"Why would you think I'd be at some theatre called the Crossroads?"

This time, the silence lasted so long that I thought she wasn't going to answer. Finally, she said, "Because your father worked there."

I found myself staring up at a spiderweb in the corner of the ceiling, admiring its intricate construction. Beautiful, really, except for the dead fly trapped in its sticky strands.

"Daddy? Did summer stock in Vermont?"

Could she feel the effort required to keep my voice calm? To give it just the right blend of puzzlement and curiosity? To judge from her impatient, "He did summer stock all over," she had no idea I was turning in a Tony Award-winning performance.

"But this was later," she continued. "After he'd been working at A.I. for three years."

A.I. DuPont, the high school where he had worked as an English teacher.

"I thought he'd gotten acting out of his system. Then he suddenly decided to go to Vermont for the weekend. To visit a college friend, he said. And when he came home, he told me he'd been offered a job at the Crossroads Theatre for the summer."

I pictured him driving slowly past the barn. Stopping for coffee at the Chatterbox. Waving to a waitress who called, "Break a leg!" as he hurried off to audition.

"Well, you can imagine how I felt. He'd finally settled down in a real job—a job he liked and was good at—and then . . ." My mother sighed. "In the end, he agreed to finish out the school year and only go up for the second and third shows. And after that, no more acting except in local productions."

"What happened?"

"He went. And when we drove up to see him—"

"Wait. I saw him? At the theatre?"

"Don't you remember? Well, you were only six or seven. And you were doped up on Dramamine because you always got carsick and I wasn't about to drive seven hours with you throwing up the whole way. You slept through most of the show. But you loved the theatre. Especially the big star on the side of the barn."

I squeezed my eyes shut and took a deep breath. "But . . . I still don't understand. You sounded so panicked when you thought I was working at that place."

"It's just . . . it's completely irrational. He was fine when he came home. Happier than he'd been in years. But later . . . things got bad. You know." Her sigh was heavier this time. "Maybe it would have happened anyway. But I always sort of blamed that place. If he hadn't gone there, if it hadn't been such a great experience . . . God, he was always talking about it. The cast. The staff. That damn director."

"What . . . what was wrong with the director?"

"Oh, he was nice enough. And the show was good. Remarkably good, for such a hole-in-the-wall place. But for the next six months, all I heard was 'Rowan this' and 'Rowan that.'"

I clamped my lips together and swallowed down a burning surge of bile. It was possible—just possible—that Rowan could have directed my father. It might have been his first season. Fresh out of college. Or wherever.

I managed a weak laugh. "Maybe I should look this guy up. See if he remembers Daddy."

"I don't want you going anywhere near that place!"

"You said yourself you were irrational about it."

"I don't care! Humor me. Besides, he's probably retired by now."

I took a careful breath. "Retired?"

"Well, he had to have been forty when I met him. And that was—what? Twenty-five years ago?"

My stomach muscles clenched as I fought another wave of nausea.

"But even if he's still there . . . stay out of it, Maggie. Please. There's no point digging up the past. You'll only get hurt."

"Yes."

"I knew I shouldn't have told you."

"No. I'm glad you did."

"I just wanted you to understand why I was so upset."

"I do. It's okay. I'm sorry I didn't tell you sooner. About HelpLink. I'll call you Monday. Let you know how the interviews go."

"You really have interviews? I thought . . . I was afraid you were just making those up."

"No. That was true."

It was everything else about my summer that was a lie.

❧❧

A few women—Kalma, Brit, Bobbie—noticed my distraction and commiserated with me when I explained that my mother had found out that I'd lost my job. Sarah squeezed my hand and whispered, "Things'll look better tomorrow."

I trudged up the stairs to the green room, groping for logical explanations, trying to understand how my mother could have met a man of forty who still looked that age twenty-five years later. I told myself that her memory was faulty, that it had been dark when they met, that Rowan's natural self-assurance made him seem older than he was. But I didn't believe any of it.

Rowan bounded into the green room, full of energy and high spirits. Then his head snapped toward me, an expression of profound shock banishing his excitement. I gripped the back of the battered armchair, fighting for control, but when the pre-show circle formed, I slipped out of the green room and hurried down the hall to the production office. Hearing footsteps behind me, I whirled around and discovered Reinhard.

"Stay away from me!"

He must have heard the hysteria in my voice. Or maybe he could sense it. He was part of this. The secret of the Crossroads. They all were.

Had my father stumbled on that secret? Had they tried to brainwash him the same way they had brainwashed Caren? Only in his case—and mine—it didn't stick. Once he left, the power wore off—and he drifted away.

I'd go crazy if I thought about that, if I allowed wild

speculations to carry me into Helen's realm of "impossible possibilities." There was no time for these questions, no time to process the answers. In five minutes, the curtain would go up. And suddenly, I was pathetically grateful for that.

"I'll be fine," I told Reinhard. "Just some personal stuff I have to work out."

I eased past him and returned to the green room. I didn't trust myself to look at Rowan. As soon as Reinhard called places, I joined the stream of cast members hurrying backstage. Safely screened from Rowan by their bodies, I escaped into the world of *The Sea-Wife*.

I turned my resentment against the swaggering Craigies. Directed my suspicions toward the strange woman who had joined their household. Took out my anger on the new schoolteacher who thought he was so much wiser than the rest of us. Channeled my roiling fear about my family's past into concern for my stage family.

Back in the dressing room after the show, my fierceness evaporated. I felt completely disengaged from the closing night high, the good-natured moaning about strike, the hugs and tears and congratulations. Every action felt slow, as I if were moving underwater. I was still hanging up my costume when the rest of the women were removing their makeup, pulling on my street clothes as they hurried upstairs for strike.

When their voices faded, loneliness threatened to choke me. Then I heard footsteps in the hallway. I let out my breath a moment later as Nancy peeked into the dressing room. I leaped out of my chair. My eyes closed as I hugged her. When I opened them again, I found Rowan standing in the doorway.

Nancy must have felt me tense. She reared back, then noticed the direction of my gaze.

"Hi, Rowan." She eased free from my embrace, but I clung to her hand like a frightened child.

"Hello, Nancy," Rowan replied, his gaze fixed on me. "Maggie, I think we need to talk."

"I have strike."

"One pair of hands won't be missed."

Nancy squeezed my hand. "Do you want to talk now? Or do you need some time?"

Rowan's mouth tightened. He wasn't used to the staff questioning him, never mind a cast member. But if Nancy felt his flash of annoyance, she gave no indication.

Knowing that no amount of time would be enough, I said, "It's okay. But would you wait for me? At the hotel?"

"Of course." She hesitated at the doorway and turned to Rowan. "I don't know what's happened, but I think you should be very careful what you say and do in the next few minutes."

He regarded her with open astonishment, then nodded stiffly. With a final glance at me, Nancy walked out.

"Not here," I said before Rowan could speak.

Cast and crew swarmed over the stage. Ignoring Reinhard's worried gaze, I strode through the chaos, threw open the stage door, and walked to the picnic area without looking back to see if Rowan was following. I chose the table closest to the theatre, the bench facing the woods. I wanted him to sit where the light from the walkway lamps would shine on his face.

As he slid onto the bench opposite me, I laced my fingers tightly together atop the table. His hands moved toward mine, stopped, then retreated.

"What happened, Maggie?"

The kindness in his voice made me ache. I hated that.

I stared down at my hands, listening to the low buzz of conversation wafting through the back doors of the theatre, the rapid thud of hammers, and Lee's voice calling out occasional directions to the crew. Then I forced myself to look up.

The lamplight revealed the concern on his face. And something else I couldn't identify.

"You were so happy this afternoon. And now it's gone."

Then I recognized the emotion I had not been able to name. Sadness. So deep it verged on grief. I didn't know whether it stemmed from his emotions or his perception of mine. But I refused to let it sway me from seeking the answers I needed.

"There are some things I have to ask you. And I need you to tell me the truth."

"I've always told you . . . as much of the truth as I could."

"Do you know a man named Jack Sinclair?"

The lines between his brows deepened, but he seemed puzzled rather than shocked. "He worked here. Years ago."

"And you were his director?"

His nod destroyed my ridiculous hope that his father had preceded him here, that Rowan Mackenzie, Sr. had been the man my mother had met.

"What does Jack Sinclair have to do with—?"

"Did you know he was married?"

"Yes. And he had a child, I think. A little—" His eyes flew wide as he stared at me. "You're Jack's daughter?"

I nodded. "My mother changed our names. After the divorce."

"Why didn't you tell me?"

"I never knew he worked here. Until a few hours ago."

"Your mother?"

"She found out I'd lost my job. And when I confessed that I was doing theatre again, the first thing out of her mouth was, 'You're not at the Crossroads, are you?'"

Rowan's gaze slid away.

"The thing that scared me was how panicked she sounded. She tried to explain it away. Said she was irrational about this place. Because of everything that happened afterward."

"What?" he demanded. "What happened?"

I described that last year with my father. The happy family reunion. His determination to make things work. And then the slow unraveling of a marriage and a life: the dreams that haunted him, the obsessive research into New Age religion and mysticism, the arguments that alternated with the ominous silences.

I described the drinking and the drug use, the first to keep the dreams at bay, the second to encourage them. The days he missed work. The weekends he raced up to Philly or New York to do research in the libraries there. The weekends he simply disappeared with no explanation at all. Losing his job at the high school. Bouncing from one job to another, each paying less than the last, each lasting a shorter while, until he simply stopped working altogether.

That was the worst time. When he had no job to anchor him and very little family life to cling to. When he locked himself in the basement with his precious books. Or vanished for a week, two weeks, a month, returning elated at some new discovery or utterly dejected. Running through the bank account and credit cards until my mother cut him off. Running through the therapists she couldn't afford, the meds he wouldn't take. And through it all, his increasingly frantic assertions that he wasn't losing his mind, that everyone was just too narrowminded to look beyond conventional religion and medicine and wisdom to seek the ancient beliefs and exalted experiences that would lead—must surely lead—to enlightenment.

I told him everything I had gleaned from my mother over the years, my voice as calm as if I were talking about a stranger. Which is what Daddy had been and still was. I didn't offer my memories of those final years; they were too clouded by confusion and unhappiness to be reliable. Perhaps my mother's were as well. Certainly they were tainted by her sense of betrayal, her anger and frustration and fear. But she was the only witness I had.

Except for the man sitting opposite me. The man who had known my father during his last summer of happiness. Who might possess the missing piece of the puzzle. Who sat unmoving, unspeaking throughout my recitation, staring down at his clasped hands.

When I finished, I waited for him to say something. When he didn't, I asked, "What are the odds? Me showing up at the same theatre my father worked at."

"Better than you'd think." He looked up then, his expression grave but calm. "I call to them, you see. Just like I called to you after Helen's heart attack. And they come here."

"Who?"

"The Mackenzies. Descendants of the original family who owned this farm."

When I picked up that bed and breakfast guide, when I chose the turn to Dale, when I slowed down to examine the barn—each time, I'd thought instinct had prompted my decisions. Just as I'd believed my love of the theatre—my desire to return to that happy period of my life—had prompted me to audition. But it had been Rowan all along. Calling me—calling all of us—who were bound to him by virtue of a blood tie I hadn't even known existed.

With as much calm as I could muster, I asked, "So we're related? You and I?"

"No! I merely . . . took the name."

Again, I waited for an explanation. When none was forthcoming, I asked, "But why do you call them? If the owners of the farm and your folk were enemies."

"Because I am cursed."

His expression was too serious for it to be a joke. But my nerves betrayed me and I blurted out, "You violated some ancient Indian burial ground or something?"

"No. I violated a girl's innocence."

His calm gaze never wavered as he uttered that damning statement. I tried to square the man I knew—the man I thought I knew—with the one sitting across from me who had just admitted to raping a girl. Then I realized he might be speaking metaphorically. I prayed he was.

"I can't believe you would commit rape."

He looked down at his hands again and cleared his throat. "Thank you for that." Then his head came up and his eyes seared me. "But I don't deserve your good opinion. I used my power to seduce her. To overcome her fear and her reluctance. And no matter how willingly she came to me, how many times she sought me out and enjoyed what I gave her, the fact remains that I abused my power—and her innocence—simply because I wanted her."

My hands had come up to clutch my arms, shielding myself from his words, from his act, from the revulsion that shuddered through my body.

"I told you—the day of our picnic—that my arrogance and selfishness had led me to hurt people when I was young. She was one of them. There were others, of course. Who suffered because I could not offer them the friendship—the love—that they wanted. Needed."

I thought of Janet's blistering accusations about Rowan's inability to love, of the sadness and tenderness on Helen's face when she described their brief affair.

"The consequences of my crime against that girl were very heavy. For her and for me. I left her, you see. At summer's end. And when I returned, I learned that she had borne a child. And that both had died during the birth."

I studied him, hoping for some sign of distress. All I found was weariness. And although I knew his ability to hide his emotions, I exclaimed, "Did you feel anything at all about what had happened? About what you'd done?"

"She asked me that, too. Her mother."

He never spoke the girl's name. Did he even remember it? Or did he refuse to say it because that would bring the tragedy too close?

"I told her that I . . . regretted the deaths."

"Two people were dead and you were regretful?"

"You asked for the truth, Maggie, and that's what I'm trying to give you."

Although his voice was still calm, I glimpsed genuine grief on his face. He looked down at his clasped hands. When he raised his head again, all traces of emotion had been banished.

"I felt regret," he said without inflection. "But if not for what happened afterward, I would have walked away and forgotten about them."

I shook my head, unable to believe what I was hearing.

"That's the kind of . . . creature I was. But I am not like that now. I have lived with the sorrow and the guilt and the shame of my actions for many years."

Janet's voice and Helen's warred in my mind, Janet's claiming that he was incapable of change, Helen's affirming that he was.

"I did not—could not—feel such things then. Perhaps if I had . . ." His mouth twisted in a bitter smile. " 'Perhaps' holds no weight. And regrets cannot change the past. I was responsible for their deaths and I was cursed. By her mother. You probably don't believe in curses—or in the witches who cast them—but they exist, Maggie. I know. That girl was the heart of their family, a being of light and music and joy. When I stole her from them, I stole those things as well. And brought them grief and sorrow."

His gaze had become distant, his voice an eerie singsong, as if he were repeating the actual words of this "curse."

"What I stole, I must return. What I brought, I must take away. What I had never felt—"

He broke off abruptly. Then he said, "Her curse bound me to the Mackenzies. To this farm. To this theatre."

I could not accept that a witch had cursed him. But I could believe that the words of a distraught mother had awakened his sense of responsibility and guilt, that an imaginative mind like his could have played those words over and over, twisting and distorting them, until he was convinced that he could neither leave this place nor abandon the work that was—for him—both punishment and penance.

Whether or not I believed in the curse, he surely did. It explained his anger at being held hostage to this place. It explained why I never saw him in town, why he cast people according to need rather than talent, why he took so seriously his responsibility to his cast. But it didn't explain why my mother feared this place and blamed it for my father's breakdown.

Rowan nodded, as if I had voiced those thoughts aloud. But again, he forced me to ask.

"Did something happen to my father that summer?"

He let out his breath as if he had been bracing himself for that question. "Yes. Something similar to Caren's experience at Midsummer. But I helped him recover. And—"

"You brainwashed him?"

He grimaced. "I helped him forget. And Helen kept in touch with him for months afterward. To make sure he was all right."

"Helen? Not you?"

"I had to use a great deal of power to help Jack. And I knew that could create a bond between us. So I thought it best to . . . keep my distance. But I thought . . . Helen said he sounded . . . fine."

"He was an actor! Didn't it ever occur to you that he was lying?"

Rowan's hesitation gave me the answer he refused to speak.

"How could you just abandon him?"

"If I had known what was happening—if I knew where he was today . . ."

"It's too late," I whispered. "He's lost."

"He was already lost, Maggie."

I shook my head.

"Your father was an unhappy man. Unhappy with himself and unhappy with his life. I know it hurts you to hear that, but it's true. He thought he'd found his purpose, his joy in the theatre, but it wasn't enough. Nothing was ever enough. Not his family, not his work. He was always seeking something more. Even he didn't know what that was. I tried to ease that restlessness, to show him all the good things he had, but—"

"But that wasn't just to help him. You were protecting yourself. Covering up whatever he had seen, whatever secrets he'd exposed."

"He should never have been in the forest that night!"

Rowan rose with such violence that the bench tumbled over. I shrank back, buffeted by the cold blast of his anger and the ragged desperation in his voice.

"What did he see?" I whispered.

As suddenly as it had surfaced, all the violence left him. He stood quite still, his gaze resting on me with an expression that was almost tender.

"He saw what Caren would have seen if I had not stopped her. He saw my folk."

He carefully righted the bench and seated himself, clasping his hands atop the table once more. For a moment longer, he hesitated. Then he raised his eyes to mine.

"We have always been among you. Slipping between moonlight and shadow. Wandering woodland groves and darkened streets. In the Old World and the New. Forever linked by curiosity and envy, by wonder and fear. By blood."

His voice had taken on the lilting cadences of a storyteller. Like my father's when he wove one of his tales about pirate gold or gnomes living under tree roots. And although his expression was as gentle as his voice, a chill spread through my flesh. I wanted to make him stop, to tell him that some secrets should never be revealed.

"We are all around you, but you rarely see us. It's safer that way. For when our paths cross, it is your folk who invariably suffer."

He leaned forward, but somehow, the movement only reinforced my sense that he was far away from me, separated by miles instead of the narrow width of the table.

"Over the centuries, you have called us by many names. The Still Folk. The Blessed Ones. The Prowlies and the People of Peace. The Daoine Sidhe and the Fey. Mostly, though, your folk refer to us as Faeries."

I stared at him. A burble of incredulous laughter escaped me, and I shoved my fist against my mouth. Finally, I whispered, "That's impossible."

"Yes. But it's still true." When I shook my head, he said, "Think, Maggie. Look back on everything you've experienced this summer. Then find another explanation."

His surprising strength. The beauty of his voice. The grace of his movements. The sudden playfulness and the terrifying mask that hid every emotion. His ability to transform a group of rank amateurs into a company of real actors, to transform a mediocre show into something magical.

All those I could explain away. Somehow. Even his strange power to beguile humans and fireflies alike. But to believe that power stemmed from an otherworldly source—that *he* was otherworldly . . . not even human . . .

"No."

I'd seen his wild mood swings. And the scars on his wrists. Maybe he had tried to kill himself after learning of the death of the girl and his child. And failing to do so, sought refuge in this impossible delusion.

And then my carefully constructed arguments collapsed. No matter how hard I tried, I could not explain away the fact that he still looked like the man of forty my mother had met twenty-five years ago.

I shook my head, unable to accept that everything I knew about the world had changed, still seeking refuge in logic and reason even though they could no longer serve me. It was as if I had spent months struggling to complete a jigsaw puzzle, picking up one piece and discarding it for another, trying to force others together when I knew they wouldn't connect, and only now discovered the essential piece that allowed me to see how all the others fit together.

"I'm still the same person I was a minute ago," he said

gently. "With the same flaws, the same strengths. I'm still . . . me."

But he wasn't. He was something new and frightening.

His expression grew remote. "I only told you about myself so that you would understand what happened to your father. May I tell you about that night? Or are you too upset to listen?"

I wasn't sure any of it would make sense, but I had gone too far to stop now.

"From the earliest days of the theatre, we've always taken precautions to ensure that the cast is occupied at Midsummer. The staff realized Jack was not at the restaurant with the others, but his roommate told them that he'd decided to take a drive. Jack was a bit of a loner. It seemed . . . reasonable. But he never made it past the theatre. Maybe he decided to take a walk instead. I don't know. By the time I sensed his presence in the woods . . ."

His brows drew together, and he looked away. With a visible effort, he forced himself to meet my gaze.

"To chance upon one of our kind is dangerous enough for a human. To chance upon an entire clan . . . at Midsummer . . ."

Again, he looked away. And again, he mastered his momentary weakness.

"Eventually, I got him away."

"Eventually?"

"Please listen. Please try to understand. My clan has dozens of members. Most far older and more powerful than I was. Than I am. If I had tried to snatch him away, they might have retaliated. I had to wait. Until they . . . lost interest."

"What did they do to him?" I demanded, my voice shaking.

"At first, they were angry. Because he had intruded on their revels. But soon—"

"They were the intruders! Sneaking into our world and—"

"It was our world first, Maggie. Humans drove us from it. That's one of the reasons there has always been friction between your folk and mine. Why there are rules to discourage . . . fraternization. Which only increases our mutual fascination. That's why their anger faded so quickly.

They began . . . playing with him. Petting him. Teasing him. Heightening their glamour to enthrall him."

My arms ached. I realized they were wrapped around my body again as if to shield me from their cruelty. I remembered my headlong flight through the woods when I heard Rowan singing, the physical sensations that had rocked me in his apartment. And he hadn't even been trying to enthrall me.

My poor father. He hadn't had a chance.

"When they tired of their game—"

"Their game?" I repeated, stung into speech. "Is that what you call it?"

Rowan shook his head wearily. "No. But that's how they viewed it. They left after that. To enjoy their revels elsewhere. When he tried to follow, I restrained him." Rowan hesitated. "He wept. Like a brokenhearted child."

My breath hissed in.

"It gives me no pleasure to tell you these things. But—"

"Go on."

"I carried him to my apartment and lulled him to sleep. For a night and a day and another night, I sat with him, using my power to get him to eat, to drink. To forget."

"Two days?"

"He didn't want to forget, you see. He had found that . . . something more that he'd always been looking for. Forcing him to give it up would have shattered his mind. I had to be careful. And gentle. Coax him into accepting a new reality. Much like the one the staff gave to Caren."

"They're . . . they're faeries, too?"

"No. But they carry the blood. I'm not the only one of my kind who has trespassed in this world."

My mind told me that was only reasonable. But it sickened me to know that these creatures regularly invaded our world, playing with us, seducing us, then discarding us like unwanted toys when they became bored.

"Blood calls to blood. That's how the staff found this place. How the cast does, too."

"But . . . you said it was the Mackenzie blood, that we weren't related . . ."

"The first Mackenzies carried the blood."

My stomach heaved.

"It was strong in the witch. Only three or four generations removed. It's strong in some of the staff as well."

Janet. Reinhard. Helen.

"In the end, Jack accepted the new reality I gave him. If he had been pretending, if he had felt any doubt, I would have sensed it. But still, we watched him carefully. All summer. He was a different person. Relaxed and happy. Mingling with the rest of the cast where before he had been aloof. He even helped them with their roles. Like you did."

Hot tears burned my eyes. I blinked them back.

"And when he left us at the end of the summer, he was eager to go home. To start over again. He was healed. And whole. For the first time in his life."

I could only stare at him, stunned at his monumental arrogance in assuming he had made my father into something better.

"I should have foreseen the possibility that the memories might come back. Realized that he loved them so much that—"

"He didn't love them! If he thought he did, it was because they made him."

"He ran to them with open arms, Maggie."

"I ran to you that day in the woods. That didn't mean I loved you."

Rowan flinched. Then his expression hardened. "I know how to use my power to seduce a human. There's fascination, yes. And excitement. But always, there is fear. And reluctance. Not with Jack. He wanted them. More than he had ever wanted anything in his life."

I pushed myself up, but I had to lean on the table for fear my shaking legs would betray me. "You have no idea what my father wanted from life. And he never had a chance to find out. He was as much a victim as that poor girl you raped."

The mask slipped smoothly into place. This was the true face of Faerie. This blank-faced stranger who knew nothing of kindness or compassion or love. Janet was right. No matter how long Rowan lived among us, he would never be like us.

"You allowed a sensitive man to be tormented and call it caution."

The mask slipped, and I was savagely glad.

"You watched his life and his world crumbling and blame him for it. You manipulated his memories and call it healing. You twisted him into something new and congratulate yourself on making him whole. And then you sent him away and regret that you didn't foresee what might happen to him. To us."

"Should I have abandoned him in the forest?" Rowan demanded. "Stood by while his mind cracked under the weight of that experience? Allowed him to go with them knowing they might toss him aside in the end and leave him even more miserable?"

"You should never have called him here in the first place!"

Rowan shook his head. "He needed me. You all need me. You're unhappy—"

"Maybe we are! But we have the right to try and heal ourselves. The right to choose our own paths, even if we choose the wrong ones. To make mistakes and try to correct them. That's what being human is all about."

"I've helped hundreds of people. Thousands."

"Just because you have the ability to change people doesn't mean you have the right to. It's an abuse of your power."

"No."

"You're the puppet master and we're the puppets who dance and sing—and spread our legs—when you pull the strings."

"No!"

"You cloak it all in colored lights and pretty scenery and kind words. But in the end, you're only using us to expiate your guilt."

His wave of fury sent me stumbling backward. I sat down hard. As he stalked toward me, I slid off the bench, wincing as splinters scraped my thighs.

"You're being completely unfair! And unreasonable." His features twisted in an ugly sneer. "You want to know the truth about your father, but only if it reinforces what you already believe. You want to discover the truth about yourself, but only if it's comfortable. You want me to be your lover and you want me to keep my distance. Well, you can't have it both ways, Maggie! Life isn't that neat. You have to take chances. You have to risk being hurt. Risk being honest. Until you do, you'll never find what you're looking for."

I whirled around and raced for the parking lot.

"That's right. Run away," he called after me, his voice rich with the scorn and arrogance and cruelty of his kind. "That's what you always do. It's a lot easier than facing the truth."

I stopped and slowly turned back to him.

"Try facing the truth about yourself, Rowan. About why you started this theatre. About what *you're* looking for. About your pathetic attempt to act human without bothering to understand us or care about us. It's easy to stand back and play God. Well, take a good, hard look at your life, pal. Maybe then you'll earn the right to lecture me about mine."

I turned my back on him. And the Crossroads Theatre.

ENTR'ACTE
THE JOURNAL OF ROWAN MACKENZIE

Miserable, irrational, ungrateful, self-centered bitch.

Why am I surprised?

It doesn't matter how long you live among them, how well you think you know them. Give them truth and they shudder in revulsion. Heal their pain and they spit in your face.

And they call us capricious.

Jack Sinclair's daughter. What a colossal irony. The old witch must be laughing.

Two hours before I trusted myself to go to the cast party. To smile and hug them and tell them how wonderful they were. They *were* wonderful. I mustn't blame them for her failings. She would only point to that as further evidence of mine.

At least they recognize my achievements. Our achievements. They understand what I'm trying to do here. What I have been doing for one hundred and fifty years.

One hundred and fifty years repudiated in five minutes.

What gives her the right to judge me? She doesn't know me. She has no conception of what it's like to spend centuries among strangers.

Jamie never thought of it as interference. He encouraged me to do this. Yes, it was a penance. An unwelcome one in the beginning. But what choice did I have? To remain aloof and give up all hope of returning home?

Maybe I should talk with Helen. Ask her if someone might misinterpret my work. No. I've already burdened her too much. And the rest of the staff is as gossipy as old women. I've spent half the summer ignoring their speculative glances. And—in Reinhard's case—his outright defiance.

She's a bad influence. On them. And on me.

Now Nancy, there's a woman to admire. Strong. Solid. Reliable. And a far better actor than I ever gave her credit for. That story about the phone call from Mother Graham that left her dear roommate too upset to attend the cast party? Brilliant. And brilliantly underplayed. Within minutes, the whole company was sighing over poor, poor Maggie.

If poor, poor Maggie were here now, I'd cheerfully strangle her. Or fuck her until she screamed. She wouldn't call me a pathetic imitation of a man after that.

Gods. I'm ranting. How humiliating. Did I do that with her? No wonder she walked out.

She'll be back, though. If only to disprove what I said about running away.

The break will do us both good. Give us time to think. Let our tempers cool. When she's calmer, she'll accept the truth. Right now, she's too blinded by what happened to her father. And what happened to her as a result.

Stupid to taunt her. To allow anger and hurt to provoke me. I should have remained calm. Pointed out his flaws. Set her on the path to forgiving him for his neglect. Instead, I gave her the perfect excuse to blame me for her unhappiness and bestow upon him the title of helpless victim.

Jack Sinclair. Now there's a pathetic imitation of a man. A trickster. Like the Jacks in the old tales. Thieves. Giant slayers. Charming, yes. And clever. About everything except himself. But completely self-absorbed. And arrogant and superior. Always making excuses for his failures. Always standing apart, judging

I am not like that.

What happened to Jack was unfortunate, yes. But it doesn't outweigh all the successes. The thousands I have helped over the years. Unless everything they learned here just leached away, too.

No. His was a special case. I did help the others. I am helping them. Look at the letters and e-mails Helen gets. The hundreds of Christmas cards people send every year. I should have told her about them.

And my folk. I should have made her understand just how powerful they are. Even the young ones. Their power burns brighter every year, while mine remains stunted.

And the agony of the iron searing my flesh, my spirit. Feeling my life and my power drain away week after helpless week until they finally removed the collar and bound my wrists and nursed me back to health. Not out of compassion, of course. They simply refused to let me escape so easily.

Would she have listened if I had told her that? Would she have felt a shred of sympathy or pity? Likely, she would have accused me of making excuses and detested me even more.

There are always mistakes. Blunders. Things you regret. People you fail to reach. But my intentions were good. Can't she at least credit me with that?

If I failed Jack

I failed Jack. I saw his neediness, and I turned away. I recognized his fragility, and I didn't protect him. I observed his desperation to grasp the impossible, and I stood by while they ripped apart his soul.

I failed Jack and I've failed his daughter. She is as lost to me now as he is.

But there are others who still need me: Kalma, who is so afraid of showing her vulnerability; Sarah, who cannot recognize her beauty; and Nick, who refuses to acknowledge his feelings or his responsibility to his family.

I cannot allow this incident to blind me to *my* responsibilities. And I cannot keep wondering if she might have been the one to finally lift the curse.

How could I have been so foolish? To imagine that I could love her.

Love makes you soar. Like Alex's music. It provides a refuge when you're tired and disheartened. Like Helen. It's built upon friendship and trust and the knowledge that in the vast emptiness of this world, there is one person who sees you with all your flaws and still accepts you. Like Jamie.

She doesn't accept me. She's never a refuge. And the only thing that soars around her is my blood pressure.

Who could love a woman who scorns your beliefs, your work, your very existence?

Who delights in pointing out your flaws and holding you up to her impossibly rigorous standard of right and wrong.

Who pushes and pushes, but turns on you in a fury when you push back.

Whose anger burns you like iron.

Whose tenderness makes you ache.

Whose laughter is the last thing you conjure before falling asleep and whose face is the first thing you long to see when you open your eyes in.

Oh, gods.

ACT THREE

WHERE DO I GO FROM HERE?

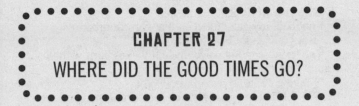

CHAPTER 27
WHERE DID THE GOOD TIMES GO?

DON'T KNOW WHAT I WOULD HAVE DONE without Nancy. After covering for me at the cast party, she sat up with me half the night. I told her that my mother had discovered I was doing theatre again. I even talked about my father's breakdown. Of course, I didn't tell her the rest. How do you tell someone, "My father had a close encounter with a bunch of faeries? And guess what? Rowan's one of them!"

Each time I burst into tears, she held me until I calmed. If her embrace failed to flood me with peace as Helen's did, her strong, skinny arms were a comforting shield against fear and grief. And they were real. She was real. Real and natural and normal.

When I finally cried myself out, she helped me undress and tucked me into bed. And when I woke the next morning, she assured me that I wasn't losing my mind, that anyone would have been overwrought after the events of the last few days, and that I would feel much better after breakfast.

I did feel better— until I walked back into the Bough and found Reinhard in the lobby. The condition of his hair and the worried expression on his face told me he already knew about my confrontation with Rowan.

Nancy stoutly volunteered to hang around as long as I needed her. I hugged her hard and reluctantly urged her to go home. Then I followed Reinhard into the deserted lounge. He motioned me toward a table, but I shook my head and remained standing.

"Are you all right?"

I nodded, my gaze fixed on the worn floorboards.

"But you cannot bear to look at me."

The sadness in his voice made my eyes burn with unshed tears. "Don't do that. It's not fair."

"Maggie . . ."

"No!" I met his gaze and felt a reluctant pang of sympathy when I took in the heavy bags under his eyes. But I kept my voice firm as I said, "Just say what you have to say."

Reinhard sighed. "In light of . . . last night's events, Rowan suggested that you might wish to skip rehearsal and drive to New York this morning."

Rowan might be too cowardly to face me, but I was made of stronger stuff.

"I'll leave as planned. At the dinner break."

"If you are this upset, you will gain nothing from rehearsal. And your anger will affect the rest of the cast. And Rowan."

He was right, of course, but I was damned if I was going to run away. Not after the taunts Rowan had thrown at me last night.

"This is not a competition between you and Rowan to prove who is stronger."

"He's a faery. Pretty hard for a measly human to compete with that."

"He still has feelings, Maggie. You are not the only one who is hurting."

"Good!"

Reinhard drew himself up, as stiff and formal as the day I met him. "If this is your attitude, I cannot permit you to attend rehearsal. I have the welfare of the entire cast to consider."

"Rowan might sense how I'm feeling, but no one in the cast will."

Reinhard shook his head. "You are very bad at hiding your feelings."

"Just watch me."

Rowan was sitting in the house when I walked into the theatre. His gaze burned into me as I marched down the aisle. When I passed his row without speaking, I heard the creak of his seat, the muffled thud of his footsteps.

"Maggie."

Calling upon my inner Meryl Streep, I summoned an expectant expression and turned toward him. I don't know why I thought I'd find some evidence of strain; unlike me, he was adept at hiding his feelings. But his air of mild puzzlement infuriated me.

"Didn't Reinhard speak with you? About—"

"I told him I'd leave at the dinner break. Is that a problem?"

Rowan studied me. "That remains to be seen."

"Was there anything else?"

He shook his head. But as I reached the steps to the stage, he asked, "Will you be coming back?"

"I have a contract, don't I?"

"That's not a good enough reason," he replied, just as he had that day in the meadow when I told him I had nothing to go home for.

"I'll be back." My shaking voice undermined the Terminator effect.

"If you can't bear to be near me . . ."

The slight tremor in his voice gave me the will to master mine.

"I'll be back," I repeated.

"Fine." His voice was cool now, and as remote as his expression. "If you change your mind, please call Reinhard. We'll need to choose another actress to play Nettie."

I strode into the wings where I glanced around to ensure I was alone before beating my fist against the wall. Then I took a number of deep breaths and got ready to turn in the performance of a lifetime.

I succeeded in convincing my cast mates that I'd recovered from my argument with my mother. But my performance in "June Is Bustin' Out All Over" was so manic that it felt like I was welcoming the storm of the century rather than the onset of summer.

"You'll Never Walk Alone" was worse. Big surprise. Any Julie hearing my words of comfort would have impaled herself on the nearest harpoon. By the third time we ran it, I sounded about as hopeful as the Grim Reaper. Rather than screech out the high G and shatter Kalma's eardrums yet again, I dropped an octave for the final line, surprising Alex so much that he gawked at me from the pit.

Without waiting for Rowan's notes or the dinner break, I fled as soon as the scene ended. Reinhard watched me go without comment.

I bombed at my interviews.

Only minutes after each began, flop sweat erupted from every pore. My manner veered from stiff formality to syrupy warmth and finally to a desperation as palpable as the waves of heat rising from the city streets.

I felt none of the relief I'd expected at being back on helping professional home turf. The office milieu felt alien, as if I'd been absent for years instead of months. The corporate-cubicle vibe at the United Way made my skin crawl, the "one heartbeat from closing our doors" shabbiness of the victims' assistance center depressed me. And as Reinhard had pointed out, I was very bad at hiding my feelings.

When I reluctantly reported back to my mother, I braced myself for a gusty sigh or a disappointed silence. Instead, she said, "Neither of them sounds like a good match for you. Wait for the right opportunity. It may seem pretty bleak right now, but you'll see the light at the end of the tunnel eventually."

Which was so reminiscent of the lyric in "You'll Never Walk Alone" about the golden light at the end of the storm that I might have laughed if I hadn't been so close to tears. Again. All I needed was a reminder to keep my chin up and walk on with hope in my heart.

"Something else will come along," Mom said. "Keep your chin up."

At which point I hurriedly signed off.

Yet I felt better. Not because she'd said anything profound, but simply because she'd offered support instead of criticism. Clearly, platitudes worked on me as well as they'd worked on Sarah. And just as clearly, Rowan had been right to take me to task for looking down my nose at them—and

at Nettie. Hard to say whether his crystalline perception
stemmed from his directorial skill or his faery power.

On the long drive back to Dale, I realized that what Rowan
was mattered less than what he had done—to my father, to
me, to everyone who had ever been dragged, unsuspecting,
to the theatre. Reluctantly, I admitted that he *was* helping
some of my cast mates. But they might just as easily have
discovered what they needed without his interference.

Perhaps my father's dreadful experience was an isolated
incident. But if there were others who had suffered lasting
damage because of the Crossroads Theatre, I had to find out
about them and make Rowan acknowledge the harm he was
doing.

But what could I do if he refused? Go to the police? Write
a blog? Find an exorcist?

Think about it tomorrow, Scarlett.

There were three weeks left in the season. I had stayed
this long because I had nothing to go home to, because I
was too intrigued by the many mysteries of the Crossroads
Theatre, and—in the wake of Saturday's confrontation—
because I was determined to refute Rowan's accusation that
I was always running away. Now, I had a more compelling
reason to stay. Maybe I wouldn't figure out what the hell
I was supposed to do with my life, but if I could prevent
Rowan Mackenzie from ever hurting anyone the way he had
hurt my father, I would have accomplished something this
summer.

CHAPTER 28
YA GOTTA LOOK OUT FOR YOURSELF

I ARRIVED BACK IN DALE to find my cast mates streaming out of the Bough. A chorus of voices eagerly inquired about my interviews. When I gave them the bad news, there were a lot of sympathetic groans and a few assurances that I'd done better than I imagined. Sarah said, "Don't get down on yourself." Lou loudly asserted that my interviewers were assholes.

"I'm okay. Really. But how come you're out so early? Dinner break's at six."

"Rowan let us go so he could run 'Soliloquy' with Nick," Lou said.

I glanced around the circle of glum faces and sighed. Nick had always been able to capture Billy's swagger, but the rare moments of tenderness and vulnerability seemed beyond him. At best, he was wooden. At worst, petulant and insincere. But who was I to point fingers?

"Look, the song just cuts a little too close to home," Lou said.

"I'll say." Bobbie shook her head in obvious disgust. "He gets his girlfriend pregnant. Dumps her. And hasn't seen his daughter since she was born."

"She's probably better off," Kalma muttered.

Lou's face had gotten redder and redder, but all he said was, "Come on . . ."

Kalma turned on him in a fury. "How can you defend him?"

"I just think—"

"He doesn't even pay child support!" Bobbie exclaimed. "Are you telling me you think that's okay?"

Lou's head swung from one to the other, like a bull confronted by twin matadors. "I'm just saying it hasn't been easy for him, either."

"Yeah, right," Bobbie said with withering scorn. "It's hard to screw around and then walk when things get tough."

"That's not—"

"Well, if you're all right with that, Lou Mancini, you are not the man for me!"

Bobbie stormed off. Lou hurried after her, crying, "Baby, wait! Listen!"

Kalma watched them go, then surveyed Gary and Bernie through narrowed eyes. "Typical. You guys always stick together."

"Hey!" Gary protested. "I'm the one who got dumped, remember?"

"And I was married for fifty-two years!"

"Yeah. Well. You're the exceptions."

"Let's eat," I suggested.

We headed for Duck Inn. Although Lou and Bobbie seemed to have patched up their quarrel, Lou remained glum throughout dinner. The rest of us avoided any mention of Nick.

When we arrived at the theatre, I noticed Rowan standing in the doorway, watching the line of cars ease down the lane. As mine passed, he turned and walked inside, leaving me to wonder if he'd been anxiously awaiting my return or was simply relieved that he didn't have to get somebody else up to speed on Nettie.

For days, we'd been bracing for this tech rehearsal. The design relied mostly on painted backdrops, a few set pieces to suggest location, and shifts in lighting to establish mood. But then there was the carousel. Lacking a turntable in the floor, the actors had to roll out the "pulpit" where Billy drums up business and the six painted horses on their stands, then connect the stands and lock each to the hub of Billy's pulpit. After which the skinniest women in the cast mounted the horses and the men gripped the handlebars sprouting from the hub to turn the carousel.

Rowan claimed the do-it-yourself carousel reinforced the theme of community, but it seemed more like a desperate attempt to get around the theatre's limited technology. Even with the glowing umbrella of colored lights that descended from the flies to shimmer above the carousel, Rowan would have to use all the magic he possessed to create the glamour the opening number required.

Javier and the stage crew had spent the afternoon putting the chorus grunts through their paces. But once we added the other performers into the mix, plus lighting and sound cues—and the necessity of timing our actions precisely to the music—mistakes were inevitable.

It took two hours of stopping and starting to get everything running smoothly. After that, thank God, there were only the usual glitches: set changes that took too long, lighting cues that got screwed up, avalanches of lobster pots.

It was after midnight when Billy marched back to heaven, leaving the rest of us in a glassy-eyed final tableau. Rowan thanked us for our patience and called a work-through of the problematic numbers the next afternoon, followed by a full dress rehearsal that night.

After driving nine hours in the last twenty-four and enduring two excruciating interviews, I thought I'd be too exhausted to obsess about Nettie or Daddy or the existence of faeries. Instead, I tossed and turned, reliving my confrontation with Rowan and every dreadful moment that had followed. Including the way he had avoided me at tech rehearsal.

The staff adopted the same guarded formality, clearly closing ranks behind him. I shouldn't have been surprised; it was their theatre at risk as much as Rowan's—and their secret. But it still hurt when Hal watched me with obvious anxiety, but avoided me just as assiduously as the others.

The last thing I expected was for Janet to wave me into the office the following morning. "It just gets better and better," she muttered as she lit a cigarette.

"At least you're talking to me. That's more than the others will do."

"Oh, grow up!" As I opened my mouth to protest, she added, "If Reinhard or Alex made their usual solicitous inquiries, you'd have either cried or bitten their heads off. You want us to comfort you *and* stay the hell away from you. Well, you can't have it both ways."

I suppressed a wince; Rowan had flung those same words at me Saturday night.

"Cut them a break, Maggie."

"Cut *them* a break?"

"Now that Rowan's spilled the beans, nobody knows what you'll do. So we're worried. Not just about ourselves, but about the show and the theatre. And believe it or not, we're worried about you, too."

Her manner was as brusque as ever, but her unexpected concern brought a now-familiar tightness to my throat.

"If you cry, I'll strangle you."

I managed a shaky laugh instead. "That would certainly solve all your problems."

"I've done a lot to preserve this secret, but I haven't stooped to murder. Yet." Janet took a deep drag on her cigarette. "Look. I know this business about your father is a shock. But you have to let it go—at least for the next couple of days—and concentrate on this damn show. There'll be plenty of time after we open to obsess about your life."

She was right, of course. I owed it to my cast mates to turn in my best performance. But I couldn't help asking, "Do you believe in what he does? Calling people here? Pushing them to discover what he thinks they need?"

Janet studied the glowing tip of her cigarette. "Rowan has a more exalted opinion of his work than I do. By putting on successful shows, the actors accomplish something they never dreamed they could. And leave with a lot more self-confidence than they had when they arrived. Maybe that's all it takes to change your life. The belief that it's possible." She shrugged. "There are always some who experience the kind of breakthrough Rowan longs for. People like Gary and Bernie. Lou and Bobbie. But there are probably an equal number who'll return to their lives, relatively unchanged by this summer."

"And then there are those like my father."

"That was a unique experience, thank God."

"But there must be others. People who resist change. Who resent Rowan's pushing."

"Like you?"

I glared at her. "You don't think there's anything inherently wrong in calling people here against their wills? In tinkering with their lives?"

"You could have refused the call, Maggie. Or gone home after auditions. You can still go home now. As far as tinkering with people's lives, how is Rowan's technique any different from method acting? That encourages actors to draw upon their emotions and memories."

I considered reminding her that method acting was a far cry from faery magic. Or brainwashing. Instead, I just said, "I never thought I'd hear you defend him."

"My issues with Rowan have nothing to do with his directing."

"Just the affair with Helen."

"Just? He knew before he began it that she wasn't the one. Worse, he knew she was vulnerable. If not for him, she might have married again. Instead of wasting her life pining after a man who could never love her. A man who isn't even a man."

"So it's true? He really is a . . ."

"We're not in church, Maggie. You don't have to whisper."

"This might be a joke to you—"

"It's not a joke. I've just had a lot longer to come to terms with the truth."

"Still, it must have been a shock. When he told you."

Janet rolled her eyes. "I knew what he was—and what I was—long before I met Rowan Mackenzie. I grew up with the stories. So did Alex and Helen. Most of the others found out about their faery blood after they joined the staff. Some were understandably skeptical. Others took it in stride. Hal, of course, was thrilled—until he found out he has no more faery blood than you do. It's rich, isn't it? The biggest fairy on staff is the one with the weakest bloodline."

"But you all have the same . . . powers."

"More or less," Janet replied. "The gift weakens with

each generation as the faery blood gets more diluted. And of course, each of us has developed various aspects of the power. Helen's green thumb, for example. Alex's extraordinary musical gifts."

"And you?"

"I can sense what people are thinking and feeling. A useful gift. And I can make them do what I want. If I choose. Also useful."

"Couldn't that just be a testament to your strong personality?"

Janet laughed. "Well, there's that, too. But if it's proof you're looking for, I could always show you my birth certificate. The real one." She took a deep drag on her cigarette and chuckled as she exhaled. "I was born in 1850."

I just stared at her. I had thought a lot about the powers faery blood might bestow, but never made the leap to longevity.

"Rowan looks . . . what? Forty?" Janet speculated. "Even he doesn't know how old he is. Faeries, apparently, don't keep track of time the way we do. His best guess is that they can live up to a thousand years. So the offspring of a faery and a human might live four or five hundred years. The next generation . . . well, you can do the math."

"Then Helen must be . . ." I shook my head, unable to imagine her real age.

Janet frowned. "You still don't get it, do you?"

"Well, she's older than you are, obviously, so—"

"Helen only looks older. Because the faery blood is thinner." Janet leaned forward. "Helen is my daughter, Maggie."

Again, I could only stare at her. Lee had told me . . . no. I'd said they were mother and daughter and he had agreed. I'd jumped to the obvious—and completely incorrect—conclusion.

"Naturally, everyone assumes I'm her daughter. It's easy to encourage that misperception." She crushed out her cigarette. "A lot easier than watching your children age faster than you do."

I quelled the impulse to comfort her; Janet wouldn't welcome any display of emotion. And what words could comfort a woman who knew her child would die long before she did? Who had never known the luxury of growing old with a man she loved?

All summer, I'd noticed the way Janet scolded Helen, fussed over her, set limits on her behavior. My mother had morphed from child to parent during Nana's final years; I'd just assumed Janet had, too.

Then I realized something.

"You said . . . children."

"Helen had a brother. He died in a car accident. Nearly sixty years ago."

Her voice was completely matter-of-fact. But like Rowan, she had the ability to hide her emotions.

"Helen and Robbie were too young to remember their father. He fell at Verdun."

I felt my head nodding, but I was numbed by the realization that her husband had died during World War I.

"When I remarried, I was reluctant to have another baby, knowing I would outlive any child I brought into the world. But accidents happen." Her bleak expression softened. "That's how I got my Alex."

Details clicked into place. Their similarity in coloring. Their mutual affection. Reinhard's assumption—puzzling at the time—that Alex would rush to the hospital after Helen's heart attack. Catherine's equally puzzling hysteria that night. I'd assumed they were all bound by friendship, by their shared commitment to the theatre. I never dreamed they were family.

"We're an incestuous little group." Janet's voice held the familiar brittle sarcasm, but her shifting expressions hinted at other emotions: bitterness, tenderness, love.

"Why are you telling me all this?"

She shrugged. "No use hiding it, is there?"

But this was Janet who always had an ulterior motive. As I continued staring at her, she acknowledged my unspoken suspicions with a tight smile.

"Rowan entrusted you with a secret that has never been shared with anyone beyond our little circle. I want to ensure that it will go no further. And the best way to do that is for you to know who we are as well as what we are. All our lives, we've had to protect ourselves. Explain away the impossible. Disappear from time to time and return with new names, new identities."

"And no one in Dale suspects?"

"Probably. But most of the people hereabouts can trace their roots back to the original Mackenzies. We're family as well as neighbors. We look out for one another. We don't make trouble. And we don't welcome those who do."

"Are you . . . threatening me?"

"Don't be silly." The coldness of her eyes belied her smile. "I know you're angry about what happened to your father. But destroying us is not going to change that."

"I don't want to destroy anyone! I just don't want someone else to get hurt."

Janet studied me for a long moment before nodding briskly. "Then we understand each other. As long as my family isn't hurt, I don't much care if Rowan Mackenzie takes a fall."

She'd probably relish it. What better way to get back at him for his affair with Helen?

"You're the only one who might be able to do it. Because he cares about you. That makes him vulnerable—and gives you power. Use it right and you might shut down his precious theatre. And stop him from ever hurting anyone the way he hurt your father."

Janet's speculative gaze disturbed me. Was that really what she wanted or was she just testing me to discover how far I would go? I didn't want to shut the theatre down, just stop Rowan from interfering in people's lives. He could still direct shows. Put on his original musicals. Run the Crossroads like an ordinary theatre.

But he wouldn't, I realized. As long as he believed that the theatre was the key to lifting the curse, he would call the Mackenzies every spring, try to heal them every summer. If I tried to make him stop, he could remain an exile forever. And I'd be interfering in his life as surely as he'd interfered in mine.

Everything had seemed so much clearer in New York. Now I wondered if my desire to prevent Rowan from hurting people was just a way to exact vengeance for my father.

I hurried out of the hotel, my mind churning. I was too close to all this, too confused to be objective. Every day, another impossible revelation battered at my understanding of what was right and normal and real. By the time I reached the theatre, I couldn't wait to slip out of my head and into Nettie's.

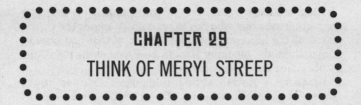

MY NUMBERS FEATURED PROMINENTLY in the afternoon's work-through. So did Nick's.

While Mei-Yin rehearsed the ballet in the theatre, Rowan ran Kalma and Nick through "If I Loved You." Judging from Kalma's stormy expression as she left the Smokehouse, it had not gone well. And judging from the shouts we could hear during the rehearsal of "Soliloquy," Nick continued to resist—loudly—Rowan's efforts to help him discover Billy Bigelow's softer side.

By the time the chorus began work on "June Is Bustin' Out All Over," Reinhard's hair was in full porcupine mode. Rowan appeared calm, but his grim expression indicated that he was feeling the strain as well.

Alex joined us onstage, but instead of giving us specific notes, he talked about the community of *Carousel*.

"Remember how in *Brigadoon* I wanted the miracle of the village's return to explode into the excitement of 'Mac-Connachy Square'? That's what's missing from this number. These people have shivered through six long months of snow and ice and rain. Now—finally—summer's arrived! And their joy and excitement and relief overwhelm their New England stoicism and make them all a little punch drunk. That's what I want to see onstage."

We all nodded wearily; he and Rowan had told us this during the early days of rehearsals. But we just couldn't bring it to life onstage.

Alex suddenly swung around and pointed his finger at me. "You're the one who has to set it up, Maggie. The antici-pation of the intro and then the release of that first chorus. Forget about the blocking Rowan gave you at the top of the number. Just do what feels right."

I glanced at Rowan, sitting in his usual aisle seat in the house, but he remained silent. Maybe he thought I wouldn't accept his direction any longer.

I thrust the thought aside as I began the intro. The events of the last week made it hard to summon Nettie's confi-dence that the long, dreary days were ending. But then the men responded, their choral line as insistent as the beat of a tom-tom. When the girls chimed in and the music grew more impatient, I recalled the giddy elation of my audi-tion, the excitement of opening nights, and—in spite of everything that had happened—the relief I had felt leaving the helping professional world behind and returning to this one.

And just like that, the number popped and June finally busted out. The boys and girls were flirty and foolish, each singer trying to top the preceding one to come up with the perfect image of June. I egged them on in the choruses and allowed Nettie's memories to infuse the slower bridges with a dreamy wistfulness.

At one point, I heard Alex shout from the pit, "That's what I'm talking about!" And when Rowan walked onstage after the number, he wore the first smile I'd seen in days.

It was Alex who helped us find the heart of the fucking clambake song as well. And once again, he did it by remind-ing us of the bonds of community, as critical to this small town's survival as the bounty of the sea.

Maybe we were simply buoyed by the success of our last number, but for once, it *was* a real nice clambake, bloated with good food and good feeling. I gazed at my cast mates, recalling that warren of cubicles at the United Way and that shabby, desperate office in the Bronx, and felt newly grateful for the community I'd found here.

Yet when it came time to perform "You'll Never Walk Alone," my confidence evaporated. Although I understood the emotions I wanted to pour into it, the song felt as flat as if I were still spouting meaningless platitudes. And the high G still sounded like a dying seagull.

"It's much better," Alex assured me. "Don't you think so, Rowan?"

Rowan nodded.

"You're still worrying about the high note, though, and it's throwing you off."

I nodded.

"Maybe we *should* take the song down a third. What do you think?"

I shrugged. Rowan shrugged. Alex's head swiveled back and forth. Then he flung up his hands. "For God's sake! Would you just talk to each other?"

I started. Rowan frowned. We stared at each other. We looked away.

"Fine! If you want to take the goddamn song down, just let me know before the goddamn show opens." Alex disappeared into the bowels of the pit, muttering about some people's stubbornness and other people's blindness and he wasn't going to get caught in the middle and he was way too old for this crap.

Rowan cleared his throat. "You did good work today."

"Not on this number."

"It's a lot closer." He glanced around the theatre as if searching for the nearest exit.

"Why can't I get it?" I blurted.

For the first time, he looked at me. "Stop thinking about the number so much and just feel it, Maggie. Then it will come alive. Like the others did."

"You make it sound easy."

"It's easy to tell someone else what to do. A lot harder to do it yourself. To let go. And allow your heart to carry you. Especially when you don't know where you're going to end up."

For a moment, I forgot what he was, what he had done. I just saw the weariness of his eyes, the wistfulness of his expression. And I wished we could go back. Not to the hectic sexual excitement we had known for those few minutes outside the theatre, but to the unrestrained laughter under the beech, the quiet joy of the plateau, the brief tenderness we had shared in his apartment.

I took a step back. His half-smile vanished.

"I'll see you at seven," he said. And hurried out of the theatre.

Our final dress rehearsal got off to a promising start. The chorus hit their marks, the carousel turned, and if the overall effect was not as glamorous as I'd dreamed, neither was it as hokey as I'd feared.

Brittany struck all the right notes in her scene with Kalma. Kalma embodied Julie's combination of strength and vulnerability in "If I Loved You." And for the first time, Nick managed to capture some of the fear lurking beneath Billy's bravado. If their kiss was stiff rather than gentle, an audience might still believe they had fallen in love.

So when Kalma hurried past me in the wings to make her costume change, her angry expression shocked me.

"The son of a bitch has been drinking," she said in a furious whisper.

Bobbie and I turned toward Lou, who held up his hands in protest. "One beer at dinner."

"And how many more in your room?" Bobbie demanded.

"None. I swear to God. Look, he was nervous about tonight. Rowan's been riding him hard. He thought a beer might loosen him up."

There was no time for more. Lou had to make his entrance.

Nick did fine in his exchanges with Mrs. Mullin and Jigger, but he just couldn't summon up the proper balance of concern and tenderness when Julie tells him she's pregnant. Then the "Soliloquy" rolled around. We'd caught snatches of the song during rehearsals and heard Nick arguing with Rowan earlier in the day, but this was our first opportunity to see the number.

Maybe that was partly responsible for what happened. He had to know we were clustered in the wings, watching him. Maybe he thought we wanted him to fail, when all we really wanted was the breakthrough Rowan had been pushing him toward for weeks.

The swagger was evident during the "My Boy, Bill" section, but there was also a strange, manic quality. I doubted the beer was responsible; I'd seen Nick put away a six-pack after a show and just get boisterous. More likely, he was afraid of what was coming next. Like me with the high G.

The music returned to the darker, more reflective theme of the opening. As Billy imagined a daughter who would be a smaller version of her mother, a sneer entered Nick's voice. And as he began to sing about the sweet attributes of his little girl, his expression alternated between sullen and truculent.

"Stop!"

All of us watching caught our breaths in a collective gasp. Rowan had interrupted numbers when technical snafus threatened to disrupt them completely, but he had never stopped a dress rehearsal.

"Go back. Take it from the dialogue into the bridge."

Alex hastily flipped pages in his score and whispered the measure number to the musicians. The slow minor vamp began. Nick spoke the lines where Billy wonders aloud what he could possibly do with —and for—a daughter. Then he began to sing.

Rowan stopped him at the end of the first chorus.

"Go back. Same place."

I saw Alex's head turn toward Rowan. Then he obediently signaled the musicians.

This time, Rowan stopped Nick as he launched into the first chorus.

"Go back. Same place."

Nick began again. And again, Rowan stopped him and ordered the music to start over.

Alex hesitated. "Rowan, I'm not sure this is—"

"Same place."

Alex shook his head, but raised his hand. The music began. Nick just stood there, staring at Rowan in his aisle seat.

"Say the lines."

I could see the tendons standing out on Nick's neck, hear the labored sound of his breathing.

"Say the fucking lines!"

Another gasp from the cast, this one louder than the first.

Nick spat out the words. Rowan rose from his seat and stalked down the aisle. Alex swiveled around on his piano bench. The music faltered, then fell silent.

"Play."

"Rowan . . ."

"Play!"

Rowan stopped in front of the stage, his gaze locked with Nick's. "Say the lines."

Nick obeyed.

"Now sing."

Hands fisted at his side, Nick sang. I couldn't tell if it was anger that choked his voice or some other emotion.

"Go back."

"Jesus," I heard someone whisper.

I'd seen directors push actors to their limits to get to the truth of a performance. But never at a dress rehearsal and never in front of the entire company. It was like stripping an actor bare, forcing him to go to the dark places he was trying so desperately to avoid and then shining a spotlight on his shame and fear.

Rowan didn't need to do that. All he had to do was sprinkle a little faery dust and Nick would turn in a great performance. But clearly, he wanted Nick to do it himself.

And the worst of it was, Nick had already learned the lesson Rowan was trying to cram down his throat. It was obvious from his trembling body, his angry grimace, the way he broke off, unable to sing the line about being a faithful dad.

Nick knew what this song was about. He understood the parallels to his own life, to his failures as a partner, as a father. He was just too proud or too scared or too ashamed to offer them up for Rowan Mackenzie's approval.

"Again," Rowan said in that same steely monotone.

Rowan talked about standing beside his actors, helping them on their journeys of discovery. This wasn't helping. This was just cruel. As cruel as the faeries tormenting my father.

"Again!"

As I strode out of the wings, the hot blast of Rowan's frustration buffeted me.

"Get off the stage, Maggie."

Rowan's voice was low, but there was no mistaking the warning in it. I continued toward Nick who had turned upstage, one hand shielding his face.

"Get off my stage. Now!"

"You have no right to do this!"

"Don't tell me how to direct."

"You're not directing. You're bullying him!"

I heard the muffled thud of his footsteps on the carpet, then the louder clatter as he ran up the steps to the stage. But I was already reaching for Nick, murmuring words of reassurance, of compassion, of caring.

Nick whirled around, smacking aside my hand with such force that I staggered.

"I don't need your help, you fucking cunt!"

For a moment, there was utter silence in the theatre. Then I became dimly aware of voices shouting, floorboards shaking as people stampeded from the wings. But all I saw was Nick's face twisted in a grotesque mask of anger. A single tear winked in the lights before it slipped, unheeded, down his cheek. His right hand clenched into a fist that grew larger and larger as he rushed toward me.

Suddenly, Nick froze, staring at his fist suspended a mere foot from my face. I shrank back, so stunned by his sudden fury and so relieved that he had reined it in that I barely noticed the blur of movement to my right.

Rowan's arm slid around my waist, steadying me. He thrust out his right hand, warding Nick away.

"Touch her again and I'll kill you."

Even more shocking than the words was the quiet savagery in his voice.

And then I understood Nick's stupefied expression. He hadn't quelled the urge to hit me. Rowan had used his magic to hold him at bay until he could reach my side.

Nick stumbled backward, his eyes wild. Everyone else remained frozen, watching us. I wondered if Rowan was holding them at bay, too, or if they were simply too stunned to move.

Rowan's arm slid free, and I turned toward him. Instead of the menace I expected to find, his expression was eager, his lips drawn back over his teeth in a feral smile. Blood lust rose from him like a malevolent fog.

A shiver raced up my back. Saliva filled my mouth. I swallowed it down, terrified and disgusted and excited.

A smile blossomed on Nick's face. His hands bunched into fists. And I knew we were both under the sway of Rowan's emotions, Rowan's power.

They wanted this fight. And so did I.

I wanted to hear the meaty smack of fist on flesh, the hollow crack of shattering bones. I wanted to feel the impact of a punch shuddering up my arm, the warm spray of blood oozing over my fist. The smell of it in my nostrils, the salty-sweet taste filling my mouth. The wild elation as my opponent reeled, the thud of his body as he crashed to the floor, the echoes of his defeat racing through the boards, through my feet, resonating throughout my body, as hot and fierce as any climax.

"Rowan."

Reinhard's voice, very close. I wanted him to go away; he'd ruin everything.

"Rowan!"

The blood lust spiked, and I bit back a moan. Then frustration stabbed me, and I did moan.

The surge of adrenaline ebbed. In its wake, I began to tremble. Firm hands gripped my shoulders. It must be Reinhard; Rowan was still beside me, panting like a winded animal.

The tension drained from Nick's body. Lou hurried over to him, softly urging him to be cool, to let it go. Nick shook off Lou's hand impatiently. His face darkened to the color of fresh liver. His gaze snapped to me.

"Fuck you. And fuck you, too." He glared at Rowan, then hawked a gob of phlegm onto the floor. "Fuck you and your whole fucking theatre!"

He pushed Lou aside, shoved his way through the crowd, and thudded down the steps. As he ran up the aisle, Rowan spun toward me.

"You had to interfere!"

Before I could reply, he took off after Nick.

"Everyone stay where you are!" Reinhard instructed.

Still shaking, I allowed him to guide me toward the collection of bales and baskets and crates that comprised the wharf set. He eased me onto a wooden box and gently probed my wrist and fingers.

"Any pain?"

My wrist ached, but I just shook my head.

"Bobbie! Would you please fetch a cold pack from the freezer in the green room?"

Bobbie raced off, probably glad to have a mission; everyone else just milled around, watching me uncomfortably and conversing in whispers.

"I just wanted to . . ."

Stop Rowan. Help Nick. Do something.

"I know."

Reinhard's voice was kind, but his frown indicated that he shared Rowan's belief that I had interfered. Maybe I had. But there were limits to what a man should have to endure.

"I couldn't just stand there—"

"But it wasn't about you, Maggie. Or what you needed."

I recalled Nick's furious expression and shuddered.

Reinhard patted my shoulder. "It is done. We move on."

Before I could ask how, an unearthly scream filled the theatre. A woman's scream. Coming through the open doors to the lobby.

"*Gott im Himmel*, what now?" Reinhard demanded. "Stay here!" he shouted to the cast as he raced for the stairs.

But no power—faery or human—could have kept us on that stage. We stampeded after him and poured up the aisles like a flood of lemmings.

The lobby was empty. Craning my neck to see past those in front of me, I made out a woman standing in the open doorway. The fingers of her right hand curled like claws over the doorframe as she stared out into the deepening twilight.

Reinhard's steps slowed as he approached her. "Madam? Are you all right?"

She started at the sound of his voice and spun around. And I found myself staring into my mother's terrified face.

CHAPTER 30
DON'T TELL MAMA

"**M**OM!"

Her gaze darted around the lobby, frantically searching for me. I flung up my hand and began pushing toward her. When she spotted me, she threw out her arms, a drowning woman reaching for a life preserver.

She clung to me for a moment, then swung me away, shielding me from the crowd. Only then did I realize how mistaken my initial impression had been. She might be terrified, but this was no drowning woman; this was a lioness defending her cub.

As ferociously as Rowan had protected me from Nick.

"Are you all right?" she demanded.

"I'm fine," I replied automatically.

But my world was teetering on its axis again. I tried to square this wild-eyed stranger with the mother I knew. The mother I thought I knew. The woman who offered brisk advice instead of hugs. Who lectured me on how to get ahead in the business world. Who greeted me on every trip home with a quick perusal of my appearance and a resigned sigh. The shirtwaist dress from Talbots was the only thing that was familiar.

Without relinquishing her painful grip on my arms, she turned to keep her wary gaze on the crowd. "I saw him," she whispered. "That man. That director. He looked the same, Maggie. Exactly the same as he did twenty-five years ago!"

I had to do something, say something before everyone heard her accusations.

"If I may."

My mother's head jerked toward Reinhard. She eyed him suspiciously, but without any hint of recognition.

"Forgive me for interrupting. I am Reinhard Genz, the stage manager."

Only Reinhard could perform a brisk little Teutonic bow at such a moment.

"I could not help but overhear. You seem to have mistaken our current director for his father. It happens often. The resemblance, I am told, is quite striking."

My mother shook her head. "I saw him, Maggie. It was the same man."

I couldn't bring myself to lie to her. Again. I could only ask the logical question and allow her to reach the logical—and incorrect—conclusion. Just as I'd done all summer.

"How could it be the same man, Mom?"

"An easy mistake," Reinhard said. "Especially if you only caught a glimpse of him, yes?"

She was still shaking her head, but her expression held doubt now. Her gaze darted from me to Reinhard and back to me. Like Caren when the staff first began their brainwashing. But this time, I was on their side.

My stomach lurched on a wave of nausea.

"Maggie, perhaps you should accompany your mother to the hotel. She must be tired after her long drive." Reinhard still wore a benign smile, but his underlying warning was clear: "Get her out of here."

"No! I want to see that man. I want to talk to him. Tonight!"

"Mom, it's dress rehearsal."

Her gaze traveled over me, belatedly taking in the heavy theatrical makeup, my prim bun, the high-necked blouse and billowing skirt.

"Things are a bit hectic tonight," Reinhard interjected, "but tomorrow, I am sure Rowan will be happy to—"

"Rowan? His name's Rowan?" Panic returned to my mother's face.

"He was named after his father," Reinhard lied smoothly.

I squeezed her hand. "Come on, Mom. We can talk about it back at the hotel."

"But what about your dress rehearsal?" she asked, unexpectedly reverting to maddening practicality.

Reinhard dismissed the necessity of my presence with a nonchalant wave. "Get your mother settled in, Maggie. You can always come back later. If time permits." Subtext: "Once you've locked her up for the night."

As I led her, still protesting, out of the barn, Reinhard shouted, "Everyone! Back into the theatre, please."

I glanced back. Through the open doors, I saw the staff huddled together, watching us.

❧❧

We took her car; I abandoned my gear in the dressing room, unwilling to leave her for fear of another meltdown. To forestall more questions that I didn't want to answer, I asked, "What are you doing here? How did you even know—?"

"The only number I could find for this place was an answering machine that wouldn't let me leave a message. So I called every theatre in Vermont. When you weren't at any of them. . . ." She shrugged.

I considered reminding her that she could have asked me. But after all the lies I'd told her this summer, she probably doubted she'd get a truthful answer.

"So you drove all the way up here."

She shot me an exasperated look. "Obviously."

She must have left work after lunch. If she'd even gone in today; God only knew how long it had taken her to track down every theatre in Vermont.

"But . . . why?"

"Oh, for God's sake! Why do you think?"

Because I'd been depressed as hell when I called her after my interviews. Because even though she knew it was irrational, she couldn't shake her concerns about this place. Because she had to see for herself that I was okay. Because she was my mom.

I found myself recalling all the times she had dragged herself to my performances. From my debut as a spinning top in kindergarten to my shows in college—including that dreadful original one-act where I'd played an hermaphrodite with a pair of socks stuffed in my leotard. Only once—after

SPELLCAST311

I'd taken the HelpLink job—had she ever revealed her fear that acting would leave me as disappointed and disillusioned as my father.

Ever since I was a kid, I'd resented what I considered her coldness, always comparing her to my father who was so free with his hugs and his kisses, who would tuck me into bed at night and play dress-up with me on the weekends. And pretend fireflies were faeries.

But my affectionate, imaginative, volatile father had left. And she was here. As reluctant as ever to talk about feelings. Maybe she thought she didn't need to. She showed them in everything she did, everything she'd ever done—feeding me, clothing me, keeping a roof over our heads, squirreling away money so we could afford a vacation every summer, so I could take piano lessons and art classes and go to an expensive private college. Offering sensible advice that I invariably rejected and keeping her mouth shut about her concerns.

Only Maggie Graham, Helping Professional, had been too stupid—or too stubborn—to see that.

I shifted in my seat to look at her. "I'm glad you're here," I said in a small voice. And in spite of the havoc it might wreak, I was.

"Are you sure you're all right? You looked . . . stressed out. In the theatre."

The understatement of the year. I was still reeling from everything that had happened and finding it hard to think straight, to know what to say, what to avoid saying.

"It's our final dress rehearsal," I said. "Everybody's stressed out."

"Touch her again and I'll kill you."

"Not that Rainer or Rupert or—"

"Reinhard. He's a doctor. He has to be calm."

"I thought he was the stage manager."

"He is. But he's also a pediatrician."

"I don't like him."

"He's really very—"

"And I don't like that theatre. There's something strange about it. I noticed it the first time I was here. Everyone was so happy. It wasn't natural."

Only my mother could observe happiness and conclude it was unnatural. Then again—given the life she'd led with my father—it probably was.

"Like that movie," she added. "The one where they replace the wives with robots."

I smiled, recalling my first impression of Dale.

"And just look at this town!" she exclaimed as she cautiously eased her Audi through the empty roundabout. "Nothing's changed! Except for that . . . pink nightmare." She waved her hand at Hallee's, awash in neon.

"It's a small town, Mom. I doubt it's changed much in the last century. The Bough's just up here on the right."

She pulled into a parking space and ducked her head to stare at the hotel through the windshield. "We stayed here last time."

"Of course we did! It's the only hotel in town. Come on. I'll help you with your stuff."

That proved easy. All she had was a small overnight bag.

Frannie was behind the front desk. She and Bea were spelling each other until Janet could hire a regular night manager. She hurried forward when she saw us.

"Reinhard called and said you'd be coming over. I'm Frannie. You must be Maggie's mom."

"Alison Graham," my mother replied, surveying the empty lobby. "It's just the same," she added with a pointed glance at me.

Frannie clucked. "Lord, yes. Those drapes will probably fall off the rods before someone replaces them. And the upholstery on the chairs is so shiny you can practically see your face. Come on over to the desk and we'll get you settled in, hon."

My mother visibly started at the "hon," but followed Frannie to the reception desk.

"Now," Frannie said briskly. "I can give you your own room for the next two nights, but after that, you'll have to bunk with Maggie. We're full up 'cause of the show."

My mother and I exchanged glances.

"Or I can put you in with Maggie from the get-go. That way, you girls can have a little slumber party."

Another furtive exchange of glances, each of us waiting for the other to make the choice.

"My room doesn't have a bathroom," I ventured. "We share the ones in the hall. But if you don't mind that—"

"No, of course not."

I tried and failed to imagine my mother trotting back and forth to the john with the women in the cast.

"All righty, then!" Frannie plucked a key off the board. "You must have had a long drive, Alison. All the way from New York City."

"Delaware."

Frannie gasped. Her admiring glance suggested my mother was akin to a pioneer woman who had just crossed the limitless prairie. "Lord love you, you must be beat. But I could open up the lounge if you'd like a cocktail before bed."

"Yes!" my mother and I exclaimed in unison. Then Mom frowned. "Or do you have to get back to dress rehearsal?"

I couldn't just desert her. And we could both use a drink. Maybe a few vodka tonics would help her forget the shock of seeing Rowan—and her desire to talk with him tomorrow.

"They'll manage without me."

Frannie beamed and fished a ring of keys out from under the counter. "Best part of being night manager. I got the keys to the kingdom."

Jingling all the way, she led us to the lounge, unlocked the door, and ushered us inside. "Just help yourselves. First one's on the house. After that, just sign the notepad on the bar. You can square up later." Noting Mom's shocked expression, she chuckled. "You're in Dale now, hon. Things are different here."

"Yes," Mom replied, shooting another glance at me. "They certainly are."

I nursed my mug of ale, refilled her glass, and kept the conversation focused on the bloodbath at HelpLink, my interviews, Leila's wedding—anything and everything except the theatre and Rowan. Three vodka tonics and an hour later, we mounted the stairs to my room. I waited until she returned from the bathroom, freshly scrubbed and attired in a lacy blue nightgown, to announce, "I'm going to run back to the theatre."

Mom yawned and crawled into Nancy's bed. "Won't they be finished by now?"

"Probably. But I need to pick up my stuff. It'll only take a few minutes."

"Take my car." She nodded vaguely in the direction of her purse, then bolted upright in bed. "And tell that man I want to talk to him."

That, of course, was my real reason for going to the theatre. In different circumstances, I might have appreciated the irony of urging Rowan to come up with a believable life history. But I was more concerned that he'd never be able to invent one that could allay her suspicions.

As I reached the lobby, the cast began filing into the hotel. Lou paused only long enough to pat my shoulder before pounding upstairs to the room he shared with Nick. Others clustered around me, asking if everything was okay. I told them Mom had been worried about me after my interviews, that she'd decided to surprise me by coming up for the show, that she'd been spooked when Nick bolted past her in the dark.

By the time I reached the theatre, the events of the evening came crashing down on me. The sight of the staff gathered around one of the picnic tables gave me a much-needed jolt of adrenaline. They turned as I approached and I glimpsed Rowan slumped on the bench, cradling his forehead in his hands.

Hal rushed forward and blurted, "Is she all right? Are you all right? God, what a night! I think I've aged ten years."

Lee's hand descended on his shoulder, and Hal fell silent.

"Mom's . . . okay. But she wants to talk with you tomorrow, Rowan."

He lowered his hands and nodded. Then he slowly rose, his gaze sweeping the staff. "There's nothing more we can do tonight. I suggest we all try to get a good night's sleep. We'll have a long day tomorrow."

Reinhard silently handed me my carryall. He hesitated, as if he wanted to say something, then joined the others trudging to the parking lot.

"What did you tell her?" Janet demanded.

"Nothing," I said, not bothering to disguise the bitterness in my voice. "I just backed up Reinhard's story."

"And she believed that?"

"It's the only explanation that makes sense."

Janet rounded on Rowan. "We need to make sure—"

"Yes, Janet. Thank you. You should go back to the house. Helen will be worried."

Of course. She would have sensed the uproar at the theatre, just as Janet had.

Rowan beckoned me to the bench opposite his. I slid onto it, all too aware that we had been sitting in these same positions only three nights ago. Just as he had done then, he folded his hands together and stared down at them.

"I'm sorry I upset your mother."

"It's not your fault."

His head came up at that. "What do you want me to do?"

"Obviously, you have to make her believe Reinhard's story."

"Is that what you *want*?"

"What I want doesn't matter!"

"It does to me."

I was the one to look away. "Do I want you to brainwash my mother? No! But I don't want her obsessing about this. She's already paranoid about you. And this theatre. If she starts asking questions, she'll never stop. You wouldn't believe how stubborn she is."

A tired smile lightened his expression. Then it vanished. "All right. Bring her to my apartment tomorrow morning at nine."

I nodded and started to rise, then sank back down on the bench. "She'll ask about my father. We didn't discuss him, but . . ."

"I'll tell her as much of the truth as I can."

"And . . . she'll be okay? Afterward?"

"I swear to you on everything and everyone I hold dear."

That comforted me a little; if he could swear on Helen's life, I knew he'd ensure that Mom came through this unharmed.

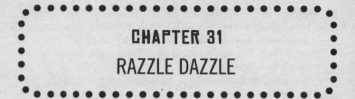

CHAPTER 31
RAZZLE DAZZLE

PROMPTLY AT NINE O'CLOCK, I knocked on the door of Rowan's apartment, noting with relief that it had been repaired. It swung open a moment later.

"Maggie. Mrs. Graham. Please come in."

I just gaped at him. He'd chopped off his hair. The loose waves that normally fell to his shoulders now brushed his jaw. Even more astonishing was his short-sleeved shirt. Some designer's misguided idea of a Hawaiian theme. Black and white fish swam in an aqua ocean studded with pink and yellow seaweed. Already unnerved by the prospect of this meeting, I needed every ounce of self-control to keep from bursting into hysterical laughter.

As I stepped inside, my desire to laugh vanished, replaced by the uncomfortable realization that this was the first time I had ventured here since . . . that night. His office was immaculate now. I resolutely avoided glancing toward the bedroom. My mother was far less circumspect, head swiveling this way and that to take in his abode. As she'd called it during breakfast.

Her eyes widened slightly as he led us into the living area. So did mine. The night of Helen's heart attack, I'd merely noted its size and its blend of comfort and elegance. Now I studied it, as I had so often studied the man who lived here.

I took in the thick rugs scattered across the floor, their tangle of vines and flowers echoing those painted on the wooden sideboard. The L-shaped sofa of deep forest green.

Easy chairs in a paler shade of misty gray-green. A spray of bare branches in a tall porcelain vase. It was almost as if he wanted to re-create the forest here.

Ceiling fans whirred softly, stirring the faint breeze that wafted through the windows nestled under the eaves on the eastern side of the room. I hadn't noticed them on my previous visit. Nor the small, antique melodeon that stood near the baby grand piano. The battered wooden trunk that served as a coffee table was a startling contrast to the other furniture; perhaps—like the melodeon—it was a treasure preserved from his early days in this world. Certainly, there were few other personal items in the room, unless you counted the leather-bound volumes that filled the bookcases and the floor-to-ceiling collection of record albums.

Hazy sunshine filtered through the skylights, but Rowan had turned on the lamps that flanked the sofa, as well as the track lights near the impressive bank of stereo equipment and the hanging lamp over the circular dining table. The overall effect was one of warmth and openness. My mother's expression conveyed just the opposite, but Rowan pretended not to notice as he waved us toward the sofa.

"May I get you something to drink? Coffee? Tea? Water?"

"No. Thank you." My mother gave him the quelling look that always drove away officious waiters.

I sat in the middle of the long L of the sofa and anxiously kneaded the soft velvet. Rowan waited for my mother to seat herself at the end closest to the door, then perched on the easy chair near her. I heard the soft scrape of her sandals on the hardwood floor as she ostentatiously moved her feet away from his.

Rowan leaned back in his chair, shifted position, then leaned forward again, clearly uncomfortable. My mother observed him, silent and unsmiling.

"I'm sorry for startling you last night," he finally said. "I can't imagine what you must have thought when I came racing out of the theatre like that."

"I thought you were the same man I'd met twenty-five years ago," she replied with devastating bluntness.

"Yes. Maggie told me." A quick smile. An awkward shrug. "I get that a lot. I've never been able to see the resemblance.

Maybe I just didn't want to." His smile faded, then reasserted itself with obvious effort. "My father was taller, of course. Not half so skinny. And his eyes were green."

I fought to conceal my shock when I realized that his eyes were a muddy hazel. Almost brown. I'd been so blinded by his shirt that I hadn't even noticed.

"But mostly," Rowan continued, "it was his air of confidence. He was so much more distinguished. In every way." Another smile, tinged with bitterness this time. A helpless flutter of his hands. Somehow, he'd managed to make the scars less visible, too.

Belatedly, I realized I was watching a carefully orchestrated performance. The stupid shirt. The "aw, shucks" manner. The subtle changes to his physical appearance. He even looked younger—or maybe his self-conscious gestures made him appear so.

And it was working. My mother's frown had deepened, obviously contrasting this awkward young man with the self-assured director she had met. So much more distinguished in every way.

Even I found it difficult to believe this was the same man I had worked with all summer. Was he using faery glamour to create these effects? Or were his acting skills just as uncanny?

"Forgive me," Rowan said. "I'm monopolizing the conversation. Maggie said you wanted to talk about . . . my father?"

"I wanted to talk *to* your father."

"That won't be . . . he moved. Out of the country."

I let out the breath I hadn't realized I was holding. Too easy for her to check the obituaries if Rowan claimed he had died.

"When was this?"

Rowan considered. "Ten years ago?" He frowned. "No, eleven now."

"Rather young to retire, wasn't he?"

"Yes. Everyone called it a tragedy." His tone made it clear he didn't share that opinion. I found myself wondering what had caused the rift between them before I remembered that this was an imaginary relationship with an equally imaginary father.

"Would you mind giving me his phone number? Or e-mail address?"

Rowan regarded his hands. A hot blush stole up his throat to fill his cheeks with color. "We don't keep in touch. But I'd be happy to ask some of the older folks in town."

My mother studied him, clearly curious. But all she said was, "There was a woman—Helen?—who called our house a number of times. A member of the staff, she claimed."

Part of me was relieved to know Rowan had told the truth about Helen checking in on Daddy. But there was something unsettling about the way Mom emphasized "claimed." Why would she think Helen had lied?

"Is she still with the theatre? Or has she retired and left the country as well?"

"She lives in Dale," Rowan replied, ignoring the barb. "But she's not in the best of health."

"She just had a heart attack," I added.

Mom's frosty smile suggested Helen had arranged it just to avoid speaking with her. "It's not important. I just wanted to ask a few questions about my ex-husband."

"I can try and answer them."

"You knew Jack?" she asked sharply.

"Not well. I was only an intern that summer. On the stage crew. We didn't mix much with the cast. I never even realized he was Maggie's father until a few days ago. But I do remember his performance."

"He did two shows."

Rowan's eager expression faded, as if crushed by his forgetfulness. "I'm sorry. I just remember the one."

"Yes?" Mom's fingers dug into the nap of the velvet, belying her indifferent tone.

Rowan's expression grew soft, almost dreamy. "He was very good. Amazing, really. He brought a sort of . . . lost boy quality to Billy. He had the toughness and the swagger, but he made you realize—"

"Wait!" I interrupted. "Are you saying . . . did Daddy play Billy Bigelow?"

Rowan and Mom turned to me, identical expressions of surprise on their faces.

"Yes, of course," Mom said. "Didn't I mention that?"

I shook my head.

"I'm sorry, Maggie." Rowan's voice was very gentle. "I thought you knew."

"That's the show we're doing," I told her.

She blew out her breath and muttered, "Christ on a crumpet."

Rowan started. I'd heard her use that expression countless times and just nodded.

"What are the odds?" she demanded. "Not only that you'd stumble on the same theatre but star in the same show?"

I felt an unexpected rush of pride that she assumed I'd have a starring role. Along with the shock of realizing I'd been so successful in steering our conversation away from the theatre last night that I hadn't told her anything about my season at the Crossroads.

"It *is* pretty incredible that both of them would end up doing the same show," Rowan admitted. "But we've had generations of families coming here. Parents tell their children about the theatre. Years later, their kids audition."

"I never talked about this place with Maggie. And if her father did, she was too young to remember. She didn't even remember coming here." My mother's head snapped toward me. "Unless . . ."

Unless I'd been lying about that along with everything else.

"The barn looked familiar. But when I drove into Dale, I was just looking for a bed and breakfast. And then somehow . . ."

My mother sighed.

Anxious to avoid dwelling on the incredible "coincidence" of Daddy and I stumbling upon the theatre, I asked her, "*Was* Daddy good? As Billy?"

I had another motive, of course. She rarely talked about my father and this seemed as good an opportunity as any to try and learn more.

Her expression softened, just as Rowan's had. "He was amazing. Just like you said." A grudging nod to Rowan. "Maybe it was the role. Or the direction. But it was the best thing he'd ever done. And I saw most of his shows."

"You did?"

"Well, not the ones where he was a chorus boy or a spear carrier. But the important ones. I traipsed all over the country. Even after you were born. I don't know how many hole-in-the-wall theatres I dragged you to. Then he got the teaching job and I thought we were finished with all that." She shot an accusing look at Rowan before asking, "Do you remember anything else about that summer? What he was like? His friends?"

"He didn't seem to have many friends," Rowan replied with obvious reluctance.

"He rarely did." Mom's voice was crisp. "Probably because he looked down his nose at the rest of the cast."

Rowan's head drooped in silent agreement.

"Jack always thought he was the best actor onstage."

"Was he?" I asked.

"Yes. But that was no great feat given the places he performed."

I inwardly cringed, wondering if she'd felt the same watching me—the best of a mediocre bunch.

"He seemed to get along with everyone," Rowan said. "I don't remember any problems, anyway. With his cast mates."

Neatly skirting his problems with faeries.

"And with your father?" Mom asked.

Rowan hesitated. "My father wouldn't have spent much time with Jack. He was rather . . . aloof."

"Well. Thank you for your time, Mr. Mackenzie. I'll be going now."

As Mom prepared to rise, Rowan's hand came down upon hers. She recoiled, then sank back onto the sofa.

Now it would begin. Already, she would be feeling that power flowing through her, the desire to stay, to hear what this man wanted to tell her. In a few moments, her head would be bobbing as she mindlessly accepted any lie he chose to offer. I wanted to close my eyes and blot out what was happening, but I was part of it. And I owed it to my mother to witness everything.

Rowan released her hand, but remained leaning forward, his knees almost touching hers.

"Maggie told me what happened to Jack. Afterward. I just want to tell you how sorry I am."

My mother nodded stiffly.

"I can understand why you blame this theatre. Suspect that we made things worse by stirring up feelings that had lain dormant. But I swear to you, when he left here, he was happy. Eager to go home and start over. If any of us had known what was happening, we would have done everything in our power to help."

Mom nodded again, more slowly this time. She didn't have that glazed look I'd seen on Caren's face. She merely looked . . . thoughtful.

"That's kind of you, Mr. Mackenzie."

"It's not kind!"

His vehemence made us both start.

"I feel responsible," he said more calmly.

"Why? You were just a boy at the time."

"Because as long as I've been a part of this theatre, we've made it our job not just to put on good shows, but to help people. And we didn't help Jack."

"I'm not sure anyone could have, Mr. Mackenzie. Jack was always a . . . what did you call him? A lost boy? It was part of his attraction." Her mouth twisted as she grimaced. "Of course, there's a big difference between being attracted to a lost boy and building a life with one."

Rowan's gaze drifted to the windows. "You always wonder, don't you? If you could have done more. If you made the right decisions. If there was a certain crossroads where you might have changed everything simply by choosing another path. Whether that might have led to greater happiness or greater tragedy. Or simply taken you to the same place in the end."

My mother was watching him with open curiosity. I was barely breathing, knowing he was speaking as much about his past as hers.

"In the end, all we can do is live with our choices and learn from them. And move on."

"Is that what you've done, Mr. Mackenzie?"

Rowan acknowledged her question with a small smile. "No. I dwell in the past. And advise others not to." Abruptly, his smile vanished. "Maybe that's why I'm a successful director. I sit in the shadows, moving people about on a stage.

Observing their successes, their failures, their lives. Much easier than shining a spotlight on mine."

Mom observed him silently. Then she said, "I think you should call your father, Mr. Mackenzie. Life is too short to spend it dwelling on the past."

"You're a very perceptive woman," Rowan said. "Your daughter takes after you."

"Do you think so?"

"Well, she called me an arrogant prick with a God complex."

There was a moment of appalled silence. Then my mother burst out laughing. When I glared at Rowan, she laughed even harder.

"Maggie does tend to be . . . plainspoken."

"A trait we share," I reminded her tartly.

"One of many," Rowan remarked. "You may have gotten your imagination and your love of the theatre from your father, Maggie, but your strength, your stubbornness, your common sense . . . those you get from your mother. You even look like her."

Mom and I exchanged frowns. I saw a small-boned, perfectly groomed woman with hair that was still black (thanks to her hair stylist Paul), a milkmaid complexion (thanks to genes and Olay Regenerist) and arresting blue eyes. She undoubtedly saw her slightly overweight, inadequately groomed daughter, auburn hair in a messy ponytail, a sprinkling of freckles on her cheeks, a budding zit on her chin, and eyes of some indeterminate color between blue and green.

"The coloring's different, of course," Rowan said. "But you've got the same jawline, the straight nose. The way you thrust your chin out when you're angry. And flash that scornful look that makes a man want to slink away. And the same wonderful bellow of laughter." Catching our astonished stares, he cleared his throat. "The kind of things anyone might notice."

My mother regarded him for a long moment before turning her speculative gaze on me. "This has been an interesting morning. But I won't take up any more of your time, Mr. Mackenzie. You must have a great deal to do today."

"More than you can imagine. Our Billy Bigelow walked out last night."

"He'll be back," I assured her. I glanced at Rowan for confirmation. "He *will* be back?"

"I'm not sure. Lou called last night after he got back to their room. Nick's things were gone."

I'd thought the staff had looked despondent because of my mother's untimely arrival. Now I realized they'd been reeling from the shock of Lou's call as well.

"What sort of an actor walks out on a show?" Mom demanded.

"It was my fault," Rowan replied. "I pushed him."

"That's what directors are supposed to do."

Rowan shook his head. "I pushed too hard. I was frustrated with his performance, yes. But there were . . . other frustrations. And I took it out on Nick. It was inexcusable."

I was the "other frustration," of course. Our blowup. His concern about what I'd do with my newfound knowledge. But I found it hard to believe that could have overridden his sense of responsibility to Nick.

"I think you're being a bit hard on yourself," Mom said. "After all, you're only human."

Rowan looked away.

"And you're still dwelling on the past."

This time, he nodded slowly. "It's been a pleasure speaking with you, Mrs. Graham."

"Likewise, Mr. Mackenzie. I look forward to seeing the show tonight."

Mom headed for the door. When she realized I wasn't following, she glanced over her shoulder.

"I'll be down in a minute."

Her gaze darted from me to Rowan. Then she nodded and strode out of the room, closing the front door firmly behind her.

"What an extraordinary woman," Rowan mused.

"You seem to have won her over."

His expression grew hard. "Well, that was my job, wasn't it?"

I was suddenly aware that the light in his apartment seemed harsh and unforgiving, accentuating the lines around his eyes. His green eyes. But of course, he didn't need to create illusions for me.

"I know you used your power to change yourself. But you didn't . . ."

"Brainwash her? No." Seeing my puzzlement, he made an impatient gesture. "I owed it to her to be honest. As honest as I could. To try and make up for the harm I'd done. And help her move on."

She wasn't even one of his Mackenzie chicks. But once she entered his world, she became his responsibility.

"Maybe this visit is a gift, Maggie. For her and for you."

I wondered if that was the reason I had come here. If so, it was an extraordinarily roundabout way to reconnect with my mother.

"Not much of a gift for you," I noted. "Or the rest of the staff."

"Neither Reinhard nor Alex was on staff that summer. Janet and Helen are the only ones she might remember. I'll just make sure they're seated in the balcony tonight."

"Helen's coming?"

"You think anything would keep her away?"

He wandered over to the piano. The score of *Carousel* rested on the music stand. The open script lay facedown on the bench.

"You don't think Nick's coming back, do you?"

"No."

Firm. Final. And devoid of emotion.

"You're going on as Billy."

"If I have to."

He had created the blocking. He knew the songs. Hell, he probably knew every line of dialogue. And if he could alter his appearance for my mother, surely he could perform in the show and work his necessary magic at the same time.

I hesitated, then said, "Last night . . . what you said to me about interfering . . ."

"I said a lot of things last night. I let my emotions rule me. That was a mistake."

"I thought we were supposed to let our emotions carry us."

He looked away. "I was talking about a song."

"But if I hadn't—"

"It's done, Maggie. And we just discussed the futility of dwelling on the past." He picked up the *Carousel* score and flipped through it. "I've scheduled a company meeting at ten. After that, you'll have the rest of the day off. I'm just going to rehearse Billy's big scenes today."

As I walked to the front door, I heard him tapping out the first few notes of "If I Loved You" on the piano. He stopped in mid-phrase.

I closed the door on his silent apartment. As I reached the bottom of the stairs, my mother hurried toward me. "I was so charmed by Mr. Mackenzie that I forgot my purse." She rolled her eyes and started up the stairs. "I'll be back in a sec."

I sank onto the bottom step. The meeting had gone better than I could have hoped. Mom seemed satisfied. Rowan had assumed responsibility for last night's fiasco—and for what had happened to my father. If Nick didn't return, he would be brilliant as Billy. And he'd assured me often enough that I could shine as Nettie.

So why did I feel so depressed?

CHAPTER 32
NOT A DAY GOES BY

ROWAN APPEARED AT THE COMPANY MEETING in his regulation linen shirt. His shorn hair caused a greater sensation than his announcement about Nick; clearly, word had already spread. And his calm statement that he would be stepping into the role evoked more relief than surprise.

Mom and I headed off to spend the day in Bennington. Instead of commenting on our meeting with Rowan, she remarked on the scenery, the steep hills, a Moose Crossing sign. It was half an hour before she said, "You avoided talking about your summer last night."

"You were already upset."

She twisted around in her seat to look at me. "Has it been that bad?"

"No. It's been . . . pretty great, actually."

I waited for the inevitable warning about getting caught up in the false glamour, the reminder that it was a brutal business, that I'd never make any money, that I was too old to be bouncing from one second-rate theatre to another. But all she said was, "Tell me about it."

I talked about the shows, about the cast. I talked about Rowan, too, careful to avoid praising him to the skies as Daddy had done. Her expression grew thoughtful when I described his philosophy of casting people in roles that would force them to dig deep and learn something about themselves.

"I never even asked who you were playing in *Carousel*.

I just assumed it was that perky best friend. But from what you just said . . ."

"I'm the inspiring anthem singer."

"The 'You'll Never Walk Alone' woman?"

"That's the one."

She digested that in silence. Then said, "I've never liked that song. It's fine at the end of the show. Quite moving, actually. Much as I hate to admit it. But if anyone told me to keep my chin up while my husband was lying dead at my feet, I would have killed her."

I laughed. "That was pretty much my reaction, too. At first."

I felt more than saw her head turn toward me. "And now?"

I told her about my struggle to find meaning in the platitudes, to construct a life history for Nettie, to make the character real. I even shared my Goddess Wheel experience.

"A tie between Athena and Aphrodite? That doesn't bode well."

"No. But it pretty much sums up my experience with men." I hesitated a moment before adding, "Maybe you should take the quiz when we get back to the hotel."

"Oh, that should be fun," she replied, her dry tone indicating just the opposite.

We strolled through Bennington, popping in and out of shops. Mom sprang for an unbelievably expensive serving platter at Bennington Potters. I settled for a mug on the seconds rack. We visited the Bennington Center for the Arts, where we lingered at the Covered Bridge Museum and I tried—in vain—to get a peek at the space where the Oldcastle Theatre Company performed. After a late lunch at the packed Blue Benn Diner, we hopped back in the car to scope out three nearby covered bridges, exclaiming over each like typical city mice.

Our covered bridge tour sparked memories of other vacations: the trip to Mystic Seaport, where I threw up; the trip to Williamsburg, where she got a massive sinus infection; our many pilgrimages to Rehoboth.

"You *will* come?" she asked. "The season will be over by then."

"Unless—by some miracle—I have a job."

"Just tell them you can't possibly start until after Labor Day. If they want you badly enough, they'll wait."

"Right now, nobody wants me at all."

"They will," she said firmly.

By the time we reached Dale, the afternoon was waning. I knew I should go to the hotel and relax before the show, but the memories we had shared—and the rare confidences—encouraged me to keep driving.

As I pulled into the empty parking lot at the theatre, I said, "I thought we could sit by the pond for a bit. It's a lot cooler than my room."

We walked in silence to the pond. Sat on a bench. Stared at the upside-down trees reflected in the calm surface of the water.

Suddenly, she turned toward me. "Look. If you love this . . ." She gestured brusquely toward the theatre. ". . . then that's what you should be doing. I'm not going to pretend I'm happy about it. But you're a grown woman."

Caught off-guard, I just stared at her. Then I admitted, "I *do* love it."

There were times during these last few days that I'd forgotten that. The joy of stepping out of the everyday world, of sloughing off Maggie to become someone else, of inhabiting that person, that world for a few hours. The sudden tension as the house lights dimmed, an excitement born of uncertainty, of knowing that in live theatre you could never predict exactly what might happen. The symbiotic relationship between performer and audience, each charging the other emotionally.

Every actor experienced that. But this summer, I'd come to value the sense of community as I never had before. Maybe because I'd usually been a jobber, coming in to do a couple of shows, then moving on to another round of auditions, another home away from home, another set of cast mates who were quickly forgotten. I'd found unexpected friendships here and unexpected support on and off the stage.

And in spite of all my difficulties with Nettie, there was a certain satisfaction in proving that I could go the extra mile, explore more deeply than I wanted, relinquish my inhibitions and trust my director and my cast mates to help me. And an even greater satisfaction in knowing that I could help them on their circuitous paths of discovery.

Even Rowan. If he'd pushed me to look into my dark places, I'd pushed him just as hard. And if I still wasn't sure what this summer was supposed to teach me, I had discovered one thing, perhaps some time ago, although I only realized it now.

"I love acting," I said. "But I don't think that's what I should be doing with my life."

Mom let out her breath in obvious relief. Then demanded, "Well, what *is*? You're thirty-two years old, Maggie. Don't you have any idea what you want to be when you grow up?"

"I'm working on it, okay?"

We glared at each other, the earlier camaraderie evaporating.

Still a little shaken by my realization, I said, "That's not what I wanted to talk about."

She nodded so wearily that I almost let it go. But this conversation had been postponed for too many years. And I needed to have it before I walked onstage tonight.

"Tell me about Daddy."

My father would have turned it into a grand tragedy. Told in my mother's measured voice, it was the largely expressionless recounting of a relationship that began in college and ended sixteen years later in divorce.

I knew the broad outlines: that he had gone off to New York after graduation hoping for his big break, that he had worked in a series of non-Equity theatres while she got her graduate degree in business administration and her first job in banking. I didn't know that she had performed in college as well. Or realize how many times they had broken up and gotten back together again.

She talked about the early years of their marriage, Daddy stealing a few days at home when he was working nearby, more often gone for months. The pain of being left behind morphing into a strange contentment at organizing her days as she pleased. The excitement of their reunions that made her feel like a newlywed. But there were also the months without work, the inevitable quarrels over money, over the future, over other women.

I gaped at her. "Daddy cheated on you?"

"He was faithful to me when he was home. As to what might have happened when he was away . . ." She shrugged.

Her stoical acceptance shocked me almost as much as the idea that he might have been unfaithful. Now I understood why she'd been suspicious about Helen's calls. Maybe Helen had been one of a long line of women calling Jack Sinclair after the season ended.

"That lost boy quality . . . it drew a lot of people to him. Including me. I thought I could make him happy, give him what he needed, make everything right. Of course, I couldn't. No one could. Which is why I never worried that much about what he was doing when he was away. It hurt my pride more than anything else."

"Your father was an unhappy man. Unhappy with himself and unhappy with his life."

Reluctant to press her about Daddy's possible infidelities, I just listened as she described the move to Wilmington, the months when it looked like the marriage would founder, the discovery that she was pregnant. All in that same expressionless voice.

When she described how Daddy had exchanged acting for grad school, I just stared at the upside-down trees. I'd always feared I'd broken up their marriage. Now I realized that I had stolen his dreams as well.

Mom seized my arm. "Nobody could make Jack Sinclair do anything he didn't want to do. If he gave up acting, it was because he was ready to. Your arrival just gave him the graceful exit he needed."

I nodded, only half-believing it. Then I recalled how he had fought Rowan's attempts to brainwash him for two days before finally surrendering.

"Those were good years, Maggie. The best we'd had since college. You gave us a common bond. And he adored you."

Saturday evenings, falling asleep to the sound of his guitar.

Sunday mornings, curled up in bed with him while he read me the funnies. Clapping and laughing as he sang along to an MTV video. Coming down the stairs Christmas Day to find the letter he had helped me write to Santa, now marked with comments in red or green ink: "In stock" next to my request for a light-up wand; "Moondancer" next to my urgent plea for a unicorn My Little Pony. And at the bottom, the name and badge number of the elf who had filled the order. By the time I realized that "Everett" and "Ernie" and "Ellsworth" were all Jack Sinclair, he had already left.

Mom released my arm and sighed. "And of course, you adored him. That's why I let things drag on as long as I did. It might have been kinder for all of us if I'd made the break sooner."

He'd always let her make the tough decisions. He indulged my whims and fed my imagination. She gave me time-outs and made me eat my vegetables.

I'd spent the first half of my life blaming her for driving him away, and the second half blaming him for abandoning us. But I'd never stopped longing for him.

"You want to know the truth about your father, but only if it reinforces what you already believe."

I wasn't sure who my father was any more. Or what to believe.

"Do you ever think about him?" I asked.

Her smile was infinitely weary. "Every day."

"You still love him."

"No. But I can't help worrying about him. Wondering where he is. If he's even alive."

"He was always seeking something more."

I almost wished that he had found what he was looking for. Then I could imagine him frolicking in Faerie, drinking nectar from a golden cup or whatever the hell they did.

"Should I have allowed him to go with them knowing they might toss him aside and leave him even more miserable?"

Rowan couldn't have done that any more than my mother could have ended the marriage sooner. Both of them had tried to redeem Jack Sinclair, to save him from himself, to reconcile him to this world. Neither had dreamed their failure would condemn him to endlessly seek the elusive portal to another.

"Does it help?" Mom asked. "Knowing any of that?"

"Yes."

I had a few more pieces of the puzzle, but I would never have them all. The lost boy was lost to me forever.

CHAPTER 33
YOU'LL NEVER WALK ALONE

THE AIR IN THE DUNGEON CRACKLED with nervous tension that night. Hal flew around making last-minute adjustments to Rowan's costumes. Catherine had a small nervous breakdown when she discovered a wheel had come off one of the carousel horses. Javier had a small nervous breakdown watching Catherine's. Reinhard's hair grew progressively higher.

I observed it all without being touched by any of it. I felt numb, my senses muffled as if I were swaddled in cotton. Even when Alex told me he had dropped "You'll Never Walk Alone" a third, I just nodded and obediently ran through the key change with him.

The man of the hour was conspicuously absent, which sent the cast into a brief frenzy until Reinhard explained that Rowan would be dressing in his apartment.

"That's a relief," Kalma said. "The guys would have freaked. Imagine seeing Rowan in his tighty-whities."

"Mmmm," Albertha purred. "I'm imagining it right now."

For the first time that evening, I smiled, picturing their reactions if I told them he wore boxers.

By the time we gathered in the green room, the anticipation of witnessing Rowan's transformation had risen to a fever pitch. When the door swung open, there was a moment of slack-jawed silence. Part of it was the novelty of seeing him in a blood-red sweater, black leather vest, and red-and-black checkered pants. But it was more than his costume or the stage makeup that lent a ruddy glow to his complexion. He exuded that explosive combination of danger and sexuality that was the very essence of Billy Bigelow.

His sudden grin dispelled that impression. "If you like this, you should see my tropical fish shirt."

As the laughter ebbed, his expression grew serious. "The last few days have been difficult for all of us. I'd like to thank you for your patience and your hard work and your belief in me." His gaze lingered a moment on me before he added, "This is the first time I've ever performed on this stage. And to be honest, I'm a little nervous. But we have a fine show and a splendid cast and I'm honored to be part of it."

We formed our usual pre-show circle. Ever since learning what Rowan was, I'd been dreading this moment, but instead of flinching when his power touched me, I felt strangely awed to recognize its source. In spite of his claim of nervousness, the energy flowing around our circle felt perfectly controlled.

When Reinhard called places, Rowan allowed us to precede him backstage. As each person passed, his hand gripped a shoulder, patted an arm, shook a hand. Like a priest blessing his congregation.

When it was my turn, he just stared at me. The black liner made his eyes look enormous and brilliantly green; I hoped he would remember to tone down the color if he ran into my mother after the show.

His hand rose. A long forefinger gently tapped my breastbone.

"Stop thinking about the number and just feel it."

I waited in the wings while the mill girls and fishermen eased in front of the scrim. Across the stage, Reinhard perched like Bob Crachit on his stage manager's stool. His head came up as Rowan and Albertha took their positions. Then he slid off the stool and disappeared into the darkness of the stage right wings. A few moments later, the murmur of conversation in the house ceased.

Reinhard cleared his throat. "Ladies and gentlemen. Welcome to the Crossroads Theatre's production of *Carousel.* For tonight's performance, the role of Billy Bigelow will be played by Rowan Mackenzie."

Even through the thick velvet curtain, I could hear the audience's whispers. As they rose to an excited babble, Reinhard slipped back onto his stool and pulled on his headset. The work light winked out, leaving only the faint glow from Reinhard's desk lamp, shining down on his open notebook of cues.

The audience grew quiet, and a shiver of anticipation rippled through me. I groped for Bobbie's hand in the darkness. Felt fingertips brushing my left wrist, a hand gripping my shoulder. Knew the same thing was happening in the stage right wings, in front of the scrim, in the lobby where others waited to make their entrance down the aisles. Clusters of performers, scattered throughout the theatre, yet linked together. Waiting.

The jolt of Rowan's power made me catch my breath. Clearly, he *was* a little nervous. But within moments, the energy subsided to a slow, steady pulse.

The curtain whispered open. The lights came up behind the scrim, twilight blues and lavenders as soft and mysterious as the music that rose from the pit. In front of the scrim, two pools of pale light illuminated the mill girls sweeping their brooms stage right and the fishermen repairing their nets stage left, their movements as dreamlike as the music, as steady as the pulse of Rowan's power.

The sweet dissonance of the piccolos. A shivering ripple of energy through our bodies. Alex and Rowan, twin conductors, perfectly attuned to each other.

Shafts of misty blue light revealed the roustabouts emerging from the wings, otherworldly figures half-visible through the scrim as they wheeled on the pieces of the carousel and paraded slowly around Billy's pulpit.

Horns called mournfully, their sound fading with each repetition. Rowan's power faded as well, only to swell again as the strings came in, lush and sweeping, to release the workers from their drudgery. As the carousel began its first slow revolution, the girls ripped kerchiefs from their heads, the men snatched up coats and hats. My body quivered with the same urgency.

The music grew faster, Rowan's power more palpable. No longer a current passing through me to Bobbie, but a

web connecting all of us. A shimmering web of power as
brilliant as the umbrella of multi-colored lights suspended
over the carousel. It carried us along with the frenzied rush
of music, the frenzied rush of the townsfolk spilling down
the aisles. Then it slowed, hovering like the music on the
brink of resolution, hovering like the crowd at the edge of the
fairgrounds, savoring the anticipation for one final moment
before the scrim rose and the music exploded into the joyous
waltz and Rowan leaped onto Billy's pulpit to sweep cast
and audience alike into the lights and spectacle and swirling
motion of the carousel.

I caught only glimpses of him during the opening number:
exhorting the crowd from his pulpit; lifting Kalma effort-
lessly onto her carousel horse; leaning casually against its
pole, smiling at her.

Then it was over and I was hurrying to the dressing rooms
with the other chorus members. Brittany's voice crackled
through the ancient speakers as she sang about "Mister
Snow." Tomorrow night, I promised silently, I would watch
her scene with Kalma. But tonight—like everyone else—I
rushed through my costume change so I could get back to the
wings in time for "If I Loved You."

When Rowan began to sing, I felt both relief and disappointment because he sounded so . . . ordinary. He drew me
in slowly, his voice sometimes rough with frustration, other
times faltering with uncertainty, only to soar, clear and strong
and sure when he reached the main theme. His quicksilver
mood changes captured Billy's struggle to remain aloof from
Julie and the reluctant fascination that pulled him relentlessly
toward her, his vain attempt to laugh off his attraction, only
to fall, helpless as the blossoms drifting down from the trees,
and surrender with a kiss so sweet and gentle it made me ache.

His "Soliloquy" explored all of Billy's shifting emotions:
the concern of an expectant father; pride in his son and confidence in the infinite possibilities that await him; the shock
of realizing he might have a daughter; disappointment turning to tenderness as he pictured her; and finally the panicked
determination to do anything to ensure her welfare.

The applause continued through the lighting change and Rowan's cross to stage right. It was still going strong when he glanced over his shoulder to where I was waiting in the stage left wings. I obediently made my entrance, but I still had to ad lib a few lines until the tumult subsided enough to move on with the scene.

That was one of the few moments when I was aware of my performance. The rest of my scenes passed in a sort of blur. Even "June" and "Clambake."

Suddenly, I found myself walking toward Kalma and Rowan, walking toward the number I had dreaded since the day I was cast.

Rowan was so still I could almost believe he was dead. Kalma was on her knees beside him, her long wig masking her face. I knew I should be watching Billy and Julie, but I just stared at the man who had pushed me so hard, at the woman who had given me the key to unlocking Nettie's character. I observed the tension in Kalma's narrow shoulders, Rowan's hand lying palm-up on the floor, those long, slender fingers far too beautiful to belong to Billy. Noting little details like a reporter at a crime scene.

I knew then that I was going to fail.

A soft cry escaped me, covered by Kalma's line. Then it was my turn to speak, to respond to her desperate plea, to tell her what she must do.

The silence stretched. Still on her knees, Kalma twisted around. For a moment, her tear-streaked face went blank. Then she shook her head, suddenly fierce.

"Nettie. Please!"

I realized my hand was covering my mouth. I let it fall.

And then I felt him, his touch as reassuring as if he cradled me in his arms. And something else, very faint, a feather brushing against my consciousness.

Alex stood in front of his piano bench, facing the stage. His eyes were closed, his face a grimace of concentration.

Rowan and Alex would not let me fail. Not on opening night. Not in front of my mother.

Kalma's features blurred as tears welled in my eyes. I squeezed them shut. Opened them.

I am standing at the top of the stairs, staring down into

the basement. Daddy is stretched out on the carpet. Mom is kneeling beside him. Her long hair hides her face. I smell throw-up. My stomach heaves.

I wonder if he's sleeping. I wonder if he's dead.

I'm so scared.

Mom raises her head. Tangled black hair. Angry white face. Is she angry with me for peeking? Or at Daddy again?

Her face smoothes out. "Everything's all right, Maggie. Go on up to bed now."

Her blue eyes darkening to Kalma's brown. His unshaven face changing to Rowan's smooth one. Rowan and Alex bringing me back, urging me to speak. And out there in the darkness, my mother. Waiting.

I heard my shaking voice urging Julie to keep on living, to recall the song she used to sing in school. The harplike arpeggio flowing from Alex's piano. Kalma's voice, splintering with grief. A silence broken only by her sobs. And then Alex again, accompanied by the hushed sostenuto of the strings.

I tottered downstage and knelt beside Kalma. Her head jerked up in surprise, but when I opened my arms, she flung herself into them.

I cradled Julie in my arms, but I sang to my mother. To the thirty-five-year-old woman in the basement and the sixty-year-old one sitting in Row G, Seat 114. To the stark-faced woman who had tried so hard to keep her family together and when she realized she could not, had torn it apart so that the two of us could survive. To the wild-eyed woman who had stormed the theatre to protect me. To the mother who would always push and pull and nag and worry and love me.

I sang my fear of the dark memories. My yearning for that promised golden sky. My doubt of ever finding it. I let hope swell my voice as I sang my determination that we would make the journey together. But the upwelling of sorrow for all we had lost made it dwindle to a whisper as I sang that final word.

". . . alone."

It seemed only moments later that we were lining up for curtain calls. The applause swelled for Brittany and J.T. and became deafening as Rowan and Kalma entered from opposite sides of the stage and met at the center.

They bowed together. Before he could gesture to her to take a separate call, she stepped back, leaving him alone as the audience rose to its feet. He acknowledged their ovation with a quick nod, then pulled Kalma forward for her bow. She thrust her free hand toward the pit. A final company bow. Then the curtains closed.

Reinhard opened them twice more in deference to the storm of applause. After our third bow, Rowan made a slashing motion with his hand and the work lights snapped on.

All that was left were the hugs and the kisses, the squeals of excitement, the relieved laughter. I said all the right things, but my face felt like it would crack as I smiled. Exhaustion shattered my numbness, bringing with it the recognition of everything I had done wrong in "You'll Never Walk Alone." When I caught Rowan watching me, I flinched, then raced downstairs to the dressing room.

I lingered in the shower, the cool spray stinging my skin without refreshing me. Returned to the empty dressing room to dry my hair, apply a fresh coat of makeup, and put on the inevitable kicky sundress. Then I fixed an unconvincing smile on my face and headed upstairs.

Mom was waiting outside the stage door. She stopped pacing when she saw me and exclaimed, "What took so long?"

I burst into tears.

She stared at me, aghast. Then hurried forward, fumbling in her purse. "Don't cry. Your mascara will run."

It was so typically Mom that a cracked laugh broke through my sobs. "It's waterproof."

She thrust out a wadded tissue. I started when I felt its dampness.

"You'll have to make do. I used up all my Kleenex."

I could feel my cheeks stretch as I smiled. "A whole pack?"

"Yes. Blow your nose."

I blew my nose and accepted a somewhat soggier tissue to dab my eyes.

"I'll never be able to listen to that song now." Her glare

made my smile grow broader. "It was so . . . it was like you were singing to . . . oh, damn!" She fished another crumpled tissue out of her purse and blew her nose with a resounding snort. Then she sighed. "I'm exhausted."

"Me, too."

Laughter and noisy conversation emanated from the breezeway where cast and audience were enjoying the opening night reception that Helen had insisted we hold because it was now "a tradition."

"Want to skip it?" I asked.

"Yes. But I should congratulate your friends. And Mr. Mackenzie."

"No one calls him Mr. Mackenzie, Mom."

"I do."

As we edged toward the refreshment table, people kept stopping us to congratulate me, which was nice considering how I'd mangled my big number. Each time I introduced Mom to someone, she found exactly the right thing to say. Not some generic "you were wonderful" compliment, but specific words of praise about a specific moment in the show. With others, she astonished me by remembering the stories I had told her that afternoon, confiding to Lou and Bobbie that she had heard terrific things about their performances in *Brigadoon*, telling Maya that she so wished she had seen her dance in "Always the Sea," asking Caren about her recent redecorating.

Then Hal pushed through the mob and swept me up in an embrace. "Oh. My. God." He stepped back and pressed his palm to his chest. "Shattered. Shattered! I had to borrow Kleenex to make it through the end of the show."

Lee shook Mom's hand. "I'm Lee. Tech director. The shattered one is Hal. Costumes and set design."

Hal embraced Mom with his usual fervor. I watched her eyes widen as she gazed at me over his shoulder. When he released her, she said, "Hal and Lee? Are you two . . . that shop? Hallee's?"

Hal beamed. "I am. Lee's just a lawyer."

Lee rolled his eyes.

"You have to stop by while you're in town. I just got in a satin bed jacket—the same misty blue as your dress, well, maybe the tiniest bit darker. It would look fabulous on you. And then you can persuade Maggie to buy the emerald green sarong I've been holding for her all summer." Hal glanced at my kicky sundress. "You know I love you in that, but every party?"

It was the first time I could remember anyone rendering my mother speechless. She blinked a couple times and glanced at me, but her gaze returned to Hal as if mesmerized.

Lee broke the spell by inquiring, "How long will you be in town?"

"Only a day or two."

The stab of disappointment surprised me. "I thought . . . I just assumed you'd stay through the weekend."

"Well, I wouldn't see very much of you with two shows Saturday and another on Sunday. Besides, your friend's coming. Nancy. No, I'll leave Friday morning. We'll have a whole week together at the beach."

Hal moaned ecstatically. "I love the beach! But my skin's so fair, I have to sit under an umbrella in a caftan. With a hat. Like Nathan Lane in *The Birdcage*."

"Well, well, well," boomed a familiar voice behind me. "The woman of the hour!"

"That would be Kalma," I replied, suppressing a sigh. "Mom, this is Longford Martindale."

"Your mother? No, I won't believe it. Your older sister, perhaps."

"Alison Graham," my mother responded with a frosty smile.

"He prefers to be called Long," I added.

My mother pursed her lips. "Most men do."

I gasped. Hal shrieked. Long just waggled his eyebrows.

"Long publishes *The Hillandale Bee*," Lee said. "He's also our local theatre critic."

Mom's smile grew noticeably warmer. "Really? Well, I hope you enjoyed the show as much as I did."

"Don't fish for compliments," I muttered.

"A beautiful woman need never fish for compliments," Long replied.

Mom shook her head, still smiling. "Maggie warned me that you were a charmer." I watched in astonishment as she rested her fingers on his bicep and stared up at him, blue eyes wide. "Would you be a dear? I'm absolutely parched and there's such a crowd at the drinks table . . ."

In spite of the press of bodies, Long actually managed a bow. "Your servant, dear lady."

As he maneuvered through the crowd, Lee began to applaud. Mom grinned and said, "I did a bit of acting myself in my younger days." Then she sighed. "It's been lovely talking with you, but I'd better beat a hasty retreat before he returns."

"I'll come with you," I volunteered. Rowan seemed to have skipped this reception just like the last one, but I was eager to escape the celebration.

"Don't be silly. The party's just beginning."

"I'll walk you to the car," I insisted.

As we headed toward the parking lot, a figure emerged from the shadows of the picnic area. Mom followed my gaze, her eyes narrowed in a nearsighted squint. Then she recognized the Hawaiian shirt.

"Why, Mr. Mackenzie," she said. "I was wondering where you were hiding."

"I'm not much for parties."

"Nonsense. You should enjoy your success. You were quite brilliant tonight."

"Thank you, Mrs. Graham. I hope . . . was it very difficult? Watching the show again?"

How typical of Rowan to recognize that. And how typical of me to overlook it. I was so caught up in my performance that I forgot she had to contend with the memory of Daddy's as well.

"It *was* difficult," she admitted. "But mostly, because your performance was so moving. And Maggie's, of course." She smiled at me, then nodded toward the breezeway. "Go back to the party. Both of you. Congratulations on a wonderful show, Mr. Mackenzie. And, Maggie, be sure and make my excuses to that man."

"What man?" Rowan inquired.

"The long one." Mom shuddered. "Be nice, Maggie. We want a good review, after all."

Before I could scurry back to the breezeway, Rowan

caught my arm. "You have to stay," he reminded me. "And make excuses."

Clearly, he wasn't referring to any apology I would offer to Long. My performance tonight might have made Hal and Mom weep, but it could only have disappointed Rowan.

He steered me into the theatre, flicked on a light, and demanded, "What's wrong?"

"What do you think? I screwed up! I butchered your blocking. Nearly blew the whole scene. I wobbled through the beginning of the song and sang the rest as Maggie Graham instead of Nettie Fowler. And I'm sorry, okay? I don't know what happened. I was just standing there, watching myself blow it, and I couldn't do anything!"

Rowan frowned. "Didn't anyone tell you what they thought of your performance?"

"Everyone said I was great. And it was nice of them to try and make me feel better. But I knew I'd let you down."

He cocked his head, his frown deepening. "Don't you have any idea how good you were? How powerful that scene was?"

"I . . . it felt right for me. But I couldn't tell what the audience thought. Or Kalma or—"

"It was right. For everyone."

I shook my head, still unable to believe what I was hearing. "If you and Alex hadn't been there . . ."

"We just gave you a little push."

"That vision of my mother wasn't exactly a little push."

"What are talking about?"

"My mother. In the basement. With . . . that wasn't you?" Rowan shook his head.

Had I been so aware of my mother's presence that I'd simply replaced Kalma's face with hers? Or tapped into some long-forgotten memory?

I started shaking. Rowan's hands grasped my shoulders, steadying me. "It's all right. Whatever happened, it's all right."

"It was so real," I whispered, recalling the cool tiles under my bare feet, the sour stink of vomit.

"Visions can be like that. Do you want to tell me about it? Sometimes that helps."

I let him ease me onto Reinhard's stage-manager stool. It seemed like the most natural thing in the world to rest my cheek against his chest, to feel his palm smoothing my hair. Yet only four days ago, we had flung horrible accusations at each other.

His heartbeat thudded in my ear with the steady pulse of his magic at the beginning of "The Carousel Waltz," the same slow rhythm I had noted during our very first encounter. I'd been more certain of everything then.

I tried to describe what had happened, what I'd felt when I became my seven-year-old self. I told him about the strange sensation of floating through the show, never fully inhabiting my own skin. Or Nettie's. I told him about my conversation with Mom by the pond. And when I finished, I said, "I feel so slow."

"You're tired."

"Not just tired slow. Stupid slow. Like it's all right there, but I can't see it."

"See what?"

"Nettie. My mother. My father. My life. And . . . you."

His chest rose and fell as he sighed.

"Mom asked when I would figure out what I was going to be when I grew up."

"What did you tell her?"

"That I was working on it."

"Good for you."

"I'm sick of working on it."

"I know."

"I'm so confused. I hate being confused."

"I know."

"You know everything," I grumbled.

"No. I'm confused, too."

My head came up. "About what?"

"My life. My work." He hesitated. "You."

I searched his face and found only kindness and concern. My head drooped. He took a step back.

"You don't have to be afraid of me, Maggie."

"I'm more afraid of myself," I whispered.

His hand rose, then fell back to his side. "It's been a long day. You'll feel stronger in the morning."

"You're supposed to say 'better.' Don't you know anything about platitudes?"

That made him smile. "I defer to your expertise." He thrust out his hands and pulled me to my feet. "Come on. I'll walk you to your car."

We detoured to the dressing room so I could pick up my stuff. As we walked through the lobby, I noticed a box of programs. The goldenrod paper was nice. A reflection of the lyric about the golden sky in "You'll Never Walk Alone," maybe.

As we walked outside, I said, "You were great tonight."

"So were you."

"I watched all your songs."

"I know."

"I just wish . . ."

"What?"

"I wanted to hear you sing 'If I Loved You' the way you sang 'The Mist-Covered Mountains.' I know you couldn't, but . . ." I shrugged.

Rowan gazed at the woods, the outline of the trees barely visible against the backdrop of the sky. "Maybe I'll sing it that way. Just once. Before the summer's over."

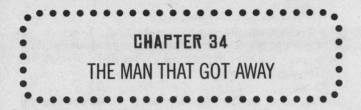

CHAPTER 34
THE MAN THAT GOT AWAY

MOM AND I PLAYED TOURIST IN BRATTLEBORO. I caught her sneaking glances at me all day. Maybe I looked as distracted as I felt.

She insisted on stopping at Hallee's when we got back to Dale. Hal swept her up in his arms, exclaiming, "I thought you'd forgotten me."

"That would be very difficult," Mom said dryly. But her smile was affectionate.

She tried on the bed jacket and—as Hal had predicted— she looked fabulous. To my surprise, he didn't even have to coax her into buying it. She also sprang for the emerald-green sarong. It was actually various shades of green. With a bamboo design. I looked like a slightly overweight wood nymph on vacation in Bali. Or that chick from *South Pacific*.

When I mentioned that, Hal promptly burst into "Younger than Springtime." If I hadn't felt older than Moses, I would have laughed.

Mom skipped the show that night. Said she just wasn't up to it. Neither was I. A great actress could have conjured the vision of opening night and tapped into the emotions it had evoked. I managed to tap into Nettie. Her strength and endurance comforted me, but after the show, Kalma seemed a little disappointed; I guess she wanted another meltdown. I couldn't tell what Rowan wanted.

The next morning, as I walked Mom to her car, she asked, "Is everything all right?"

"It's just been a really long week."

She examined me critically, then said, "Don't obsess about your father. Mr. Mackenzie was right about dwelling on the past. You have to put it behind you and move on."

"The way you have?"

"Yes."

"Oh, come on! You haven't had a serious relationship since Daddy left."

"I've had several, in fact."

"Who?"

"Adam Peterson."

I vaguely remembered him. She'd brought him to one of my junior high school plays and I'd instantly decided I loathed him.

"And then there was Joe Laurence."

"That skinny, bald guy who looked like Ichabod Crane?"

"He looked like James Taylor," she corrected. "And recently, I've been seeing Chris."

I stared at her blankly.

"He volunteers with me. At the Nature Society?" Impatiently, she added, "I told you all this weeks ago, Maggie."

I vaguely recalled someone named Chris. But she'd definitely skipped the part about dating. For that matter, I was pretty sure she'd skipped the part about Chris being a man. When I mentioned that, she had the grace to look abashed.

"So? What's he like?"

"Please. Whenever I tell you about one of the men I'm seeing, you either take an immediate dislike to him or act like we're a pair of puppies rolling around on the floor."

"You roll around on the floor with this guy?"

To my astonishment, her cheeks turned pink. I nodded thoughtfully. "Now I understand why you were so eager to buy that bed jacket."

"I'm leaving."

"Without telling me anything about Chris?"

She smiled sweetly. "I'll tell you all about him. When you come to the beach."

We stood there, suddenly awkward; neither of us had ever mastered the art of the fond farewell.

"I'm glad you came up."

"So am I." She hugged me quickly and stepped back. "And I'm glad I met your friends. They're really very nice." She sounded mildly surprised. "Hal's sweet. I wish you could find a man like him."

"I did. Michael."

"Michael . . ." She sighed. "He was a love."

"Just not my love."

She opened the car door, hesitated, then turned toward me. "Be careful, Maggie."

"What?"

"He's very charming. And sensitive. And talented. But there's something . . . strange about him. Mysterious is fine in novels, but it usually spells trouble in real life."

"We're just . . . we just work together."

"Any man who can sum up all our similarities after knowing me for fifteen minutes has to have studied you for a good, long while."

"He studies everyone! He's a . . . studier."

"Just be careful." She slid into her car, then rolled down the window. "You were wonderful in the show, Maggie. Really."

Before I could reply, the window slid up and she backed out of her parking space. Typical Mom. Say something from the heart and make a quick getaway to avoid the emotional fallout.

I paid some bills. Browsed some jobs. Considered the irony that my mother's love life was more robust than mine. Recalled her comment about Rowan studying me, the comforting warmth of his arms on opening night. Then I thrust the memories aside and tried to get on with my life.

❧

Nancy joined us in the lounge after that night's show. I made her laugh with the tale of my mother storming the theatre. But when everyone began vying with each other to describe Rowan's showdown with Nick, her eyes grew wide.

"I've never seen anyone move that fast in my life," Bernie said. "One minute he was on the steps and the next, he was standing beside Maggie."

"Like a vampire," Kalma said. "You know how they always move in this incredible blur in the movies?"

Anxious to steer the conversation away from such otherworldly speculations, I said, "The whole thing was pretty much a blur."

"If you could have seen his face . . ." Brittany shuddered. "I thought he'd kill Nick."

"He called."

Every head at our table swiveled toward Lou.

"Nick? When?" Bobbie demanded.

"During the show." Lou scowled. "When he knew I wouldn't be around to pick up."

"Did he leave a message?" I asked.

"Yeah. He said, 'Leave me the . . . eff . . . alone.'"

"You can say fuck," Sarah assured him. "I've heard it before." She darted a wary glance at her grandfather, but Bernie just waved his hand dismissively.

"I called back and left *him* a message. Told him he was acting like a fucking crybaby and Rowan was right to push 'cause he was doing a shitty job and if he didn't visit that kid of his, I was writing him off as a bum."

Bobbie squeezed his hand. Kalma nodded approval. I said, "I guess that means we won't be seeing Nick again."

"Good riddance," Kalma said. "He *is* a bum!"

"Rowan didn't think so," I said. "Or he wouldn't have cast him."

Any chance of a breakthrough was lost now. And although Rowan had assumed the blame, I knew I bore part of the responsibility, too.

"Do you think I should tell Rowan about the call?" Lou asked.

"No!" Brittany and Bobbie exclaimed in unison. "It'll only upset him," Brittany added. "He's been so down lately."

"He has?"

Bobbie rolled her eyes. "I love you, babe. But sometimes . . ." She shook her head.

"Haven't you noticed how quiet he's been?" Kalma demanded.

Bernie stared morosely into his beer. "This Nick thing has really thrown him."

"He hardly smiles at all any more," Sarah said. "And when he does . . ."

Brittany sighed. "It just about breaks your heart."

"Wait a minute!" Lou demanded, still staring at Bobbie. "You love me?"

Everybody laughed. Even I had to smile.

"Of course I do, you big ape." Bobbie punched Lou's shoulder. Lou just shook his head, a dazed smile on his face.

Nancy was unusually quiet for the rest of the night. Several times, I caught her studying me. Rowan, Mom, Nancy. Everybody was eyeing me these days. Did I look that fragile?

As we were climbing into our beds, Nancy said, "It's not Nick."

"What?"

"Rowan may be upset about him leaving, but that's not the reason he's been down."

I stared at the quilt, unable—unwilling—to answer.

"He won't make the first move. You know that, too."

"It's not like that, Nance." I gave her an edited version of my father's summer at the Crossroads that roughly paralleled Nick's.

"Maggie, your father didn't go off the deep end because of some blowup with Rowan."

"I know. But we're both better off keeping our distance."

She regarded me with a mixture of fondness and exasperation. "I love you to death," she said, "but sometimes, you're a dope."

❦

I'd had no time to visit Helen since my return from New York. So after Nancy left Sunday morning, I drove over to the Bates mansion.

Janet answered my knock. She gave me a long, considering look, then said, "If you're going to get all weepy . . ."

"Cut me a break," I snapped. "It's been a shitty week."

"Well, just don't—"

"I won't upset Helen!"

"Good. She's in the sunroom."

Helen must have heard our voices; she was already on her feet when I walked in.

"Oh, Maggie! I'm so glad to see you." Her embrace enfolded me with love and concern. "Come sit down and tell me everything."

"First, tell me how *you're* doing," I said. I thought she looked pale, but the wooden blinds were down, rendering the sunroom rather shadowy.

Helen waved away my concern. "I'm fine. Just feeling cut off from everyone. Momma should have been a prison guard instead of a producer."

"I heard that!" Janet called from another part of the house.

It was a shock to hear her refer to Janet as "Momma." But there was no longer any need to pretend for me, no secrets left to hide.

"I put my foot down opening night. I refused to miss that." Helen clasped her hands. "I cried through your whole number."

"You cried through the whole damn show." Janet appeared in the doorway, holding a silver tray with a pitcher of lemonade and glasses.

"I did not! I laughed at all the right spots." Helen eyed the two glasses on the tray. "Don't you want to join us?" she asked Janet.

"I thought I'd let you girls have a *tête-à-tête*. So you can talk about me behind my back."

"Oh, Momma. Don't be such a grumpy puss."

Helen pressed Janet's hand to her cheek. The hard angles of Janet's face softened as she smiled. Then she frowned and said, "Don't drink the lemonade too fast. You'll get a headache."

I watched her walk out of the sunroom and continued staring after her for so long that Helen asked, "Maggie? What is it?"

"I just realized who she reminds me of."

The same brusqueness. The same dislike of emotional displays. The same immaculate grooming and self-assurance. God, my mother had even handled Long with the same ease as Janet. Mom was a little less outspoken, a little more gracious. But I'd seen both of them at moments of crisis, their careful facades shattered as they rushed to the aid of their daughters.

It made me a little queasy to reflect upon my dislike for a woman who shared so many of my mother's qualities. Only now could I admit that I usually valued Janet's frankness—even when it made me squirm—and that she used that brusque manner to hide her vulnerability. The same way I used humor as a shield. Or tried to. Lately, I seemed incapable of shielding any of my emotions.

Helen was watching me with a small smile. "It's your mother, isn't it?"

"Yeah."

"You sang to her opening night."

I nodded.

"So it was a good visit."

"A long overdue one in a lot of ways."

"I'm sorry I didn't have a chance to talk with her. Although I doubt she would have welcomed that. She seemed so . . . formidable."

"When you met her before?"

"I don't remember that visit very well. If anything, she seemed more frightened than formidable. But of course, she didn't want Jack to be here, did she? No, this was later. When I called. She was polite at first. But after a few months, she told me to stop calling."

I closed my eyes. Clearly, Mom *had* viewed Helen as a threat. If not a rival for her husband's affections then a reminder of his wonderful summer. But if she had just let Helen talk with him . . .

"I'm so sorry, Maggie." Helen's voice was little more than a whisper. "Rowan told me what happened to poor Jack. I thought . . . when you stopped visiting . . . I thought you blamed me.

"And no wonder. If I had just kept in touch with him, I would have realized something was wrong. And then maybe . . ."

"It's not your fault, Helen. Or Mom's." I hesitated, then said, "Or Rowan's."

"Have you told him that?"

"I think I just realized it."

I realized something else, too. And wondered why it had taken me so long.

At that afternoon's show, I sang to my father. To the play-
mate who had fed my imagination and my dreams. To the
reassuring presence at my bedside. To the lost boy he had
been and the lost man he had become.

I sang reassurance for his dark fears and clouded memories. I sang understanding for his restless nature that drove
him to search for the impossible. I sang the hope that his
solitary journey would lead him to a calm harbor. But I also
sang my sorrow—for what we had shared and lost, for what
we had never had, for all the years that we had both walked
alone.

I forgave him for leaving us and asked his forgiveness for
failing to cherish the gifts he had given me. And then I said
good-bye.

When the curtain swung shut after our final bow, there was
the usual Sunday rush for the dressing rooms. Rowan and I
were two islands in the stream of bodies flowing around us.

Our gazes met. I needed neither words nor the touch of
his power to realize that he had understood my song. And
that this was why he had called me to the Crossroads.

His smile held quiet joy and an extraordinary sense of
peace. But Brittany was right; it did break my heart.

CHAPTER 35
MAYBE THIS TIME

WITHOUT REHEARSALS TO FILL OUR DAYS, I joined my cast mates on day trips. Instead of enjoying the incredible vista from the Mt. Olga lookout, I found myself recalling the one from the plateau. When we picnicked in Woodford State Park and sunbathed on the miniscule beach, I closed my eyes and envisioned another picnic and a very different beech. Each excursion outside of Dale reminded me that Rowan was trapped on those twenty acres and might remain a hostage for centuries more.

On show nights, I tried to lose myself in Nettie's world. But Rowan was part of that world, too, onstage and off. He still gave his little blessing as we filed past him for places, but I received only an encouraging smile rather than the touch he offered everyone else.

I worked with Helen in the garden when it was nice. Went out to lunch with Alex, Catherine, and Javier. Out to dinner with Hal and Lee. I had the strange feeling I was being vetted for a club I wasn't sure I wanted to join.

The staff was much more relaxed now, finally able to talk about themselves and their reactions to discovering the source of their powers. Whenever Rowan's name came up, they shared anecdotes about him eagerly—almost too eagerly—but deflected my questions about the curse, the "witch," anything that touched on the reason he was trapped in this world and the ways we might help free him.

Reinhard remained aloof from the camaraderie. He would

listen if I needed to talk, but he would not press me to do so. Nor would Rowan. As Nancy observed, he would never make the first move. And I couldn't decide if I wanted to.

Time hurtled past in a headlong race toward season's end. After Sunday's matinee, I returned to the hotel, painfully aware that in one week, I would be back in Brooklyn.

I showered and changed, then headed down to the lounge where people had started to gather for a special Sunday movie night; Kander and Ebb were on the docket—*Cabaret* and *Chicago*. When I made an abrupt U-turn in the lobby, Lou called out, "Hey, Brooklyn! You're going the wrong way!" I walked out the front door and down the street to my car, hoping I was finally going the right way.

The light rain that had been falling all afternoon had stopped. As I pulled into the theatre parking lot, a watery sun peeked out between the breaks in the clouds. A good omen, I concluded. As I started down the walkway, the stage door opened. Rowan hesitated on the threshold.

"Maggie?"

I'd spent the last week wondering if I would ever reach this moment, but I'd neglected to think about what I was going to say if I did.

"Is something wrong?"

Was it nervousness that sharpened his tone or merely concern? I'd be concerned, too, if a woman showed up at my home and walked toward me as silently as a goddamn zombie.

"Maggie!"

"You know when I went home after you cast me?"

An understandable silence greeted that question. Then he nodded.

"I made a list of pros and cons. To help me decide if I should come back. I filled a whole column with reasons why I shouldn't. But I just wrote one thing in the other column: I want to."

Another silence, longer than the first. "Yes. Well . . ."

"I spent the last week putting together a similar list in my head. About you. And me. And I came up with the same answer."

His hand gripped the doorframe. "I don't think this is a good idea."

"You thought it was two weeks ago."

"That was before I knew you were Jack Sinclair's daughter."

"Does that matter?"

"It does to me. I hurt him. I don't want to hurt you. I've thought about this a lot, too. I'm happy that we're friends again. But it would be best if we left it there. That would be the wise course. The safe course. For both of us."

"What happened to taking chances?" I asked quietly. "That's what you said the night we quarreled. That I had to risk being hurt. Being honest."

"I was—please don't come any closer!"

The hoarse rasp of his breathing filled the silence. His fingers tightened on the doorframe until the tendons stood out on the back of his hand. Yet in spite of those outward signs of turbulence, he still had his power under tight control.

"I was angry that night," he said more calmly. "And I said things I shouldn't have. What you should remember—what you must remember—is the danger for any human who gets too close to my kind."

"You also told me to stop thinking. And let my heart carry me."

"I was talking about the song!"

His power lashed me, but the sensation faded immediately.

"One week, Maggie. We just have to be sensible for one more week."

In that brief instant when he'd lost control, I'd felt desperation, anger, desire. He was just as conflicted as I was. As I had been. If he truly wanted me to leave, all he had to do was shut the door in my face. Instead, he hovered on the threshold, heart and head battling for supremacy as mine had for so much of the summer.

I took another step, and heard his breath hiss in. Touch had unleashed his emotions before. If I could just get close enough to touch him, I could break through his rigid self-control.

"I understand the risks. And I know that, a week from now, we'll say good-bye and we'll probably never see each other again. But I don't want to be sixty years old and wonder what might have happened if we had just taken this chance."

I never saw his hand move. One moment I was reaching for his face and the next, my wrist was snared by his imprisoning fingers.

"So you want me to fuck you, is that it?"

His face was as expressionless as his voice; he might have been discussing the weather.

"You want it the way I gave it to you after the Follies? Or would you prefer a human fuck? Either way, you'll come hard and fast. They always do."

Stung by the studied cruelty of his words, I wrenched my hand free and whirled around. Then I froze, finally recognizing what he was doing and why.

He had promised never to use his power against me. He might use words to drive me away, but even now, he was honoring that promise.

I slowly turned toward him, and the mask slipped. His hand moved suddenly to his throat, slipping under the silver chain to knead the scar around his neck.

"It's okay," I told him. "I'm scared, too."

His eyes flew wide. Then he stumbled backward, the first time I'd ever seen him move gracelessly.

I followed him into the theatre and found him sitting on the stairs. When I touched his hair, he flinched. I stroked it gently, just as he had stroked mine during the reception, then pulled his drooping head to my breast. He made a strangled sound that might have been a laugh or a sob or a muffled protest. Then he flung his arms around my waist and buried his face between my breasts.

I felt the bone-deep ache of his loneliness. A tremulous longing. A shiver of desire. And a relief so palpable that I sighed. So many emotions pouring over and through me like waves crashing against the shore. But none threatened to overwhelm me. Even now, he was holding them back, trying to protect me.

I let my hands speak for me, one smoothing his hair, the other stroking his back. We swayed gently, drifting with the flow of our emotions. The arms squeezing my waist gradually relaxed. His cheek rested against my breast like a sleeping child's.

I had felt this peace before—the afternoon I drove into

Dale, the moment I stepped into the theatre, the day of our picnic when we had stood hand in hand on the plateau with the world stretching out before us. Then and now, it felt like coming home.

His head came up and I found peace in his face as well. I took his hand and led him up the stairs. He pushed the door open, but hesitated on the landing.

"I haven't done this in a long while."

"Neither have I," I assured him.

"A really long while."

"It's okay."

"You were probably in diapers."

Laughter had been lost to us, but we rediscovered it then and I knew everything would be all right.

I expected a mad scramble to rip off our clothes, the same wild rush of sensation, the same cataclysmic results. Instead, he kept a tight rein on his power, clearly wanting to savor every moment. The simple act of unbuttoning each other's shirts seemed to take forever because his hands were trembling even more than mine.

My shorts were easier. Thank God for drawstring waistbands. When they lay in a puddle around my ankles, he stepped back, his gaze drifting over my body.

I could feel my face growing warm and fought the urge to snatch up my clothes, suddenly conscious of every extra pound, every tiny mole, every imperfection. I took refuge in desperate humor. "I guess after thirty years any woman looks good, huh?"

His gaze returned to my face. "But only you would look so beautiful."

It was impossibly sweet. Of course, I didn't believe a word of it. But it gave me the courage to unhook my bra and let it fall to the floor.

He sighed. Then slowly knelt before me.

He explored me with his eyes, his hands, his mouth. There was such wonder in his gaze, such reverence in his touch—as if my body were a precious gift, as if I were truly Aphrodite and he, the worshiper at my shrine. I felt humbled and powerful and just as beautiful as he had claimed.

He skimmed off my panties and sank back on his haunches. Then he looked up, an astonished grin stretching his mouth wide.

"It's so . . . red! Redder, I mean. Than your hair. On your head. Like the sun just after it's been born in the morning. Or just before it dies at night."

I had to laugh. Never in my life had a man composed an ode to my pubic hair.

He twisted a few curls between his thumb and forefinger, then rubbed his cheek against them. His hands slid up my thighs to grasp my bottom and pull me closer. He nuzzled me like an overeager puppy, and I laughed again. Then his tongue flicked out, satiny smooth, teasing deeper, and the laughter caught in my throat.

The temperature in the bedroom suddenly soared. Sweat popped out on my forehead, under my arms, my breasts. Desire curdled between my trembling legs. I dug my fingers into the smooth, bare skin of his shoulders to keep from sinking onto the floor.

He rose swiftly, and I breathed in the thick, sweet aroma of honeysuckle. Not cologne. His scent. The scent of desire. And beneath it, another: wilder, gamy, an animal musk.

Golden sparks glittered in his eyes. His features seemed sharp, his expression almost feral. And suddenly, I was afraid.

He sensed the shift in my mood immediately and drew back. The golden sparks still flashed in the depths of those green eyes, but the feral avidity had vanished, replaced by concern and then frustration.

"This is what I am, Maggie."

"I know."

"If you're afraid of me—"

I groped for his hand and raised it to my mouth. The clenched fingers slowly uncurled. I pressed my lips to his palm, to his fingertips, and finally to the jagged scar on his wrist. His left hand shook as I lifted it and performed the same ritual. Then I leaned forward, lifted the chain off his neck, and kissed the red ridge of the scar. It tasted strangely bitter.

His throat moved under my mouth as he swallowed. His

groan rumbled against my lips. I raised my head, and he captured my mouth. A starving man who had finally reached the feast table. His tongue rasped against my lips, sandpaper-rough now. The cat's tongue I remembered from that rainy night of the Follies.

We stumbled backward, awkward in our urgency, and I tumbled onto the bed with a startled grunt. He sprawled beside me, but when I reached for the buttons on his jeans, he seized my hands.

"Later."

"I want you inside me."

His power leaped, making me shudder with pleasure. He licked his lips and regarded me through heavy-lidded eyes.

"Later," he repeated a bit less firmly.

My hand moved over his chest, his belly. Then slid lower.

His head fell back and he stretched, languorous as a cat, while I stroked him. Then he suddenly twisted and pinned my hand to the mattress.

"If I can wait thirty years, you can wait thirty minutes."

He teased me with his mouth, his hands, his power, by turns sweet and tender and rough. Once, he murmured, "Slippery as seaweed." And later: "You even taste like the sea." I opened my eyes and discovered him sucking his fingers, his expression rapt.

I wondered briefly how he knew what seaweed felt like, what the sea tasted like. Before I could ask, impatient hands grasped my hips and swung me around until my legs dangled over the side of the bed. He stood before me, his green eyes enormous and glittering. Strands of hair clung to his damp cheeks. Sweat streaked his face and pooled at the base of his throat where a pulse throbbed with the same inexorable rhythm of his power.

His fingers closed around my knees and parted them, exposing me to his avid eyes. He sensed the exact moment I realized what he intended. His lazy smile flushed my body with a fresh wave of heat.

He knelt between my legs, still smiling. His fingertips slid lightly up my thighs, trailing tingling sensation in their wake. His mouth followed the same path, pressing damp kisses to my skin, nipping me gently with his teeth. Anticipation clenched my thigh muscles tighter. His breath eased out on a shaky groan.

"I've dreamed your scent."

When his cat's tongue rasped against my sensitive flesh, I shot halfway across the bed. He leaped up and bent over me, his expression anxious.

"Did I hurt you?"

"No. Just . . . that tongue."

"I'm sorry. It gets like that. When I'm . . ."

"Yeah."

"Should I stop?"

"No! Just . . . go easy."

He slid off the bed again and took a series of deep breaths. God help me, all I could picture was Shelley Winters, getting ready for her epic underwater swim in *The Poseidon Adventure*.

"Stop giggling. I'm trying to concentrate."

Which made me giggle even more. Then he lowered his head and I stopped.

For several delicious minutes, he went easy. Then his groan vibrated through my flesh and his fingers tightened on my thighs. The satiny texture of his tongue grew rough, his mouth more demanding. He licked me, kissed me, teased me with tongue and lips and teeth. I fought to escape, even while my fingers tangled in his hair, pulling his head closer, wanting more.

Too much. Not enough. Excruciating tension twisting inside me, harder, tighter. The relentless throb of his power, a wild tattoo that carried me along with the same frenzied rush of excitement that I had felt during "The Carousel Waltz," the same momentary hesitation at the brink of fulfillment, a note held, aching with anticipation. Then it shattered and I shattered with it.

⌐≈

I surfaced slowly, feeling bruised and tender and swollen. My legs oozed off the bed like the melting clock in that painting by Salvador Dali. A heavy weight rested against my thigh. My hand stirred feebly and ascertained that it was Rowan's head. He raised it with a damp squelch of flesh parting from flesh and kissed me lightly on the knee.

I stroked his hair; it was as wet as if he'd just emerged from the shower. Mercifully, the stifling heat in the bedroom had faded along with his power. I even shivered a little as a breeze wafted over me.

He rose then and pulled the lambs' wool throw over me before sliding onto the bed. We lay there, side by side, staring into each other's eyes.

"Are you . . . is everything . . .?"

I smiled. "I am. And it is. You?"

Spiky lashes veiled his eyes. "I've never tasted a woman before," he confessed.

"Did you . . . like it?"

"You were delicious." A shiver of power rippled through me. "Can we do it again?"

"Oh, Lord . . ." I moaned.

"Not right away."

"Thank you."

"After dinner, maybe. Are you hungry?"

"Starving."

"I'll cook for you." He smiled, happy as a child at the prospect. Then his smile faded and he cleared his throat. "First, though, I need to use the bathroom."

I studied him, wondering why he seemed embarrassed. "Okay."

He slid off the bed and walked stiff-legged toward the bathroom. And suddenly I understood. Sloughing off my lethargy, I forced myself upright.

"I'm sorry. I've been completely selfish."

He turned back to me, frowning. "What?"

"You did all the work and got nothing in return."

His frown deepened. "That's not true."

"Look, that's got to be uncomfortable. Come back to bed and let me take care of it."

He opened his mouth, closed it, ran his fingers through his damp hair, and finally said, "It's already . . . taken care of. Now I have to take care of the aftermath."

The light finally dawned.

"But I didn't even touch you!" I exclaimed.

"If you had, I'd never have lasted as long as I did."

A wave of tenderness filled me. And with it, an incredible

sense of feminine power. I'd never made a guy come in his
pants before. And although I realized that had a lot more to
do with his long years of celibacy than anything I had done,
I felt like I'd out-Aphrodited Aphrodite.

"It's so . . . great!"

His surprise gave way to a rueful smile. "It was at the
time. Now, it's just . . . soggy."

"Sorry. It's just . . . I feel like I have faery magic, too."

He leaned down and kissed me on the nose. "Your own
magic is quite powerful enough."

As he straightened, I asked, "Want some company? In the
shower?"

His gaze slid away. "I'm a little . . . shy."

"After what we just did?"

"Not about your body. Just mine."

"What are you talking about? You have a beautiful body."

He grimaced, so clearly uncomfortable that I let it go.

After he had showered, I treated myself to a cool soak in
the tub. It was like bathing in a forest glade: pale green tiles
and wooden beams and the last golden rays of the sun slant-
ing through the skylight. But my pleasure faded as I recalled
Rowan's discomfort and wondered who could have made
him so self-conscious about his body.

A woman's ethereal voice interrupted my thoughts. As
other voices joined hers, I recognized the haunting tune of
"The Mist-Covered Mountains." I quickly dressed and hurried toward the living area, only to draw up short on the
threshold.

Candles glowed in the silver candelabra on the sideboard,
the silver candlesticks on the dining table. Votives in dozens
of glass containers created shimmering pools of green, blue,
and gold. Rowan walked toward me, a stately shadow moving in and out of the flickering light.

He wore the leather pants and silk shirt I'd seen at the
opening of *The Sea-Wife*. I felt hopelessly underdressed in
my shorts and blouse, but his eyes assured me that I was
beautiful.

"I'm afraid dinner's pretty simple," he said as he led me
to the table.

By his standards it was: lollipop lamb chops with morel

sauce, asparagus spears, and a crusty baguette. The first sip
of wine made me shiver with pleasure. I lifted the bottle and
inspected the label. Chateauneuf du Pape. Then I saw the
date and gasped.

"Rowan, this bottle of wine is older than I am."

"I was saving it. For a special occasion."

The warmth that suffused my body owed little to the wine.

We shared stories as we ate. Rowan told me about his
early years in this world when the land was still a wilderness.
And he described the genesis of the theatre: the first musicale
he attended where he used his magic to comfort the families
grieving for their loved ones who had fallen at the battle of
Gettysburg; the first shows he had staged—Gilbert and Sullivan, Victor Herbert; the leap to "professional" productions
when charging two bits for admission seemed like an impossible gamble; the first call to the Mackenzie descendants and
the astonishment of seeing them arrive on foot, horseback,
and bicycle, and a few in their spanking new automobiles.

My descriptions of acting in school plays and stumbling
through my first piano recital seemed impossibly dull by
comparison, yet he listened as if fascinated. He seemed
to find our family vacations even more fascinating, but of
course, his only glimpses of the world had come from photos in newspapers and books and—much later—images on
television and computer.

I was surprised to learn he even owned a television. He
laughed and said he no longer did; there was little need when
you could stream video on a computer. But when Helen purchased one for him back in the 1950s, he had spent entire
days in front of it, enthralled.

"And when color television arrived . . . that was simply
extraordinary. As magical as anything in Faerie."

I hesitated a moment, then asked, "What's Faerie like?"

His gaze drifted to the windows under the eaves as if Faerie lay just beyond. "What I remember most is the clarity.
Of the light. The air. The colors. Everything so perfect and
pure. As if the world were freshly made each morning."

"Why would anyone leave, then?"

"Because it's also . . . muted. Insubstantial. This world
is so raw. Sometimes beautiful, often ugly, but always real.

The rain stinging your face. The earth pressing against your feet. Flavors bursting in your mouth. And so many emotions slicing through you, filling you up. For all its beauty, Faerie lacks passion."

"You don't."

"Maybe passion is the wrong word. Humans are as raw and real as their world. Burning with such intensity. Maybe that's why your lives are so short. We're drawn to that heat. The Fae burn as well, but it's a cold fire. Like ice."

For a moment, his expression clouded. Then he smiled. "That's what makes this theatre so extraordinary. The crystalline perfection of Faerie translated into something even more powerful through the intensity of the human experience."

He might have been describing himself—that combination of cold and heat, aloofness and intensity.

As if I'd spoken aloud, he said, "This world has rubbed off on me. Because I've lived here so long. One of the reasons my power is weak."

"Weak?"

"Compared to the rest of my clan. Imagine any adolescent—a mass of raging hormones. Well, it's worse for us. Fae children age much like human ones until puberty. Then our power just . . . explodes. And the aging process begins to slow. I was roughly fifteen when I was trapped here. My power was still developing. The iron collar drained much of its strength, but—"

"The iron . . . ?" My horrified gaze snapped to the scar at his throat. I swallowed hard, tasting that metallic tang again.

"Crude, but extraordinarily effective." His shudder belied his dismissive words.

"Does it . . . does it still burn?"

"No." His tender smile faded. "But when I hurt someone, it throbs." He drained his wine and quickly refilled his glass.

How many times this summer had I seen him kneading the scar? And the burns on his fingers—he must have gotten those while clawing at the collar, trying to rip it off.

I suddenly understood what had happened the night of Helen's heart attack. Steel burning his fingers as he wrenched open the door, steel surrounding him—sickening him—as he leaned inside the car. Yet he had ignored the pain, remaining at Helen's side until Reinhard arrived.

"And your power never recovered?"

He shook his head. "The best I can do is maintain what was left to me after they removed the collar. Being in nature helps. I spend part of every year at the cottage. Longer during one of my periodic . . . absences. But without Faerie to nourish it, my power will always remain stunted. And so will my ability to control it."

I understood how that lack of control must frustrate him. Yet, somehow that very helplessness made him seem more human.

"Why didn't your folk help you?" I demanded. "How does a single witch trump an entire clan of faeries?"

"After I was . . . lost, they avoided these woods. Nearly a century passed before they returned. A few wanted vengeance for what the Mackenzies had done. But by then, of course, the witch and her brood were dead." His mouth twisted. "Most, though, made it clear that if I was too weak to overcome a human curse, I didn't deserve their help."

"But you were one of them!"

"And I had broken the rules. Worse, I'd been stupid enough to get caught. If it had happened to another, I would have laughed and thought he deserved his punishment. Then."

"So they just . . . abandoned you?"

"They've returned more frequently this last century. They even seem happy to see me. But our chief declared it was too risky for anyone in the clan to help me break the curse."

"And they accepted that?"

"The chief is the final arbiter. There's no court of higher appeal. No Faerie Queen in spite of what the legends say. And to be fair, I doubt they could have helped me. The heart of the curse is beyond the power of Faerie to comprehend."

"They could have tried! I would have. So would your staff. We wouldn't have laughed or shrugged it off or washed our hands of you."

"Because you're human, Maggie. And humans have an infinite capacity to change. To forgive. To . . . love."

"Well, fuck them! Cruel, unfeeling little fuckers."

He regarded me with a small smile. "Pity the poor Fae who comes up against the wrath of Maggie Graham."

"You've come up against it often enough."

"And I pitied myself every time."

"How can you joke about this? More than two hundred years of your life!"

"Because it *has* been more than two hundred years, Maggie. I've learned a lot in that time. Including patience."

"But why go back? I don't care how beautiful it is. You don't belong with them."

"I wonder if I belong in either world. Sometimes I feel I'm neither Fae nor human, but some monstrous amalgam of both."

I shoved back my chair. "Don't you ever say that! You are not a monster."

"You thought I was. Not so very long ago."

"I was wrong! I was angry and hurt and wrong. You're not perfect. You can be arrogant and dictatorial and stubborn and blind and standoffish and temperamental and impossible to understand and a major pain in the ass . . ."

"Please tell me it gets better soon."

"But you're also perceptive and clever and amazingly talented. And tender. And kind. And you try to help your cast, even if you don't always succeed. And sometimes, you're so sweet that it breaks my heart."

He bowed his head. "I'm not . . . you're the one who's kind."

"Shut up."

He watched, wide-eyed, as I marched around the table.

"I don't know what the hell kind of faery you are, but you're a good man, Rowan Mackenzie. Got it?"

His breath eased out in a shaky sigh. "Got it."

"Good."

CHAPTER 36
SECRET SOUL

ROWAN DIDN'T URGE ME TO STAY. Maybe he sensed that I needed to be alone. Maybe he needed that, too. Sleeping beside another person was a greater act of trust than making love; in sleep, you were truly naked, incapable of maintaining the barriers around your soul.

His kiss was tender, but doubt shadowed his face when he asked, "Will you come back tomorrow?" When I nodded, relief chased away his doubts.

Mine remained. There was so much I didn't understand about him, so many shadows I could not penetrate.

I slept restlessly and woke to the warbling of a mockingbird. The Bough awoke more slowly, a sporadic symphony of trilling alarm clocks and squeaky springs, thudding footsteps and groaning pipes.

The aromas of coffee and frying bacon lured me to the Chatterbox, where I invented excuses for missing movie night and skipping today's planned trip to Bennington. After everyone departed, I threw some things into my carryall and drove back to the theatre.

Rowan was waiting in the picnic area. A huge smile filled his face as he hurried toward me, and I felt an answering one blossom on mine. He swung me off my feet and kissed me, apparently unconcerned that the residents of the Bates mansion and the Mill might see us.

"What should we do today?" he asked as he set me down.

"You choose," I replied, caught by his boyish enthusiasm.

"Let's go on another picnic."

"I just ate breakfast!"

"Well, we don't have to eat right away. Not food, anyway." He offered a leer as convincing as Long's and laughed when I smacked him. Then suddenly asked, "You haven't told your mother about us?" When I shook my head, he muttered, "That's a relief."

"Oh, come on. She's not that bad."

"The day you brought her to my apartment. Remember how she came back afterward?"

"Oh, God. What did she do?"

"She picked up her purse, smiled very sweetly, and told me if I hurt you, she would geld me with a spoon."

When I stopped laughing, I repeated, "A spoon?"

"Maggie. The implement she chooses is not my prime concern here."

"Oh, she'd never . . ." I considered the matter further and shook my head. "No. She might murder you, but I doubt she'd waste time gelding you first."

"Well. That's a relief," he repeated, far less fervently than before.

We took a more roundabout route to the beech. Just as Reinhard had declared after Midsummer, Rowan knew every inch of the woods. And every inch seemed to have a story. The little pool where he had bathed in the summer. The clearing where he had brought down his first deer with bow and arrow. The shallow grotto beneath a rock formation where he had lived—a dark, dank hole so small that his head would have brushed the ceiling when he sat, so cramped he would have been unable to stretch out full-length when he slept.

"Fifty years?" I whispered. "You lived in . . . that . . . for fifty years?"

"I lived in the woods. I only slept there."

"But fifty years . . ."

"They brought me blankets that first winter. And food. They even left me weapons so I could hunt. And were solicitous enough to fashion the knife blade and arrowheads from flint instead of iron. They wanted me to live, you see. And when I tried to escape . . ." He shoved back the sleeve of his shirt and stared at the jagged scar on his wrist. ". . . they nursed me back to health. They wanted me to live a long, long time."

"You still hate them, don't you?"

He turned to me, clearly shocked by my question. "They stole my life, Maggie! They didn't just drain my power and bind me to this world. They drained my very essence. I might have lived a thousand years in Faerie. But because of that collar, I'll be lucky to live half that long. Five centuries may seem endless to you, but I can never recapture all the years they stole. Not even if I return to Faerie one day."

I took his hand, torn between my horror at the terrible price he had paid and my reluctant understanding of the motives of those who had exacted it.

"I'm not trying to excuse what they did. It was horrible. But they were frightened of you, and angry and grieving and—"

"I never set out to harm her."

"No. You set out to seduce her. And succeeded. Are you telling me you didn't know the risks she might face?"

Cold air buffeted me as he wrenched his hand free and stalked away. Then he faced me and sighed. "No. I just didn't care enough to protect her."

Cautiously, I took his hand again. "What they did was incredibly cruel. But their hatred is easier for me to understand than your own folk abandoning you."

"It wasn't just hatred, Maggie. The witch loved her daughter. They all loved her. Hatred, my folk have always understood. But love . . . love is the most powerful, most human of all emotions. And it is alien to us."

"To them, maybe. Not to you."

"How do you know?" he demanded.

"I've seen how much you care about your cast. About Helen."

"Caring is not the same as loving."

"No, of course not, but—"

"I've never loved anyone."

His voice was as expressionless as his face, yet the air around us crackled with tension. Was this some kind of a test to see if I would abandon him as his folk had? Or was

he warning me that—whatever else we shared this week—it
was not, could not be love?

"Maybe you just haven't found the right person," I finally
said.

"Or maybe I'm incapable of love."

I shook my head. "I don't believe that."

I couldn't tell if he was relieved or disappointed.

We visited the beech and picnicked on the plateau. Rowan's mood slowly improved, but the weather deteriorated.
Scudding gray clouds and ominous rumbles of thunder soon
had us scrambling to pack our supplies. We reached the hut
as the first fat drops of rain gave way to a pelting downpour.

Even with the top half of the Dutch door open, it was
gloomy inside. The table and benches looked as worn and
battered as the narrow bed. The cold fireplace resembled a
gaping maw, its stones blackened from centuries of smoke.
Although it was a huge improvement over that awful hole he
had lived in, I couldn't imagine spending months in this one
small room.

Then I noticed the candlesticks and crockery in the tall
wooden hutch, the frayed rag rugs, the small cross-stitched
sampler carefully preserved under glass. And suddenly, the
hut became a home, his first refuge in this world. Isolated,
perhaps, but not entirely lonely. There had been people
nearby who had cared about him, friends who had woven
that rug, stitched that sampler, brought him those bowls.

I found him watching me and asked, "Were you happy
here?"

"Yes," he replied, sounding faintly surprised. "Mostly. It
was good to have a real home. And as much as I enjoy the
comforts of my apartment, this is the place I always come
back to. Maybe because Jamie and I built this cottage. And
everything in it."

Rowan had mentioned Jamie Mackenzie last night—the
great-grandson of the woman who had cursed him, the man
who had dragged him out of the shadows and urged him to
create the theatre.

"He was my first friend—my only friend for many years.
The first of the witch's clan to speak to me. Forty years without hearing the sound of any voice save those of the birds

and the animals. By then, I was as wild as they were. And then a ten-year-old child walked into this glade and said he thought it was fitting we should meet face-to-face. Being neighbors and all."

A fond smile filled Rowan's face. "One of the first gifts he ever brought me was a jug of milk and a basket of strawberries."

I could only gape at him.

"So now you understand why your gift took me aback."

Rowan caressed the smooth wood of the table. I pictured him sitting there with Jamie, sharing food and drink and laughter. Just as we had last night.

Jealousy stabbed me, so startling and unexpected that my stomach churned. I realized he had begun speaking again and forced myself to focus on his words.

". . . and when Jamie insisted that I become a part of the community, the easiest thing was to pass me off as a distant Mackenzie cousin."

"People believed that?"

"The witch had seven sons. There were plenty of distant cousins to go around," he said dryly. "I chose my first name. Pretty much on the spur of the moment when I met Jamie. Rowan is a sacred tree—to humans and faeries alike. The Scots thought it provided protection against witches."

"That's appropriate."

"And faeries."

His grin made me shake my head. "You have a strange sense of humor."

"More of a gift for appreciating irony. I've had a lot of names over the years. But Rowan Mackenzie is still my favorite."

As he smoothed the faded quilt atop the bed, the fond smile returned. And jealousy pierced me again. Stupid to be jealous of a man who had been dead for more than a century. Yet I couldn't help wondering if Rowan had led Jamie to the bed they had built together, had loved him with the same passion and tenderness and ferocity he had shown me last night.

Rowan's smile faded as he studied me. "We were never lovers, Maggie."

I shook my head. "It's none of my business."

"I *have* slept with men. It was . . . simpler. No risk of pregnancy, of course. But also less chance of any romantic entanglements."

"I've known plenty of gay men who've gotten romantically entangled."

"Yes, of course. But I chose my partners carefully. Men who wanted pleasure, not love. Men like . . ."

"Your folk."

With a curt nod, he walked to the door and stared out at the rain. "The Fae rarely have sex as you know it. There's little need when you can give and receive pleasure without even touching."

"But you must . . . they must . . . reproduce."

"Occasionally. To replenish the clan. And introduce new bloodlines."

It sounded as cold and clinical as I'd expect from beings that could taunt my father and abandon one of their own without a backward glance.

"That's why children are such a gift," Rowan continued in the same flat voice. "There's rarely more than one birth every few decades. We don't know our parents. The whole clan raises the child. And he is spoiled and pampered and doted upon."

And grows into the kind of arrogant, self-centered creature Rowan had once been.

"And then another child is born. And becomes the center of our world."

Maybe that was why he had trespassed in this one, why they were all drawn here. Not just to sample the intensity of human experience, but to recapture—if briefly—that time when they were the center of the world.

"The rain is letting up," he said. "We should be able to leave soon."

I walked over to him, slipped my arms around his waist, and rested my cheek against his back. His body was as unyielding as a tree trunk. Then his hand came up to clasp mine.

We walked back to the theatre in silence. The whole way, he seemed to be undergoing some silent, internal struggle. For once, I didn't press him.

As soon as we reached the apartment, he excused himself and disappeared into the office. I unpacked his knapsack, washed the empty food containers, and wandered through the living area, scanning the books on his shelves. Leather-bound classics and modern fiction and collections of poetry. Art books. Travel books. The King James Bible, the Koran, the Tao te Ching. An eleven-volume history entitled *The Story of Civilization*. A dozen books by and about explorer John Muir. Other than an edition of Shakespeare's plays, there were no books on the theatre, no scripts or scores; maybe he kept those in his office.

On one shelf, I discovered a black-and-white photograph in a silver frame. As I picked it up, Rowan walked back into the room, a small sheaf of papers in his hands.

He nodded at the photograph and said, "That's Jamie and his family. His wife, Jeannie. Duncan, Andrew, Wee James, Meg, and little Jennet. She's the one who made the sampler you saw in the cottage."

It was one of those stern-faced family portraits so typical of the Victorian age. Jamie wore a frock coat, Jeannie a long, black gown. She looked far more fearsome; even with a mustache and beard, I could see the hint of a smile curving his mouth.

"Was Jamie a redhead?"

"Yes. Wee James and Jennet got his coloring. The rest were dark, like Jeannie."

"Was she as terrifying as she looks?"

"Almost. She was the disciplinarian in the family. Jamie was . . . its heart."

Suddenly, he thrust the papers at me. I read the heading on the first page and started. "*By Iron, Bound?* This is . . . your story?"

He nodded. "These scenes are from Act One. I thought they might . . . explain things."

"You don't have to—"

"I know. But I'd like you to understand. Not just about me and Jamie, but . . ." He shrugged. "I'll take a walk. Be back in half an hour."

Before I could respond, he strode out of the apartment. A little flustered, I sank onto the sofa.

As I read the first scene, I understood why he had entitled it "Simple Gifts." Three times, the character of Young James brought food and drink to Ash, stubbornly refusing to be deterred by his coldness. I smiled a little to discover Rowan had chosen yet another tree name for his character. But it was hard to smile at the stage directions that described Ash as a barefoot creature in tattered clothes who seizes a half-eaten bone from his campfire and gnaws at it.

Scene two skipped forward fifteen years. Jamie was now a man on the verge of marriage, full of dreams and hopes for the future. I bit my lip as he attempted to describe love to a being who had never known it, cringed as Ash coldly rejected his attempt to forge a true friendship. But when Ash turned his power against Jamie to drive him away, I had to put the manuscript down until I grew calmer.

At least with me, Rowan's power had simply escaped his control; he had deliberately used it to hurt Jamie and shame him. And still, Jamie left the gifts he had brought, including the *McGuffey Reader* from which Ash—Rowan—learned to read and write. And when Jamie returned months later, he forgave Ash for his cruelty.

The man's sweetness flowed through the ensuing scenes: when he calmed Ash's nerves before that first musicale, when he urged him to find a nice level-headed widow to spark, when he brokenly confessed that he was in danger of losing the farm.

I gasped when Ash presented him with a gift of faery gold that saved both their homes—a necklace intended for the girl who had died. Smiled as Ash wrangled with Jamie's wife—as tough a cookie as she looked in the photograph. She was the one who brought the news of Jamie's passing— along with a forged birth certificate and Jamie's bequest of five acres, including "the parcel with that big beech you love so much."

Jamie's letter to Ash was almost too painful to read. It was filled with such love and humor and kindness, the words of a man who had lived a full life and a happy one, yet even on his deathbed, worried about the future of his friend. The final scene showed Ash singing at Jamie's wake. The words of "Amazing Grace" had never seemed so powerful: "Through many dangers, toils and snares/I have already come; 'Tis grace that brought me safe thus far/And grace will lead me home." When Ash stared front at the end of the act "into a future filled with uncertainty, but also possibility," I broke down.

I was almost as shaken as the night Rowan confessed his otherworldly origins to me. It wasn't just that I understood Jamie. It was that my experiences with Rowan so closely paralleled his. In a weird way, I *was* Jamie.

But that was nonsense. The man in the play was sweeter, kinder, and far more forgiving than I was. Whether or not Rowan acknowledged it, his love for Jamie filled every page. Who could ever mean as much to him? Fill that void in his life, in his heart? Even Helen had failed.

I had tried to accept this week as an unexpected gift and resolutely avoided speculating about our future. Only now could I admit that we had none.

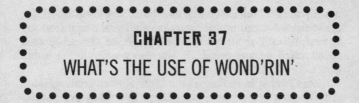

NEITHER ROWAN NOR I SPOKE about our inevitable parting. Nor did we offer comforting lies about seeing each other after the season ended. We both realized it would be better to make a clean break.

Knowing he was still in love with a man who had died more than a century ago made that decision a little easier. Otherwise, I doubted I could simply walk away. Yet when I told him I understood why he had loved Jamie, Rowan looked startled. As if he had never realized it. And then he shook his head and said, "Not enough."

I hated to think that he would spend another century grieving. Jamie wouldn't want that. "Go out into the world," he had exhorted Ash. "Seek the happiness you deserve. And the love. Surely, then, you will find your way home." Although Rowan had joined the human world, he still hovered on its periphery. He might have found happiness, but he had not discovered the way home. And I was powerless to help him.

Afraid of betraying my turbulent emotions, I avoided talking with my mother. Instead, I left a message, claiming that I was already going through withdrawal and would probably be a complete mope at Rehoboth. I must have sounded convincing because her return message assured me that it was better to mope on a beach than swelter in Brooklyn.

It would be impossible to fool Nancy so easily. When she

came up for the final cast party, she'd discover I was sleeping elsewhere. I worked up the courage to tell her that I'd made the first move after all, but got off the phone fast when she started making plans to see me when I came up to Vermont in the fall.

I found the greatest peace with Helen. Mostly, we just sat on the patio, sipping lemonade and chatting about unimportant things. On Thursday, she greeted me with a basket over her arm and we walked down to the garden to harvest lavender. Only the snip of our shears, the hum of the bees, and the gentle splash of the fountain broke the heavy stillness of the August morning.

But as we walked up the stone steps to the house, she said, "I'm so happy you found each other, Maggie."

I realized then that she knew Rowan and I were lovers, that the entire staff probably knew. I felt as if I had stolen something precious from her. Recalling the staff's bird-dog-on-point sensitivity to Rowan, I was struck by the horrifying possibility that Helen had felt his emotions, that all of them had shared the heat of his desire, the shuddering release of his climax.

Helen rested tentative fingers on my arm. "Are *you* happy?"

"I'm . . . all over the place."

She nodded as if this was only to be expected. "You've given him a great gift, Maggie."

I felt like I was the one who had been given a gift. And in three days, it would be snatched away from me.

"Has he talked about . . . going home?"

I nodded.

"Does he seem . . . happy?"

"More like confused. He doesn't seem to know where he belongs. He even said that he's not sure whether he's faery or human any longer."

Helen surprised me by smiling. "You know, Saturday will be so busy with the two shows and the cast party. Let's have a little farewell lunch here tomorrow."

I was startled by the sudden shift in the conversation, but happily agreed. When I suggested that Rowan join us, Helen said, "I think we should make it just us."

"Just us" took on a new meaning the next day when Janet answered my knock. Her appraising look confirmed my fears that she knew exactly what had been going on in Rowan's apartment this past week. But for once, she held her peace and simply ushered me inside.

I followed her to the dining room and drew up short when I saw the entire staff seated around the table. I shot Helen a pointed look, and she flushed.

"This is not a farewell lunch," I said.

"As a matter of fact, it is," Janet replied. "Only it's Rowan's farewell we're concerned about."

I stared blankly at her. "What are you talking about?"

It was her turn to look blank. Glancing around the table, I saw her expression reflected on the faces of all the staff members.

"We believe he intends to return to Faerie," Reinhard said. "As soon as the season ends."

"But . . . the curse . . ."

"Maggie, dear." Helen squeezed my hand. "The curse is lifted."

"Didn't you know that?" Janet asked.

I shook my head, dazed. I was vaguely aware of Reinhard rising, guiding me to the empty chair, easing me onto it.

"When? How?"

There was another exchange of glances. This time, it was Helen who answered.

"I'm not sure exactly when it happened. Certainly by that first weekend of *Carousel*. As to how . . ." Helen smiled. "Why, that was you, Maggie."

I heard Janet demanding, "Didn't he tell you?" Helen replying, "That's not his way." And Alex pleading with everyone to stop talking and let me take it all in.

But it was happening too fast and there was too much to take in. I looked up at Reinhard, as if he might provide the answer, but his face held the same concern and confusion as the others. Only Helen seemed . . . peaceful. But she was probably the first to realize what had happened.

I sifted through her words again. The first weekend of *Carousel* I had sung to my father. Perhaps, my ability to forgive him and to forgive myself had been the keys to Rowan's breakthrough as well as mine. The first step in my healing, the final act of his.

I realized how many clues he had given me. His determined efforts to drive me away, pleading with me to be sensible for just one more week. His pain at losing Jamie, so visceral in the pages of his play. The terrible knowledge that he would have to relive that pain over and over again with each parting, each death. The way he had clung to me these last few days. I thought he was sad because I was leaving, never realizing that he intended to make that final, irrevocable break.

Back to the muted world of Faerie, where partings were so much more infrequent, so much less painful. Where everyone shared the same long lifetimes, and pleasure came without the risk of love or loss.

They were all watching me, their expressions ranging from concern to pity to affection. Oddly, Janet seemed angry. I would have expected her to be pleased that Rowan was leaving.

I finally managed to say, "You should be happy for him. I am."

"Then why are you crying?" Hal asked.

I glared at him and swiped at my cheeks. "It's what he's wanted. For hundreds of years."

"He's changed," Helen said.

Mei-Yin thumped the table with her fist. "THIS is his home."

Alex nodded. "And you're the only one who can convince him of that."

I wondered why they thought I possessed such power over Rowan. Yes, I had pushed him into making changes. But it was one thing to demand that he attend a cast party, quite another to demand that he abandon his world and his folk and—possibly—his only hope for peace.

"Even if I had the power to convince him to stay, I wouldn't use it. That would be holding him hostage as surely as the Mackenzies did."

"Would you rather lose him?" Catherine asked. "Forever?"

"I'd still lose him. He'd hate me for doing that. Just as he hated them."

I pushed my chair back. I had to lean on the table to ensure that my trembling legs would support me, clear my throat to ensure that my voice wouldn't break again when I spoke.

"This is Rowan's choice. And we have to let him make it."

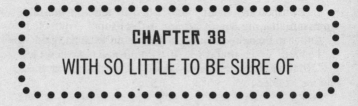

CHAPTER 38
WITH SO LITTLE TO BE SURE OF

SATURDAY ARRIVED, REEKING OF ENDINGS: the last matinee, our last company dinner, our final performance of *Carousel*. I felt strangely calm; I wasn't sure if it was because I had accepted what was going to happen or because it still seemed unreal.

I shook off my daze for the evening show. This performance was my gift to Rowan. I wanted it to be one we could both recall with pride.

The exuberance of June burst inside of me with the remembered giddiness of our shared laughter under the beech and his undisguised delight in my body. The repletion of the clambake suffused me with the same languorous afterglow of our lovemaking.

He offered me the same gift: his boyish enthusiasm as he sang about his son, his protectiveness as he imagined his daughter, his fierce attempt to resist his attraction to Julie, only to surrender with impossible tenderness.

You are all these things to me, we told each other in every song. The gentle emotions and the angry ones. The push and pull of dissension and the melding of minds and bodies into oneness. The fears and the doubts one tries to hide and the shelter the other offers when darkness threatens to suffocate the light.

When I saw him lying on the stage in Kalma's arms, all those emotions tumbled in upon me. I listened to the vamp repeat once, twice, three times. I felt Alex watching me, and Kalma. But I waited until I found my voice.

And then I sang to Rowan. To the director who had pushed me so hard. To the friend who had comforted me when I felt lost. To the lover who had delighted me with his tenderness and his wonder.

I sang the marvelous impossibility of his existence and the sorrow that it carried. I sang healing for his pain, and the recognition of the centuries of healing he had shared with the wounded souls of this world. I sang forgiveness for what had happened to my father and asked his forgiveness for doubting that his intentions were honest and good and true. I sang my gratitude for all that he had helped me discover, the pain of losing him, the fear that I would never know his equal. The joy of sharing his life—however briefly—strengthened my trembling voice so that I could sing the hope that his journey would be safe, that his life would be happy, that his spirit would find peace.

For a moment, I found peace as well, but it shattered during the reprise of "If I Loved You." It was impossible to hear the lyrics about Billy leaving this world forever without recognizing that Rowan would soon do the same.

While he was still singing to Kalma, his gaze shifted to where I huddled in the wings. He offered me a gift to ease my pain, the gift I had longed for since I first heard him sing "If I Loved You." For just a moment, he freed his power. And it infused his voice with such passion and longing and regret that tears spilled down my face.

His gift gave me the strength to master my emotions and sing to him one last time. In the number that ended the show and our season, I assured him that he would never walk alone, that the love and respect of each member of his cast—of all his casts—would follow him. That we would always remember the lessons of the Crossroads. And that I would always hold him in my heart.

When the curtain swung shut after our bows, we were all strangely silent, recognizing the end of an extraordinary chapter in our lives. Everyone turned to Rowan, like flowers seeking the sun, and his power embraced us with love and encouragement and the reassurance that this was a beginning rather than an ending.

Our pent-up emotions burst free in tears and hugs just like any other closing night. I glanced around the stage, knowing I was unlikely to encounter most of these people again. But some would always be part of my life. Lou and Bobbie. Bernie and Sarah. Kalma and Brittany. Gary. I might have to let Rowan go, but these few I would hold onto twice as hard. And Nancy, of course. They were as great a gift as any of the others I'd received this summer.

Lee shattered the tremulous emotion by yelling at us to change and get our asses back for strike. As everyone rushed to the dressing rooms, I discovered Rowan in the stage right wings, hovering between shadow and light.

I closed my eyes, imprinting that picture on my memory. Somehow, it captured all the contradictions of his nature and the dichotomy of his existence. When I opened them, I found him striding toward me. In the harsh glare of the work lights with the crew swarming over the set, he took me in his arms.

"It's all right," I whispered. "Everything will be all right."

He pulled back and regarded me with a bleak smile. "Maggie Graham, you're the worst liar in this world or the other."

"Points for trying?"

"Always."

He kissed me gently, and I heard someone gasp. Only then did I realize that the pounding of hammers and the shouts of the crew had ceased.

Rowan scowled at the rapt crew. "Don't you have a set to strike?"

Lee was the first to recover. "Yeah. And maybe if you two would stop making out center stage, we could actually strike it."

"You know nothing of romance," Javier complained. He grabbed Lee— hammer and all—and dragged him into a waltz, singing "Love Makes the World Go Round." Then Catherine cut in and spun Javier away, warbling "I'm in Love with a Wonderful Guy." Within moments, the entire crew was dancing around the stage.

Rowan shouted, "You've all lost your minds!" But he was smiling. We both were. And for a moment, at least, the fear retreated.

The cast seemed more shocked by Rowan's presence inside
Janet's house than the fact that his arm was around me. Brittany and Ashley sighed. Kalma nodded wisely and whispered, "Aphrodite. I knew it all the time." Nancy beamed
like a Jewish yenta, while Lou pounded Rowan on the back
and said, "Love, man. There's nothing greater."

My pained smile drew understanding looks; it was, after all, a night filled with an equal measure of celebratory
joy and the sadness of incipient partings. Rowan handled it
much better than I did. Only during the obligatory end-of-
the-season speech did his facade crack. But practically everyone was weeping by then; if he had to pause to compose
himself, it was merely proof that this summer had meant as
much to him as it had to us.

I seized his hand before he slipped away and blurted,
"You'll . . . wait up, right?"

"Yes. I'll wait."

"I can leave now—"

"No. Stay. You have other good-byes to say."

So I lingered. I'd already exchanged e-mail addresses and
phone numbers with everyone I was determined to keep in
touch with, but there were a few last minute additions, including Caren, who seemed so unhappy at the prospect of
leaving and so desperately relieved when I invited her to
visit me in Brooklyn.

It was nearly 2:00 A.M. when I finally turned to Nancy and
asked, "Did you ever think we would become friends? When
all this started?"

"I thought we'd loathe each other. You seemed so smart
and confident and funny. I was . . . well . . . me."

"I'd never have made it through without you. You know
that."

"Same here." She hesitated, then asked, "You're ending
it, aren't you?"

I nodded, unable to speak.

"Are you sure, Maggie? The two of you . . . you're so
good together."

I nodded again.

"I can hang around tomorrow if you need me. And if you don't want to drive home, you can spend a few days with me."

I clutched her desperately, then forced a smile. "I might take you up on that." Then I bolted for the front door.

The staff was gathered on the porch. Janet stopped pacing when she saw me.

"When are you leaving?" she demanded.

"Tomorrow morning. Early." Drawing out our farewells would be far too painful.

"Have you thought any more about . . . what we talked about?" Alex asked.

"I can't do it, Alex. It's not that I want him to go, but . . ."

"Enough!" Reinhard rounded on the others. "Maggie has made her decision. It is not fair to try and bully her into changing her mind."

"I wasn't bullying!" Alex protested.

"No. But this discussion is over." Reinhard gave me a brief, hard hug and quickly stepped back. "We are always here. You know that."

I swallowed down the lump in my throat and nodded.

One by one, I hugged them. Tears welled in my eyes when I reached Hal. They overflowed when I came to Helen.

She dabbed at my cheeks with her handkerchief. "No matter what happens tomorrow, Rowan will always carry you in his heart. We all will. Remember that, my dear. And know that you will always have a home at the Crossroads."

I mounted the stairs to his apartment for the last time. Each step carried the memory of other visits, other emotions. If the stairs could do more than creak, they could tell the whole story of our relationship.

The door swung open, and he appeared above me, surrounded by light. He held out his hands and smiled. "I never even told you how pretty you look in your new dress."

"Sarong," I corrected. "Please don't break into 'Younger than Springtime.'"

" 'Some Enchanted Evening' is your song, as I recall."

What I recalled was the closing wisdom of that song: once you had found your true love, you should never let her go. But I wasn't Rowan's true love. And I had to let him go.

Our loving was tender and slow, yet it was still over too soon. And in spite of my resolve to remain awake all night, to share every minute with him, I dozed off.

When I rolled over sometime later and found him gone, I bolted upright in bed, my heart pounding. A moment later, I heard the scrape of a chair from the office, the quick slap of his feet on the floorboards. The door flew open, and I blinked as light streamed into the bedroom.

The mattress sagged as he gathered me in his arms and whispered, "I'm here."

Before I could stop myself, I said, "Until morning."

His silence was answer enough.

I pulled away and took a deep breath. "I'm not going to make a scene. Or ruin these last hours. I just . . . are you sure, Rowan? About going back?"

"Yes, Maggie. I'm sure." His voice was as calm and steady as his gaze. "How long have you known?"

"Just since yesterday."

"You know it's the right choice. Don't you?" His eyes pleaded with me to agree.

"THIS is his home."

"You're the only one who can convince him . . ."

"You've given Rowan a great gift."

And now I had the opportunity to give him another.

"Yes. It's the right choice. The only choice. It's just . . . hard."

"For me, too. I never expected . . . any of this."

He hesitated as if he wished to say more, then strode toward the balcony where he stared out into the night. Then he turned.

"I want you to see me. As I really am."

He'd never allowed me to see him naked. During the day, he loved me with his hands and his mouth. At night, he slipped into the bathroom to put on a condom, then came to me in darkness. By now, I'd concluded that it was more than

shyness that prompted his behavior. But his discomfort only
fed mine, and I shook my head.

"Rowan. You don't have to—"

"I know. But I'm tired of hiding in the shadows."

He walked toward me and turned on the lamp on the
nightstand. Then he stepped back. His hands rose to his
waist. For a moment, he hesitated. Then he untied the sash
and shrugged off his dressing gown. It slid to the floor with a
soft hiss of silk. And he stood naked before me.

I had expected him to be hairless. But none of my imag-
inings prepared me for the soft white folds of flesh between
his legs.

I felt neither shock nor revulsion, only a deep sense of
confusion. He looked completely sexless, neither male nor
female. Yet I had felt him inside my body. Could he have
created that illusion with his magic?

His face was expressionless, all emotion hidden behind
that unblinking mask. I had to say something to reassure
him. He had offered me the great gift of his trust. Every moment I hesitated would only deepen his conviction that I was
unworthy of it.

As I groped for the right words, he snatched up his dressing gown. "Now you know why I've never allowed anyone
to see me like this."

That drove me to my feet. "You're beautiful, Rowan."

He flinched as if I'd told him he was hideous.

"Everything about you is beautiful and strange and impossible. And I want to make love with you."

I tugged the dressing gown from his hands and led him
to the bed where I kissed and caressed him until the tension
drained away, replaced by his growing desire. My fingertips brushed the smooth expanse of his chest. My gaze swept
over his body. I gave a strangled squeak.

A pink rosebud of a penis peeped out of the folds of flesh
between his legs.

Rowan cleared his throat. "It . . . does that."

"What else does it do?"

"The usual things."

I dragged my gaze from the rosebud and regarded him

with exasperation. "Then why in God's name did you make such a fuss about it?"

"Because it's . . . well, look at me! I'm not like . . . I'm different."

"I figured that out the first day I met you, you big goof."

I silenced his protest with a very thorough kiss. When we came up for air, he offered the sweet smile I loved so much. "You always astonish me."

"I don't know why. I'm the least astonishing person I know. Whereas you are—oh."

The rosebud had . . . bloomed. Was blooming. The kind of astonishing growth spurt you see in time-lapse photography on a nature show. Or a cartoon.

Without thinking, I murmured, "Hello, Pinocchio."

I clapped my hand over my mouth, horrified at the words that had just popped out of it. Rowan's expression underwent a series of changes ranging from shock to disbelief to embarrassment. Then he burst out laughing. My babbled apologies made him laugh harder.

Finally, he subsided into a succession of long, wheezing sighs.

"Maggie Graham. You are the only person in the world who could make me laugh at such a moment." Suddenly, he glanced down. " 'Look what you've done!' " he screeched. " 'I'm melting, melting . . .' "

Once we regained some measure of control, I set myself to the task of reviving his drooping rose. It recovered far faster than we did. We were giddy and breathless, surprised by our unexpected laughter, by the ease with which we had coped with this secret. Playfulness quickly shifted to tenderness, and tenderness to desire.

When his body covered mine, I felt as if I were filled with light and heat. I pulled him closer, my urgency tinged with the painful awareness that I could never bring him close enough.

The hoarse rasp of his breath, the rhythm of his movements, the honeysuckle musk of his body . . . they pierced me with the same silvery music I had heard at Midsummer. It vibrated with his power, striking an answering chord in me that blossomed into fullness, harmonizing with his and

building to a fierce crescendo until we lost ourselves in helpless dissolution.

Only afterward, as we lay in each other's arms, did the
sadness set in. For no matter how close we had become or
how many barriers had fallen, the ending would remain the
same.

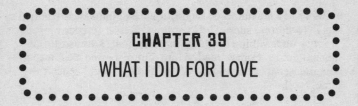

CHAPTER 39

WHAT I DID FOR LOVE

WHEN THE FIRST HINT OF BLUE APPEARED in the skylights, I slipped out from between the sheets and hurried into the bathroom with my clothes. I left the door open so I wouldn't be tempted to cry. I washed my face, brushed my teeth. I didn't wash my body, though; I wanted his scent on me—the sweet, musky smell of him. That, at least, I could keep for a while.

By the time I returned to the bedroom, he had dressed. I wore last night's finery, feeling anything but fine.

He took my hands and said, "I want to give you something. In return for all you've given me this summer."

Before I could protest that he had already given me so much, he leaned close and whispered in my ear. When I began to repeat the words, he pressed his fingertips to my lips.

"My true name. The one I chose as a boy. In the wrong hands, it could be used to bind me. Or steal my power."

"You mean if I had said it just now, something awful would have happened?"

He smiled. "No. I'm just superstitious. To harm me, you'd have to use it in a spell. If the witch had known it, she could have bound me to this world without the iron. And there are those who still practice the old ways who could use it against me. Including my folk." His expression became very serious. "No one knows that name, Maggie. Not in this world or in Faerie."

If I had been humbled by his trust last night, I was stunned now. To entrust such a gift to me who was forever blurting out the wrong thing at the wrong moment. I vowed to safeguard his name and speak it only in my mind. For me, of course, he would always be Rowan.

"Thank you. For telling me. For trusting me."

He kissed me gently. For a moment, we clung to each other. Then I eased free.

"Let's go down to the stage," he said.

That's where it had begun, after all. It seemed only fitting that it should end there as well.

I followed him through the living area and into the kitchen. My puzzlement grew as he opened a door that I had assumed was some sort of pantry. Instead of shelves of dry goods, I saw a dark stairway. He flipped on a light switch and led me down the stairs.

I waited outside the cramped lighting booth while he bent over the control board. Moments later, a pool of golden light illuminated the stage.

Hand in hand, we walked down the stairs from the balcony, followed the aisle through the orchestra section, and slowly mounted the steps to the stage. Rowan switched off the ghost light and together, we stared out at the darkened house.

"The last audition of the day," he said. "I heard you trotting down the aisle after Reinhard . . ."

"Bitching and moaning the whole way."

"What made you choose 'Some Enchanted Evening?'"

"I heard Bernie singing it. To Nancy."

"The whole of our summer in the way you performed that song," he mused. "So flip and sarcastic in the beginning. And then—halfway through—you sang. Really sang. With so much passion and hope that I knew you had to be Nettie." He smiled. "And I knew what an uphill battle I'd have on my hands to help you discover her. I just never imagined how much I would discover, too."

His face suddenly went blank. Then he whirled around, his gaze raking the wings.

Once by one, the staff emerged from the shadows. I wondered why Rowan had failed to sense their presence earlier;

perhaps he'd been concentrating so hard on restraining his emotions.

"What are you doing here?" Rowan asked.

I'd expected anger at their interruption. Instead, I felt confusion and a cold shudder of fear, quickly banished as he regained control.

"We didn't know when you were leaving," Helen said. "Or if you intended to say good-bye."

"I would never have left without . . . I was going to come up to the house. Later."

"And the rest of us?" Lee asked.

"I . . . I wrote letters."

"Jesus, Rowan." Alex looked shocked. "I've known you my whole life. Worked with you for forty years. And you were going to leave me a letter?"

"Oh, for God's sake, Alex!" Janet glared at her son. "He was trying to spare us—and himself—from exactly that kind of grotesque emotional outburst. An instinct I approve of as much as I disapprove of this melodramatic intervention. It's like the ending of some goddamn Agatha Christie mystery."

"Then why are you doing it?" I demanded.

Janet just shot me the same exasperated look she had given Alex. Of course, she was doing this for Helen. But I couldn't help saying, "It's unfair to mount this last-ditch effort to convince him to stay."

"That's what this is?" Rowan asked.

"They wanted me to do it. But I said it was your decision."

"There are things you need to know," Helen said, "that might affect that decision."

Rowan's expression grew wary. "What do you mean?"

"You think of us as your colleagues," Helen said. "And in some cases, your friends. But we're your family, too."

"I understand that, Helen. But it doesn't change—"

"No, you *don't* understand," Janet interrupted. "You've never understood." For a moment, she hesitated, regarding Rowan with a frown. Then she said, "Marsali Mackenzie died in childbirth. Just as her mother told you. But the child—your child—lived."

Rowan's shock broke over me with such force that

I gasped. He backed away, shaking his head. "No. That's not . . . the witch said—"

"She told you the child was taken," Helen said, her face full of pity. "You preserved her words in your play, remember?"

Rowan's memories assailed my mind: a forest glade; a circle of men, red hair glinting in the shafts of sunlight; a gray-haired woman, hatchet-faced like Janet, clutching something that hung on a chain around her neck.

"They named her Margaret," Helen said quietly, glancing at me.

A girl running toward him through sunlight and shadow, her laughter as joyous as birdsong. Not Margaret, of course. Her mother, Marsali.

"She was raised by one of the Mackenzie brothers," Janet said. "A blacksmith in Dale." Her voice was as flat as if she were narrating some dull piece of local history. "Later, of course, they had to move to another town. To protect Margaret and avoid arousing suspicion."

"Where is she?" Rowan demanded.

"She died," Helen said. "In 1854."

Rowan's hand came up to shield his face.

"She killed herself," Janet said. "Family legend claims it was because her faery blood drove her mad."

"We don't know that!" Helen added quickly. "Not for sure."

Wave after wave of shock and misery pummeled me. I flung my arm around Rowan's waist to support myself as much as him.

I couldn't believe Helen would allow Janet to concoct such a monstrous lie. Easier to believe that Janet had convinced her it was the truth and was using it to exact vengeance against Rowan for becoming Helen's lover. But nothing in Janet's manner conveyed satisfaction or pleasure. She looked tired, almost pained, as if she just wanted to get this over with.

"Before Margaret died," Janet continued, "she gave birth to twin daughters. I was one of them."

"It's a lie!"

Even Janet took a step back in the face of Rowan's fury.

"You're making this up! All of it! You've always hated me. Even before Helen."

"Yes, I hated you. Your lust killed my grandmother. Your blood drove my mother mad. Your selfishness ruined Helen's life. You couldn't even leave me Alex. His life revolves around you as much as Helen's does. And because they were determined to remain here, I was bound to this place as surely as you were."

Suddenly, Janet's passion evaporated and she shook her head wearily. "I've spent most of my life hating you. But after Helen's heart attack, I didn't have the energy for it. It never changed anything. And left me with . . . ashes. Ironic, isn't it? I've finally made my peace with you and you want to leave."

Rowan's gaze swept the faces of the staff. "Why didn't you tell me, Helen? Why didn't any of you ever tell me?"

"It was my secret," Janet said. "My precious secret. I held onto it for years, waiting for the right moment to use that knowledge. To wound you. When I realized that Helen was falling in love with you, I told her, thinking that would keep her from you." Janet's smile was bitter. "But my little plan backfired. So I'm as much to blame as you for ruining Helen's life."

"No one ruined my life," Helen said. "I wanted to be the one who opened the gateway for you. I knew you'd never allow yourself to love me if you knew the truth. Later, I was afraid you'd be angry that I had kept it from you. Please try to understand. And forgive me."

Rowan had his power under control again, his emotions carefully hidden. Only the tremors coursing through his body betrayed his shock.

"I was afraid, too," Alex said. "Afraid we wouldn't be able to work together. And the work was what kept me going after Annie died. That and Catherine, of course."

Rowan's gaze moved from his face to Catherine's to Helen's. "So you're all . . . family."

"And so am I," Reinhard said.

Rowan's breath hissed in. His hands came up as if to hold back another assault.

"Janet's sister, Isobel," Reinhard said quietly. "She was my mother."

"And my grandmother," Lee added.

"Lee is my sister's son," Reinhard said. "She and I were . . . estranged for years. I never even knew she had married. Or had a child. Until Lee came here. He looks . . . very like her."

Rowan was shaking, his hoarse pants loud in my ear. As if he had been running for miles, a stag pursued by baying hounds.

"There was also my son from my first marriage," Janet said. "Robert. He settled in California after World War II."

Rowan's gaze snapped to Mei-Yin and Javier.

"I'm his grandson," Javier said.

"I'm his daughter. A BASTARD. Big surprise, huh? Which makes Reinhard my second half cousin or something." Mei-Yin smiled up at Reinhard. "Doesn't change ANYTHING for us."

"Or us," Catherine said, squeezing Javier's hand. "Dad told us when we started dating."

"I, of course, didn't know anything about anyone until yesterday." Hal shot a reproachful glance at Lee. "I'm just . . . me. No relation to anybody." He sounded forlorn.

"Dearest, I know how hard this is for you," Helen said. "And please forgive us for breaking it to you like this. We hoped you would stay because of Maggie. If you had, we would have told you then. But when we realized you were going back . . . it was my decision. I thought you had to know that you would not only be leaving the woman you love, but your family, too."

"Wait," I said. "No. You're . . . you don't understand. Rowan isn't in love with me."

Nine blank faces stared back at me.

"But that's how the curse was broken," Helen said. "I thought . . . we all thought you understood that."

I turned to Rowan, but he was staring at the floor.

"The curse was about music and light and healing. There was nothing about love."

Janet's mirthless laugh broke the silence. Alex shook his head. Reinhard glared at Rowan and said, "You never told her."

My desperate gaze returned to Helen.

"There were three parts to the curse, Maggie. To return light and music to the world. To use his power to heal the Mackenzies' grief. And to feel the one emotion he had never known."

"What I stole, I must return. What I brought, I must take away. What I had never felt—"

"But it's not . . . it can't be me. It's Jamie. Rowan finally realized that he loved Jamie."

Again, I looked at Rowan for confirmation, but he refused to meet my gaze.

"For God's sake, say something!" Alex exclaimed.

Helen sighed. "Oh, Rowan. How could you leave without telling Maggie the truth?"

"Maybe he left her a letter," Lee said.

"Enough!" The word burst from Rowan on a blaze of anger. Then he turned to me and seized my arms. "I wanted to tell you. A hundred times this past week. But I thought you knew how I felt. After everything that happened, all the things we've shared—things I've never shared with anyone. I thought you were trying to make it easier for us. Just as I was."

The words reached me, without bringing the sense of them any closer. I took them apart and attempted to put them together again, a child struggling with a puzzle far too complex for her inadequate brain and fumbling fingers. Apparently, he had given me the last piece of that puzzle, but still, I could not determine its proper setting.

I searched his face and found desperation there, and concern, and the fear that he had wounded me. His power fluctuated wildly with those same emotions. But not love.

Then his hands came up to cup my face. And his love poured over me. Not the turbulent stream I had imagined, but the deep, still waters of a lake. Not the rock I had battered against for so many weeks, but one I could lean on for strength and support. No longer a shadowy sensation, half-sensed but always dismissed as fancy, but the strong, clear sunlight flooding the plateau.

"But if you love me . . .?"

"It doesn't change anything," he said gently.

"It does for me."

"If I asked you right now if you loved me, you'd say yes.

You'd always say yes, Maggie. Because you will always feel my power—my emotions for you."

I shook my head, but I couldn't help recalling all the times his power had left me giddy and breathless, when his emotions had swamped mine and carried me along, helpless as a leaf in a stream.

His smile was filled with sadness and understanding. "Even if you were certain of your feelings, I'd still have to go." He regarded his silent staff. "You came here to convince me to stay. Instead, you gave me the best reason to leave."

He took my hands, his expression still sad but determined now. "You deserve a man who can share your life without forever looking over his shoulder, hiding his real self from the world. A man who can give you a child without fearing that his tainted blood would destroy it. A man who can grow old with you. I can't give you any of those gifts, Maggie. And I'd rather lose you forever than stand by helplessly and watch you die."

I doubted I could bear that either. To watch him transform from a lover into a caretaker. To see him struggling to control his emotions lest they add to my grief. I had tried not to consider a future beyond this week, and when rebellious daydreams intruded, they extended only to next week, next month, next year, never twenty years from now or fifty. I had imagined the anticipation of seeing him, our combustible reunion, its drowsy aftermath. Walks in the woods and picnics on the plateau. Although I had known he would no longer be chained to this small parcel of land, I'd never even envisioned him beyond its borders.

Someday, I might laugh at the bitter irony that a faery made me realize what a completely impossible fairy tale I had created. Now, as his grief stabbed me, I became calm.

I had to help him, lend him the strength he needed to walk away. Time enough later for me to fall apart. Right now, he needed Maggie Graham, Helping Professional.

I watched him bid farewell to his staff, offering a handshake to some, a quick embrace to others. He held Helen for a long moment. I saw his lips move as he whispered something. She was weeping when he finally stepped back.

"Forgive me if I've seemed cold. Or if I ever gave the

impression that your friendship was unimportant. It was. It is." His gaze lingered on Alex, then Reinhard. "I had hoped to avoid a painful farewell. Even though I knew it was wrong to slink away. But you'll have to forgive me if I leave now. Before—"

His voice caught. Blindly, he flung out his hand and I stumbled forward to grasp it. He led me quickly toward the stage right wings, but paused there to look back.

"May the gods bless you all. And keep you ever safe."

We hurried out the stage door and into the picnic area. His words flowed at the same breathless pace.

"The letters to the staff are in my desk. There are two for Reinhard. Make sure he reads the first one before you leave. There's also a copy of *By Iron, Bound* for you. Act Two is a mess. I couldn't capture you. Foolish to try."

Like a dying man, dictating his last will and testament, disposing of his possessions, tying up the threads of his life.

He halted abruptly at the edge of the meadow. "I'm going to the cottage. I'll cross at sunset. Don't wait. It will be harder if I feel you here. Will you do that for me?"

I nodded, unwilling to trust my voice.

His hands fumbled at the back of his neck. The silver chain slipped free. He thrust it out. When I just stared at it, he seized my hand and dropped it into my palm, the metal warm from his skin. He closed my fingers around it. Immediately, he released my hand and stepped back.

I studied his face, just as I had the day I met him.

Remember everything about this moment. Those wild-winged eyebrows drawn together in a frown. The hard line of his mouth. The golden sparks, shining like tears in his eyes. Remember.

One final time, I held him.

Remember how his breath comes short and hard. How his fingers dig into your back. How those antler tine buttons dig into your breastbone. The thud of his heart against yours. The softness of his hair against your cheek. The sweet aroma of honeysuckle filling your nose.

And then I let him go.

Remember his eyes, soft and green as moss.

His hand came up to touch my cheek.

*Remember the scars on his fingertips, on his palms. The
slide of them against your flesh.*

His mouth came down on mine.

*Remember his lips, hard and bruising. The scrape of his
tongue. The warmth of his breath.*

"You are my heart."

*His voice, shuddering through you like his power. Raw
and harsh, in spite of the tenderness of his words. Remember
the contradiction. All his contradictions.*

He turned away and started walking toward the woods.

*Remember his long, purposeful stride. His fingers knot-
ted into fists. Remember how the grass bends before him.
How his hair gleams in the early morning sunlight, shiny
and black as a raven's wing.*

*Remember how he lurches to a halt at the very edge of the
pond, as if he forgot it was there, then stumbles around it, a
blur of beige and black against the green of the grass, the
pewter of the water.*

Remember the liquid song of a robin in one of the maples.

*Remember the breeze caressing your face, the sun warm-
ing your back.*

*Remember the creak of the weather vane atop the barn.
How you heard it that first day.*

At the edge of the woods, he paused and turned back.

*Remember how small he looks, dwarfed by the trees.
Small and alone and vulnerable.*

His hand came up.

*Remember his fingers, long and slender as a girl's. Re-
member the scars on his wrists. Is he smiling or weeping?
Weeping. His power tells you that. But remember his smile,
remember all of his smiles, but especially the one that surprised you so much with its unexpected sweetness.*

I raised my hand, still clenched around his silver chain.

*Remember that he loves you, that you are his heart, that
he will carry you with him all the days and nights of his long
life. Remember how much you love him, that it's not merely
an echo of his feelings, but as real as the sun on your back
and the tears on your face.*

His hand came down. He turned away. In three strides, he
was lost among the trees.

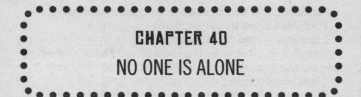

THE NEXT THING I REMEMBERED was the absence of warmth and sunlight. That seemed fitting, somehow. Then I realized I was inside a building. Janet's house, cool and shadowy.

Hands guided me up the stairs, led me into a room, urged me onto something soft. A bed. I was sitting on a bed. Hands stroked my hair, my back, my arms. Voices murmured quiet words that lapped against me, warm and soothing as bathwater.

"No! Don't take it away! Don't make me forget!"

A hand squeezing mine. Helen's face, blotchy from crying. "No, dear. Never. Just a blessing. For strength."

He was still here. In the woods. He probably hadn't even reached the cottage yet.

I lurched to my feet, pushing past the clustered bodies, the restraining hands. "There's still time!" If I called his secret name, if I asked the staff to help me . . . together, we could find some way to stop him from leaving.

Reinhard's hands grasping my shoulders. Reinhard's eyes looking down into mine. "Is that what you want?"

"Yes!"

But that was not what he wanted, not what he had asked of me.

"It will be harder if I feel you here."

"I have to go home."

"Rest a bit first," Reinhard urged.

I let him guide me back to the bed, ease me onto it.

"Why don't you lie down?" Helen suggested.

I shook my head. There was something important I was supposed to do. Instructions to pass along. I recited them to Reinhard, surprised that my voice sounded so calm.

"I will take care of everything," he assured me.

What else? What else was I forgetting?

"Nancy. She's waiting at the hotel."

"She's probably still asleep," Helen said. "It's not even seven. Are you sure you won't lie down, dear? Just for an hour."

He wouldn't be sleeping. How could I?

Helen sat beside me and clasped my hand. "He would want you to be peaceful, Maggie. He would want us to give you that peace."

"I have to do something."

"What?"

"Something. Anything."

"Fine." Janet pushed through the crowd. "You can help me make breakfast."

Reinhard shook his head impatiently, but I said, "Yes. All right."

Janet gave me a brisk nod of approval. "Helen can show you where everything is. Alex, Lee—help Reinhard at the apartment. Javier, gas up Maggie's car. Catherine, Mei-Yin—go to the hotel. Pack Maggie's things. Bring them here. And Nancy, too. Just tell her Maggie and Rowan have broken up and Maggie needs her support. Not the rest."

"You think I'm an IDIOT?" Mei-Yin exclaimed.

"What about me?" Hal asked. "What can I do?"

He looked so miserable that I lowered the fist I'd been pressing against my breastbone and uncurled my clenched fingers. "You can help me with this."

He stared at the silver chain coiled in my palm, and his face crumpled.

"If you're going to cry," Janet said, "go out on the porch."

Hal threw back his head and glared at her. "I can do this. I'm a costume designer!"

I surrendered the chain and rose. Cold fingers fumbled at the nape of my neck. How unlike Hal to be clumsy. The

chain nestled atop my collarbone. I caressed the braided silver with trembling fingers and glanced over my shoulder at
Hal.

He gave me a wobbly smile. "It's beautiful. Now. We'll
go to the bathroom and I'll help you fix your pretty face.
We'll both feel better after that."

❦❦

I looked better, but I felt just as numb. That was a good thing,
Hal assured me. When the numbness wore off, I'd be a mess.
Which is why, he insisted, I should stay with him and Lee.

Everyone seemed to have the same idea. As they trickled back to the house, I was inundated by invitations, surrounded by worried faces. When Janet herded us all into the
dining room, I picked at my eggs for a few minutes. Then
I put down my fork and said, "I have to go." Ignoring the
storm of protest that ensued, I added, "The longer I stay, the
harder it'll be. For both of us."

"Yes," Reinhard agreed. "But we will all worry if you
drive alone. So. I will drive you in your car. Wait. Listen. I
will not pester you with questions. I will not talk at all if you
prefer. But it will ease my mind if you allow me to do this.
Lee will follow in his truck and bring me home."

I nodded wearily. It was easier to agree than to argue.

"Good. Then say good-bye. And we will go."

I hugged Catherine and Javier. Received a rib-bruising
embrace from Mei-Yin, a tender one from Alex. And with
Janet's brisk hug, the stern advice to cry my eyes out for a
day and then get on with my life.

Nancy's hug was every bit as bruising as Mei-Yin's. "I'll
call you tomorrow. And I'll come down to Brooklyn next
weekend if you want me to. Any weekend."

I felt like Dorothy leaving Oz. I wished for a Glinda who
could magically transport me . . . somewhere. Not over the
rainbow. Or to Brooklyn; it had never felt much like home.

When I reached for Hal, he stepped back, his expression
fierce. "I'm coming with Lee. Don't even think of trying to
stop me."

Helen enfolded me in her arms. When she'd welcomed
me to the Crossroads that first day, I had thought she was a

fairy godmother, little realizing the truth behind that fanciful impression. She had offered blessings to lull me to sleep, a kind and open heart when I needed advice, a maternal embrace when I needed solace. Even now, I felt comfort and peace flowing from her. And I hated to think how little I had given her in return.

"Hush," she whispered. "You made me feel young again, and hopeful. And you gave me the greatest gift I could ever wish for—to see him happy. You must be happy, too, Maggie. He'd want that. And don't ever regret loving him."

Reinhard guided me down the path, a strong arm around my waist. Lee and Hal followed behind, like official mourners. Reinhard was speaking. Something about Rowan's journals. I tried to focus, but it was difficult.

"He wanted you to have them. It was in his letter to me."

Yes. I remembered the letter. The one he was supposed to read before I left.

"There were more than we expected. They filled five boxes."

"Five boxes?"

Reinhard smiled. "It would seem he was always a writer. The first journal was written in 1838. I've packed it—and this year's—in a separate box as Rowan requested. With his play and the other things. The rest of his journals I will store. Or ship to you when you are ready. Yes?"

I nodded, too dazed to inquire about the "other things" Reinhard had packed.

When we reached my car, I rubbed my streaming eyes, ruining all of Hal's efforts. My gaze moved from the cluster of people on the front porch to the deep green of the woods.

Can you feel me? Do you know I'm about to leave? If you know that, you must feel my love as well. Carry it with you to that other world. And I will carry yours with me.

I raised my hand in farewell—to my friends on the porch, to the man in the woods. Then I collapsed into the passenger seat.

I stared straight ahead as we drove up the lane and out into the road. Only when we started up the hill did I twist around. Through my tears, the Crossroads Theatre was little more than a pale blob floating between green grass and blue sky. Then we crested the hill and it disappeared.

◄◄ ►►

It was still early afternoon when we arrived in Brooklyn. Reinhard expressed cautious approval of tree-lined Eastern Parkway with its rows of brownstones, but seemed surprised by the diversity of the neighborhood where black-coated Hasidim shared the sidewalks with weekend soccer leagues, yuppie couples pushing strollers, teenagers calling to each other in Spanish and Creole, and formally dressed African-American families heading home from church.

Sweltering heat and reggae music blasted me as I threw open the car door. My apartment was an oven, but at least my tenant had left it clean. The three men tried unsuccessfully to conceal their shock at its size; if I had told them the rent I paid, they would have been even more shocked.

Reinhard gazed around the room and announced that we were going out to lunch. I took them to Tom's Restaurant. It was a bit of a hike, but we all needed to stretch our legs after the long drive. Even if they didn't want to try the out-of-sight egg creams, they'd find something familiar on the menu; I wasn't sure how Reinhard would fare at the West Indian places near me.

Afterward, we trudged back to the apartment, heavy with food and heat. Lee and Hal hesitated at the steps to my building, looking at Reinhard for guidance.

"We could stay a while," he told me.

Their presence would be a bulwark against the inevitable pain that sunset would bring, but I shook my head. They had already done more than I could have asked—today and throughout the summer. These three men—all so different— who had leaped to my aid so many times. Lee, fiercely protective the night of the Follies. Hal, whose sweet, open nature had been apparent from the very first day.

And Reinhard. Two months ago, I could never have imagined that the man who had bullied me into auditioning would become my staunchest ally. I had cast Alex as my surrogate father, but it was Reinhard who had stepped into the role.

Never obtrusive, never pushing me for confidences I was unwilling to share, but always there, guarding my back and ensuring my welfare, hiding his affection and concern beneath a gruff veneer, never realizing that the state of his hair always revealed his emotions.

It was in full porcupine mode now. I resisted the urge to smooth it and simply hugged them one by one. Hal wept. Lee kicked the step of my brownstone. Reinhard frowned.

"You will be all right. You have our numbers. You will call if you need us."

"I'll call even if you don't," Hal said.

I shoved a napkin into Reinhard's hand with scrawled directions to the Whitestone Bridge. Waited on the steps, smiling and waving until Lee's truck rounded the corner. Then my smile faded, my arm fell to my side, and I walked slowly up the stairs to my apartment.

I cranked the A/C up another notch. Washed my face. Exchanged my sarong for a T-shirt and shorts. Stared at the cardboard "Store-All" box sitting under my front windows and decided I wasn't ready to tackle it.

I unpacked my carryall and my suitcase. Put fresh sheets on the futon, hung fresh towels in the bathroom. Scoured the tub and the sink. Picked up some supplies at Food Town. Each task distracted me, kept me calm, allowed me to focus on the immediate problem confronting me. French baguette or seeded Italian loaf? Cottonelle or Charmin?

I called Jorge and thanked him for doing such a great job on the bathroom ceiling. Called my mother to let her know I was home. Pleaded exhaustion to avoid a long conversation and promised to call tomorrow. Only then, as afternoon was sliding into evening, did I sit down beside the box.

I took a deep breath and removed the lid.

I saw the envelope first. With some surprise, I realized I had never seen his handwriting before. I studied the small, precise letters of my name, then set the envelope aside.

The first leather-bound journal I picked up was the size of a notebook. The other was more like a diary, the leather cracked with age and torn at the corners. Those, I set aside as well. And the script of *By Iron, Bound* that he had placed inside a large manila envelope.

I found his script and score of *Carousel*, both filled with tiny, penciled notations. A battered copy of the 1836 edition of the *McGuffey Reader*. A CD entitled *The Rankin Family*.

I studied the back cover and caught my breath when I saw a track entitled "Chì mi na mórbheanna." The Gaelic title of the song I knew as the "The Mist-Covered Mountains." I put the CD on my player, skipped ahead to the track, and sank onto the floor again as the sweet, unearthly female voice I had heard in his apartment filled mine.

I pulled out the soft lamb's wool throw, the knapsack he had carried on our picnics. Inside I found a bottle of Chateauneuf du Pape. And—carefully wrapped in a linen napkin—a faded beech leaf.

I had to pause then and wait until I collected myself before opening the second manila envelope. It was larger than the one that held his script, softer and lumpy. And the handwriting on the outside belonged to someone else.

Maggie. This was not on Rowan's list. But I thought you would wish to have it. Forgive me if I presume too much.

I opened the clasp. My fingers brushed the nubbiness of linen. And something hard and pointy.

I held the wrinkled shirt to my face, the shirt he had worn only yesterday, and breathed in his animal musk and his honeysuckle sweetness and the faint tang of his sweat. I wept for the loss of the man I loved, but also in gratitude to the one who had given me this gift. Reinhard had guessed rightly that the memories it evoked and the sheer physical closeness of Rowan would far outweigh the pain.

Reluctantly, I let the shirt fall to my lap while I examined the last item. A rectangular wooden box, roughly the size and shape of a box of tissues. The painted green vines on its cover and sides were so faded with age that I had to squint in the dying light to make them out.

I raised the lid and gasped.

Hundred dollar bills in ten neat bundles, each secured with a rubber band. With shaking hands, I counted one.

Fifty thousand dollars.

"My salary doesn't allow me many luxuries, but it does put clothes on my back and food on my table."

Long summer days blocking the shows, exhorting his casts, helping them discover what was lacking in their lives. Long winter evenings collaborating with Alex, shaping and reshaping their newest creation. A century of directing and writing. A century of savings. Tucked away in a wooden box. And given to me.

It was far more than a gift of money. It would give me time to decide what I wanted to do with my life. With my unemployment, I could live on half that money for a year. Longer if I moved out of New York.

And the balance? That would go back to the Crossroads. To give the staff the time it needed to create a plan for the theatre's future. And to take care of some of the immediate necessities: augmenting those wretched salaries, painting that tired-looking lobby. New chairs—comfortable ones—for the Smokehouse. And furniture for the green room to replace the chairs and tables that were literally falling to pieces. Maybe there would even be enough left over for Hal to splurge on some snazzy costumes next year.

For the first time in days, I was excited, looking forward to the future. And I blessed him for that gift, too, amazed that I could feel those emotions when the light filtering through my windows told me it must be close to sunset.

I wondered if his power was strong enough to touch me here. He had reached me before; I'd been looking through travel books then. But he had been calling all of us. Maybe it was harder to call one person. Maybe he would prefer to slip away. Spare us both that final pain.

Then I realized he *was* calling me. Not with his magic, but with his words.

I slipped my arms through the sleeves of his shirt. Carried his play, his journals, and his letter to the futon. Grabbed a Mike's Hard Lemonade from the fridge; the Chateauneuf du Pape was meant to be shared.

I would not sit and watch the light fade, wondering when he chose to make his crossing. I would let his words bridge that moment, fill the hole left in the world, fill me with his thoughts, his hopes, his fears, his love.

My dearest Maggie,

Before I can write the words of my heart, I must say a few words about the things I have instructed Reinhard to pack for you. Most are sentimental in nature. Not—I hope—maudlin. You will have to judge.

The journals are a window into my life, my thoughts, my heart. I should warn you: some of the sections from this summer are ugly. I reread the worst passages while you slept and winced. I was angry when I wrote them. And hurt. I worry that you'll feel the same after you've read them. But I am through hiding in the shadows.

Other sections are—I don't know, maybe you'll wince at those, too. Because they're so graphic. Not pornographic. I hope. Your body is such a wonder to me. I go on at embarrassing length about it. I will not do so here.

There is money in the wooden box. Not much for more than a century's labor. But it is free of all encumbrances, including those imposed by the government. I have never had a bank account or an Internet account, a credit card or a phone. There are inconveniences in having no identity—I used Helen's Internet account to purchase my clothes, did I ever tell you that?—but there are advantages as well. So keep the money in the box as I did, so that you can benefit from it rather than Uncle Sam.

I suspect your first reaction will be to give it to the theatre. I beg you to keep some of it for yourself. It will give you time to consider what you will do next. Take that time, my love. Allow yourself to drift and dream as I urged on our first picnic. Trust yourself to find your true path. And when you do, don't be afraid to take it.

I have just reread what I've written. I sound more like a lawyer than a lover. Except for the remarks about your body. Were I a lawyer, I'd be disbarred for those.

Are you smiling? I hope so. I am. Almost.

I'm procrastinating. Because when I finish writing this letter, all that's left is the waiting. For morning. For our farewells. I pray I'll have the strength. I know you will. You're much stronger than I am.

Know that I will always love you. For making me laugh. For making me doubt. For making me change. I love your kindness and your stubbornness and your courage. Your great bellow of a laugh. Your quick wit. Your blush. The sight and the smell and the taste of you.

Loving you is the most impossible thing that has ever happened to me. And the most humbling. I never expected love to bring equal measures of joy and sorrow, delight and fear. And those unexpected moments of peace. I imagine this is what it must be like to shoot the rapids in a leaky canoe and then emerge from heart-stopping tumult into a quiet pool.

You will be with me every day, every night. My shield against loneliness. The bright, pure flame that burns at the core of my being. And if there is an afterworld where humans and faeries meet, we will find each other again and our spirits will dwell together until the world's end.

My love. My heart. My beautiful girl. Be well. Be happy.

Yours,
Rowan

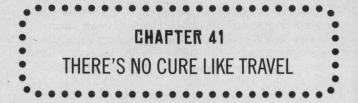

I FILLED MONDAY MORNING BY PICKING UP MY MAIL at the post office, running a load of wash at the Laundromat, dusting, vacuuming. When I ran out of tasks, I called Mom at work and asked if I could come down to Delaware a little early.

Three hours later, I was sitting on her horribly uncomfortable settee, calmly explaining that I had been involved with Rowan Mackenzie but we both realized it wouldn't work out and we had gone our separate ways and I was fine, really, not really fine, but okay, would be okay, I just needed a little time, and could we please not talk about it any more.

Her gaze rested on the silver chain around my neck, but all she said was, "All right. Would you like to go to Domaine Hudson for dinner?"

I spent much of that week just wandering along the Brandywine. Sometimes, I sat by the river reading Rowan's journals and his play. I thought a lot about *The Sea-Wife*. The parallels to our situation were obvious. The selkie who had to return to her home. The lover who had to let her go. I'd told Rowan that the schoolteacher would find love again because he had learned to hope, to change, to embrace the impossible. I wanted to believe that was true for me, too. But Rowan had left the ending ambiguous. And that's how my future felt.

Mom did her best to distract me in the evenings, taking me to a concert at the Riverfront, a concert at Longwood

Gardens, a concert at the Chadds Ford Winery. "Thank God
we're going to Rehoboth," she said near the end of the week.
"I'm running out of concerts."

She studiously avoided taking me to the theatre—and
talking about Chris. Finally, I asked if I was ever going to
meet the mystery man.

"I wasn't sure . . . I thought it might be . . . difficult."

"Well, as long as you don't make out in front of me or
anything."

"Maggie!"

After extracting a promise to say nothing that might
embarrass her, she invited Chris to dinner on Friday night.
He turned out to be a lawyer with a neatly trimmed gray
beard, an earnest expression and—after two glasses of
wine—a wicked sense of humor. We took turns embarrassing my mother, who blushed and protested and enjoyed it
immensely. As happy as I was for her, it was hard to suppress
the feelings of regret and longing and envy that filled me
each time she and Chris exchanged smiles.

Rehoboth was crowded and noisy—your typical beach
town in August. Maybe because it held fewer memories than
Wilmington, it was easier for me to relax there. I still woke
to the pain of Rowan's absence and went to sleep with that
pain at night, but in between I tried to drift as he had urged,
to live in the moment, to enjoy the cool slap of the waves, the
tackiness of the boardwalk, and the quaint shops in nearby
Lewes.

By the end of our week, Mom had stopped studying me
for signs of a nervous breakdown and allowed me to take
solitary walks on the beach in the evening without fearing I
would swim out to sea and drown myself. I could even talk
about the summer—at least parts of it—without the threat
of tears. To Mom and to the astonishing number of people
who called.

After inundating me with calls those first few days in
Wilmington, Helen and Hal apparently decided to give me
time off during my week at Rehoboth. But Nancy called every couple of days. Although I was happy to hear from her, I
was reluctant to talk about Rowan; it just brought everything
crashing down on me again.

Chatting with Kalma and Brittany was easier, sighing over the annoyances of the "real" world and speculating about what the next few months would bring. Bernie called to complain about the boring old people at the senior center, Sarah to complain about her mother. Gary called to make sure I was okay. Caren wanted to know how soon she could visit Brooklyn. Bobbie wanted to do the "list thing" over the phone to help her weigh the pros and cons of moving in with Lou.

"You certainly have a lot of friends," Mom remarked after I hung up with Kevin who called to invite me to a gig in Queens.

I smiled; three months ago, I couldn't name one friend I could comfortably call on for help. Now I could name dozens.

Two weeks after leaving the Crossroads, I was back in Wilmington, packing yet again—this time for my return to New York. I was no closer to discovering my path in life than when I'd arrived in Delaware, and the prospect of returning to that empty apartment left me anxious and depressed.

When my phone broke into the "People" ringtone I'd programmed to identify Hal, my spirits revived a little.

"Maggie?"

Hearing the quaver in his voice, I immediately assured him I was okay.

There was a brief silence. Then something that sounded like a sob.

"Hal. What is it? What's wrong? Is it Lee?"

"No. It's Helen."

CHAPTER 42
I BELONG HERE

FIVE DAYS LATER, I WAS BACK IN DALE, still hearing Hal's tearful voice, still struggling to cope with this new loss. According to Hal, she had died quietly in her sleep—how like Helen—and Janet had discovered her the next morning.

She had lived more than a century, but even her faery blood could not protect her from the rheumatic fever that stole her strength. What a terrible irony that it should be Helen's heart that betrayed her.

I'd railed at Hal for failing to call me sooner, then felt horribly guilty when he burst into tears. "Janet wouldn't let me call anyone," he said when the storm subsided. "She insisted on a small, private funeral. Not even an obituary."

"But after the funeral? Why didn't you call me then?"

"That was Reinhard. He said you needed your vacation. And since we'd convinced Janet to hold a memorial service, I thought . . . oh, I knew I should have called! I don't know why I let people talk me into doing things I don't want to do. Now you'll hate me forever."

I assured Hal I wouldn't hate him, didn't hate him. I even volunteered to call my cast mates and let them know about the memorial service.

Helen had touched so many lives; people would want the chance to say good-bye. But I could understand Janet's desire to keep things private. What if some octogenarian former cast member arrived? How did you explain that

Helen—middle-aged when he had worked at the Crossroads fifty years ago—had lived so long? Or the seemingly ageless appearance of Reinhard and Alex and Janet?

Reinhard provided the answers when I called him to get phone numbers for some of my cast mates. "We will only be contacting those who worked at the theatre in the last ten years," he told me, his voice heavy with grief. "After the memorial, we will notify the others. It is a pity. There are many who would want to attend. But the dangers are simply too great."

Most of our cast was making the trip back to Dale. Some, including the Rastas, couldn't afford the airfare. Others, like Kevin, had weekend jobs. Nick never returned my call, but I'd expected that.

Even those who had been forced to seek accommodations in neighboring towns showed up at the Bough Friday evening. There had to be close to two hundred people, spilling out of the lounge into the lobby, clustering on the stairs and porches. Although many had decided to speak at the memorial service the next day, we held an unofficial one that night, sharing stories about Helen, about the theatre—and about Rowan.

Everyone had a similar account of his patience, his insight, his mysterious gift for pulling astonishing performances from his cast. And many shared personal stories about how their lives had changed after their season at the Crossroads. Like the young guy I'd seen around town who told me that playing little Winthrop in *The Music Man* had helped him overcome his shyness. And the woman who explained that her role as Louise in *Gypsy* had convinced her to attempt a reconciliation with her mother.

Late that night, I pulled out Rowan's final journal and jotted the stories down. A sort of memorial for him and a testament to the effects of his healing on so many lives.

Reinhard had prepped me about the party line on Rowan's absence. He had gone home to Scotland. He had no plans to return. They had not even notified him of Helen's death yet. My job was to convince my cast mates that our failed relationship had been partly responsible for his decision. I would also have to convince them that I had only learned of his departure in the last few days; otherwise, close friends

like Nancy and Kalma would surely wonder why I'd said
nothing earlier.

Yet another unforeseen acting job. But if I could manage
to let him go, I could surely lie about where he had gone.

The happy memories of the summer helped offset some of
the sadness that flooded me when I entered the theatre the
next day. Reinhard directed the memorial service with a firm
voice and a ravaged face. He expressed the staff's love for
Helen and their gratitude for all she had done for them and
for the theatre. Then he invited others to share.

The tributes lasted more than three hours. So many stories, all citing Helen's generosity and kindness, her unfailing
cheerfulness and warmth. When the last person finished, Reinhard returned to the stage and read Rowan's farewell letter
to Helen. He skipped over any passages that hinted at the
intimate relationship they had shared, but even with those
omissions, Rowan's letter was filled with humor and tenderness, with his gratitude and his love, his sorrow to be leaving
her and his joy that she had been part of his life for so many
years. And hearing his words, picturing him as he struggled
to write them—to write all those letters—I wondered how he
could ever have imagined that I was the strong one.

I was walking out of the theatre when I glimpsed someone
talking to Lou and Bobbie. When I realized who it was, my
mouth fell open. I hesitated, wondering if he'd want to talk to
me. When he nodded brusquely, I decided to chance it.

"How are you, Nick?"

"Okay. You?"

"Okay."

I glanced at the skinny blonde beside him, teetering on
the gravel in her spike heels, a squirming infant in her arms.

"This is Deb. Maggie."

"Nice to meet ya," Deb said. "Nicky, I gotta put Angie
down for a nap."

"Okay." He nodded to us awkwardly. "Good to see you
guys."

"Janet's having a reception at the house," I said. "Why
don't you come for a little while?"

Nick shrugged. "We only got the one car."

"So I'll give you a lift after," Lou said.

"We're staying out of town."

Lou punched Nick's shoulder. "So I'll still give you a lift, asshole."

Nick grinned. Then glanced doubtfully at Deb. "You came all this way," she said. "You should spend time with your friends. I'll see ya at the motel."

"Come back after Angie's had her nap," Bobbie urged. "Janet puts out a great spread. You should spend time with Nick's friends, too."

This time it was Deb who glanced doubtfully at Nick.

"That's a great idea," Lou said. "Isn't it, Nick?"

Nick muttered agreement. Deb smiled wanly, then tottered off in search of their car.

"It'll never last," Bobbie muttered as we followed Lou and Nick up the path.

"Probably not," I agreed. "But at least, he's making an effort."

"Damn, I wish Rowan could've seen this."

"Yeah. Me, too."

Janet was conspicuously absent from the reception, but the rest of the staff was there. Alex put up a brave front, but I knew how hard it must be to pretend that Helen was merely a good friend, not his sister. At one point, I saw him sitting on a bench in the garden and made my way down to him. For a long while, I just sat with him, listening to his childhood memories of Helen; even then she had been as much mother as sister to him.

"How's Janet?" I asked.

Alex shook his head. "You know Momma. She keeps everything inside. Even with me. Especially with me."

Her only child now.

He squeezed my hand. "How are *you* doing?"

"You know. A wreck some days. Other days, okay."

"It's like he died, too."

I bit back my protest. In the space of a week, Alex had lost two people who had been part of his life for more than seventy years. But I could not—would not—think of Rowan as dead. For me, it was more like when my father went away. A sort of limbo.

As afternoon turned to evening, people began drifting away. I was walking to the door with Nancy when Lee stopped me.

"Would you mind hanging around, Maggie? There's some stuff we need to discuss. About Helen."

"That sounds mysterious," Nancy said as Lee walked off.

"Maybe she left me a letter or something."

An hour later, I found myself seated at the dining room table, trying to banish memories of the last time I had been there. Janet walked in and greeted me with, "Good. You're here. Let's get started." Which did little to relieve my growing anxiety.

"If this is about the money Rowan left me, I've already decided to give half of it to the theatre. I didn't think today was a good time . . . I mean . . ."

My voice trailed off as I took in their expressions. Only Reinhard seemed unsurprised; clearly, Rowan must have told him about the money in his letter.

"This meeting is about Helen's bequests," Reinhard said. "Not Rowan's."

"I don't know whether you realized this," Lee said, "but I was—am—Helen's lawyer. A couple of weeks ago, she called us together to discuss some changes she wanted to make to her will. Make sure we were okay with them. Her new will leaves two specific bequests to you. The first is what she called her Recipe Book."

What I had called her book of spells.

"But that's an heirloom," I protested. "It should stay in the family. With you," I added, looking across the table at Catherine.

"There are two herbals," Janet said. "Helen left Catherine the original written in the Gaelic."

"I have such a black thumb it wouldn't matter if it was in English," Catherine replied with a small smile. "Besides, you're a Mackenzie, too. That makes you family."

"The other," Janet continued, "is a copy my great-grandmother transcribed in English near the end of her life."

"But—"

"Helen wanted you to have it," Janet said, putting an end to further argument.

She placed a worn leather volume on the table. I opened it and peered at the spidery handwriting on the first page, the ink faded to tan.

The Herbal of Mairead Mackenzie. 1817.

The paper crackled as I carefully turned the pages. There were remedies for chilblains and "joint-ill," insect bites and green fractures, "costiveness" and quinsy. Directions for preparing ointments and poultices. Rituals to observe when harvesting plants. Incantations and charms to soothe the heart and the bowels, to attract a lover or repel one, to curse an enemy or bless a loved one. Talismans to protect the wearer from witches and faeries.

A treasury of folklore and knowledge and superstition— and a gift of love from the woman who had hesitantly told me about her nighttime blessings.

I blinked back tears and whispered, "This belongs in a museum."

"Probably," Lee agreed. "But Helen's instructions are very specific. By accepting this bequest, you agree to pass it on only to a blood descendant of Mairead Mackenzie. Do you accept that proviso?"

I nodded, still a bit overwhelmed.

"The other bequest is a little . . . bigger," Lee said.

I glanced at the sideboard. One of the lovely Chinese vases, maybe? Or Helen's candlesticks? I was still trying to decide which she might have chosen when Lee announced, "Helen left you the Golden Bough."

"Yeah. Right." I glanced around the table; no one was laughing. "You can't be serious!"

Lee nodded.

"But that's yours!" I exclaimed to Janet.

"I transferred ownership to Helen decades ago."

"But it's still yours."

"No, Maggie. It's yours. If you want it."

"What am I going to do with a hotel?" I blurted.

"It was Helen's hope that you would run it," Lee said.

"But I don't know anything about running a hotel!"

"I do," Janet said. "I can teach you. And then I can wash my hands of that old rattletrap."

"It's a lovely example of the Greek Revival style," Hal retorted. "It just needs sprucing up. Especially that lobby. The furniture's ancient and the moths are devouring those draperies. And those horrible portieres might have been fine for Scarlett O'Hara but—"

"Hal," Lee interrupted. "You're jumping the gun a bit. Obviously, this isn't a decision you can make in five minutes, Maggie. I'll go over all the documents with you: recent capital improvements, profit and loss statements—"

"Mostly loss," Janet muttered, prompting Alex to demand, "Do you want her to stay or not?"

"Is that what this is about?" I asked. "God. First Rowan, now me. Trust me, you'd be better off hiring me to direct the shows rather than run the hotel."

A furtive exchange of glances greeted that statement.

"I was joking. You knew that, right?"

"Suppose we finish up with the hotel first," Lee suggested.

"I haven't directed since college. And that wasn't even   "

"The hotel? Please?"

I didn't follow half of what Lee said. Finally Reinhard interrupted.

"I know this is a lot to take in. But Lee will help you understand the legal and financial ramifications. You should also know why Helen left you the property."

"That's in the letter," Lee said.

"Which you have not mentioned," Reinhard pointed out.

"I was getting to it! If everybody would just let me talk." Lee took a deep breath and blew it out. "Okay. Here's the deal. Helen dreamed of this theatre becoming a nonprofit. An educational facility that would not only present plays and musicals, but offer classes in acting and dance and directing. Children's programming. Summer internships for college students. Maybe even a residence hall for actors. Obviously, it'll take years to accomplish all that. But Helen thought—we all thought—that you were the right person to run that organization. To be its executive director."

My heart was beating so hard I was having trouble breathing. I managed to say, "I've never run a nonprofit. Or done a lot of fundraising."

"Well, you could learn, couldn't you?" Janet demanded.

"Of course! But this a huge step. For you, I mean. You need someone experienced."

"We want someone we know," Alex replied. "Someone who knows *us*."

"Someone we TRUST," Mei-Yin added.

"And not just because Rowan left," Hal said. "Because he would have been awful. I mean, he's brilliant and everything, but he's an artist. You are, too," he added hastily. "But you're practical. You can handle the details. And you get along with everybody. Even Janet. I mean . . . well . . . sorry."

"But what does that have to do with the hotel?"

Lee glanced uneasily at Reinhard, who said, "That bequest was a subject of some discussion. Some of us—myself included—felt it was too soon for you to return. That you needed time to . . . heal. And consider your options."

"But Helen was afraid you'd find another job," Alex said. "That by the time we were ready for you, you would have moved on."

"We need you NOW. We want you in on the PLANNING. The VISION. The DREAM."

"She never saw managing the Bough as a permanent gig," Javier said. "Just a way to tide you over while we were getting the new and improved Crossroads Theatre going."

"But more than that," Reinhard said, "Helen wanted you to have something of your own."

"Know that you will always have a home at the Crossroads."

"At the time, none of us knew about Rowan's bequest," Alex said. "That might affect your decision."

"It's not about money," Hal said. "It's what you want to do with your life, who you want to be."

"You're thirty-two years old, Maggie. Don't you have any idea what you want to be when you grow up?"

"No matter what you decide, you're going to need Rowan's bequest," Lee said. "For the first couple of years, you'll

be making the same kind of crap salary we get. So. The
Golden Bough."

I glanced around the table. My gaze lingered on Janet.
"If I do this, you and I are going to have to work together
pretty closely. Managing the hotel. Getting the new Crossroads Theatre up and running. Can you do that? Do you *want*
to do that?"

Janet smiled. For a moment, I saw Helen in her.

"Yes, Maggie. I want to do that. You're smart and you're
tough. And you've got a good heart. I don't know if I'll be
able to call back the Mackenzie descendants without Rowan.
So—"

"You helped him?" I interrupted.

"Well, it was my blood that he used." As I was digesting
that astonishing statement, she added, "Because I'm the el-
dest." As if that explained everything.

"The point is, the Crossroads Theatre is at . . . a crossroads. It has to change and grow if it's going to survive. And
if you could get Rowan Mackenzie to change, you can surely
do the same for this theatre. And that rickety old hotel."

"The more the theatre is in the spotlight, the more dangerous it could be for you."

"Alex and Reinhard and I discussed that. And we all
agreed that it's worth the risk to realize Helen's vision."

Janet would risk almost anything for that.

"I . . . I don't know what to say."

"You will say nothing now," Reinhard replied. "You will
talk with Lee. You will think about it. And then you will tell
us what you've decided."

"Never mind all the legal stuff," Hal said. "You *want* to
stay, don't you?"

I looked at the circle of expectant faces and swallowed
hard.

"Oh, yes, Hal. I want that more than I've ever wanted
anything in my life."

Except Rowan.

FINALE AND CURTAIN CALLS

CHAPTER 43
OPEN A NEW WINDOW

WAKE WITH THE BIRDS, INSTANTLY ALERT although I've probably slept a grand total of fifteen minutes. The floorboards creak as I hurry toward the kitchen. I gulp my first cup of coffee at the sink, pour another, and begin sifting through the papers and folders and notebooks that I pored over for hours last night.

I force myself to stop. I'm as ready as I'll ever be.

Radiators clang as the heat comes on. It sounds like the Seven Dwarfs and their extended family are performing a demented version of "The Anvil Chorus." Iolanthe's head jerks up. The tip of her pink tongue curls as she yawns. After a minute or two, the dwarfs settle down and, after kneading the sofa cushion into submission, so does Iolanthe.

Shower. Dress. Another cup of coffee. A magnet on the fridge reminds me: "I will not obsess! I will not obsess! I will not obsess!"

I head into the office to check e-mail and glance at the little card on the cluttered bulletin board: "Though time be fleet and I and thou are half a life asunder, Thy loving smile will surely hail the love-gift of a fairy tale." Although it's unsigned, I know Rowan must have given it to Helen. Janet urged me to redecorate when I moved in, but I like feeling Helen's presence in these rooms. And Rowan's. To feel they're both watching over me as I work.

Besides, Caren will be moving in after Memorial Day. God only knows where I'll be living after that. I may take Janet up on her offer to stay at the Bates mansion. Maybe by the end of the summer, I'll have worked up the courage to move into Rowan's apartment. Or at least walk inside. And Caren might have figured out what she wants to do with her life.

At least, managing the Bough this summer will ease her through these first months after the divorce. Give her something positive to focus on. She's already started in with redecorating ideas. Thank God, Hal approves her suggestions, although he describes her taste as "fussy." This from the man whose current window display features a jungle theme with feather boas and garter belts hanging like snakes from the artificial foliage, and mannequins wearing bras and panties with leopard spots and tiger stripes.

And if Caren works out . . . if she becomes the permanent manager . . .

Think about it tomorrow, Scarlett.

I answer the flood of "break a leg" messages in my inbox. Nothing in the hotel's mailbox that can't wait until tomorrow.

I pour another cup of coffee and cross to the wooden milk crates that hold my father's record collection. Pull out *The Fantasticks* and place it on the turntable—one of the few personal purchases I made with Rowan's money. Wait for the crashing chords of the overture to segue into the gentle intro of "Try to Remember." Then I remove Rowan's journal from the bookcase Catherine made me.

Last-of-the-Mohicans-Menswear.com, indeed. She'll be a tough nut to crack. It will be interesting to see what happens if she comes back . . .

Naturally, she had to be the one to hear me sing. And see the scars. Her concern moved me. I must tread carefully . . .

She's puzzled by my distance. And hurt. I need to find some middle ground where we are both comfortable . . .

Only she can decide how much to risk, how far to travel. My job is to keep her safe on the journey. To let her choose her own path, but remain close enough to support her . . .

When he wrote those words, neither of us could have imagined how far we would travel or how many twists and turns our paths would take. And if there were times that summer when I felt he had failed me, I understand now; his journey was far more difficult than mine.

I glance at my watch and gasp. Grabbing my briefcase and travel mug, I race for the door.

As I burst into the lobby, Bea calls, "Break a leg!" from the front desk. Thank God, she's holding down the fort today. I just pray the fort needs holding down. That the ritual Reinhard, Alex, and Janet have been performing for the past month works. Reinhard assured me there was very little blood involved. And that the Mackenzies will come. God, I hope so. I hate turning away guests to hold rooms for actors who may not even appear.

I console myself with memories of our brisk business over the winter. And bless the Rastas for designing our new Website. I still feel guilty about letting them do it for nothing; their business is still new and needs all the support it can get. When it's time to design a Website for the theatre, they're getting paid for every hour.

I dart into the Chatterbox and smile as patrons call out greetings and good wishes. As I slump onto a stool at the counter, Frannie clucks sympathetically. "Long night, huh?"

"Very."

"The usual?" She reaches for the pot, then scrutinizes me. "Or maybe decaf today."

"Definitely decaf."

"Be ready in a jiff. Help yourself to a muffin."

"I'm too nervous to eat."

"Save it for later, then. It'll taste even better after auditions."

She fills my travel mug, adds a dollop of cream, and snaps the lid on. Then lifts the glass dome over the muffins. I sigh and select one.

"Didn't think to see you so early."

"I'm stopping by to visit Helen first."

Her plump hand comes down atop mine. "She'd be real proud of you, hon. They both would."

My throat tightens and I lose any desire to nibble at the muffin. Although everybody in town talks freely about Helen, Frannie is one of the few who mentions Rowan. He was much more a part of the community back in Jamie's day. Now they remember the work, not the man.

As I slide off the stool, Frannie flings back the counter's

bridge and follows me to the door. "Now don't worry. You'll do fine. And your hair looks terrific. All tousled."

"Probably because I spent most of last night pulling it out in handfuls."

"It'll be fun. You'll see."

She follows me outside. So do most of the patrons. Mr. Hamilton in his John Deere cap. Sally and Trish, two of the waitresses at Duck Inn. Gina and Tony from Nonna's. Mr. Banerjee from the pharmacy. They wave as I ease my car into the street. Frannie shouts, "Break a leg, hon!"

"From your lips to God's ears," I mutter.

Everyone refers to Maple Lawn Cemetery simply as the new cemetery to distinguish it from the old one where Mairead and Marsali Mackenzie are buried and the second one nearby where Jamie and Jeannie lie. The oldest headstones here date only from the beginning of the twentieth century. The surnames speak to the growing diversity of Dale, but there are still a lot of Mackenzies.

I pick my way carefully through the wet grass, avoiding the muddy spots left by last night's storm. I pass the headstone for Reinhard's first wife, Greta. One row over is Victor Ross, Janet's second husband. Annie Ross, Alex's wife. And Helen.

I brush away the damp leaves clinging to the top of the headstone. Pluck out those that are tangled in the heather Janet and I planted. Read the five words etched into the stone: "Helen Mackenzie O'Mara. Always beloved."

"Well, here I am. Ready or not for my big day. This time a year ago, I was in Brooklyn, packing up for a getaway weekend. Who knew? Maybe you did. Maybe you knew from the beginning how it would end."

I glance reluctantly at my watch. Nine-thirty already.

"I can't stay long. I just wanted to thank you for everything. Again. You must be getting sick of hearing that. I say your blessing every night—when we have guests, that is. Hopefully, we'll have a lot tonight. I'll come back tomorrow and let you know how everything went. And if you know a blessing for a first-time director, say it for me. I need all the help I can get."

A breeze gusts through the leaves of a nearby maple,

spattering drops of water onto my head and neck. I smile, imagining Helen scolding me for my doubts.

Everyone on staff seems convinced that I can do this. "We'll help," they keep telling me. "We'll lend you our magic. We'll make it work."

So now I'm about to plunge into *The Fantasticks*. A small show—only eight actors. A good way to get my feet wet. I have Rowan's script and score with his neatly penciled notes. And Alex and Reinhard at my back. I can't go too wrong.

Except for sloshing through a giant mud puddle. Not what I had in mind in terms of getting my feet wet. I slow my pace to avoid slipping. Muddy shoes, I can hide. Muddy ass, not so much.

As I reach the parking lot, my phone breaks into "I'm Still Here."

"Hey, Mom."

"Has anyone shown up yet?"

"I'm not at the theatre."

"It's nine forty-five, Maggie."

"I'm on my way."

"You don't want to be late for—"

"Mom! I won't be late."

A silence. "No, of course not. I'm just nervous. Call me when you get a break. Let me know how it's going."

I pull onto the road and smile as I spy the giant banner on the side of the barn that screams "The Crossroads Theatre— Auditions Today!" My smile fades when I discover that the only cars in the lot belong to the staff.

You are not going to cry. There are still ten minutes before auditions begin. Someone has to show up.

Thank God I sent out those press releases. Some of the staff members weren't wild about the idea, claiming we'd get a bunch of "strangers," professional actors only looking for their next job. I assured them few professional actors would traipse out to Dale to audition, especially for a hundred dollars a week. And if they did, they probably needed healing as much as any Mackenzie.

My smile returns as Hal races out of the theatre, warbling "Everything's Coming Up Roses." We link arms and march into the lobby. It still smells of fresh paint.

"I finished the stencils last night," he tells me.

I survey the intertwining vines twisting along the tops of the walls. "They look terrific."

So does Bernie, although it gives me a brief pang to see him sitting in Helen's place. Still, it's great to have him handling the box office this summer. He even took a computer class so he could help with the programs. And came a week early to reorganize the production office.

"How about those posters Hal framed for us?" Bernie asks.

More than a dozen line the walls of the lobby, including the one from last year's production of *Carousel*. I swallow down the lump in my throat and say, "They're gorgeous, Hal. Very professional."

The bulletin board studded with flyers from local businesses looks less professional, but it's comforting to see the bright pink one advertising Hallee's "Spring into Summer" Sale. And to know that—once again—all corsets are twenty-five percent off.

The house door swings open. Reinhard emerges, clipboard in hand. Mei-Yin and Janet trail behind him.

"So," Reinhard announces. "We are ready."

I can't help blurting out, "No one's here!"

"They will come."

"And if they don't," Mei-Yin says, "WE'LL put on *The Fantasticks*. I'll play the MUTE! HA!"

"Last year, the first people didn't show up until ten-fifteen," Janet assures me. But in spite of her confident words, she looks worried, too.

Hal takes up his post at the front door. The rest of us troop into the house.

The air of hushed anticipation is even thicker than the dust motes floating in the pool of light center stage. Alex's head peeps over the rim of the orchestra pit. In the center section of the house, I spot the dark silhouettes of Lee, Javier, and Catherine. Everyone's here to offer their support and their insights into casting.

My stomach goes into freefall. Then I straighten my slumping shoulders and try to walk down the aisle as if I own it.

Lee's laid a piece of plywood across several rows of seats. A surface for scripts, notebooks, scenes, and coffee mugs. I slide into a seat. Janet and Mei-Yin position themselves on either side of me. Reinhard checks his watch before edging sideways down the row of seats behind me where the others are sitting.

His hand comes down on my shoulder. Other hands pat my back, squeeze my hands. Warmth and calm and affection flow through me. "The cousins," Hal calls them. Mine now, too.

A door opens, admitting a shaft of light from the lobby.

"A car just pulled in!" Hal exclaims.

As the light vanishes, a jolt of energy makes me catch my breath. There is no single battery charging us any longer. We all charge each other. I've begun to recognize the subtle differences in their power: the zinging spikes of Mei-Yin's, the steady throb of Reinhard's. Janet's is just as steady but more intense.

Another shaft of light. "Two more are coming down the lane. The first one has out-of-state license plates!"

I feel their relief and confidence filling me. And a quick thrill of excitement. It is time.

As Reinhard heads to the lobby, Hal slips into the row behind me, whispering that more cars are coming, that he always knew it would work, that this is going to be our best season ever.

I close my eyes. I can almost feel him. That calm presence. That soothing voice.

"You are my heart."

The door behind us opens. Reinhard marches down the aisle. A middle-aged man walks hesitantly onto the stage. His bulky green sweater makes him look heavier than his thin, worried face suggests. He blinks as he steps into the light. Pulls off his Irish tweed cap and smoothes his thinning hair. Kneads the soft cap between nervous fingers and peers out into the house.

I caress the silver chain at my throat.

"Welcome to the Crossroads."

Celia Jerome
The Willow Tate *Novels*

"Readers will love the first Willow Tate book. Willow is funny, brave and open to possibilities most people would not have even considered as she meets her perfect foil in Thaddeus Grant, a British agent assigned to look over the strange occurrences following Willow like a shadow. Together they make a wonderful pair and readers will love their unconventional courtship."

— *RT Book Review*

TROLLS IN THE HAMPTONS
978-0-7564-0630-1

NIGHT MARES IN THE HAMPTONS
978-0-7564-0663-9

To Order Call: 1-800-788-6262
www.dawbooks.com

DAW 170

P.R. Frost
The Tess Noncoiré Adventures

"Frost's fantasy debut series introduces a charming protago-
nist, both strong and vulnerable, and her cheeky companion.
An intriguing plot and a well-developed warrior sisterhood
make this a good choice for fans of the urban fantasy of
Tanya Huff, Jim Butcher, and Charles deLint."

—*Library Journal*

HOUNDING THE MOON
978-0-7564-0425-3
MOON IN THE MIRROR
978-0-7564-0486-4

and new in paperback:
FAERY MOON
978-0-7564-0606-6

To Order Call: 1-800-788-6262
www.dawbooks.com

Seanan McGuire

The October Daye Novels

"...will surely appeal to readers who enjoy my books, or
those of Patrica Briggs." —*Charlaine Harris*

"Well researched, sharply told, highly atmospheric and as
brutal as any pulp detective tale, this promising start to a
new urban fantasy series is sure to appeal to fans of Jim
Butcher or Kim Harrison."—*Publishers Weekly*

ROSEMARY AND RUE
978-0-7564-0571-7
A LOCAL HABITATION
978-0-7564-0596-0
AN ARTIFICIAL NIGHT
978-0-7564-0626-4
LATE ECLIPSES
978-0-7564-0666-0

To Order Call: 1-800-788-6262
www.dawbooks.com

DAW 142

Gini Koch
The Alien *Novels*

"This delightful romp has many interesting twists and turns as it glances at racism, politics, and religion en route. Darned amusing." —*Booklist* (starred review)

"Kitty's evolution from marketing manager to member of a secret government unit is amusing and interesting ...a hilarious romp in the vein of 'Men in Black' or 'Ghostbusters'." —*Voya*

TOUCHED BY AN ALIEN
978-0-7564-0600-4

ALIEN TANGO
978-0-7564-0632-5

ALIEN IN THE FAMILY
978-0-7564-0668-4

To Order Call: 1-800-788-6262
www.dawbooks.com

Sherwood Smith
Inda

"A powerful beginning to a very promising series by a writer who is making her bid to be a major fantasist. By the time I finished, I was so captured by this book that it lingered for days afterward. I had lived inside these characters, inside this world, and I was unwilling to let go of it. That, I think, is the mark of a major work of fiction…you owe it to yourself to read *Inda*." —Orson Scott Card

INDA
978-0-7564-0422-2

THE FOX
978-0-7564-0483-3

KING'S SHIELD
978-0-7564-0500-7

TREASON'S SHORE
978-0-7564-0573-1 (hardcover)
978-0-7564-0634-9
(paperback)

To Order Call: 1-800-788-6262
www.dawbooks.com